MW00770496

American Literature Readings in the Twenty-First Century

Series Editor

Linda Wagner-Martin
Unit 402
Chapel Hill, North Carolina, USA

American Literature Readings in the 21st Century publishes works by contemporary critics that help shape critical opinion regarding literature of the nineteenth and twentieth centuries in the United States.

More information about this series at
http://www.springer.com/series/14765

Alison Graham-Bertolini • Casey Kayser
Editors

Carson McCullers in the Twenty-First Century

palgrave
macmillan

Editors
Alison Graham-Bertolini
Dept. 2320, Dept of English
North Dakota State University
Fargo, North Dakota, USA

Casey Kayser
University of Arkansas
Fayetteville
Arkansas, USA

American Literature Readings in the Twenty-First Century
ISBN 978-3-319-40291-8   ISBN 978-3-319-40292-5   (eBook)
DOI 10.1007/978-3-319-40292-5

Library of Congress Control Number: 2016955735

This Palgrave Macmillan imprint is published by Springer Nature
The registered company is Springer International Publishing AG Switzerland
The registered company address is: Gewerbestrasse 11, 6330 Cham, Switzerland

PREFACE

By 1947, when *Quick*, a weekly news magazine, selected Carson McCullers as "one of the best postwar writers in America" (qtd. in Carr 294), she had already found success with *The Heart Is a Lonely Hunter* (1940) and *Reflections in a Golden Eye* (1941), published several short stories and novellas including *The Ballad of the Sad Café* (1943), and had received wide critical acclaim for *The Member of the Wedding* (1946), a novel that she would soon adapt into a successful Broadway production. Around the same time, Gore Vidal declared McCullers "the best American woman novelist" (qtd. in Rodwan). In 1951, the *New York Times* "expressed thanks that America was the country of Carson McCullers" and *Time* magazine declared Carson McCullers one of America's most important contemporary writers (qtd in Savigneau 207–8). McCullers' success and productivity were especially impressive in light of the illnesses she battled throughout her life, suffering as a child from respiratory disorders and misdiagnosed rheumatic fever as a teenager; three strokes before the age of thirty that led to multiple operations to improve loss of muscle function and mobility; a heart condition; and finally, a brain hemorrhage that resulted in her death at the age of fifty. Writing of McCullers' 1967 death, biographer Virginia Spencer Carr concludes, "Twentieth-century America had lost its lonely hunter" (3). Such compelling critiques and accolades all situate McCullers as one of the major writers of the twentieth century. However, the chapters to come will demonstrate that McCullers' legacy and influence continue into the twenty-first century, and that readers and scholars are finding new and increasing social applicability within her themes and ideas.

The impact of McCullers' work on scholarship, art, and popular culture in the twenty-first century continues to grow. Moreover, her work has found new relevance with a wide-reaching international audience. 2001 saw the English translation and publication of Josyanne Savigneau's *Carson McCullers: A Life*, originally published in French. It is without question the most comprehensive biography of McCullers' life since Virginia Spencer Carr's *The Lonely Hunter* (1975) and is enriched by quotes from additional letters and unpublished work by McCullers, as well as material supplied by Dr. Mary Mercer, McCullers' once psychiatrist and close friend. Additional evidence of the influence of McCullers' work on readers and scholars in the twenty-first century include the following examples: In 2001, the Library of America published a collection of her novels followed by a second print run in 2004. In 2002, Women's Project and Productions and Playwrights Horizon of New York City collaborated to stage *Carson McCullers (Historically Inaccurate)*, by playwright Sarah Schulman, which the *New York Times* deemed the "latest evidence of renewed interest" (A5) in McCullers and her work. In 2004, Oprah Winfrey selected *The Heart Is a Lonely Hunter* for her book club, a move that widened the influence of the novel significantly. In 2005, McCullers appeared in Sherill Tippins' biographical history *February House*, an account of the Brooklyn Heights home and artistic experiment she shared with W. H. Auden, Paul and Jane Bowles, Benjamin Britten, Richard Wright, and Gypsy Rose Lee during the 1940s. Tippins' book was followed by a 2012 Broadway musical adaptation of the same name, in which McCullers is also a significant figure. Also in 2012, Sarah Gubbins' play *fml: how Carson McCullers saved my life* opened in Chicago at the Steppenwolf Theater and played more recently in Atlanta in 2015. This play situates the work of Carson McCullers in a contemporary context, the world of texting teenagers at a Catholic high school, where a new English teacher assigns *The Heart Is a Lonely Hunter*. In 2014, the state of Georgia chose *The Heart Is a Lonely Hunter* as part of the National Endowment for the Arts Big Read program, an initiative that is designed to promote reading in American culture, and the Atlanta production of *fml* provided several opportunities for Atlanta and surrounding communities to discuss the novel and play in conjunction. And in 2011, singer songwriter Suzanne Vega performed a hybrid piece of narrative and music titled "Carson McCullers Talks About Love" at New York's Rattlestick Playwrights Theater, in which she portrays McCullers reflecting on her life and work. Finally, in 2014, the Carson McCullers Society (formed in 1990) once again became active, electing a new board of officers and drawing a small but dynamic membership of individuals who are dedicated to the study of this great American author. The fifteen chapters included in this volume explore how McCullers and her writing are being read and understood in a twenty-first-century context. To begin, **Casey Kayser**, in "From Adaptation to Influence: Carson McCullers on the Stage," considers some of the aforementioned plays and performances and the ways in which contemporary playwrights, artists, and audiences are interacting with McCullers, her work, and her legacy. The contemporary explorations of McCullers on stage are appropriate in light of her own experiences with theater, with the successful dramatic adaptation of *The Member of the Wedding*, which ran on Broadway from 1950 to 1951, and the not so successful production of her single stage play *The Square Root of Wonderful* (1957). Kayser explores McCullers' successes and challenges in adapting her work to the stage during her lifetime and examines potential explanations for ambivalent critical responses, in addition to considering twenty-first century stage engagements with McCullers' life and work.

Several other essays included in this volume are the product of opportunities to study McCullers in new contexts. Columbus State University has converted McCullers' childhood home in Columbus, Georgia, into the Carson McCullers Center for Writers and Musicians, which is dedicated to preserving McCullers' memory through educational and cultural programming for the campus and community. The Center offers The Marguerite and Lamar Smith Fellowship for Writers, named after McCullers' parents, for which they annually receive numerous applications from writers and artists hoping to engage in a productive period while in residence in the home. In 2011, Columbus State hosted an interdisciplinary conference for McCullers' 94th birthday, drawing an international group of scholars and featuring a performance by Suzanne Vega of her one-woman show. In celebration of McCullers' 100th birthday, John Cabot University, the Carson McCullers Society, and the Carson McCullers Center for Writers and Musicians at Columbus State University are hosting "Carson McCullers in the World (1917–2017): An International Conference to Celebrate the 100th Anniversary of Carson McCullers' Birth." This event will take place in July 2017 in Rome, Italy. Finally, Columbus State recently acquired a collection of McCullers-related papers, mementos, correspondence, and other materials from Dr. Mary Mercer upon her death in April 2013. These materials are housed in the archives at Columbus State, in a collection that rivals that of the University of Texas at Austin and Duke University.

The archives, including nine transcripts of Mercer's therapy sessions with McCullers recorded on a Dictaphone between April and May of 1958, are attracting international scholars who are interested in new insights into McCullers' life and work.

In the chapter, "Impromptu Journal of My Heart": Carson McCullers's Therapeutic Recordings, April – May 1958" **Carlos Dews**, who is known for bringing McCullers' unfinished autobiography *Illumination and Night Glare* to publication in 1999, discusses the details that the transcripts reveal regarding McCullers' friendships and relationships, including her relationship with Swiss heiress Annemarie Clarac Schwarzenbach, with whom McCullers was infatuated. Dews additionally provides further insight into *Illumination and Night Glare* and "The Flowering Dream: Notes on Writing," a piece published in *Esquire* in 1959 that was partly based upon inspiration from the sessions, which Mercer and McCullers saw as "literary experiments" to help her overcome a period of writer's block.

Melanie Masterton Sherazi, in "Collaborative Life Writing: The Dialogical Subject of Carson McCullers' Dictaphone 'Experiments' and Posthumous Autobiography, *Illumination and Night Glare*," also engages with these transcripts, exploring their connection to McCullers' unfinished autobiography and Dews' approach to its editing and publication. She reads *Illumination and Night Glare* as a work of women's autobiography, marked by its nonlinear nature of storytelling and "the collaborative nature of its posthumous supplementation." Sherazi demonstrates that although the text was composed in 1967, *Illumination and Night Glare* is an assemblage of McCullers' sustained engagement with life writing as a collaborative practice, which is also affirmed by the content of the Dictaphone experiments. Then, in "Telling It 'Slant': Carson McCullers, Harper Lee, and the Veil of Memory," **Jan Whitt** explores the arbitrary boundaries between the autobiographical novel and the memoir. Whitt compares the autobiographical novels of Harper Lee and Carson McCullers, both of whom grew up in the South and lived periodically in New York City. Examining McCullers' work from the perspective of the autobiographical novel and comparing her writing to that of Harper Lee is especially relevant today, given the release of Lee's recovered manuscript *Go Set a Watchman*. In an alternate biographical approach to McCullers, **Carmen Trammell Skaggs**, in "Musings between the Marvelous and Strange: New Contexts and Correspondence about Carson McCullers and Mary Tucker," focuses on the close relationship between McCullers and her childhood piano teacher, Mary Tucker, and the importance of

McCullers' musical training to her fiction. Skaggs considers archival materials that reveal Tucker's formative influence on the young writer by examining correspondence between McCullers and Tucker from the Mary Sames Tucker Papers, 1936–1967, which are housed in the David M. Rubenstein Rare Book and Manuscript Library at Duke University. Her perspective is enriched further by materials recently acquired by the Margaret S. Sullivan Papers and the Dr. Mary E. Mercer/Carson McCullers Collection at Columbus State University, including the therapy transcripts, which also provide primary insight into McCullers' thoughts about Tucker and her influence. It was McCullers' early experiences as Tucker's pupil and her response to Tucker and her husband's 1934 move away from Columbus to Maryland that helped give voice to her expression in *The Member of the Wedding* "the we of me," as she felt that the Tuckers completed her in this way and was devastated by what she perceived as their abandonment of her (Carr 35–6).

Though McCullers would ultimately give up her dream of becoming a concert pianist to focus on her writing, her childhood love of music would remain a mainstay in the form and content of her writing. **Kiyoko Magome** investigates McCullers' use of musical form in "The Image of the String Quartet Lurking in *The Heart Is a Lonely Hunter*." Magome demonstrates how the relationships among the five main characters of *The Heart Is a Lonely Hunter* evoke the image of a musical performance like a string quartet. John Singer, she argues, is the center of the musical composition, which invokes the image of four musicians performing a string quartet without a conductor. Magome also discusses evidence of a similar structure within McCullers' early short story "Court in the West Eighties," arguing that the image of "the string quartet existed in her imagination as early as 1934" and that the string quartet can be identified as part of "a much larger musico-literary, socio-historical context."

McCullers' fiction depicts characters and situations that only now, in the twenty-first century, are we in the academy finding the language and theory to explore. In "Entering the Compound: Becoming with Carson McCullers' Freaks," **renée c. hoogland** analyzes Frankie, the adolescent narrator of *The Member of the Wedding*, by moving away from previous sociopolitical readings of this character to consider her function and effect as a literary and aesthetic being. Using the theory of French philosopher Gilles Deleuze, **hoogland** foregrounds the novel's protagonist as an aesthetic creation, a literary design with possibilities and movement that cannot be reduced to the strict operations within established forms of literary criticism.

The twenty-first century's increased concern with human interactions with the environment and all of its living creatures has given rise to critical animal studies, a rapidly growing interdisciplinary field that examines human treatment of animals and their role and value in an unprecedented era of challenges related to exploitation, extinction, and ecological threats. **Temple Gowan**, in "'To be a Good Animal': Toward a Queer-Posthumanist Reading of *Reflections in a Golden Eye*," adds a posthumanist lens to queer readings of this text, to foreground the importance of both human and nonhuman bodies in the novel. She focuses her analysis on Firebird, a horse that is notably listed as a "participant" in the tragedy in the first pages of the text and that she argues is a "full character." Though the horse is lowest on the hierarchical listing of the novel's participants: "two officers, a soldier, two women, a Filipino, and a horse" (309), Gowan argues that the horse has an agency that produces self-knowledge in the human subject and collapses human and nonhuman binaries. However, the ideology and physical violence that are used to maintain hierarchical categories that organize and govern our world are highlighted in Captain Penderton's mistreatment of the horse, as he attempts to regain power over his queer tendencies and reinstate species hierarchies. Gowan argues that through this violence, McCullers "foregrounds the insidious nature of disciplinary structures that are grounded in species difference and links the oppression of the nonhuman to the oppression of the queer."

McCullers-related criticism in the field of queer studies has generally fit within two categories: work that considers McCullers' own gender and sexuality and that which examines depictions of gender and sexuality in her work; while there is "considerable controversy" about McCullers' own sexual identification, her textual representations of gay and lesbian characters and themes related to gender and sexuality are "less ambiguous" (Dews 382). McCullers presents transgressive images as a means to resist the status quo, images that have been and remain important to the emergence of a queer activism in gay and lesbian communities (Brasell 65). McCullers' characters, many of whom don't fit within traditional gender and sexuality conventions, offer important models of identification for adolescents who identify as queer. One such example is the character Jo of Gubbins' *fml*, for whom texts by McCullers provide an avenue of resistance to the taunts of her peers as well as examples of alternative sexualities. Further, McCullers' themes contribute to the contemporary dialogue surrounding bullying and the tragic suicides of young LGBTQ individuals. In "Coming of Age in the Queer South: Friendship and Social

Difference in *The Heart Is a Lonely Hunter,*" **Kristen Proehl** explores the ways in which McCullers' own queer friendships, including those with playwright Tennessee Williams and her cousin, Jordan Massee, contribute to the non-normative models of friendship that appear in her work. While Singer and Antonapoulos might be the most commonly considered example of queer friendship in *The Heart Is a Lonely Hunter,* Proehl expands such definitions to involve transgressive relationships between people of many different identity categories, such as age, race, and gender, reading other pairs in the novel, like Mick Kelly and Biff Brannon, and Singer's various relationships with particular characters as queer. Proehl argues that the depiction of these queer relationships is "a vehicle through which McCullers imagines the possibilities, as well as the limitations, of political alliances across social differences."

Miho Matsui, in the essay "Queer Eyes: Cross-Gendering, Cross-Dressing, and Cross-Racing Miss Amelia," interprets *The Ballad of the Sad Café* as a story of a white woman's resistance to white male dominance. The character's cross-gendering, cross-dressing, and cross-racial performance allows readers to interrogate the meaning of the word "queer," as it is used in the story, especially when employed to describe Miss Amelia's crossed eyes. Through analyzing both Amelia's gaze and the narrator's perspective in opposition to the male, authoritative, normalizing gaze, Matsui concludes that being queer allows the characters to attain an alternate subjectivity, one that is not always possible in a world that is typically constructed of binaries. **Alison Graham-Bertolini**, in "'Nature is Not Abnormal; Only Lifelessness is Abnormal': Paradigms of the In-valid in *Reflections in a Golden Eye,*" argues that McCullers deliberately undermines conceptions of "normality" in the characters Captain Penderton, Alison Langdon, and Anacleto by demonstrating how performances of "the normal" lead them to unhappiness and tragedy. Moreover, she observes that the atypical attributes of the aforementioned characters allow them to resist and challenge a social order that denies equal treatment to all. **Stephanie Rountree** is also concerned with disability studies in her essay, "An "archaeology of [narrative] silence": Cognitive Segregation and Productive Citizenship in McCullers' *The Heart Is a Lonely Hunter,*" in which she argues that the novel bears out the racist and classist rhetorics that led to the growth of mental institutions in the early-twentieth-century South and the marginalization of cognitively disabled persons during this time, individuals like Antonapoulos, a lesser-explored character in criticism of the novel. She views this history as "manifest in Carson McCullers' *The*

Heart Is a Lonely Hunter in ways that expose national, neoliberal ideals of U.S. citizenship while simultaneously organizing the narrative." Through the lenses of disability studies and new historicism, her essay demonstrates how the practice of cognitive segregation to make way for the productivity of normative citizens that informed institutional practices in the 1930s still impedes disability politics in the twenty-first century.

Since the reformation of the Carson McCullers Society in 2014, a noted increase of interest in McCullers' work among international scholars, students, and other overseas readers has taken place. **Lin Bin**, in "Seeking the Meaning of Loneliness: Carson McCullers in China," discusses two iterations of the "McCullers craze" in China, first in the 1980s and now in the twenty-first century, periods shaped by sociopolitical forces that have led Chinese people to negotiate two frameworks she introduces: that of "isolation by community" in the 1980s, and in the twenty-first century, "alienation in a crowd." Bin postulates that the tension between the individual and community, one also explored in McCullers' work, holds particular relevance for Chinese readers because of the historical focus on community in Chinese culture. Bin concludes that Chinese readers and scholars avidly study McCullers' texts with the hope of "deconstructing McCullers' loneliness" and finding something redemptive in the bleak isolation of her characters. This interpretation, in turn, writes Bin, offers some resolution to Chinese readers who are themselves seeking to balance the needs and values of the individual with those of the community. In another international context, **Barbara Roche Rico** uses postcolonial and transatlantic theories to present a new comparative reading of McCullers' *Ballad of the Sad Café* and Nicholasa Mohr's *In Nueva York*, a work of the best known female writer of the Puerto Rican diaspora. In "The Ballad of Two Sad Cafés": Nicholasa Mohr's Postwar Narrative as 'Writing Back' to Carson McCullers," Rico analyzes similarities related to narrative and characterization in the two texts, suggesting that Mohr was not only influenced by McCullers, but engages purposefully with *Ballad*, "writing back" to McCullers and her text. Rico argues that Mohr has adapted pieces of McCullers' text to achieve "an artful dismantling of clichés often found in the literary representation of the working class." Further, she explores the ways in which both texts consider affiliation and membership versus exclusion within their particular communities.

Finally, while McCullers' final novel, *Clock Without Hands* (1961), is not always given the high praise assigned to her other work, the fact that she saw it through to the end despite the advanced stage of her illnesses is a great achievement. The novel's focus on death and dying in the character of JT Malone, who is diagnosed with leukemia, parallels what might have been McCullers' own confrontation with her mortality in the last decade of her life. Some critics fail to see the unity and coherence in this novel, but **Craig Slaven** offers an explanation for this apparent lack in "Jester's Mercurial Nature and the Hermeneutics of Time in McCullers' *Clock Without Hands*." Slaven reads Jester Clane as a trickster figure, who both disrupts and reaffirms cultural narratives of white supremacy, and argues that the inner conflicts of Jester Clane become an allegory for the historical moment that undergirds the novel, the *Brown v. Board of Education* Supreme Court decision regarding desegregation. Slaven demonstrates that the text's incoherence "reflects a heightened sense of discord between personal, regional, and national narratives of selfhood," and suggests that through Jester, McCullers "exposes the cultural processes by which such narratives are reproduced and propagated." The concern with racial injustice and violence in McCullers' work may be even more relevant in the contemporary cultural climate of America, as we consider the supposed "post-racial" period marked by Barack Obama's election to the presidency in 2008, a label that was later exploded by controversies and protests surrounding the ubiquitous and violent deaths of young black men at the hands of police in Ferguson, Missouri, and other American cities. Considering the *Brown v. Board of Education* decision, the threat of racial violence, and the mob mentality featured in *Clock* alongside today's conversations about power dynamics and clashes between government, military, police, and people of all colors may provide us with new insight into our history, our present, and our future.

The essays in this collection provide a cohesive and dynamic sampling of the ways in which McCullers is relevant to reading audiences, artists, and scholars in the twenty-first century and demonstrate ways in which her work is being read with new and innovative lenses and approaches by our contributors and others. We believe that now is a timely moment to return to McCullers and re-examine her texts and life from new perspectives, and we hope that this collection builds on and enriches the body of criticism her work and legacy have engendered up to this point. In 1961, Gore Vidal famously wrote that "of all the Southern writers, [McCullers] is most likely to endure" (50). We believe that McCullers has indeed endured, and that her work's ongoing relevance to the social issues of today suggests that we can look forward to continued opportunities to reconsider her life and work, and that readers will engage with her texts, in both analysis and pleasure, for years to come.

WORKS CITED

Brasell, Bruce R. "Dining at the Table of the Sensitives: Carson McCuller's Peculiarity." *Southern Quarterly* 35 (4): 1997. 59–66. Print.

Carr, Virginia Spencer. *The Lonely Hunter: A Biography of Carson McCullers.* Athens: University of Georgia Press, 1975. Reprinted 2003. Print.

Dews, Carlos L. "Carson McCullers." *Reader's Guide to Gay and Lesbian Studies.* Ed. Timothy Murphy. New York: Routledge, 2000. 381–383. Print.

Mandell, Jonathan. "When She Wrote, the Dross of Her Life Became Gold." *New York Times* 20 January 2002. A5. Print.

McCullers, Carson. *Reflections in a Golden Eye.* 1941. *Complete Novels.* New York: Literary Classics of the United States, 2001: 309–93. Print.

Rodwan, John G. Jr. "Carson McCullers and Her Crowd." *Open Letters Monthly: An Arts and Literature Review.* n.d. Web.

Savigneau, Josyane. *Carson McCullers: A Life.* Translated by Joan E. Howard. New York: Houghton Mifflin, 2001. Print.

Vidal, Gore. "The World Outside." Rev. of Clock Without Hands. *The Reporter* 25 (28 Sept 1961): 50–2. Print.

Fargo, ND, USA   Casey Kayser Fayetteville, AR, USA

Alison Graham-Bertolini

ACKNOWLEDGMENTS

Grateful acknowledgment is made to Columbus State University Archives, Columbus State University, Columbus, Georgia, for permission to quote from the letters, transcripts of therapy sessions, and other materials in the Margaret S. Sullivan Papers (MC 298) and the Dr. Mary E. Mercer/ Carson McCullers Collection (MC 296).

We also gratefully acknowledge the David M. Rubenstein Rare Book & Manuscript Library, Duke University, for permission to quote from the Mary Sames Tucker Papers.

Finally, we would like to thank The American Literature Society of Japan for permission to publish material that was originally published in Japanese as "*Shisen, isou, jenda ekkyou: The Ballad of the Sad Café ni okeru 'kuia na me.'* Gaze, Cross-Dressing and Cross-Gender: Queer Eyes in The Ballad of the Sad Café," by Miho Matsui, *Studies in American Literature 41 (2005): 37–52.*

CONTENTS

From Adaptation to Influence: Carson McCullers on the Stage

Casey Kayser

While Carson McCullers is primarily known as a novelist, she also found success as a playwright with the stage adaptation of her 1946 novel *The Member of the Wedding*, which ran on Broadway from 1950 to 1951. This production was universally praised, winning several Donaldson awards and the New York Drama Critics' Circle Award. Unfortunately, her next attempt at writing for the stage, with the 1957 play *The Square Root of Wonderful*, was a critical disaster that closed after only 45 performances. Biographer Virginia Spencer Carr pronounces this play "the square root of humiliation" ("Novelist Turned" 49) for McCullers. In 1963, Edward Albee adapted *The Ballad of the Sad Café* to the stage, and while the play received fairly positive reviews, it only ran for two and a half months, and McCullers felt that Albee had not translated her novel well (Carr, *Lonely Hunter* 504).

Despite McCullers' ambivalent experiences with the theater during her lifetime, and the lack of critical attention given to her plays in relation to her novels, her oeuvre has retained compelling connections with the theater world into the twenty-first century, both in adaptations and

C. Kayser (✉)
Department of English, University of Arkansas, 333 Kimpel Hall, Fayetteville, AR 72701, USA

© The Author(s) 2016   1
A. Graham-Bertolini, C. Kayser (Eds.), *Carson McCullers in the Twenty-First Century*, DOI 10.1007/978-3-319-40292-5_1

in drama influenced by her life and work. In 2002, Women's Project & Productions and Playwrights Horizons teamed up to present Sarah Schulman's *Carson McCullers* (*Historically Inaccurate*), and seven years later, playwright Rebecca Gilman's adaptation of McCullers' novel The *Heart Is a Lonely Hunter* (1940) was staged at the New York Theatre Workshop. More recently, several interesting pieces of McCullers-inspired work have appeared on the stage, such as "Carson McCullers Talks About Love," a show by singer songwriter Suzanne Vega, and Sarah Gubbins' *fml: how Carson McCullers saved my life*, which premiered in Chicago in 2012. In the same year, following the publication of Sherill Tippins' 2005 book of the same name, *February House* debuted at the Public Theater, a musical exploration of the Brooklyn Heights home McCullers lived in with other artists during the early 1940s. Clearly, there are some interesting connections between McCullers' own experiences in the theater in her lifetime and the ways in which McCullers' life and work have influenced or been adapted for stage productions in the twenty-first century, all of which compel this chapter's exploration of McCullers' successes and challenges in adapting her work to the stage, and potential explanations for the ambivalent critical responses to her stage adaptations. Ultimately, I am interested in the ways in which contemporary playwrights, artists and audiences are interacting with McCullers, her work and her legacy, and how these inform our contemporary understandings.

McCullers experimented with playwriting as a child, staging productions in her living room for her family and neighbors ("How I Began" 249–50); however, she seemed to move away from the genre after her success with the novel. Then, in the spring of 1946, she received a letter from Tennessee Williams, who by this time was well-known for *The Glass Menagerie* (1944). Williams, who had never met McCullers, was so affected by the story that he wrote to McCullers, expressing his appreciation of the affinity between her work and his own plays. He later recalled that he knew "at once that we were kindred souls. There was something wounded in Carson, you know, as I was quick to discover" (qtd. in Carr, "Novelist Turned" 38). At the time, Williams had been suffering from heart pains and palpitations, and he was certain that he was dying, even though he was only 34 years old. His dying wish, he wrote in his letter, was that he might meet this young artist with whom he already felt a strong connection. Carson accepted his invitation to visit him in Nantucket, where he suggested that she adapt *Member* for the stage.[1]

Ironically, it was a critique of *The Member of the Wedding* that provided her with additional motivation for adapting her text. McCullers said, "I was challenged in one malicious part of myself because *The New Yorker* in reviewing the novel said that I had many of the components of great writing, but the chief thing I lacked was a sense of drama. Clifton Fadiman attacked the book because it 'was not dramatic'" (qtd. in Madden 87).[2] Williams was sure that Carson's work possessed the necessary components for drama, and she became determined to try. The two artists wrote together daily, she diligently on *Member*, and he with new passion on the *Summer and Smoke* script he had nearly abandoned. Williams describes the process:

> We sat opposite each other at a long table on which we worked mornings and dined at night. And—yes—the story about our shoving that bottle of whiskey back and forth between us is pretty much the way it happened—but it never interfered with our work. Carson was the only person I have ever been able to work in the same room with, and we got along very well. She was deadly serious about her writing, and I admired her for that. Otherwise, our friendship never would have survived. (qtd. in Carr, "Novelist Turned" 39)

Carson too felt great admiration and fondness for Williams: theirs "proved to be one of the most enduring friendships and loves she was ever to experience with a fellow artist" (Carr, *Lonely Hunter* 277). However, despite Williams' expertise in the dramatic genre, McCullers was stubbornly insistent on taking no advice from Williams in the process of adaptation, as he remembers:

> If she wanted to ask me something or to read some lines aloud for my reaction, she would. But that was rare. Carson accepted almost no advice about how to adapt *The Member of the Wedding*. I did not suggest lines to her more than once or twice, and then she would usually have her own ideas and say, 'Tenn, honey, thank you, but I know all I need to know.' (qtd. in Carr, "Novelist Turned" 39)

In fact, the allure of the image of the two artists working side by side that summer, the period that "began one of the most affecting and strange friendships in American literary history" (Spoto 126) in itself inspired southern writers David Madden and Peggy Bach to imagine that time period in dramatic form. In "Tennessee and Carson: Notes on Concepts for a Play," Madden outlines his and Bach's vision for a play exploring that summer in Nantucket and ultimately, the relationship between Williams and McCullers. While the two never turned the play into a final product, it was staged as a work-in-progress at Lynchburg College and in a bookstore in Baton Rouge, Louisiana ("Re: Play on Tennessee and Carson").

McCullers encountered logistical difficulties, suffered health complications, and endured battles over artistic visions throughout the process of adapting *Member*, and it may have been her resiliency and insistence on her own vision that contributed to the play's success, in addition to her newly established literary reputation. Virginia Spencer Carr and Judith Giblin James have both examined the process of her adaptation and the critical response to *Member*, pointing to factors such as these as key to its success.[3] However, while the play was praised by the *Commonweal* and others "as a complete delight" (Phelan 437), many critics felt that the story had not quite transitioned from novel to play, and as a result, it lacked the dramatic movement that critics had commented on in novel form. In fact, the director, Harold Clurman, remembers his initial reservations: "It had no regard for theatrical conventions, little plot, no big climaxes or sweeping movements—in short, it was not Broadway material and the public won't like it. The play was to be my fiftieth production and probably one of my biggest failures" (qtd. in Carr, "Novelist Turned" 44). While the play was not the failure Clurman had feared, critics agreed that it did not seem to fit within the genre: Robert Garland comments that it was "something special but not quite a play" (18), and Brooks Atkinson points out in the *New York Times* that its original status as a novel might have "some bearing on the fact that the play has no beginning, middle or end and never acquires dramatic momentum. Although Mrs. McCullers has taken the material out of the novel she has not quite got it into the form of a play ... It may not be a play, but it is art" (26). Critics seemed to agree that *Member* was effective and moving, but not a traditional play.

Despite the faults critics found with its qualifications for the dramatic genre, *The Member of the Wedding* received 17 of a possible 25 votes of the New York drama critics for top honors in 1950, including awards in the categories of "best play of last season," and "best first play by an author to be produced on Broadway" (Carr, "Novelist Turned" 45). There were nominations for the performances as well; in fact, the quality of the acting and reputation of the performers may have been a major selling point of the play. Reviews deemed the performances by Ethel Waters as Berenice, Brandon de Wilde as John Henry and Julie Harris as Frankie as "magnificent" (Wyatt 468; Gibbs 44), and "of a high order" (Barnes 12). Further, evidence suggests that McCullers' reputation preceded her and because of her acclaim, critics were able to overlook the limitations of the play. Critics proclaimed that "its writing largely excuses its playwrighting" ("New Play in Manhattan" 45) and "in lesser hands" the play may not have succeeded ("New Plays" 74). *Member's* shortcomings were excused because its author was Carson McCullers, who had become New York's "new literary darling" (Carr, *Lonely Hunter* 98) with the publication of *The Heart Is a Lonely Hunter* at only 23 years old.

The reception of *The Square Root of Wonderful* also seems to suggest that McCullers' style did not immediately lend itself to dramatic adaptation or form. *Square Root* is the story of a dysfunctional family and several boarders living in their home, which culminates in the suicide of failed writer Phillip Lovejoy, tortured by his lack of success and his wife Molly's decision to leave him for another man. It moves slowly, without the allure of the central adolescent female character that had captured audiences in *Member*. The story instead presents "grotesque" (McClain 22), "uninteresting characters and surprisingly flat writing" (Morrison 72). Though McCullers first conceived of *Square Root* as a play, her tendency to create storylines without the dramatic momentum many critics expected may have proved a challenge. Further, her health had worsened and she was grieving the deaths of both her mother and Reeves, who had committed suicide (and for whom the character Phillip Lovejoy was a clear parallel). McCullers did not insist on the final word with the production as she did with *Member*, and it ultimately suffered from too many collaborators. This resulted in a deviation from her vision of the play (James, *Wunderkind* 136) as it went through "more than a dozen drafts, six or eight by McCullers alone, and a handful of assorted other scripts written in collaboration with her several producers and directors" (Carr, "Novelist Turned" 47). The manuscript was ultimately "carved up beyond recognition" (49). Despite her frustration with *The Square Root of Wonderful*, in her final years McCullers collaborated on a musical version of *The Member of the Wedding* with Mary Rodgers, but she was in poor health at the time, and ill-prepared to write lyrics for a musical, according to Rodgers, who told Carr that "poor Carson died thinking still that her musical would some day be produced" (qtd. in "Novelist Turned" 50). There was a musical version of *Member* that opened on Broadway in 1971, scripted by Theodore Mann and titled *F. Jasmine Addams*, but it was not the script that Rodgers and McCullers had worked on, and it too failed, closing after a mere 20 performances. Despite the ambivalent experiences she had with theater in her lifetime, I believe McCullers would be pleased to see the proliferation of her work and the continuation of her legacy into the scope of twenty-first-century drama and performance.

In 2002, *Carson McCullers (Historically Inaccurate)*, a play by Sarah Schulman, was produced by Women's Project and Productions in collaboration with Playwrights Horizon. It opened at the Women's Project Theatre at a juncture when "interest in McCullers [was] stronger than ever" (Sommer), a sentiment echoed by the *New York Times*, which claimed that the "play [was] the latest evidence of renewed interest" (Mandell) in McCullers. While the abundance of recent stage engagement with McCullers' life and work might support this claim, unfortunately audiences, fans, critics, and scholars were not quite pleased with Schulman's approach or the final production directed by Marion McClinton. Schulman uses 16 scenes to sketch McCullers' life, focusing first on her early talent for the piano and closing with a deathbed scene, along the way exploring her tumultuous relationship with Reeves; friendships with other artists like Gypsy Rose Lee and Richard Wright; and her art, discussing her works in progress and the adaptation of *The Member of the Wedding*, and inserting figures like Ethel Waters and other seemingly random or tangentially related characters. Schulman does not quote from any copyrighted work, so while she draws on some well-known McCullers' quips, such as her comment about her need to return to the South every once in a while to renew her "sense of horror" (Carr, *Lonely Hunter* 313), excerpts from McCullers' texts themselves do not appear, giving Schulman considerable creative space to imagine dialogue and action, which she clearly acknowledges within the parenthetical piece of her title.

In a *New York Times* interview, Schulman discusses having read some of McCullers' texts in her adolescence, but not fully understanding them. When she began to look more deeply at McCullers' life and work, she was "riveted and amazed. She had major depressions, she was chronically ill, she was a terrible alcoholic, she drove her husband to suicide, she was cruel, she was incapable of love—she was a nightmare. But her work is so generous. It is shocking to open her books and realize from the first sentence how brilliant she is" (qtd. in Mandell). This characterization (which in itself, as many familiar with McCullers' life and work would argue, is not quite accurate)[4] may not bode well for a sensitive portrayal of a complex woman, and indeed, reviewers and audiences seemed to find Schulman's depiction problematic. Schulman goes on: "Floria Lasky, who was Carson McCullers's lawyer, called up and said she is coming to the play. I know that the first thing out of her mouth is going to be, 'It's historically inaccurate.' She's going to be right, but it's like, 'O.K., we all agree on that.' That's not what it's about. It's emotionally accurate" (qtd. in Mandell). In response to this interview and a review in the *Times*, Carlos Dews, editor of McCullers' unfinished autobiography *Illumination and Nightglare*, wrote a letter to the editor lambasting Schulman's view:

> Unfortunately, the representation of McCullers in the play is as emotionally inaccurate as it is historically inaccurate. The negative aspects are not given any redeeming balance, leaving the impression that McCullers was, in Ms. Schulman's words, 'a nightmare.' Ms. Schulman observes that, during McCullers's lifetime, 'mainstream critics dismissed her as morbid and grotesque.' Given Ms. Schulman's characterization of her, audiences could only leave the theater with the mainstream critics' impression.

The playbill poses the question: "Can a life be created, an identity forged, through prose"? In response, Schulman seems to be attempting to raise questions about the failure of biography to capture history and the nuance of lived experience in explicitly accurate ways, and perhaps, in emphasizing the more "nightmare" qualities of McCullers, meditate on the ways in which we remember people after they have passed, especially those whose art we admire. Yet critics and audiences could not reflect fully on these questions, blinded by Schulman's depiction of McCullers and the "freedom she's granted herself to treat McCullers the way no one should treat a dog" (Finkle). David Finkle claims that the real parenthetical title should be (*Dramaturgically Inept*). The crux of the problem may lie in the lack of attention and respect Schulman demonstrates for McCullers' lived experience as we know it through her own prose, since she draws on no copyrighted material. As one reviewer points out, "the writing of McCullers is of, at most, secondary importance here; it never really appears in the play. Rather, it's Schulman's words that carry the evening, and her own special wit and creativity that see us through the many, many dark spots present in its torturous 130 minutes" (Murray). Unlike *Carson McCullers (Historically Inaccurate)*, the more successful stage engagements with McCullers give precedence to McCullers' own words, and it seems that stronger attention to those words and to the details of McCullers' life would have better served Schulman.

The eventual stage adaptation of *The Heart Is a Lonely Hunter* came to fruition in the hands of one of the most talented and successful playwrights working today, Rebecca Gilman, who has earned commercial success and critical acclaim for plays such as *Spinning into Butter* (2000), *Boy Gets Girl* (2001) and *The Glory of Living* (2001). Gilman's adaptation effectively captures the lyrical tone of McCullers' novel; draws on direct dialogue and follows the novel's plotline; and for the most part, translates accurately the novel's presentation of the characters. Yet, Gilman made a controversial choice which would dominate discourse surrounding the play: she cast a hearing actor in the role of deaf-mute John Singer and endows him with speech. While he communicates mostly via his notebook and sign language, his voice opens and closes the play. He narrates his childhood history; the special nature of his relationship with his friend Antonapoulos; the conflict in which Antonapoulos is institutionalized by his uncaring cousin; and then in the final scene, his thoughts following his suicide. This monologue is a suicide note of sorts, closure we don't get in the novel, and one that some readers might take comfort in—as one reviewer acknowledges: "before you get your britches in a bunch, ask yourself: Haven't you always wanted to know what was going through John Singer's mind … especially at the end?" (Bernardo). The 2005 premiere at Atlanta's Alliance Theater opened to strong reviews and little acknowledgement of the casting and speech of Singer, but when it received more attention at the New York Theater Workshop, the production prompted deaf activists to protest that only a deaf actor should have been cast. Criticism was harsh; for instance, Linda Bove, a deaf actress and activist for minority, disabled, and deaf artists, claimed that "a hearing actor playing a deaf character is tantamount to putting a white actor in blackface" (qtd. in Healy).

Gilman justified her artistic choices, pointing out that Singer was taught to speak as a child (qtd. in Healy), and noting that she does draw Singer's words in the final monologue from letters he writes Antonapoulos throughout the novel. She received the criticism well, stating that she was open to considering potential revisions for her play so that a nonspeaking actor could play Singer in future productions (qtd. in Healy), and indeed, in a subsequent production at the Steppenwolf in Chicago, a deaf actor assumed the role. The 2010 published acting edition clarifies in the production note that "Except where indicated, Singer's signing should not be translated for a hearing audience. Singer's direct address at the beginning and end of the play should be voiced by either the actor playing Singer or the actor playing Biff. Or, for those two sections, the text may be projected" (3).

Aside from the controversy concerning Singer's speech, there were many positive reviews which called it "an eloquent, unsentimental and ineffably sad tapestry" (Zoglin), a play that "[succeeds] in capturing the essence of McCullers' book" (Feldberg). As for the criticisms, as in the case of McCullers' other plays, *Heart*'s failures may have been partly due to the difficulty of translating to the stage a style or story that is not driven by dramatic movement, but, in this particular case, the inner workings of the character's minds. Like young Mick Kelly's "inside room" (McCullers, *Heart* 138), the inner worlds of the characters in the novel are so complex that while critics praised the actors' performances, they felt that "the poetry inside them is left unarticulated," resulting in an overall "respectful but lifeless stage version" that is merely "a surface sketch of the book, one that fails to communicate any of its emotional substance. It's a mere blueprint of a cathedral, not the majestic building itself" (Isherwood, "Wounded Souls"). Reviews reflected the general challenges that McCullers' work has consistently presented for dramatic translation: ultimately claiming that it is a "sprawling story" (Bernardo), "not an easy novel to dramatize" (Jones), and "a story for the page and not the stage" (Windman). Despite these challenges, Gilman is deferential and faithful to McCullers' vision, and even when she deviates (as with the choices surrounding Singer), she does so with reason and attention to the text. Ultimately, she is effective in translating to stage the novel's themes of loneliness and isolation, ones that may well ring truer today in different form, as one reviewer notes: "In big cities and small towns, individuals pursue specific goals or languish in despair, often with their heads attached to a pair of earbuds or necks permanently bent toward a cell phone. *The Heart Is A Lonely Hunter* takes place two decades before Steve Jobs was even born, but its portrait of lost souls yearning to connect but never succeeding for very long is achingly relevant today" (Whalen).

While Gilman's adaptation presented a rather traditional take on McCullers' work, in 2011, singer-songwriter Suzanne Vega, best known for her 1980s hits "Tom's Diner" and "Luka," channeled McCullers in an innovative musical-narrative hybrid piece "Carson McCullers Talks About Love," which ran for a month at the Rattlestick Playwrights Theater in New York. As a teenager Vega was drawn to McCullers when she came across her biography in the library and felt a connection to her, thinking that, "Her face looked like photographs of myself as a young girl" (Light AR6). Later, while studying at Barnard College, Vega adapted several of McCullers' short stories to song and ultimately devised a one-act play based on these songs for her undergraduate thesis (Light AR6; Kelley 1). Thus she had been working on versions of what ultimately became "Carson McCullers Talks About Love" for a number of years, finally first trying out her solo production for an audience in February 2011 at the Carson McCullers Interdisciplinary Conference and 94th Birthday Celebration sponsored by Columbus State in Columbus, Georgia, McCullers' home-town. The Rattlestick production was directed by Kay Matschullat, fea-tured music co-written with *Spring Awakening* composer Duncan Sheik, and Vega performed with the accompaniment of Joe Iconis, on piano and offering occasional dialogue, and Andy Stack on guitar and other instru-ments. The 90-minute show features 14 songs, highlighting the major parts of McCullers' biography through narrative and music. Vega begins the show by recalling the influence that McCullers had on her as a 17-year-old, when, "Somehow at that moment I felt she picked me out, tapped me on the shoulder and had things to say to me." Many critics do comment on the physical resemblance between Vega and McCullers, whose persona Vega takes on in this transitional moment, through wiping make-up from her face, and donning a cigarette and page-boy wig.

McCullers' biography is explored through songs like "New York is My Destination," which explores the awe McCullers had for the north-ern city she journeyed to at age 17 with dreams of studying at Juilliard and taking writing courses at Columbia, then later returned to after she achieved literary success. Also included is "Song of Annemarie (Terror, Pity, Love)," a ballad to the Swiss heiress Annemarie Schwarzenbach for whom McCullers developed a mostly unrequited infatuation, and "The We of Me," words *The Member of the Wedding*'s Frankie Addams uses to imagine the unachievable union she wishes to share with her brother and his bride, and one echoed in many of McCullers' own relationships and love triangles. The narrative and lyrics are in some cases creative, yet generally grounded in real details related to McCullers' work and life. For instance, this stanza from the song "Harper Lee," a comical piece in which McCullers compares herself and other artists in a proud, taunting way: "Virginia Woolf, she leaves me cold./ I recognize the genius, but I'm twice as bold./ I have more to say than Hemingway./Lord knows, compared to Faulkner,/I say it in a better way." She once did say that Harper Lee was "poaching on my literary preserves" (Carr, *Lonely Hunter* 433), and Vega explains that the reference to Woolf comes from a lecture McCullers gave at the 92nd Street Y with Tennessee Williams (Kelley 2–3). McCullers did make those remarks about Hemingway and Faulkner one evening to her friend Thomas Ryan, who wrote the screenplay for the film version of *The Heart Is a Lonely Hunter* (Carr, *Lonely Hunter* 464), and her words have become well-known since. Other lines from that song and others are drawn from Carr's biography of McCullers, or even, in one case, an Amazon review from a reader of *The Ballad of the Sad Café*, which Vega felt McCullers would have liked (Kelly 3), a unique example of twenty-first-century discourses shaping McCullers narratives.

Some critics, such as Charles Isherwood of the *New York Times*, found Vega's performance a bit bizarre: "an odd format," wondering "under what surreal celestial circumstances, we can only wonder, would McCullers be recounting her tumultuous history in the form of a club act?" ("Alienated Souls"). Vega is not, after all, an actress, a fact noted by Michael Giltz of the *Huffington Post*, who remarks on her lack of confidence as a performer and her difficulty remembering lines, and so his assessment that the songs are "the show's strong suit" makes sense. Still, for a singer-songwriter like Vega, who has not released any work that has gained the popularity of "Tom's Diner" and "Luka"—she recounts to Alan Light one moment when a father pointed her out to his daughter on the street, saying, "She's from the 80s"—to reemerge in such a risky format is testament to the level of influence McCullers still carries. Vega's unconventional choices mirror those that McCullers herself made throughout her life and in that way it makes a fitting tribute; as one reviewer notes: "the awkwardness of the show is surprisingly endearing and true to the spirit of McCullers" (Shewey). She received a standing ovation after her first work-in-progress performance in Columbus, Georgia, at a gathering of international McCullers scholars and admirers, and reflecting on that, Vega notes her satisfaction: "If we can win this crowd over, then nobody in New York can say anything to me" (qtd. in Light AR6).

Further, Vega seems to understand the importance of McCullers' work in the twenty-first century, and no doubt her performance piece has led new readers to discover McCullers. Vega notes, "I think people understand her more than they might have 30 years ago because of the alternative sensibility … [She] was sort of an alternative personality before that phrase was coined" (qtd. in Light AR6). In fact, Vega may have even stumbled on textual analysis not yet noticed by twenty-first century literary critics: she says in an interview, "In one part of *The Heart Is a Lonely Hunter* she imagines a tiny radio that could sit in your ear, and I thought, 'She's describing an MP3 player!' So a lot of this world that she kind of intuited has come to pass" (qtd. in Light AR6). Overall, Vega's piece is an interesting modern take on McCullers' life and work that defies traditional expectations for performance and genre conventions.

Another example of McCullers' lasting influence, and perhaps the finest tribute of recent stage engagements, is the work of playwright Sarah Gubbins, who was commissioned to write *fml: how Carson McCullers saved my life* for the Steppenwolf Theatre Company of Chicago, where it premiered in February of 2012, and was later staged in 2015 at 7 Stages in Atlanta. It draws on the adolescent-centered nature of much of McCullers' work, and themes of loneliness and isolation, especially for characters who do not fit into traditional boundaries of gender and sexual identity. The setting is distinctly a twenty-first-century one, the action punctuated by on-screen projections and auditory pings of text messages between teenagers at a Catholic school in LaGrange, Illinois, a suburb of Chicago. That context is also reflected in the title, which embraces the contemporary usage of popular acronyms, like fml ("f*ck my life"), and is enriched by the syntax of many of the text messages: smh ("shaking my head"); lol ("laugh out loud"); "u" instead of "you." The setting is further emphasized in the play's content, which includes references to artists "crushin'" (18) on *The Voice*, Lebron James, and concern over the ubiquitous presence of corn in food. The play centers around Jo (short for Josephine), a high-school junior who plays basketball and is writing a graphic novel titled *fml: how Carson McCullers saved my life*, excerpts of which appear as panels and chapter titles projected on stage and that help tell the play's story. Jo is a lesbian with an ambiguous relationship with Emma, a transfer student who can't seem to decide whether she wants to hang out with Jo or her homophobic and jealous boyfriend Tyler, who never appears on stage, only through text messages to Emma. In addition to spending time with Emma, mainly helping her with her homework, Jo hangs out with Mickey, her gay male best friend. For Jo, her school is "St. Paul the Unbearable," where the other students "step at least a foot away when I walk ... past" (13) because of her unfeminine appearance and presumed sexuality.

The action is propelled by the arrival of Ms. Delaney, a new English teacher who revises the previous teacher's reading list and adds McCullers' *The Heart Is a Lonely Hunter*. Ms. Delaney begins by reading aloud the first sentence of *Heart*: "In the town there were two mutes, and they were always together" (1), telling the class that "the first sentence of any story is the moment the author begins his or her relationship with you—the reader ... But no matter their tactic that opening sentence defines the kind of relationship the two of you will have. 'Cause that's what reading is, right? A relationship between you and an author" (12). Like the relationship between the two mutes and the relationship between reader and author, Jo develops a relationship with McCullers and her work, as well as one with Ms. Delaney, which both become sources of inspiration and support as she navigates the difficulties of being unconventional in a strictly governed environment.

As Ms. Delaney reads McCullers' opening about the friendship between the two mutes, John Singer and Antonapoulos, Jo's voice joins hers, explaining, "In school there was one of my kind. I was always alone" (13). She recounts life in LaGrange with the same sense of boredom and malaise of Mick Kelly in *Heart* and Frankie in *The Member of the Wedding*, characters who, like Jo, do not fit into the strictly prescribed expectations for adolescent girls related to gender and sexuality. She also relates to McCullers' own ambivalent expressions of sexuality throughout her life, rebelling against the school's uniform policy, which requires that girls wear skirts until the cold of mid-January, by wearing pants and racking up pink slips until the school finally relents and allows the girls to wear pants regardless of weather. She says, " OK, maybe I was slightly inspired by Carson McCullers, who went around wearing men's clothing even back in the 1940s" (39). She connects with Mick's "inside room and the outside room" (*Heart* 138), explaining, "I knew exactly what Mick was talking about. But it wasn't something you could just describe in words" (30). Like Mick's "foreign countries and plans and music" (*Heart* 138), Jo's inside room is her drawings and "huge feelings and big dreams" (31). Jo unconsciously develops a crush on Ms. Delaney, who Mickey points out is "one of our tribe" (16). Ms. Delaney reading McCullers and Jo's voice and panels of her graphic novel combine into a crescendo where Jo is no longer "alone in this space … hearing Ms. D reading out loud, she was with me, and the sounds of Mick's symphony were washing over us" (32).

Jo's difficulty surviving high school escalates from alienation to explicit attacks: first, her locker is vandalized with the word "faggot" sprayed across it, and finally, a locker room beating lands her in the hospital. However, the story of Jo and Ms. Delaney parallels that of Singer's journey to visit Antonapoulos at the asylum via train, only to find his friend has died. At the end of the play, Jo's beloved teacher is no longer teaching at the school because of "irreconcilable differences" (83), presumably related to her sexuality or efforts to support students in establishing a Gay Straight Alliance. Initially depressed at the loss of Ms. Delaney and uncertain about finishing her novel, Jo says, "It's just not the same. I wanted her to read it." But Mickey encourages her: "But she could. And someone else will read it. Someone you don't even know" (86). Just as McCullers' work is an influence for Jo and other twenty-first-century readers, Gubbins' play, which is simultaneously Jo's graphic novel, reaches adolescents who might be struggling to accept their differences.

Both McCullers and Ms. Delaney serve as models and inspiration for Jo, in accepting her sexual and gender identity and in using literature as an outlet for exploring and coming to terms with these feelings. It seems appropriate that the play explores the influence and eventual disappearance of a teacher, in light of McCullers' own close personal relationship with her piano teacher Mary Tucker, who she felt had abandoned her when Tucker and her husband moved away from Columbus when McCullers was 17 years old. While some critics felt Gubbins' play needed more centrality and a tighter focus, overall, it was received as "a smart, engaging work" (Farmer) and "a play for today's LGBT youth" (Morgan). Clearly, the conflicts surrounding sexuality and gender identity that McCullers explored in 1940 have lasting resonance for audiences, especially young people, today.

In 2005, Sheryl Tippins' book *February House* was published, an account of the artistic living experiment at 7 Middagh Street in Brooklyn Heights where McCullers lived with a group of artists in the 1940s, including W. H. Auden, composer Benjamin Britten, and Gypsy Rose Lee. Their friend and writer Anais Nin coined it February House because so many of its residents had birthdays in that month. In 2012, a musical adaptation of Tippins' book, also called *February House*, premiered at the Public Theater and later played at the Long Wharf Theatre in New Haven, Connecticut, the book by Seth Bockley and music by Gabriel Kahane. This historic housing arrangement was George Davis' idea, who had just lost his editor's job at *Harper's Bazaar* and found himself broke. He and McCullers had talked about the possibility of living together along with other artists, "like living at Bread Loaf, except it would be year-round" (Tippins 31). Communal living would assist with finances, provide camaraderie, and hopefully help facilitate artistic production. In 1940, soon after the publication of *The Heart Is a Lonely Hunter*, McCullers moved into the home, partly to escape her husband Reeves and his hard drinking and to accomplish some writing among other artists serious about their work. In addition, now that she had had become a famous author in her own right, she had ambitions to join the literary elite (Tippins 18), and Davis could help facilitate this goal with his friends and contacts. Though many artists came and went through February House, the musical version features McCullers; Erika Mann, the German actress and daughter of writer Thomas Mann; writer W. H. (Wystan Hugh) Auden and his much-younger lover, Chester Kallman; the composer Benjamin Britten and his partner, the singer Peter Pears; and burlesque performer Gypsy Rose Lee, who worked on her mystery novel *The G-String Murders* (1941) while in residence. Davis, the organizer of the group, and Reeves McCullers appear as well, with Reeves mostly showing up to argue with or beg Carson to return home with him, telling her that "a serious artist needs a home. A real home. Not some fairy world, playing house with a bunch of high-brow queers" (29). The writers chose to explore Carson's penchant for developing crushes on women through the character of Erika Mann, who functions as the object of Carson's obsession in the musical, but is really a conflation of a few historical personalities, including Annemarie Schwarzenbach ("Re: A Message from Bandcamp").

Like Tippins' book, the musical brings to life that period, depicting each character's personalities; their anxieties surrounding their work, finances, and love triangles; their hard drinking and drug use; and the joys and downfalls of communal living. Most importantly, the beginning of World War II undergirds the narrative, with several of the artists in exile from Europe, and tensions building to news on the radio of German raid attacks on Great Britain. Critics praised the music (played by Andy Stack, who, incidentally, had joined Vega for her performance piece), commenting that it reflects "the sound of the age of anxiety, echoing through the voices of artists who can't avoid feeling its tremors" (Brantley). The show portrays the artist's struggle between seeing the futility in creating art alongside destruction and suffering and feeling a responsibility to use their forum in troubled times. Despite the ominous overtone, the comic aspects of life at 7 Middagh Street—leaking ceilings, bed bugs, and artists' quirks and egos—are highlighted, for a "campy" feel, which reflects how Carson described the atmosphere in her lifetime (Carr, *Lonely Hunter* 126). Of course, the play's focus is a tad esoteric, placing some of the greatest artists of the twentieth century at a particular historical juncture, with Auden's poetry set to verse at times—it clearly finds its fullest understanding in audiences familiar with the artists' work and biographies—further, it then sets these erudite topics within the realm of musical theater. However, "what saves *February House* from annoying gaucheness and pretension is the obvious affection that its creators feel for their subjects. This show suggests a sweet collection of fans' notes, set to music that is something more than that" (Brantley).

Despite the joy of the ensemble, Ben Brantley rightly assesses that "the show and its appealing cast are at their best when the focus is on individual artists who feel alone, even among their own, and hear uncommon melodies that no one else hears." One such example is the song "Coney Island," where McCullers sings about her desire to go to the freak show at Coney Island, where among the "Siamese twins" and the "pinheads" is truly where "I feel at home" (32), a sentiment she felt from an early age seeing freak shows in Georgia (Carr, *Lonely Hunter* 1). While not many others shared this affinity, George Davis, who had assembled his own "freak show" of sorts with this home, understood her fascination (Carr, *Lonely Hunter* 126), as does Frankie Addams in *The Member of the Wedding*, who is both captivated and fearful that "it seemed to her that they had looked at her in a secret way and tried to connect their eyes with hers, as though to say: we know you" (272). Ultimately, as she did in real life, Carson leaves the home with Reeves because she is ill, and they return to Georgia where her mother can help care for her. One by one, the artists leave and Davis is alone, until 7 Middagh Street is torn down to make way for a wider automobile approach to the Brooklyn Bridge in 1945. It is Carson and Davis's voices that finish the show, Carson's first through a letter to Davis:

> I hear they're knocking our old boardinghouse down ... I think I've got my novel nearly done. It's about that little hunchback and the giant bartender woman who loves him. There's no reason for their love, which is the whole point ... Things are changing so fast. December 7th turned the world upside down and I am glad in a queer way just to know what we are going to do. I wonder, George, if I am a lonely person by birth or inclination ... I was thinking this morning about those five days when I was scared I'd never see again. How you brought me cheesecake for breakfast and tucked me in at night. I hope I could do that for you some time. And I hope that 1942 will bring us all peace and peace of mind. (118)

Carson and Davis then "sing goodnight/sing goodnight/to the boardinghouse" and lie together on the floor, with "sounds of Coney Island, faintly" as the play ends (119), a reminder of the connections that people do find, even in periods of personal and sociopolitical turmoil.

Each of these productions provide ample evidence that interest in McCullers' life and work continues, and it is compelling to see that legacy played out on stage, a place where she herself had ambivalent experiences, but wished to see her work performed again. If that was her desire, she would likely be pleased by many of these twenty-first-century performances. They all offer a different approach to McCullers' life and work, with variations on genre and content, and critics, fans, and audiences have found some more satisfactory than others. The ones that have found the most success have done so by foregrounding McCullers' texts, weaving them in a way that makes them a central component of their own, and by demonstrating a respect and admiration for the author and her work. Ultimately, "the best way to know Carson McCullers is to read Carson McCullers" (Sommer), but undoubtedly each of these productions has led at least one reader to discover or rediscover Carson McCullers and her work, which remains their most important achievement as we consider the meaning that McCullers holds for us in the twenty-first century.

NOTES

1. McCullers biographer Virginia Spencer Carr has documented the time that McCullers and Williams spent together that summer through interviews with Williams and his companion Pancho Rodriguez in both "Carson McCullers: Novelist Turned Playwright" and *The Lonely Hunter*.
2. McCullers may have misspoken here about the critic who reviewed her novel, as it was Edmund Wilson who wrote a *New Yorker* review in which he states that McCullers seems to "have difficulty in adjusting her abilities to a dramatically effective subject," and that *The Member of the Wedding* has "no element of drama at all."
3. See Carr, "Carson McCullers: Novelist Turned Playwright" and *The Lonely Hunter*, and James, Giblin Judith. "Carson McCullers, Lillian Smith, and the Politics of Broadway." *Southern Women Playwrights: New Essays in Literary History and Criticism*. Ed. Robert L. McDonald and Linda Rohrer Paige. Tuscaloosa: University of Alabama Press, 2002. 42–60; "Two Plays— *The Member of the Wedding* (1950, 1951) & *The Square Root of Wonderful* (1957, 1958)." *Wunderkind: The Reputation of Carson McCullers, 1940–1990*. Columbia, SC: Camden House, 1995. 125–142.
4. While Schulman's characterization of McCullers' depressions, alcoholism, and illness are accurate, those who have studied McCullers' life find evidence of "mischievousness" (Savigneau 329), but they would probably not characterize her as "cruel." Additionally, there is ample evidence of her ability to love others deeply. Further, while her relationship with Reeves was deeply troubled and turbulent, and "more often than not they damaged one another" (Savigneau 328), it is grossly inaccurate to claim that Carson drove him to suicide, a claim that does not take into account his alcoholism and his own personal feelings about his failures as a writer and the jealousy he felt at her success, as well as the emotional abuse he inflicted on her, including his unhealthy request at one point that Carson commit suicide with him (*Lonely Hunter* 400).

WORKS CITED

Atkinson, Brooks. Rev. of *The Member of the Wedding*, by Carson McCullers. Empire Theatre, New York. *New York Times* 6 Jan. 1950: 26. *ProQuest*. Print.

Barnes, Howard. Rev. of *The Member of the Wedding*, by Carson McCullers. Empire Theatre, New York. *New York Herald Tribune* 6 Jan. 1950: 12. Print.

Bernardo, Melissa Rose. Rev. of *The Heart is a Lonely Hunter*, by Rebecca Gilman. New York Theater Workshop, New York. *Entertainment Weekly*. Entertainment Weekly, 4 Dec. 2009. Web.

Bockley, Seth and Gabriel Kahane. *February House*. Unpublished book, music, and lyrics. 2012. Print.

Bockley, Seth. "Re: Fwd: A message from Bandcamp, on behalf of Casey Kayser." Message to the author. 9 Sept. 2015. Email.

Brantley, Ben. "Tuneful Rooms of Their Own in Brooklyn." Rev. of *February House*, by Seth Bockley and Gabriel Kahane. Public Theater, New York. *New York Times*. New York Times, 22 May 2012. Web.

Carr, Virginia Spencer. *The Lonely Hunter: A Biography of Carson McCullers*. 1975. Athens: University of Georgia Press, 2003. Print.

——. "Carson McCullers: Novelist Turned Playwright." *The Southern Quarterly* 25.3 (1987): 37–51. Print.

"Carson McCullers Talks About Love". By Suzanne Vega. Dir. Kay Matschullat. Rattlestick Playwrights Theater, New York City. 5 May–5 June, 2011. Performance.

Dews, Carlos. "Carson McCullers; A Question of Balance." Letter to the Editor Re: When She Wrote, the Dross of Her Life Became Gold' by Jonathan Mandell. *New York Times*. New York Times, 3 Feb. 2002. Web.

Farmer, Jim. "The Teacher/Student Dynamic Marks 7 Stages' Enchanting Carson McCullers." Rev. of *fml: how Carson McCullers saved my life*, by Sarah Gubbins. 7 Stages, Atlanta. *ArtsATL.com*. ArtsATL, 11 Feb. 2015. Web.

Feldberg, Robert. Rev. of *The Heart is a Lonely Hunter*, adapted by Rebecca Gilman. New York Theatre Workshop, New York. *The Bergen Record*. *Northjersey.com*, 4 Dec. 2009. Web.

Finkle, David. Rev. of *Carson McCullers (Historically Inaccurate)*, by Sarah Schulman. Women's Project Theatre, New York. *TheaterMania*. TheaterMania, 22 Jan. 2002. Web.

Garland, Robert. "Something Special But Not Quite a Play." Rev. of *The Member of the Wedding*, by Carson McCullers. Empire Theatre, New York. *New York Journal American* 6 Jan. 1950: 18. Print.

Gibbs, Wolcott. "Brook and River." Rev. of *The Member of the Wedding*, by Carson McCullers. Empire Theatre, New York. *New Yorker* 14 Jan. 1950: 44, 46. Print.

Gilman, Rebecca. *The Heart is a Lonely Hunter*. New York: Dramatists Play Service Inc., 2010. Print.

Giltz, Michael. "Suzanne Vega Dips Her Toes Into Live Theater." Rev. of "Carson McCullers Talks About Love," by Suzanne Vega. Rattlestick Playwrights Theater, New York City. *Huffington Post*. Huffington Post, 10 May 2011. Web.

Gubbins, Sarah. *fml: how Carson McCullers saved my life*. Woodstock, IL: Dramatic Publishing Company, 2012. Print.

Healy, Patrick. "Hearing Man in Deaf Role Stirs Protests in New York." *New York Times* 14 Oct. 2009: C1. Print.

Isherwood, Charles. "Carson McCullers's Wounded Souls, Quietly Holding in Yearnings." Rev. of *The Heart is a Lonely Hunter*, by Rebecca Gilman. New York Theater Workshop, New York. *New York Times*. New York Times, 4 Dec. 2009. Web.

——. "The Alienated Souls Whisper." Rev. of "Carson McCullers Talks About Love," by Suzanne Vega. Rattlestick Playwrights Theater, New York City. *New York Times*. New York Times, 5 May 2011. Web.

James, Judith Giblin. *Wunderkind: The Reputation of Carson McCullers, 1940–1990*. Columbia, SC: Camden House, 1995. Print.

Jones, Chris. "Plenty of Heart, Not Enough Tension in *Lonely Hunter*." Rev. of *The Heart is a Lonely Hunter*, by Rebecca Gilman. Steppenwolf Theatre, Chicago. *Chicago Tribune*. Chicago Tribune, 18 Oct. 2011. Web.

Kelley, Rich. Interview with Suzanne Vega. *Library of America Summer E-Newsletter*. 2011. Print.

Light, Alan. "Talking About Her Love of McCullers." Interview with Suzanne Vega. *New York Times* 1 May 2011: AR6. Print.

Madden, David. "Re: Play on Tennessee and Carson." Message to the author. 12 Sept. 2015. Email.

——. "Tennessee and Carson: Notes on a Concept for a Play." *Critical Essays on Carson McCullers*. Ed. Beverly Lyon Clark and Melvin J. Friedman. Intro. Lisa Logan. New York: Hall; 1996. 87–95. Print.

Mandell, Jonathan. "Carson McCullers: Bringing Her Gold Prose to the Stage." Interview with Sarah Schulman. *New York Times*. New York Times, 20 Jan. 2002. Web.

McClain, John. "*The Square Root of Wonderful*—Diffuse Doubletalk Adds Up to Big O." Rev. of *The Square Root of Wonderful*, by Carson McCullers. National Theatre, New York. *New York Journal-American* 31 Oct. 1957: 22. Print.

McCullers, Carson. *The Heart is a Lonely Hunter*. New York: Houghton Mifflin, 1940. Bantam edition 1953. Print.

——. "How I Began to Write." *The Mortgaged Heart*. Ed. Margarita G. Smith. Boston: Houghton Mifflin: 1971. 249–251. Print.

——. *The Member of the Wedding*. *Collected Stories of Carson McCullers*. Intro. Virginia Spencer Carr. New York: Houghton Mifflin Company. First Mariner Books Ed. 1998. 257–392. Print.

Morgan, Scott C. Rev. of *fml: how Carson McCullers saved my life*, by Sarah Gubbins. Steppenwolf Theatre, Chicago. *Windy City Times*. Windy City Media Group, 7 Mar. 2012. Web.

Morrison, Hobe. Rev. of *The Square Root of Wonderful*, by Carson McCullers. National Theatre, New York. *Variety* 6 Nov. 1957: 72. Print.

Murray, Matthew. Rev. of *Carson McCullers (Historically Inaccurate)*, by Sarah Schulman. Women's Project Theatre, New York. *Talkin' Broadway*. Talkin' Broadway, n.d. Web.

"New Play in Manhattan." Rev. of *The Member of the Wedding*, by Carson McCullers. Empire Theatre, New York. *Time* 16 Jan. 1950: 45. Print.

"New Plays." Rev. of *The Member of the Wedding*, by Carson McCullers. Empire Theatre, New York. *Newsweek* 16 Jan. 1950: 74. Print.

Phelan, Kappo. Rev. of *The Member of the Wedding*, by Carson McCullers. Empire Theatre, New York. *Commonweal* 27 Jan. 1950: 437–38. Print.

Savigneau, Josyane. *Carson McCullers: A Life*. Trans. by Joan E. Howard. New York: Houghton Mifflin, 2001.

Shewey, Don. Rev. of "Carson McCullers Talks About Love," by Suzanne Vega. Rattlestick Playwrights Theater, New York City. *CultureVulture*. CultureVulture, 5 May 2011. Web.

Sommer, Elyse. Rev. of *Carson McCullers (Historically Inaccurate)*, by Sarah Schulman. Women's Project Theatre, New York. *CurtainUp*. CurtainUp, 2002. Web.

Spoto, Donald. *The Kindness of Strangers: The Life of Tennessee Williams*. Boston: Little, Brown and Company, 1985. Print.

Tippins, Sherill. *February House: The Story of W. H. Auden, Carson McCullers, Jane and Paul Bowles, Benjamin Britten, and Gypsy Rose Lee, Under One Roof in Brooklyn*. New York: Houghton Mifflin Company. First Mariner Books Ed. 2006. Print.

Whalen, Lauren. Rev. of *The Heart is a Lonely Hunter*, by Rebecca Gilman. Steppenwolf Theater, Chicago. *Chicago Theater Beat*. Chicago Theater Beat, 19 Oct. 2011. Web.

Wilson, Edmund. "Two Books That Leave You Blank: Carson McCullers, Siegfried Sassoon." Rev. of *The Member of the Wedding*, by Carson McCullers. *New Yorker* 30 Mar. 1946: 87. Print.

Windman, Matt. Rev. of *The Heart is a Lonely Hunter*, by Rebecca Gilman. New York Theater Workshop, New York. *On Off Broadway: New York Theater News, Videos, Reviews, and Rambling*. 4 Dec. 2009. Web.

Wyatt, Euphemia Van Rensselaer. Rev. of *The Member of the Wedding*, by Carson McCullers. Empire Theatre, New York. *Catholic World* Mar. 1950: 467–68. Print.

Zoglin, Richard. "The Top Ten Plays and Musicals of 2009: *The Heart is a Lonely Hunter*." *Time*. Time, 8 Dec. 2009. Web.

"Impromptu Journal of My Heart": Carson Mccullers' Therapeutic Recordings, April–May 1958

Carlos Dews

INTRODUCTION

Early in 1958 Carson Mccullers made an appointment to see Dr. Mary Mercer, a child psychiatrist who lived and worked in South Nyack, New York, a short drive from Mccullers' home in Nyack. In the autobiography she worked on during the final two years of her life Mccullers wrote of her motivation for seeking the help of Dr. Mercer: "I went professionally to Mary Mercer because I was despondent. My mother had died, my dear friend John La Touche had died, and I was ill, badly crippled. Several psychiatrists who are social friends of mine … had suggested strongly that I go to see Mary Mercer" (Mccullers *Illumination* 73). In making the appointment to see Dr. Mercer, Mccullers sought relief from the accumulated physical, emotional and professional difficulties she had faced in the previous five years. Medically, Mccullers had suffered since she was an adolescent with the ramifications of a misdiagnosed and untreated case of rheumatic fever, primarily a series of cerebral strokes, including progressive paralysis on the left side of her body. In 1956 her paralyzed left arm had begun to atrophy, and her doctors had suggested

C. Dews (✉)
Department of English Language and Literature, John Cabot University,
Via della Lungara 233, 165 Rome, Italy

© The Author(s) 2016   21
A. Graham-Bertolini, C. Kayser (eds.), *Carson Mccullers in the
Twenty-First Century*, DOI 10.1007/978-3-319-40292-5_2

amputation as a remedy for the pain it caused. She ultimately chose not to opt for amputation and the pain continued. Due to these and other medical difficulties, the year 1956 would prove to be the least productive of McCullers' adult life.

In addition to her physical ailments, McCullers faced myriad emotional difficulties. Beyond the losses she described in her autobiography, in the years preceding her first appointment with Dr. Mercer, her husband, Reeves McCullers, had committed suicide in Paris on 18 November 1953, and her favorite aunt, her mother's sister, Martha Waters Johnson, had died in late December 1953.

Professionally McCullers did not fare any better during the mid-1950s. In addition to the significant drop in her creative output, on 7 December 1957, McCullers' play *The Square Root of Wonderful*, closed after only forty-five performances on Broadway. Perhaps the only significant positive experience between 1953 and 1958, beyond minor publications, some public appearances and lectures, and sporadic continued writing on works in progress, was the successful production of McCullers' play *The Member of the Wedding* at the Royal Court Theatre in London that opened on 16 February 1957.

McCullers sought help from Dr. Mercer not only for relief from physical and emotional suffering but also a block in her creative life. It is important to note that McCullers' life and work were inseparable. Her emotional life was so often directly reflected in her creative work that it is inappropriate to try to separate her need for assistance with her emotional life and help with her creative life. Difficulty in writing was seen as a personal failure and personal difficulties strongly influenced her productivity. Early in her work with Dr. Mercer, it became clear that McCullers was struggling with her writing and was looking for help with her work through her therapy. She had found herself unable to continue writing what was to be her final novel, *Clock Without Hands*, and at least two nonfiction projects, an autobiography and a work on the lives of other creative people who struggled with physical or emotional difficulties, were stalled. At the time she began seeing Dr. Mercer, McCullers was nearly finished working on a nonfiction piece that would soon be published in *Esquire*, in December 1958, as "The Flowering Dream: Notes on Writing."

In May of 1958, during the early months of their therapeutic work together, McCullers suggested that she and Dr. Mercer record some of their therapy sessions. According to a 1970 letter, drafted but never sent, from Dr. Mary Mercer to McCullers' agent, Robert Lantz, Mercer indicates that the idea to record the sessions came from McCullers herself:

> ... let me remind you that Carson herself made the best use of all her ideas and writing ... Carson did not have trouble talking. Instead, her concern was how she was going to pay for treatment. Out of this concern came her request to record the sessions so that a book could be published someday to support her therapy. It was her idea of killing two birds with one stone and it made her very happy ... She was a writer and she couldn't write, so somehow she must get back to her own work. She did and *Clock Without Hands* was the result. Those conversations between us had their proper place, were used up by Carson in her own way, and that is why she did not go back to that material or the title ["The Flowering Dream"] when she came to start to write her autobiography. (6 March 1970)

Mercer agreed, at least for a time, to record some of their sessions and the recordings were made with the Dictaphone machine that Dr. Mercer used to dictate correspondence and notes for her clients' files. These recorded sessions performed a dual role—they provided an opportunity for McCullers to free-associate in a traditional psychoanalytic mode and also for her to try to continue to write, speaking the text into the microphone of the Dictaphone machine and using the transcripts of what she had spoken as a first draft of her work. Dr. Mercer's secretary, Barbara, then transcribed the Dictaphone belts, providing two copies, one for Dr. Mercer to review, correct, and emend, and one for McCullers to do the same. There are no significant differences between the two copies of each transcript. Many of the same corrections were made both by McCullers and Mercer, inserting content where the secretary who transcribed the Dictaphone belt had misunderstood what one or both of them had said or had left blanks in the transcripts when she was not able to hear what Mercer or McCullers said on the recordings.

The original Dictaphone belts are no longer extant, perhaps because they were re-used for subsequent recordings by Dr. Mercer. However, as a sign of her dedication to the preservation of all materials related to McCullers' life and work, Dr. Mercer kept the Dictaphone machine that had been used to make these recordings. The machine was among the materials left to the Carson McCullers Center for Writers and Musicians in 2014 as part of Dr. Mercer's estate. The Dictaphone machine is now housed in the Smith-McCullers House museum in Carson McCullers' childhood home in Columbus, Georgia.

DESCRIPTION AND HISTORY OF TRANSCRIPTS

These recording "experiments," as they were titled at the top of the first transcribed session ("The first experiment with THE DICTAPHONE."), lasted for approximately one month. The first recording was made on 11 April 1958 and the final recording is dated 16 May 1958. It is unclear if recordings were made during all of McCullers' sessions with Dr. Mercer during this period. And it is unclear if sessions in their entirety were recorded or if only portions of sessions were recorded; however, given the relatively few number of pages in each session's transcript, it would appear that only partial sessions were recorded or that only partial transcripts were produced. There were a total of nine recorded and transcribed sessions, recorded on April 11, 14, 21, 25, 28 and May 5, 9, 12, and 16, 1958. All the transcripts are double-spaced and all the words of the transcripts are capitalized throughout.

Due in large part to the intervention by Dr. Mary Mercer, McCullers' psychological and medical condition improved significantly and McCullers lived until 29 September 1967, when she succumbed to a massive cerebral stroke. If one of the goals of her therapeutic work with Dr. Mary Mercer was for McCullers to regain her creative productivity, then the work they did together can be deemed a success. During the nine years between the time she first went to Dr. Mercer and her death in 1967, McCullers was able to complete her final novel, *Clock Without Hands*, which was published on 18 September 1961; write an illustrated book of comic verse for children, *Sweet as Pickle and Clean as a Pig*, published in 1964; and, although they were not published during her lifetime, McCullers continued to work during the final years of her life on her autobiography, with the working title *Illumination and Night Glare* (the autobiography would eventually be published by the University of Wisconsin Press in 1999). Although there are very few extant manuscript pages from it, McCullers also worked during the final nine years of her life on a book that detailed the creative work of those with significant physical limitations, including Cole Porter, Peter Freuchen, and Sarah Bernhardt. This work was sometimes referred to by its working title, "Despite All."

At the time of her death in 1967, one copy of the transcripts of the Dictaphone sessions remained in the files of Dr. Mercer at her office and the other with McCullers' papers and manuscripts at her home in Nyack. Both copies of the transcripts are now held in the Dr. Mary E. Mercer/Carson McCullers Collection at the Schwob Library of Columbus State University, part of the collections brought together by the Carson McCullers Center for Writers and Musicians at Columbus State University. One copy of the transcripts is labeled, in the handwriting of Dr. Mary Mercer, "M.E.M.", for Mary E. Mercer, and one is labeled "Mrs. McCullers." The existence in the Dr. Mary E. Mercer/Carson McCullers Collection of both copies of the transcribed Dictaphone recordings is the result of a complicated and interesting story regarding the transcripts that transpired in the years following McCullers' death.

After McCullers died in September of 1967, the responsibility of overseeing her literary estate passed primarily to her agent, Robert Lantz; her attorney, Floria Lasky; and her sister, Margarita "Rita" Smith. Per her last will and testament the proceeds from McCullers' literary estate were to be divided equally between McCullers' two siblings, Rita and Lamar Smith, and Dr. Mary Mercer. By 1970, three years after McCullers' death, three significant decisions had been made by Lasky, Lantz, and Smith. They decided to pursue publication of a posthumous collection of work by McCullers that would bring together in a single volume most of McCullers' previously published short fiction and nonfiction work, published mostly in American magazines; McCullers previously published poetry; as well as a few previously unpublished short stories. As the author's sister and a professional editor herself, Rita Smith would serve as the editor of this volume. This collection, eventually titled *The Mortgaged Heart* (the title taken from one of McCullers' poems included in the volume), would be published by Houghton Mifflin in 1971. Lantz, Lasky, and Smith had also decided to pursue the sale of McCullers' papers, as McCullers' intention had been to find an appropriate repository for her literary manuscripts, letters, and miscellaneous other materials. Finally, the three literary executors of McCullers' estate decided to identify a biographer to write an authorized biography of McCullers. They intended to grant this biographer exclusive access to McCullers' papers either before or after they were sold to an appropriate repository. This search for an official biographer would eventually prove futile, as Virginia Spencer Carr, without access to McCullers' papers and without the estate's support, was well into writing a significant biography of McCullers, the volume that would appear in 1976 as *The Lonely Hunter: A Biography of Carson McCullers*. Once they discovered the extent to which Carr had already researched the biography, Lasky, Lantz, and Smith decided not to grant Carr access to the McCullers materials and to no longer pursue an authorized biographer.

McCullers' estate, via Floria Lasky, hired the antiquarian bookseller and manuscript appraiser Lew David Feldman and his company, House of El Dieff, to catalog, appraise, and prepare McCullers' papers for sale to an appropriate institution (Dickinson 65). Rita Smith worked to identify items in the materials assembled by Feldman to include in the collection she wished to edit. She found in McCullers' papers the draft manuscript of the autobiography on which McCullers worked during the final years of her life and the transcripts of McCullers' therapy sessions with Dr. Mary Mercer. These therapy transcripts had been labeled as "meditations during analysis" by Feldman, a description that would confuse Dr. Mary Mercer when she first saw the catalog of McCullers' manuscripts and papers. Smith would eventually decide not to include the text of either of these items in the collection she edited.

Robert Lantz wrote to Mary Mercer on 7 January 1970 to update her on the progress of the posthumous collection, the search for an authorized biographer, and to ask her to write down her own recollections of McCullers' struggles during the final years of her life. Of her recollections of her time with McCullers, Lantz wrote to Mercer:

> I want the living, extraordinary, unique, incredible lady recreated and this fantastic tale of gallantry recaptured for generations to come, and we all will have to help because we were the people who knew her and to some degree understood her. You are in a unique position, and what I have in mind is that the right biographer will eventually be able to get from you, within the boundaries of all propriety, the details of the story of the many illnesses, the many operations, the many triumphs in the long war for life that she fought and always always always won. I am sure that much of your records can and will be made available at that time. As a matter of fact it was always my secret hope that you will one day find the time to write it all down or dictate it yourself in your own words, so that at some point this could all become available as seen from your unique vantage point, not only with your medical understanding but with your remarkable love and devotion to Carson. (7 January 1970)

Lantz also asked Mercer about the transcripts of McCullers' analysis that McCullers had asked him to take home and read when he saw her when she was once hospitalized. Lantz wrote:

> Incidentally at one point, not the last time or the time before that but at some time when she was at Harkness Pavilion, she asked me to open the

drawer in her night table and take out a bundle of pages, between fifty and seventy five I seem to remember, which supposedly were the transcripts of part of the analysis she had gone through with you but had taped at some stage. You then apparently had these tapes transcribed so that she could look at them in manuscript form and your idea to treat the reality of Carson's past as a piece of literature for her was of course a stroke of genius on your part. I remember that I took the pages with me overnight, at her insistence, and there were marvelous scenes in the Brooklyn house, scenes with Gypsy Rose Lee, the whole involvement with gangsters, etc. Have you any idea where those pages are? They had vitality, directness, immense humor and of course are now of great historic value. They should certainly become part of the material to be made available to an approved biography. (7 January 1970)

It was clear that Lantz wanted to make sure that these transcripts were available for an authorized biographer. This letter perhaps motivated Dr. Mercer to see if McCullers' copy of the transcripts of the therapy sessions had been included with the materials being organized and prepared for sale by Lew David Feldman.

On 10 February 1970, Mary Mercer replied to Robert Lantz's letter of 7 January 1970. She pointed out that the pages McCullers had asked him to take home to read while she was hospitalized were not a "manuscript" as he had described it in his letter and were instead part of McCullers' psychiatric record and thus should be kept in strict confidence and not shared with a biographer. Mercer wrote to Lantz:

Robby, you have solved a mystery for me. Floria asked me not long ago if I knew of a manuscript called 'The Flowering Dream,' which Carson brought with her to the hospital on one of the many hospitalizations and which you read. I did not know about this. The only "Flowering Dream" I knew about was published in *Esquire* in 1959. The material which you read was not a manuscript but part of Carson's psychiatric record. Carson was in psychiatric treatment with me for one year. That particular hospitalization must have occurred while she was still my patient. Her psychiatric records, like those of any other psychiatric patient, are strictly confidential. Carson and I became friends socially after her psychiatric treatment was terminated. We remained friends, as you know, through all of those roller-coaster years. There are no secrets to be responsible for in those last remaining years, just 'illumination and night glare'." (10 February 1970)

In the final sentence of this letter Dr. Mercer is referring to "illumination and night glare," using the term McCullers adopted as the title for her autobiography, but that she also used, as Dr. Mercer does in the letter, to describe the alternating moments of creative inspiration and personal tragedy that informed McCullers' life, for which Mercer used the words "roller coaster." Given the struggle between her and McCullers' estate that was to follow, Dr. Mercer felt strongly that the transcripts of McCullers' therapy sessions, at least at that time, should not be made public and that McCullers' copies of the transcripts should be returned to her to be placed, along with her own copy, in McCullers' medical/psychiatric records. This dispute over the therapy transcripts came in the midst of a broader conflict between Dr. Mercer and Floria Lasky over personal items designated to go to Dr. Mercer per McCullers' will and over the specific definition of "personal items" and how some items Dr. Mercer saw as "personal items" were instead considered to be part of McCullers' literary estate.

Robert Lantz responded to Dr. Mercer's letter of 10 February 1970 with a letter dated 27 February 1970. In this letter Lantz addressed Dr. Mercer's concerns about the confidentiality of the therapy transcripts. He expressed his assumption that McCullers had intended to use these materials in her autobiography on which she had worked during the final years of her life.

On 6 March 1970 Dr. Mercer drafted a response to Lantz, but after consulting with her accountant and attorney, Mr. Nathanial Sales, she chose not to send it. The manuscript of the letter includes the notation "Not sent." This draft letter does provide significant information about Dr. Mercer's thoughts on the transcripts and how she, and perhaps McCullers, saw them in relation to her autobiographical work. The draft letter, in part, reads: "Just for the record and also so you don't feel bad that anything of Carson's work will not be properly handled, let me remind you that Carson herself made the best use of all her ideas and writing. You are too wise and experienced to fail to realize that a recorded conversation between a patient and a psychiatrist is not literature, even when the patient is Carson" (6 March 1970).

Due to her concerns about the disposition of some of what she concerned to be McCullers' "personal belongings" and the therapy transcripts, Dr. Mercer asked McCullers' estate for a copy of the list of materials prepared by Lew David Feldman's company. In a letter of 3 February 1971, Floria Lasky wrote to Dr. Mercer to assure her that she would receive a copy of the list of items in McCullers papers . Dr. Mercer replied to this letter on 5 March 1971 saying that she had yet to receive the promised list of McCullers' literary papers.

Dr. Mercer finally received the list of McCullers items to be valued and sold to an archive, along with a letter from Floria Lasky, on 18 March 1971. This list, a copy of the one made by Lew David Feldman's company, was twenty-four pages in length and included 362 items (Lasky 18 March 1971). The exchange of letters between Dr. Mercer and Floria Lasky and Robert Lantz in 1970 began a sometimes heated struggle between Mercer and the representatives of McCullers' estate over the disposition of what Dr. Mercer considered to be the personal items among McCullers' materials, including the transcriptions of their therapy sessions. This struggle would last until 1973.

After three years and four months, many letters and phone calls, at least two heated meetings, and the threat of a court order, Floria Lasky agreed to return some of the items requested by Dr. Mercer. McCullers' copy of the therapy transcripts was among the items returned to Dr. Mercer. However, Floria Lasky, perhaps due to how the item was assessed by the House of El Dieff, decided that the original of the third transcript, dated 14 April 1958, would be included in the materials that would eventually be sold via the House of El Dieff to the Harry Ransom Center at the University of Texas at Austin. This decision was made because McCullers' handwriting had been identified on the transcript and so it was thus considered one of McCullers' literary manuscripts.

With mixed results Dr. Mercer would continue to litigate for at least two more years for the return of what she considered McCullers' other personal items. The letters and transcripts related to McCullers' medical and therapeutic work with her that Dr. Mary Mercer had received back from Floria Lasky would be held along with the copy of the transcripts in Dr. Mercer's office until Dr. Mercer's death in 2013, when they were included with a wealth of other McCullers-related materials bequeathed to the Carson McCullers Center for Writers and Musicians at Columbus State University in Columbus, Georgia, and formed part of the Dr. Mary E. Mercer/Carson McCullers Collection held in the Columbus State University Archives of the Simon Schwob Memorial Library.

"A Face that I Knew Would Haunt me to the End of my Life": Annemarie Schwarzenbach

As one might expect from the free-associative, wide-ranging nature of therapy transcripts, it is impossible to cover all that was discussed in the recorded sessions in a single essay. This essay is necessarily a selective consideration of the content of the transcripts. The nine extant transcripts of McCullers' therapy sessions with Dr. Mary Mercer contain a wealth of information for those interested in the life and work of McCullers. In particular, the details regarding McCullers' relationship with Mary Tucker, her most influential piano teacher, provide insight into one of the most important relationships of McCullers' life. As well, the stories McCullers told during the therapy sessions regarding the time she spent in the 1940s living in a house in Brooklyn Heights with, among others, W. H. Auden, George Davis, Benjamin Britten, and Gypsy Rose Lee provide a more detailed version of the stories from that time than McCullers included in her autobiography *Illumination and Night Glare.*

But of the stories found in the transcripts, the most content dedicated to a single individual are those passages during which McCullers reflects on her relationship with the Swiss heiress Annemarie Schwarzenbach. McCullers mentions Schwarzenbach in seven of the sessions and five of the transcripts are dedicated almost entirely to her. This content, along with the account of their brief time together recounted in McCullers' autobiography, provides a more complete story of their difficult and ultimately ill-fated relationship. Along with the content related to the Tucker family, the content related to Schwarzenbach indicates that the deep emotional connections McCullers had with the Tuckers and with Schwarzenbach remained of great significance to her, thirteen years after Schwarzenbach's death and more than twenty-four years following the departure of the Tuckers from her life in Columbus, Georgia, in 1934.

If McCullers used the free-associations in her therapeutic sessions to develop content for her autobiographical work, as the transcripts seem to suggest, she placed great significance on the relationships she had with the Tuckers and with Schwarzenbach and wanted to record these experiences, just as she did when writing her autobiography nearly a decade later. The story of her relationship with Schwarzenbach is considerably more detailed in the therapy transcripts of 1958 than in *Illumination and Night Glare.* It should not be surprising that the version of the stories about those people most important in her life were more detailed in the transcripts of the therapeutic sessions in 1958 than in the autobiography she worked on during the final two years of her life, as McCullers' health had deteriorated significantly in the final two years of her life and writing had become increasingly difficult.

Given the similarities between much of the content in these transcripts related to Annemarie Schwarzenbach and the content regarding her that McCullers included in *Illumination and Night Glare*, one might surmise that the content regarding Schwarzenbach in the transcripts was actually intended to serve as text of the autobiography underway as early as 1958, as Robert Lantz indicated in his 7 January 1970 letter to Mary Mercer. Since these transcripts were returned to Dr. Mercer, and not included in the materials sold to the Harry Ransom Humanities Research Center at the University of Texas at Austin, they were not available for comparison or perhaps inclusion when the scholarly edition of her autobiography was prepared for publication by the University of Wisconsin Press in 1999.

The following sections include all the text from the transcripts of the recorded therapy sessions of McCullers with Dr. Mary Mercer that involve Annemarie Schwarzenbach. Editorial intervention has been kept to a minimum to preserve the impromptu nature of the transcript texts. The only editorial changes were regularization of spelling and punctuation. Explanatory notes have been inserted in square brackets, as are words spoken by Mary Mercer. These sections from the transcripts provide the most detailed recounting of McCullers' relationship with Annemarie Schwarzenbach.

14 April 1958

I've been thinking of Annemarie S. "There was a time when stone was stone/And a face on the street was a finished face./Between the Thing, myself and God alone/There was an instant symmetry./This symmetry is twisted:/So that stone is not stone/And faces like the fractioned characters in dreams are incomplete/Until the child's unfinished face/I recognize your exiled eyes./The soldier climbs the evening stairs leaving your shadow./Tonight, this torn room sleeps/Beneath the starlight bent by you." [A slightly varied version of McCullers' poem "Stone Is Not Stone."]

So after that dream, you remember about the mountains and the snow, when I took the train back to New York I went straight to Freddy's and I found them both. Freddy is a real angel. He had put a sheet to separate his studio to give her privacy and there was Annemarie playing Mozart on the gramophone, playing it endlessly, endlessly, endlessly. This glass which Freddy thought was water was just gin, see? She was just drinking that and listening to Mozart when I got there (McCullers 14 April 1958).

21 April 1958

Ernst loved Annemarie, loved me. And Janie loved Annemarie and loved me. And John loved Annemarie, loved me. Do you understand that pattern in love? People who love one person, loves another person. They are very much alike and loved each other. Do you understand?

He [Ernst] has his problems ... loves people like Annemarie, like me, like Vani and he says there are only lesbians in the world and he's not lesbian. It's funny, he said yesterday, just homosexuals, nothing but homosexuals and I'm not homosexual and I'm lost.

When I came, I rode on a train all night, you see, to Annemarie and went straight to Freddy's place. When I got there, Annemarie was there and she looked at me in a kind of startled way at first. My first impulse was to lie down on the bed I was so tired, you know. But she looked at me and said, who are you? And I said, it's Carson. And she said, I want Dr. February. She had told me about once, once when she was staying at the Pierre, she told me she was one of the first people to have insulin shock treatment. And she was analyzed by this Dr. February. Anyway, Dr. February fell in love with her. Annemarie seduced her. Dr. February would give her insulin shock treatments every morning and she would die, she said, and in the afternoon, she would make love, see?

And so I was kind of shocked. Anyway she was one of the first people to have those insulin shocks. It was an experiment and she was scared.

So I was terribly shocked. Now that was when we were at the Pierre. Now at Freddy's place she told me that in the autumn and now it was December. Night was gathering. And she was calling for Dr. February. So I was in Freddy's room and she was calling for Dr. February. So I said to Freddy, what about Dr. February? And he said, well, Annemarie, dying twice a day, once at 6:00 in the morning and then again in the afternoon. One of those days when Dr. February was taking her out in the car, just suddenly pushed her out and headed for the Italian border. And Dr. February, elderly, had to walk home, a sadder and wiser woman. But I was so tired lying on Freddy's bed and just cried, you know. She screamed, Dr. February.

You see, Dr. Mercer, I was 22 years old and not trained to be anything but just a writer, I wasn't a nurse or anything, just nothing, just a writer. And there was Annemarie also a writer, and made, very sick. And I had traveled all that way and Dr. February was all I got!

So then, Annemarie accepted the fact that I was I. And I asked Freddy if she had eaten anything and he said she wouldn't eat, you know. I went to the icebox and got some food and I was taking it in. I was going to get the knives and forks, you see, and Annemarie just suddenly started eating with her hands. And so I wiped her hands on a cloth and gave her a fork and she still wanted to eat with her hands, anyway, she was eating.

So then she wanted to send me out to get drop, you see? She had eaten to please me, you see?

[Dr. Mercer: I think we won't make any sense if we don't have what you say too. Can you remember what you were saying? (We've talked of the word "use." And here she was using you after having pleased you. To use you to try to get dope for her wasn't "taking care of," was it?)]

Annemarie and dope ... now Ernst is a doctor, you know, and also Erica's father is a doctor. She would try to get dope from the doctors, but she would be quite frank about it. She'd say, listen, I know I'm giving you a rough time but I'm having a rough time too. And Ernst would never give her any, see? He felt terrible. She had saved his life, saved so many people's lives.

So I said, Annemarie, why don't we have some Martinis? She said, I don't have any Martinis. I went to get some. It was on Sunday I realized when I got in the street and I went to this place and said, I need to get two stiff martinis. And so a bar was open. I brought one in one hand and the other in the other hand, double ones, see, triple ones. And so we were sitting there drinking Martinis. And I thought then, this is going to be a night. I didn't know what it was going to be (McCullers 21 April 1958).

25 April 1958

There is such a thing as requested love but it is rare. There has to be a mutuality. A trust, a respect ... because otherwise ...

You asked me why I didn't make love with Annemarie. I tried to tell you it was that I couldn't make love with her when she was in a different world. I couldn't make love to her like an animal, you know. Because I loved her. Because I respected her. Because I mean I could have slept with her but she also had that feeling. I slept with her. She was so tormented. Her moods were so ... reality ... and she also has ... She was beyond my reach and I was beyond reach of her too, and she sensed it. Well, she wrote me, everything we have is joy. She wrote me when at first she was in Bellevue. She would not let me come to see her, but when she was getting over terrible first day ... that withdrawal. She could get other people, other patients there. ... I sent her flowers ... and then she said something that seemed to me very cruel. "Don't send flowers or even think of me now." She sent the flowers to another ward. When I think they are really appreciated, and then in her final letter, she said "I don't think I'm able once one has been taking morphine since one has been eighteen years old. I can't understand how she could have studied philosophy, and taken a Ph.D., a doctor's degree. I couldn't understand it." Only the last summer, she said, "once you have morphine since you are eighteen and been under that terrible dream of morphine, you never, never be free, the only thing would be a greater lunacy ... And the judge said that I could either stay here or be deported. I would rather be deported, for in choosing to go into the world even with morphine ... I'll be able to join my people in the resistance." So she finally got to the headquarters of De Gaulle.

What a great pity when one's heart is given to someone without hope. We don't ask where our heart is given to someone without hope. We don't ask where our heart is given, and it is just our great misfortune when the person who has it, cannot possibly take care of it. I know, Dr. Mercer. When I go on to that night.

I will tell you at one point I felt I had Annemarie, at last. I didn't know I never had Annemarie until C—wired me that she was dead. I knew I had her then. She would never leave me again. I saw her blessed face and rejoiced for she could never be hurt again ... and that she was safe now in my heart. I lived in her for my work (McCullers 25 April 1958).

28 April 1958

When I talked to Freddy about that last night I saw Annemarie, he said, ... Uh, I forgot to start it with this. When I walked in the door, there was Freddy, there was a broken window and Freddy trying to dangle something, trying to get the telephone into the apartment. What? Thrown out the telephone, and Freddy was trying to get the cord back into the apartment. And that was the very beginning when I first came in, see, so I thought ... and Annemarie was in her own little cubby hole with the sheets ... hung with the sheets. I described that to you, didn't I? And she was playing Mozart and quite unconcerned about Freddy getting the telephone back. She was just withdrawn. Huh, no ... what? ... yeah, no, no, I'm not ... it is the most painful thing in the world to say no to the ones you love, you know, but neither Freddy nor I were going to get morphine that night. And she began to have this morphine reaction, you know. Just yawn and she was in terrible pain. Stretch and yawn. You asked why I never made love to her. You can't make love under those circumstances, Dr. Mercer.

[Dr. Mercer: Because you did not take advantage of her ... you did not use her ... for to use a person, who is sick, for one's own selfish reasons is revolting.]

I thought Dr. February was dreadful, too. Well, anyway, then Annemarie started another tactic and said, you call Margot. Margot is the wife of Fritz ... it is his cars in Europe ... I don't know how many millions ... He was a great pal of Hitler ... and banking ... He backed the Nazi party, you see, and to the very end and then he escaped with his moneybags to Switzerland. And Margot is his wife. She used to be a singing girl in a café and he married her.

When Annemarie was in love with Margot ... very sexually in love with her ... and they used to bathe ... sunbath at the Plaza, see, and then people in the park would find them out and there were complaints and they moved to the Pierre Hotel. So Annemarie was living with Margot and Margot would do very strange things. Like in Paris she fitted Annemarie with a thousand dollars worth of clothes and stuck her with the bill. And I said, well I wouldn't pay it. But the poor tailor was the only one who was out.

So Annemarie was living with Margot. Margot went to Florida and Annemarie was taken to the sanatorium. Didn't I tell you about that and the dream and the ice and the water? Is it all down there? And then she said, you must call Margot. Freddy told me that she had hurled the telephone out the window because of it ... because Margot hung up ... so she threw the telephone out the window. It was a kind of dangerous thing ... but after a great deal of pleading on her part and carrying, I put in a call to Margot, see, who was in Miami, Coral Gables or something like that. Anyway, by the ocean, she had bought a house.

When I called Margot she said, what are you doing there? I said I came back form Georgia. She said, you better get out of that apartment fast and she began talking German. She said, get out, get out! I said what for? Why she will kill you! She tried to strangle Fritz in the elevator of the Pierre Hotel. They made us move. We moved to the Sherry Netherland ... and she tried to kill me. She was sitting on my chest one night and strangling me. She's dangerous! Wanting dope. Get out of that apartment right now. Who is with you? I said, Freddy.

At that moment Geoffrey came in. Geoffrey was a friend, who because of expenses, you see, shared the apartment with Freddy. They had a big living room and an alcove he had fitted for Annemarie and Geoffrey had the bedroom. Geoffrey was a very great alcoholic. He stumbled in the middle of the night and sleeps all day, and Freddy went on with his work. It was all kind of expensive, Dr. Mercer, because we were very poor. Everybody was very poor then. I lived on one hundred dollars a month. Easily. Because I had friends, who bought my clothes ... Let's go back to Annemarie.

So I called Margot and she said, get away ... who is there? And I said Geoffrey just came in ... stumbling in and went to his bedroom going to sleep. And I said, Freddy is with me. She said, you tell Freddy to call Alfred Schwarzenbach and tell him to get out too ... she is dangerous ... you don't seem to understand. I said, I'm not scared and Freddy's not scared. I said, I think you ought to let her come to you. Let her come to me, no! And she shrieked. Tell, Annemarie that I have a barbed wire fence all around this house. Just tell her that. Well, I couldn't tell Annemarie that, see? I said, Margot I can't tell her that. You just tell her that! And if she comes here she will have barbed wire fence she cannot climb and a night watchman.

So I put down the receiver and Annemarie wanted to know what she said. And I said, she said she couldn't have her now, she was having trouble with Fritz ... and made up a story, you know ... You see Fritz was kind jealous of Annemarie of when Margot was with Annemarie, you know. I like Fritz though and later on I'll tell ... can we go back and forth ... later on in Nantucket ... Tennessee, Margot and I ... we hauled in Margot to read Rilke for us. She has a very good reading voice and she would real real good. And we would go to her house and she was a wonderful cook. And we never had a square meal, see, at a restaurant so Margot would cook for us. And she asked my forgiveness for not letting Annemarie come to me after her death. Can you forgive me, Carson? I said. I said, yes, I know you love her in your fashion. And she said, how can I ever atone? And she said another thing which shocked me terribly, oh she suffered like a dog. I said she didn't suffer like a dog, dogs suffer like dogs. She suffered but not like a dog.

So back to that night. When I told her she was quarrelling with Fritz and she said Erick Anderson was there with her and she began to curse, you know. I said, maybe she needed a place to stay. She was not only broke, she was penniless. Her father trying to get a license and just penniless. No food to eat. And she was staying with Margot.

And Annemarie was terribly jealous about that arrangement. So then she said, take off your clothes. So I took off my clothes and she began to touch me. And I felt this flowering jazz passion, you know, and I felt I had her. I thought at last, I had Annemarie, at last, at last. And all the sacred fluids of my body were secreting, you know, sweat, tears, love juice, that's not the medical word but you know what I mean. So then, Annemarie just suddenly jumped out of the bed, went to a little box that she had there, see? On by the way, the food was still on the floor, a little box she had there, and showed me a clipping she had there about the house in Brooklyn and Gypsy Rose Lee and who is sleeping with who, see. Wystan, Peter, Oliver, Gypsy, Carson, who is sleeping with who? Someone sent it. It was cruel, like Walter Winchell. Just one of those little gossip columns.

So then she began saying, I was Gypsy Rose Lee. That's the only reason I came to America because I wanted Gypsy Rose Lee. Yeah, yeah, when I was just … when I was … that flowering, that passion, Dr. Mercer, do you understand … when just suddenly, I went Gypsy. I don't want you. You're too skinny. I was Gypsy Rose Lee and you, you've been seen in nightclubs with her. I know. I've kept tract of you. You go around with her. Stay weekends with her. I know. You, you bring her to be right now. You get gypsy and bring her right here and I'll sleep with her and you can watch if you want to.

So then … I ran out of the room, naked, see, snatched my clothes and ran out of the room. Freddy was there and I said, Don't you think we ought to call a doctor?

Well, I didn't know any doctor to call. We didn't know any psychiatrist? William wasn't in my life then. So I didn't know any doctor to call. I had just come to New York and had no friends. So Freddy was trying to help me get dressed, see? (McCullers 28 April 1958).

9 May 1958

So Freddy was helping me get dressed. Suddenly Annemarie dashed from the room and went into the bathroom. And I was getting dressed. Freddy suddenly made an ejaculation and rushed to the bathroom and there was Annemarie cutting her wrists and trying to cut her throat. So he was wrestling with her to get the razor out of her hand, see, and he said go quickly and I rushed quickly, and at the end of the staircase, it was three flights up, I bumped into this cop, policeman, I was running so fast he caught hold of me and asked, where are you going? I said somebody is trying to kill herself. So then I said, where is a doctor? He blew on a whistle which I didn't want at all, you know? Get me a doctor. So he went upstairs and went into this hotel, where I had gone for the drink before, you know, and asked if they could tell me the nearest doctor. So they pointed out a doctor about three blocks away. So I was running to get to the doctor and he took so long, it seemed that this was deliberately, kind of stalling, you know, and I didn't know what had happened.

So then I came back with the doctor. There were about forty copies in the place. I never saw a room with so many cops in my life. And the doctor immediately started sewing her up. It seemed as if he did it as roughly as possible. Some doctors can't stand suicides. You understand that? So then she was talking all this talk and the cops were wondering what was going on. And Annemarie said, why did you punish me like this? I said, how do you mean? Calling the cops on me. I said, I didn't call the cops. And then she was going on and on to the cops about Margot wouldn't sleep with her. Who was Margot? All this wild talk, you know. And so the cops were thinking what the hell is going on here? They look from Freddy to me to Geoffrey.

And the doctor at one point was staying, here now, Annemarie ... And I said, she is not Annemarie to you, she is Mademoiselle Schwarzenbach.

She was just doing everything to hurt us. Annemarie was sweating, trembling, and so was I. Every second she would turn on me, see, and the next second she would hold on to me, see? Saying why, why did you call these people here? The place was just swarming with cops. She was trying to explain about Fritz, Margot, and getting dope. All of that. And I would try to be gentle with her thinking they wouldn't understand, see? Freddy would start German, but she would go right on to English, see? Do you understand? I would try to go on in French but no, she would go right back to English. Trying to get dope, saying I would have to get dope for her. That was why she hated me. And she called for Gypsy Rose Lee too. It was terrible that night.

At first the cops were looking at the broken window, the whole thing was just disorder, the broken window, the phone had smashed through. They wanted to know what it was about. I didn't know what to say. It was the most disorderly thing in the whole room to have that jagging hole where the telephone had gone through the window. Do you understand?

I called Freddy about that night and he said that night wasn't the last night you and the last night you were not there. I said that happened? A Swiss nurse had been called in and left the razor right there and Annemarie just tried again. Do you understand? But I'll tell you about that ...

So everything was terrible. And Annemarie blaming me all the time. Why do you punish me like this? Can you understand how painful it was? Well, I almost did the worst thing possible. Finally, all this madness was going on and suddenly I just picked up a chair. I guess the cops were just too surprised to rush me, you know. So I had this chair over my head. I don't know how long it was, all the cops, you know. See it was getting terrible, you know, they were trying to take her off right then and there. Trying to force her, you know, so I picked up the chair.

And then, I said, now listen here, you are all good Irish cops and my grandfather was an Irish cop too. And already I was beginning to lie. I said, my father was an Irish cop too. Fear makes people lie and I was afraid they would take Annemarie. And I put the chair down very carefully. I said my father was Thomas E. Walters and came from Dublin during the famine and he had a success story since he was ten years old and when he was a young man he founded the Georgia Railway ... Jordan Massey ... my cousin ... and they also went on to other things and are very rich men ... and because we have the same blood, I am not going to let you take this girl until we get a doctor, a real doctor, not just one ...

And Freddy said, I think it is about time we called her brother, see? And she said, Don't call Albert. Because she was hiding, see? Albert would take me back to Blythewood, the hospital where she escaped. But we were too distressed to do anything else. So Freddy called Albert. He called a psychiatrist. He was mean too. Everybody was mean.

But the cops were very nice to me. I said all of you don't have to stay in this room. Two or three can stay here. Nobody is going to try to escape. So they all left but about three. I said more to the cops, if anyone one in your family life is under the influence of alcohol, or does something crazy, or anybody you love who is under some strange influence that you can't control, do you understand, I said I am appealing to you as human beings.

They were so very startled when I picked up that chair. They could have rushed me then and there and it would have been all over. Then I began to speak with them.

[Dr. Mercer: Everything you have said lent sanity to an insane situation. Freddy stood by but you were acting. You had to act under that much pressure. You could act. This is heroism.]

And when the psychiatrist came, Annemarie was still blaming me and you know that hurt. She blamed, she blamed and could not help it. So the psychiatrist came in and he was the first to blame me too. How old are you? I said I am 22. And he said, Why don't you go away? He had known

Annemarie as a patient. He's the one who blamed me too. I don't know what for. I don't know whether I should have given Annemarie dope or not. I don't know what he blamed me for. Annemarie said she wanted to have a German-speaking nurse. So this Swiss nurse was called in and just as I was leaving Annemarie came into the vestibule with me and said, Forgive me, I love you, forgive me.

So by that time it was almost dawn and I got the train to go back to Brooklyn. In getting to Brooklyn I lost my directions. Somebody found me at the end of the line and took me back home. By then it was already daylight. So then Wystan was there. I went to the back door. Wystan was always our furnace man. He stoked the furnace every morning and I would make toast with him. He is a very good friend of mine, very close. And so I was kind of blanked out. I had a kind of convulsion. So Wystan tried to find out what the hell. He didn't know I was anywhere near. He thought I was in Georgia, Wystan did. I tried to say something about Annemarie and he said he would call Alfred S., the brother, so Goldmyer was in my bed asleep so Wystan put me in his bed. He was very good that night. And the next night or so he showed me his diary and said, read, read about Kierkegaard, *Fear and Trembling* and *Sickness Unto Death*.

[Dr. Mercer: He was a very kind man.]

He is great. I wonder if you can be truly great without being kind.

So then Annemarie took a different tack. She said she was never going to expose me to her way of life. And she would tell Freddy and Wystan that I was too young to be exposed to so much agony. She even wrote me to say don't send flowers. Go home, go home, go back to your parents, go home. That's the only thing she said to me, go back to your parents, go home.

She was sent to Bellevue first and then she was sent to Bloomingdales. It is a better hospital. And she was calling for me too.

The judge said if she would stay on in Bloomingdale, she could, or any state institution but if she wanted to leave she would have to be deported. So she wrote me the most heartbreaking letter, I think, I know, I have ever received, about lunacy and that she would never be able to change this morphine habit. Please understand that I would rather live in the world. I would never be able to lick this morphine habit unless I have another lunacy. Do you know what I am trying to say? That would be stronger ... so therefore I am going back to the resistance, morphine or no, I can be used.

And so she was then stuck in Portugal, Lisbon, for almost a whole year, trying to get visas. Lisbon just swarmed with people trying to get visas at that time during the war. Don't forget, Dr. Mercer, this was the time of the war. Annemarie was also sent to England.

Reeves was a courier for combined offices. A very high position, taking letters from Churchill to Montgomery, things like that.

Yes, we were divorced. He wanted me very much to marry him again. And I didn't. So next year I went to see him at his camp. He was going overseas with all the ranger boys, one of the best outfits in the whole war. It was a real death battalion. Every one knew he would be the first one to be expendable. Of course, they were the ones who landed on the beaches. Reeves was three times in Europe before D-Day. He would go in with a commission and they would burn up Germans. Camps, you know, and kill Germans. I knew all that was going on. He never wrote me that.

So there I was, with Annemarie in Lisbon and trying to get to Africa and Reeves in England and trying to wait for D-Day. I was working on Member of the Wedding. And poems.

I was trying very hard to get overseas, naturally. I went to PM. I had all my friends working for me. Most of my friends were working against me. And the newspaper people I talked with, good god, trying to get an overseas assignment. Whether I was going to Africa or England I didn't know just to be somewhere in this battle area.

So to come back to Annemarie somebody called me about that time I was in New York and said, you are a friend of Annemarie Schwarzenbach, are you? I said yes. Is she crazy? I said what do you mean crazy? Well, I have two rooms in my office. He was a consul, see, and Annemarie has taken over one room in my office and all these journalists come. Is she crazy? I said, if this is crazy I hope I'm that crazy. She had taken over this poor man's office, she for interviews. If she is crazy, I hope I am that crazy. There was no room in Lisbon, see, too many people around. Everyone was trying to get a passport and Annemarie ... and me most of all. And he said, she said to me to send you her love. She'll be moving on to DeGaulle's headquarters soon. She wanted to tell you that. So I was trying to get a passport (McCullers 9 May 1958).

12 May 1958

... suffering, ghastly withdrawal agony ... usually a person does not think of anyone but themselves, herself ... and when she hurt me and struck out at me ... she was not under any control of herself ... have you ever seen those withdrawal symptoms, withdrawal pains? ... yawning, her bones

cracking, pain. I know, Doctor Mercer, I should done quite otherwise ...
I should have ... but I did not know ... now I would have taken her to a
doctor for treatment ... to have given her that last shot before she would
have been hospitalized again ... but how did I know at that time ... I
didn't know anything about it then (McCullers 12 May 1958).

A NOTE ON MEDICAL/BIOGRAPHICAL ETHICS

It is impossible to write of and quote from the transcripts of the therapeutic sessions of Carson McCullers without considering the ethical issues
involved in doing so. There are obvious professional ethical concerns in
using therapeutic or medical records in scholarly work. The most recent
analogous situation to the use of McCullers' transcripts in this work is
the 1991 publication of Diane Wood Middlebrook's biography of Anne
Sexton for which Middlebrook had access to audio recordings of Sexton's
therapy sessions recorded from 1961 to 1964. But the Sexton case differs significantly from that of McCullers because the Sexton tapes were
provided to Middlebrook by Sexton's psychiatrist, Martin T. Orne, who
explicitly said he had Sexton's permission to use the tapes, if possible,
to help others. The controversy surrounding the use of these recordings
was considerable at the time of the publication of the biography, with
experts and medical ethicists arguing both for and against the publication.
Without explicit instructions from McCullers regarding the disposition of
the transcripts it is hard to mount a justification for using the materials.
However, considerable circumstantial evidence exists to infer consent on
both Dr. Mary Mercer's and McCullers' parts in making the transcripts of
their sessions available to scholars.

It is clear from the vehemence with which Dr. Mary Mercer fought
for the return of the transcripts from McCullers' estate to her that Dr.
Mercer wished to control the preservation and eventual deposition of the
transcripts. It is also clear, given their reluctance to return them to Dr.
Mercer, that the executors of her estate (her sister, Rita Smith, her former
agent, Robert Lantz, and her long-time attorney, Floria Lasky) did not
have reservations about including the therapy transcripts in the materials
to be sold after the author's death and to be made available to scholars.
In the end, their insistence that the one transcript on which they had
identified McCullers' own handwriting, and thus characterized it as a literary manuscript, indicates their desire for the materials to be available to
scholars.

As well, in his letter to Dr. Mary Mercer in which he asks about the pages of the transcripts Carson had shown to him, Robert Lantz clearly felt that the transcripts included important biographical details and significant writing by McCullers and that McCullers herself had planned to use the materials in her planned autobiography. But perhaps most significantly, Dr. Mary Mercer's actions in relation to the transcripts of McCullers' therapy sessions indicate both the care which she took in preserving the documents and her desire to ensure their eventual deposition in an appropriate place so that they could be studied by scholars.

Robert Lantz's 7 January 1970 letter to Dr. Mercer and her 10 February 1970 reply to him both indicate that McCullers herself considered the original recordings of the therapy sessions and the subsequent transcripts of them as part of her creative work. The transcripts of the therapy sessions are most appropriately considered as one would any other manuscript of a work in progress in the archives of her work, just as McCullers had treated them herself, and as she did in sharing them with Robert Lantz.

Just as it might be inappropriate to consider publishing excerpts from these therapy transcripts without considering the ethical implications of doing so, it might also be inappropriate to decide not to publish these materials due to ethical concerns alone, without considering the actual content of the transcripts themselves. The transcripts are so similar to the manuscripts of McCullers' other work, in particular the manuscript of her unfinished autobiography, that they are practically indistinguishable from them, both in subject matter and style of writing. In fact, there is very little content in the transcripts that appears to address directly the therapeutic atmosphere of the sessions or that explicitly concerns itself with therapy or the therapeutic process, accepting of course that all the free associations in therapeutic sessions can be considered relevant to the overall therapeutic project.

A straightforward interpretation of the principles spelled out for psychiatrists' behavior in relation to the medical records of their patients' records would clearly prohibit the release of the transcripts of McCullers' therapy sessions. According to the American Medical Association's Code of Ethics, in particular, its "Opinion 5.051—Confidentiality of Medical Information Postmortem":

> All medically related confidences disclosed by a patient to a physician and information contained within a deceased patient's medical record, including information entered postmortem, should be kept confidential to the greatest

possible degree. However, the obligation to safeguard patient confidence is subject to certain exceptions that are ethically and legally justifiable because of overriding societal consideration. At their strongest, confidentiality protections after death would be equal to those in force during a patient's life. Thus, if information about a patient may be ethically disclosed during life, it likewise may be disclosed after the patient has died. Disclosure of medical information postmortem for research and educational purposes is appropriate as long as confidentiality is maintained to the greatest possible degree by removing any individual identifiers.

Dr. Mary Mercer apparently was pursuing the same protection of her former patient's privacy when she fought McCullers' estate in the early 1970s for the return of the therapy transcripts to her. Clearly Dr. Mercer changed her mind regarding the disposition of the transcripts of the sessions with McCullers between the time she fought so strongly for their return to her and her eventual bequeathal, forty years later, of the materials to a university library. What caused Dr. Mercer to change her mind and preserve the transcripts and consciously decide to include them in the materials she left as part of her estate to Columbus State University's Carson McCullers Center for Writers and Musicians? Perhaps I can provide a partial, first-hand explanation for this change of heart.

Following the 1999 publication of *Illumination and Night Glare*, Dr. Mary Mercer became much more willing to discuss McCullers' life and work with scholars, most notably Josayne Savigneau and me. She told me, during a conversation in late 2001, that she had come to realize that many of the things that McCullers had shared with her in a therapeutic context, or in confidence in the context of their friendship, after she and McCullers had terminated their therapeutic relationship, McCullers had already shared with others or had written about in the autobiography. This allowed Mercer to discuss these purely biographical or literary matters without fear that she was violating a confidence. However, Dr. Mercer maintained a strict policy of not discussing with biographers or scholars her medical or therapeutic relationship with McCullers.

It is a testament to Dr. Mary Mercer's professionalism that she fought, out of principle, to prevent the transcripts of McCullers' therapy sessions from being included in the collection of materials that were eventually sold to the University of Texas, especially given that there is little content in the transcripts that would have been considered particularly private or intimate. As well, and perhaps yet another reason Dr. Mercer felt comfortable in depositing the transcripts of these sessions in an academic archive, as Dr. Mercer neared the end of her life—she died at age 102 in 2013—she realized that practically all the persons discussed in the transcripts of the therapy sessions were dead and thus could not be harmed by any revelations about them in the transcripts.

In the nearly more than forty years since McCullers' death, Dr. Mercer may also have realized more clearly that the transcripts that were composed in the context of a therapeutic relationship were actually more akin to the manuscripts of a literary work, coincidentally written while in therapy or under the treatment of a psychiatrist. Dr. Mary Mercer provided McCullers with the tools, a Dictaphone machine, and services of a secretary to transcribe the tapes, to use in trying to overcome her difficulty in writing in the way in which she was accustomed. McCullers wrote very similar content to the materials described as transcripts of therapy sessions, including letters to Dr. Mercer, during her treatment that are quite similar to these transcripts. In one letter to Mercer, McCullers refers to their therapeutic work as "my heart laid bare" (4 April 1958).

As was stated earlier, there was a near-seamless connection between McCullers' life and her creative work. This connection went beyond the mere inclusion of autobiographical content in her work. McCullers' emotional and psychological well-being was dependent on her ability to continue her writing and to a great extent her sense of well-being was intimately related to her continued creative work. As well, her work was dependent not only on the details of her life but on her ability to gain access to her emotional core, what psychologists might call her primary process, to provide the integral and honest psychological portrayal of the characters and situation found in her work. These transcripts are an intimate portrayal of this synergistic relationship between her life and work. Dr. Mary Mercer was aware of this and perhaps preserved these important documents and made certain that they would eventually be made available to the public so that readers and scholars of McCullers could further understand this intimate connection between the lived life of an artist and her creative work.

WORKS CITED

American Medical Association. *AMA Code of Medical Ethics.* "Opinion 5.051 Confidentiality of Medical Information Postmortem." n.d. Web. 6 October 2015.

Dickinson, Donald C. "Lew David Feldman." *Dictionary of American Antiquarian Bookdealers.* Westport, CT: Greenwood, 1998. 65–66. Print.

Lantz, Robert. Letter to Mary Mercer. 7 January 1970. MS. Dr. Mary E. Mercer/ Carson McCullers Collection (MC 296). Columbus State University Archives, Columbus, Georgia. Print.

———. Letter to Mary Mercer. 27 February 1970. MS. Dr. Mary E. Mercer/Carson McCullers Collection (MC 296). Columbus State University Archives, Columbus, Georgia. Print.

Lasky, Floria. Letter to Mary Mercer. 3 February 1971. MS. Dr. Mary E. Mercer/ Carson McCullers Collection (MC 296). Columbus State University Archives, Columbus, Georgia. Print.

———. Letter to Mary Mercer. 18 March 1971. MS. Dr. Mary E. Mercer/Carson McCullers Collection (MC 296). Columbus State University Archives, Columbus, Georgia. Print.

———. Letter to Mary Mercer. 8 February 1972. MS. Dr. Mary E. Mercer/Carson McCullers Collection (MC 296). Columbus State University Archives, Columbus, Georgia. Print.

———. Letter to Mary Mercer. 1 March 1971. MS. Dr. Mary E. Mercer/Carson McCullers Collection (MC 296). Columbus State University Archives, Columbus, Georgia. Print.

———. Letter to Mary Mercer. 18 December 1972. MS. Dr. Mary E. Mercer/Carson McCullers Collection (MC 296). Columbus State University Archives, Columbus, Georgia. Print.

———. Letter to Mary Mercer. 19 December 1972. MS. Dr. Mary E. Mercer/Carson McCullers Collection (MC 296). Columbus State University Archives, Columbus, Georgia. Print.

———. Letter to Nathanial Sales. 13 March 1973. MS. Dr. Mary E. Mercer/Carson McCullers Collection (MC 296). Columbus State University Archives, Columbus, Georgia. Print.

———. Letter to Nathanial Sales. 5 April 1973. MS. Dr. Mary E. Mercer/Carson McCullers Collection (MC 296). Columbus State University Archives, Columbus, Georgia. Print.

McCullers, Carson. *Illumination and Night Glare: The Unfinished Autobiography of Carson McCullers.* Ed. Carlos L. Dews. Madison: U of Wisconsin P, 1999. Print.

———. "Dictaphone Sessions." 11 April 1958. MS. Dr. Mary E. Mercer/Carson McCullers Collection (MC 296). Columbus State University Archives, Columbus, Georgia. Print.

———. "Dictaphone Sessions." 14 April 1958. MS. Dr. Mary E. Mercer/Carson McCullers Collection (MC 296). Columbus State University Archives, Columbus, Georgia. Print.

———. "Dictaphone Sessions." 21 April 1958. MS. Dr. Mary E. Mercer/Carson McCullers Collection (MC 296). Columbus State University Archives, Columbus, Georgia. Print.

——. "Dictaphone Sessions." 25 April 1958. MS. Dr. Mary E. Mercer/Carson McCullers Collection (MC 296). Columbus State University Archives, Columbus, Georgia. Print.

——. "Dictaphone Sessions." 28 April 1958. MS. Dr. Mary E. Mercer/Carson McCullers Collection (MC 296). Columbus State University Archives, Columbus, Georgia. Print.

——. "Dictaphone Sessions." 5 May 1958. MS. Dr. Mary E. Mercer/Carson McCullers Collection (MC 296). Columbus State University Archives, Columbus, Georgia. Print.

——. "Dictaphone Sessions." 9 May 1958. MS. Dr. Mary E. Mercer/Carson McCullers Collection (MC 296). Columbus State University Archives, Columbus, Georgia. Print.

——. "Dictaphone Sessions." 12 May 1958. MS. Dr. Mary E. Mercer/Carson McCullers Collection (MC 296). Columbus State University Archives, Columbus, Georgia. Print.

——. "Dictaphone Sessions." 16 May 1958. MS. Dr. Mary E. Mercer/Carson McCullers Collection (MC 296). Columbus State University Archives, Columbus, Georgia. Print.

——. Letter to Mary Mercer. 4 April 1958. MS. Dr. Mary E. Mercer/Carson McCullers Collection (MC 296). Columbus State University Archives, Columbus, Georgia. Print.

Mercer, Mary. Letter to Robert Lantz. 10 February 1970. MS. Dr. Mary E. Mercer/Carson McCullers Collection (MC 296). Columbus State University Archives, Columbus, Georgia. Print.

——. Draft of letter to Robert Lantz. 6 March 1970. MS. Dr. Mary E. Mercer/ Carson McCullers Collection (MC 296). Columbus State University Archives, Columbus, Georgia. Print.

——. Letter to Floria Lasky. 5 March 1971. MS. Dr. Mary E. Mercer/Carson McCullers Collection (MC 296). Columbus State University Archives, Columbus, Georgia. Print.

——. Letter to Nathanial Sales. 19 March 1971. MS. Dr. Mary E. Mercer/Carson McCullers Collection (MC 296). Columbus State University Archives, Columbus, Georgia. Print.

——. Letter to Floria Lasky. 31 January 1972. MS. Dr. Mary E. Mercer/Carson McCullers Collection (MC 296). Columbus State University Archives, Columbus, Georgia. Print.

——. Letter to Floria Lasky. 21 February 1972. MS. Dr. Mary E. Mercer/Carson McCullers Collection (MC 296). Columbus State University Archives, Columbus, Georgia. Print.

——. Letter to Floria Lasky. 8 March 1972. MS. Dr. Mary E. Mercer/Carson McCullers Collection (MC 296). Columbus State University Archives, Columbus, Georgia. Print.

——. Letter to Floria Lasky. 5 July 1972. MS. Dr. Mary E. Mercer/Carson McCullers Collection (MC 296). Columbus State University Archives, Columbus, Georgia. Print.

——. Letter to Floria Lasky. 1 August 1972. MS. Dr. Mary E. Mercer/Carson McCullers Collection (MC 296). Columbus State University Archives, Columbus, Georgia. Print.

——. Letter to Floria Lasky. 11 December 1972. MS. Dr. Mary E. Mercer/Carson McCullers Collection (MC 296). Columbus State University Archives, Columbus, Georgia. Print.

——. Letter to Floria Lasky. 11 January 1973. MS. Dr. Mary E. Mercer/Carson McCullers Collection (MC 296). Columbus State University Archives, Columbus, Georgia. Print.

——. Letter to Nathanial Sales. 14 March 1973. MS. Dr. Mary E. Mercer/Carson McCullers Collection (MC 296). Columbus State University Archives, Columbus, Georgia. Print.

Collaborative Life Writing: The Dialogical Subject of Carson Mccullers' Dictaphone "Experiments" and Posthumous Autobiography, *Illumination and Night Glare*

Melanie Masterton Sherazi

In poor health and unable to grasp a pen or type at length after a series of debilitating strokes, Carson McCullers dictated the autobiographical content of *Illumination and Night Glare* to nurses and friends from mid-April to August 1967. McCullers suffered a final stroke and lapsed into a coma that resulted in her death at age fifty on September 29, 1967. In 1991, nearly twenty-five years later, scholar Carlos L. Dews came across McCullers' autobiographical text among her papers at the Harry Ransom Center. Dews undertook a nearly ten-year-long process to gain permission from McCullers' estate to publish the work and to find a press that was interested in the project. This chapter explores McCullers' posthumously published autobiography, *Illumination and Night Glare* (1999), as an under-recognized work of women's life writing that emphasizes the

M.M. Sherazi (✉)
Department of English, University of California, 149 Humanities, Los Angeles, CA 90095, USA

© The Author(s) 2016
A. Graham-Bertolini, C. Kayser (eds.), *Carson McCullers in the Twenty-First Century*, DOI 10.1007/978-3-319-40292-5_3

sociality of being, both at the level of its thematics and its material production by dictation. McCullers' autobiography is imbricated with other
forms of life writing with which she engaged in the 1950s and 1960s,
namely, the Dictaphone recordings of her 1958 therapy sessions with Dr.
Mary Mercer.

McCullers was referred to see Mercer while McCullers was suffering from depression and writer's block in the wake of the suicide of her
husband, Reeves McCullers, in 1953 and the death of her mother, Vera
Marguerite Waters, in 1955, and in the face of myriad health issues that
affected her ability to handwrite or type. Compounding these emotional
losses and physical challenges was the commercial failure of her Broadway
play *The Square Root of Wonderful* in 1957, which flopped, in stark contrast to the great success of McCullers' 1950 Broadway adaptation of
The Member of the Wedding. Determined to write in spite of physical and
emotional turmoil, McCullers began using a Dictaphone, recording her
sessions with Dr. Mercer and having them transcribed as literary "experiments." The content of these experiments indicates that the sessions
fueled McCullers' final writing projects: both her last novel, *Clock Without
Hands* (1961), and her posthumously published autobiography.[1]

This chapter emphasizes the Dictaphone experiments' relationship to
the autobiographical text published three decades after McCullers' death
as *Illumination and Night Glare: The Unfinished Autobiography of Carson
McCullers* (1999). *Illumination and Night Glare* opens with an introduction by Carlos Dews, in which he aptly characterizes the text as "an unfinished and collaborative work" (xviii).[2] The autobiography that McCullers
dictated in 1967 is seventy-eight pages in length, printed in its entirety from
a 128-page typescript labeled "First Draft" and entitled "Illumination and
Night Glare." McCullers narrates her autobiography in an episodic, non-
linear fashion, shifting across time and space with each reflection. Each
new episode is set off in the text by a space break that calls further attention to the project's discontinuous form and style. Dews interlaces this
portion of the text with archival photographs of the author with her family
and friends. The second half of *Illumination and Night Glare* is comprised
of an additional seventy-eight pages of selected letters exchanged between
McCullers and her then ex-husband Reeves McCullers during his World
War II service.[3] Dews provides a brief introduction to the letters, explaining that McCullers collected some threehundred wartime letters for her
autobiography (*ING* 84), signaling in the typescript, "INSERT WAR
LETTERS HERE" (*ING* 27; original emphasis). Following the letters

selected by Dews from those available in the archive is the full outline of "The Mute," the basis for McCullers' debut novel, *The Heart Is a Lonely Hunter* (1940); an excerpt of the outline is quoted in the opening pages of the autobiography (*ING* 4–5). Finally, Dews concludes the text with appendices providing a detailed chronology of McCullers' life, a list of editorial corrections, a bibliography and an index.

These interrelated, but distinct, textual elements—McCullers' 1967 life writing (paired with archival photographs selected by Dews); her 1944–45 war correspondence with Reeves McCullers; and the 1938 outline of "The Mute"—commingle in the modernist mode of juxtaposition, brought together by the editor's archival selections and supplemented by his intro-duction and appendix. In this way, Dews' editorial labor demonstrates the Derridean *supplement*, or that which augments, but is never fully inte-grated into a totality (144). These elements do not cohere as a whole but exist instead in a dynamic mode of (re)configuration that is imbri-cated with the thematic content and material production of McCullers' Dictaphone experiments of the late 1950s. McCullers' autobiography operates as an experimental model of life writing that is collaboratively fashioned, both by Dews at the turn of the twenty-first century, but also by the largely unnamed "corps of friends, family, and student secretaries" (Dews xiv) to whom McCullers dictated her autobiography in the months before her death in 1967. McCullers stresses her interactions with oth-ers in her reminiscences, addressing her musings to a future listener, just as she does in the 1958 dictaphone sessions with Mercer, to which she alludes in the autobiography (*ING* 52). *Illumination and Night Glare* is a memory scrapbook: by way of a posthumous juxtaposition, or the pairing of disparate parts collaboratively composed across time and space, it effects meaning, emphasizing the social fabric of existence.

Though McCullers' estate considered publishing the text of *Illumination and Night Glare* in the years after her death, it was deemed too fragmen-tary and in need of editorial crafting. No one assumed the role of edi-tor, so the material remained in the archive until Dews resurrected it and approached the estate about editing the project himself.[4] To date, the text has received scant scholarly attention, and its reception by reviewers upon its initial release in 1999 was mixed.[5] Virginia Spencer Carr's 537-page, 1975 biography *The Lonely Hunter* refers only in passing to "an unfinished journal," a "book [McCullers] reportedly entitled *Illuminations* [sic] *and Night Glare*" (507). Such a fleeting assessment implies that this last work was deemed a minor one, likely owing to its perceived unfinishedness, but also in the sense that McCullers' fiction is privileged over her life writing, poetry, and playwriting. *Illumination and Night Glare*, however, warrants our attention as a compelling work of feminist life writing.

McCullers' collaboratively crafted autobiography and its thematic focus on sociality reimagines the Enlightenment subject of traditional life writing. Early autobiography studies scholars like Georges Gusdorf regarded autobiography as the domain in which the individual "engage[s] in an autonomous adventure" (31). The emphasis here is on the teleological development of the Cartesian individual—who is implicitly white, propertied, heterosexual, and male. McCullers' non-linear life writing project resists this formulation of the proper subject, emphasizing instead the dialogical constitution of experience and the ambiguities, rather than certainties, of social identity. This, in other words, is not a traditional autobiography that unfolds in chronological time, tracing the autonomous protagonist's journey from birth to death, from ignorance to maturity. With its interpellation of a listener, as well as an imagined future audience, *Illumination and Night Glare* performs life writing's always already implicit solicitation of an other to recognize the writer's triumphs and sufferings, her illumination and night glare. This privileging of the social eschews the conventional, solitary "I" for a boisterous we, or what *The Member of the Wedding*'s Frankie Addams calls the "we of me" (42).

The text follows the associative wanderings of memory, as each episode contributes to a narrative that remains in flux, "unfinished" at the time of McCullers' death. She flaunts a self-reflexive awareness of her own inconsistencies of memory, at times overtly stating that she does not fully remember the details surrounding an event (*ING* 40), and she aligns life's illuminations with creative production, and night glare with the inability to write or create (*ING* 36–38). As her text moves in the generative directions of elaboration and embellishment (Dews xviii), she avoids the confessional logics of traditional autobiography, playfully violating Philippe Lejeune's "autobiographical pact," which implicitly frames autobiography in a juridical context that demands veracity and accuracy. *Illumination and Night Glare*, in contrast, remains invested in sociality, as McCullers recollects her literal and symbolic moves between South and North, the United States and Europe, sickness and health, adulthood and childhood, and male and female companionship. Such discontinuous moves demonstrate the possibilities, as feminist autobiography studies theorists such as Leigh Gilmore and Sidonie Smith and Julia Watson advocate, of distancing ourselves from the illusion of autonomy and "truth" in life writing.

McCullers' posthumously published text showcases that the affective connection between author and reader is a co-existence brokered by the labor of the editor, who, in McCullers' case, supplements the late author's text with archival materials. This collaborative dynamic reaches back to McCullers' 1967 *New York Times* interview with Rex Reed, in which she described the project of *Illumination and Night Glare* in these terms: "I think it is important for future generations of students to know why I did certain things, but it is also important for myself" (15). Blending the professional with the personal, she collapses the arbitrary distinction between public and private that has conventionally aligned women's writing with the latter. She also signals a self-reflexive awareness of the genre—McCullers was an avid reader of biographies (Carr 27)—and of her own author function, as objects of study. Rather than taking McCullers' authorial intentions as stated in her autobiography as a "key" to unlocking her fiction, I offer a reading that remains aware of *Illumination and Night Glare*'s posthumous status and juxtapositional form as a collaboratively authored life writing text that exceeds generic and masculinist expectations for continuity and closure. Reading *Illumination and Night Glare* as a work of women's autobiography affirms its elliptical and non-linear telling, which is elaborated by the collaborative nature of its posthumous supplementation and belated circulation.

"Our Flowering Dream": Reading the Dictaphone "Experiments" as Life Writing

McCullers' *Illumination and Night Glare* shares an imbricated relationship with the life writing she generated while in treatment with Dr. Mary Mercer in the spring of 1958. Though Mercer saw McCullers for a year, there are a total of just nine Dictaphone transcriptions or "experiments" available in the Dr. Mary E. Mercer/Carson McCullers Collection housed at Columbus State University, not far from McCullers' childhood home in Columbus, Georgia.[6] The experiments range from between one to seventeen pages each and are dated between April 4, 1958, and May 16, 1958. Upon her passing in 2013 at the age of 101, Mercer gifted the Dictaphone session transcripts to the archive, or what are almost certainly excerpts from the transcripts; moreover, the tapes themselves are not available. Notably, Mercer created her own handwritten inventory that she maintained through the decades, which was largely preserved in the shaping of the Columbus State University archive's formal finding aid.[7] Though many of McCullers' papers went to the Harry Ransom Center in the early 1970s, Mercer maintained her own domestic archive, cataloguing in pen and pencil on lined paper her own correspondences with McCullers, McCullers scholars, and McCullers' estate—to which Mercer was appointed, along with McCullers' agent, lawyer, and sister. She also collected articles related to McCullers and mementos gathered during their years of companionship. Mercer's labor as an archivist extends to her purchase of McCullers' house in Nyack, NY, whose units she rented out to artists in order to preserve it as a cultural landmark. After concluding therapy in 1958, McCullers and Mercer spent considerable time together, continually expressing their love for one another in written correspondence—an intimacy metaphorized by this archive's creation and maintenance.

The Dictaphone transcripts, however, made available some fifty years after their creation raise ethical questions about how to approach and write about material that is at once private and public. My own investment is in contemplating the literary value of these experiments in the context of life writing and their rich rapport with McCullers' autobiography, *Illumination and Night Glare*. My aim, in other words, is not to present biographical evidence, or "secrets," selected from the sessions, for instance, in order to decode McCullers' fiction as being in correspondence with her life experiences or her stated intentions; rather, I consider the feminist narrativizing practices at work in the experiments' thematics and by their material production by way of dictation. Regarding the overdetermined content of the transcripts, McCullers tells Mercer in the first experiment, "IT CERTAINLY WOULD CRAMP A PATIENT'S STYLE IF THEY THOUGHT YOU WERE PLAYING IT BACK TO OTHER PEOPLE......... I DON'T MIND ... IT IS NOT A SECRET AT ALL, ... IT IS A SECRET AND NOT A SECRET, BOTH" ("1st Experiment" 1; original emphasis).[8] McCullers' self-awareness regarding the recordings' paradoxical nature, of their being both private and public, and of their being recorded, and so transcribed into a record to be (re)read as she and Mercer worked together, prompts contemporary readers to grapple with their ethical and aesthetic complexity.

McCullers addresses Dr. Mercer in the sessions as her interlocutor, calling the Dictaphone sessions "letters between them" ("1st Experiment" 3), and "our book ... Our Flowering Dream" ("2nd Experiment" 4). The experiments have an oral quality that is consistent with McCullers' addressing of a listener while dictating her 1967 autobiography, *Illumination and Night Glare*. McCullers shares with Mercer in the second Dictaphone experiment that she showed the beginning of one of these "letters" to her best friend Tennessee Williams, telling him, "it was a kind of encyclopedia of suffering, you know, and he asked how many volumes it was going to be" ("2nd Experiment" 2). Such an interpellation, "a kind of encyclopedia," underscores the juxtapositional nature of this therapeutic model, as well as McCullers' consistent appeal to sardonic humor as a mode of perseverance. The experiments, what she also calls "an impromptu journal of [her] heart" ("1st Experiment" 2), emerge in the manner of a stream of consciousness: McCullers recites poems, tells jokes, rehearses anecdotes, and so on with few clear prompts from Mercer or transitions from McCullers, underscoring their literary quality and investment in the social. There is a frequent absence of punctuation, so that Mercer's interjections about childhood development, sometimes bracketed in the margin retrospectively in pencil with the note, "Dr. Mercer," dwell alongside McCullers' recollections.[9]

If the phenomenology of writing heretofore had been about the holding of a pencil and the typing of keys, McCullers reorients her writing practice to the Dictaphone, ever aware of its materiality, which is never quite naturalized—"It is like a maniac taxi going on and on," she says of the sound it produces ("2nd Experiment" 4)—but perhaps also of the method of talk therapy itself. The Dictaphone, nevertheless, becomes a vital extension, a prosthetic whereby the voice takes precedence over the hand(s) to facilitate the act of writing. Her voice is then transcribed by nurses and friends back into the documents now housed in the archive. The experiments begin with a parenthetical: "(It has to be held close like this)"; there are also often insertions of "end of reel" and so on, embedded within the text that generate a grammar whereby to read these transcripts in McCullers' and Mercer's (and the tapes') absence. Holding the Dictaphone close recalls McCullers' metaphor of a journal of the heart and signals the textual intimacy of these transcripts, which are both private and public, as McCullers notes, complicating both the knowable subject that life writing often purports to disclose and the reader's desire to know her.

The dialogics of the sessions are brought to a meta-level throughout the transcripts; for instance, at one point in the third experiment, McCullers interjects to Mercer, "I think we won't [sic] make any sense if we don:t [sic] have what you say too. Can you remember what you were saying?"

("3rd Experiment" 5). This reference to making "sense" raises the question: to whom? Apparently, this polysemic statement refers, on one level, to a book project that McCullers had in mind that would pay for her therapy. Mercer acknowledges in a letter penned in March 1970, which she did not ever send to Robbie Lantz, McCullers' agent, that McCullers proposed recording the sessions so "that a book could be published someday to support the therapy. It was her idea of killing two birds with one stone."[10] To this end, in the first session, McCullers rehearses with Dr. Mercer anecdotes with clever punch lines, then alludes to a book deal: "If I am going to get an advance from my publisher ... I have to have some kind of ... humor and fun ... or else he will never give me an advance" ("1st Experiment" 3). Later in the first session, she revises this statement, calling attention to narrativizing practices: "about the humor thing cut that ... and get back to our flowering dream" ("1st Experiment" 4). This oscillation between public and private, humor and the dream, not secret and secret, commercial and authentic, pervades the material. McCullers consistently emphasizes the "we of me," or the *our* of "our flowering dream," which fuels the creative spirit, or the illumination of her autobiography, what she names "livingness" in her final novel, *Clock Without Hands* (115).

Against the didactic function of conventional autobiography, McCullers often privileges the appeal of the comic and the *outré* in the experiments. Before her impulse to cut that "humor thing," she remarks, "So this leads to humor, which is a fine ... a nice way to go on for this is getting very serious" ("1st Experiment" 3). In turn, in the first experiment, McCullers recalls spending nights at Gypsy Rose Lee's house, where the famed burlesque performer and pulp novelist had regular nighttime trysts with a man who always arrived with an entourage of bodyguards; it eventually dawned on McCullers that her friend's lover was Waxy Gordon, a notorious gangster. McCullers narrates the same anecdote in 1967 for *Illumination and Night Glare* (33); just as in the Dictaphone sessions, in her autobiography, McCullers frequently turns to the comic for insight and comfort. In *Illumination and Night Glare*, McCullers recalls her therapy with Dr. Mercer and telling her all manner of "silly things" (*ING* 76), such as Gypsy's gift to McCullers of a monkey, Herman, who returned the favor by latching onto McCullers' hair, biting her head. Gypsy is with McCullers when the latter experiences her "illumination" about *The Member of the Wedding* that "Frankie is in love with the bride of her brother and wants to join the wedding" (*ING* 32). This queer insight flashes in McCullers' mind while she and Gypsy were running in the street, chasing the sound of a fire engine. Such recollections, dictated as they are to an other, perform a feminist recognition of an alternative sociality.

The tension between the public and private content of these transcripts, however, and their interrelation with *Illumination and Night Glare*, fully emerges in the wake of McCullers' death in 1967. McCullers' agent, Robbie Lantz, wrote to Mercer in 1970, as the estate was assessing McCullers' papers for publication possibilities before sending them to the Ransom Center, to ask her about an autobiographical manuscript that he had read, at McCullers' request, when she was in the hospital in 1958, taking the draft home with him overnight. He recalls, in particular, reading the aforementioned anecdote about Gypsy Rose Lee's involvement with gangsters. Mercer responds that "that material which [he] read was not a manuscript but part of Carson's psychiatric record. Carson was in psychiatric treatment with me for one year. That particular hospitalization must have occurred while she was still my patient. Her psychiatric records, like those of any other psychiatric patient, are strictly confidential."[11] In the same letter, Mercer alludes to Floria Lasky, McCullers' lawyer, having asked her about a manuscript entitled, "The Flowering Dream." Mercer maintains that while McCullers published an essay by that title in *Esquire*, the manuscript in question is not a manuscript, at all, but, she insists, McCullers' psychiatric record, not material for publication. Mercer goes on to maintain that their sessions "were used up by Carson in her own way" when she later composed her autobiography, but that the transcripts themselves were not intended for publication.[12] Though McCullers herself collapses the distinction between public and private during the first session, it was only over the course of many decades that Dr. Mercer came to revise her own view of the content of the Dictaphone experiments as strictly confidential, gifting them, or at least some of them, to the archive. Such a move merits further scholarly engagement and interpretation.

The most explicitly personal material in the available transcripts relates to McCullers' sexuality and her feelings of unrequited love for Swiss author and heiress Annemarie Clarac-Schwarzenbach. I include this biographical content not to promote a definitive reading of McCullers' much discussed sexuality, but rather to affirm McCullers' privileging in her life writing, just as she does in her fiction, what we would now term queer belonging and non-heteronormative affinities.[13] As Rachel Adams explains in related terms, the term queer "more accurately describes the heterogeneity of intimate erotically charged relationships and currents of desire in McCullers' fiction" (21), and, I would add, life writing, than does the term homosexual. Central to the Dictaphone experiments—McCullers refers to the same episodes in at least half of the available transcripts—are McCullers' feelings of despair over Schwarzenbach's attraction to other women, Schwarzenbach's morphine addiction and withdrawals, her suicide attempts and her subsequent commitment to Bellevue—traumatic events for which McCullers was present. McCullers recalls that while she was writing *The Member of the Wedding* during World War II, she was desperately trying to get an assignment as a correspondent overseas, *either* to join Schwarzenbach in Lisbon as she awaited a passport to join De Gaulle's resistance forces in the Congo *or* to join her then ex-husband Reeves McCullers, who had been injured in the War and was convalescing in England ("8th Experiment" 6). These wishes are espoused as simultaneous, not mutually exclusive; the heterogeneity of experience and desire, in other words, is a hallmark of these Dictaphone experiments as life writing texts.

Curiously, Reeves McCullers' spectral presence haunts the transcriptions with its absence: he is mentioned rarely in the archived Dictaphone sessions, but much more frequently in *Illumination and Night Glare*. In the autobiography, McCullers refers specifically to discussing her "relations with Reeves" with Mercer (*ING* 76; 78), explaining how "from being a man of glory, he descended little by little to forgery, theft, and attempted murder" (*ING* 76)—all crimes Reeves committed and attempted to commit against McCullers. These discussions, however, are not to be found in the archived Dictaphone sessions. Conversely, McCullers' attachment to Schwarzenbach pervades McCullers' work in therapy in the archived material, but forms a structuring absence in *Illumination and Night Glare*. Schwarzenbach is mentioned multiple times—"I don't know of a friend whom I loved more," McCullers avows (*ING* 36), and McCullers quotes excerpts from Schwarzenbach's wartime letters to her (*ING* 35–36)—but not to the extent nor with the candor with which McCullers' addresses her love and physical desire for Schwarzenbach in the Dictaphone experiments. The nested temporalities of McCullers' imbricated autobiographical accounts in this period refuse generic and juridical expectations of accuracy and chronology, offering a far more nuanced presentation of lived experience.

Following the 1958 experiments and emphasizing their literary quality, McCullers sublimated their contents into the essay, "The Flowering Dream: Notes on Writing." The essay was printed in the deluxe 1959 Christmas Jubilee Issue of *Esquire*, which came packaged in a metallic gold envelope, and featured new writing by literary luminaries including William Faulkner, Arthur Miller, Dorothy Parker and George Bernard Shaw. Notably, McCullers' proposed title for the Dictaphone sessions book project, "Our Flowering Dream," becomes "The Flowering Dream." "Our" dream, in other words, may be read as "*The*" dream. To this end, McCullers' essay concludes: "Writing in essence, is communication; and communication is the only access to love—to love, to conscience, to nature, to God, and to the dream. For myself, the further I go into my own work and the more I read of those I love, the more aware I am of the dream and the logic of God, which indeed is a Divine collusion" (164). McCullers shares similar, almost verbatim, sentiments in the first Dictaphone experiment with Mercer, musing, "the further I went into my own work, the longer I live with the work I love, the more I was aware of the dream and the logical [sic] God" ("1st Experiment" 1). This divine collusion speaks to a celebration of an alternative sociality and to writing itself as an inherently social practice often fueled by care and love and an intense desire for recognition by an other.

DIALOGIC SOCIALITY (AND ITS LIMITS) IN *ILLUMINATION AND NIGHT GLARE*

The Dictaphone experiments' imbrication with *Illumination and Night Glare* is manifest in the 1967 autobiography's "ending." Carson McCullers lived some fourteen years after Reeves McCullers' suicide in Paris; her autobiography, nevertheless, ends with his words. Following a passage wherein McCullers recounts working with Mercer through the experience of her difficult marriage to Reeves, Mercer is quoted as having suggested, "But you must have had happy times," to which McCullers responds, "Yes." *Illumination and Night Glare* then concludes with a reminiscence that disrupts mid-century gender norms: "He was of enormous value to me at the time I wrote [*Heart*] and [*Reflections*]. I was completely absorbed in my work, and if the food burned up he never chided me. More important, he read and criticized each chapter as it was being done. Once I asked him if he thought [*Heart*] was any good. He reflected for a long time, and then he said, 'No, it's not good, it's great'" (*ING* 78). This, the text's last line, returns us to the autobiography's opening passage, which also recounts the period of "illumination" accompanying the inception of her relationship with Reeves and her authoring of *The Heart Is a Lonely Hunter*. The fact that this "ending" also cites Mercer's intimate presence, further defamiliarizes mid-century heteronormativity, gesturing back to the 1958 dictaphone experiments as an intertext that informed McCullers' final work, much of which took the form of life writing. In the autobiography, McCullers describes her time with Mercer as "the happiest and most rewarding experience of [her] life" (*ING* 52).

In the process of dictating *Illumination and Night Glare*, McCullers indicated in all caps "(INSERT WAR LETTERS)" (*ING* 27): not being able to deduce just which of the three-hundred letters McCullers had gathered were intended for inclusion in the autobiography—perhaps, for instance, she wanted all of them included—Dews culled some eighty pages worth of McCullers and Reeves' wartime correspondence from the Ransom Center.[14] The letters that form the second half of *Illumination and Night Glare* rehearse compelling spatio-temporal asymmetries, as the letters would often arrive during the War out of chronological order, or in a bunch, generating a temporal complexity accentuated by Dews' own selection of available letters in the archive decades later. The supplement—again, as that which augments, but is never fully integrated into a total-ity—presents us with the impossibility of the finished text, of plenitude. This is literalized by the fact that the letters are included after the auto-biographical text; they are not inserted beginning on page 27: the point at which McCullers dictated their insertion in capital letters. They form, in other words, a second half, juxtaposed with the first. Similarly, the full outline for "The Mute" follows upon the supplementarity of these letters, included only in excerpted form in the opening pages of the text, in jux-tapositional fashion.

We cannot know whether McCullers would have selected these particu-lar letters for inclusion, nor if she would have included personal photo-graphs like those Dews selected; nevertheless, her instructions to insert her and Reeves' letters affirms a desire to share their wartime experience with future readers as integral to her life experience. Such a textual coupling commingles longing with national belonging, while also revising hetero-normative relations—the two were divorced at the time—expanding the narrative of love and care to McCullers' simultaneous love and concern for Schwarzenbach during this period, as witnessed by the Dictaphone sessions. McCullers espouses deep pride over Reeves' bravery on the frontlines in the letters, but she also experiences paralyzing concern for his well-being: often describing her partial loss of vision when she attempts to read his letters and telegrams, fearing their contents. This attention to embodiment in the letters sustains the dialogical, asymptotic dynamics of *Illumination and Night Glare*'s non-linear autobiographical practice.

McCullers described her life writing projects in terms of the social, and the scope of her final project widens to encompass race, class, gender, and sexuality. In order to assess her strength to visit director John Huston at his home in Ireland toward the end of her life, McCullers stayed briefly with her longtime friend and African American caretaker, Ida Reeder, in the Plaza Hotel in New York City. In the 1967 interview mentioned earlier in this chapter, Rex Reed reported that "her next books, she says, will be a collection of stories about Negroes she has known in the South ('The speech and feeling of one's childhood are always inherent to me as author and Negro speech is so beautiful') and, eventually, a journal about her life, her books, and why she wrote them" (15). Significantly, what McCullers describes here as *two* different projects merge into one in the text of *Illumination and Night Glare*, as biographical sketches of African American men and women in her hometown of Columbus, Georgia, are recounted in her autobiography alongside her own childhood experiences and creative practices. Such a formal coexistence further dispels the solitary "I" of conventional autobiography and manifests the ongoing material and psychic processes of desegregation and interracial sociality.

Illumination and Night Glare's accounts of interracial intimacy register the fact of her last two writing projects becoming one in the typescript draft she left behind at the time of her death. This formal convergence demonstrates the socio-cultural reality that black and white Americans were never truly materially or psychically separated from one another, in spite of Jim Crow's structural aims. Though McCullers left Georgia for New York when she was seventeen, her fiction and life writing consistently return to the South, ever grappling with its hierarchical structures of domination and delimitation. In the text, McCullers describes witnessing as a child her family's beloved fourteen-year-old nurse and cook, Lucille, being refused a taxi cab ride home outside of their house during the Depression. When the driver called out, "I'm not driving no damn nigger," McCullers shouted at him, "You bad, bad man." Her little brother, Lamar, burst out crying and crawled into the dank space under their house (*ING* 54). McCullers observes of segregation that it was not always "physical brutality, but the brutal humiliation of human dignity which is even worse" (*ING* 56). Such a scene, dictated for inclusion in her life story decades after its occurrence—McCullers notes that "Lucille comes back to me over and over" (*ING* 56)—foregrounds racist rhetoric and its psychic ramifications on black and white subjects. McCullers' life writing returns to "those hideous aspects of the South" (*ING* 62) with which she wrestled throughout her career, beginning with *The Heart Is a Lonely Hunter*, whose outline, again, is included in *Illumination and Night Glare*'s scrapbook of memories.

The limits, however, of narrating another's experiences alongside one's own—the implicit challenge of all life writing—are clear in Lucille's biographical sketch. McCullers speaks more surely of her brother Lamar's response to overt racism than of Lucille's; this effect is amplified by McCullers' assertion that when Lucille was later sentenced to the penitentiary for a year after being accused of poisoning the white family she went to work for after McCullers' family let her go during the Depression, "the experience did not harm her" (*ING* 56). McCullers bases her conclusion that Lucille's jail sentence did not affect her negatively upon her own sense that in prison Lucille "learned to sew and practice reading and writing ... [and] got a pretty good liberal education" (*ING* 56). McCullers' claim that being incarcerated on false allegations—an unthinkable scenario for most whites—was not a harmful experience reveals the limits of speaking for the other and the paradoxes of recognition.

Nevertheless, attention to racial inequality is a throughline in many of McCullers' reminiscences in *Illumination and Night Glare*. She recalls, for instance, being phoned by the Ku Klux Klan when she was convalescing at home in Columbus, Georgia, following the controversial publication of *Reflections in a Golden Eye*; her father stood guard the rest of the night after a caller threatened, "[We] are the Klan and we don't like nigger lovers or fairies. Tonight will be your night" (*ING* 31). In spite of such harassment, McCullers refused to give her papers to a segregated library that would deny access to her writings to African Americans (Carr 493). McCullers' sustained emphasis on sociality in both her fiction and life writing addresses our experiences as always already conditioned by the intersectionalities of race, class, gender, and sexuality.

Such themes are given explicit attention in her final novel, *Clock Without Hands* (1961), which is set in a small Georgia town and whose plot takes up the social flux, psychic dissonance, and brutal violence prompted by court-ordered integration. The novel registers inflections from McCullers' own struggles and insights in the Dictaphone experiments as one of the key characters, Malone, is terminally ill and comes to grips with his fragile mortality over the course of the novel. Interracial love and male same-sex desire are prominent thematics; Sarah Gleeson-White notes that Jester Clane, the grandson of a racist judge, is one of the very few characters in McCullers' fiction to be directly presented to the reader as gay (39); his love object is a black man, the child of a black woman with whom Jester's father fell in unrequited love, leading to his suicide. McCullers' privileging of and attentiveness to embodied experience in her final novel is enmeshed with her life writing in this period; her final works evoke our shared vulnerability and imbricatedness with one another, rather than the illusion of autonomy signaled by the traditional authorial subject.

CONCLUSION

McCullers' experimental, non-chronological life writing remains ever-cognizant of embodiment. Such an approach affords us a social intimacy with the author, as we encounter McCullers' mortal body, gripping a pencil, or typing with one finger of the right hand, in spite of daily pain, then eventually dictating sentences to an other, but writing, always writing, to share her insights with posterity and in communion with herself and others.[15] The writing of the self is always already bound up with dynamics of recognition, and an ethics of and attachment to the other. Having been dictated to multiple others, whose identities are not all verifiable or known (Dews xiv), *Illumination and Night Glare* re-purposes autobiographical conventions to allow for bias, humor, and inspiration. Its composition and publication history position us to read differently by affirming the dialogical thematics of McCullers' œuvre.

Circulated over thirty years after its dictation, McCullers' posthumously published autobiography generates complex temporalities by way of its elliptical omissions, non-linearity, and its tension with what Dews calls the "strict biographical record" (xxi). Her text affords us insights into her creative production in a manner that complicates a mere striving for one-to-one correspondences between her stated intentions and her fiction, or her exceptional life circumstances with that of her fictional characters. My emphasis in expanding our approach to biographical criticism by way of feminist autobiography studies performs a reckoning with the unique forms of the editorial and archival supplement that register our desire to sustain the author in the world. By way of her heterogeneous writing acts and their irreducible relationship to the archive, McCullers ever greets us at the door in her white robe and sneakers, with her cinnamon-ey drawl—somehow both known and unknown to us as scholars and readers.

NOTES

1. McCullers worked on *Clock Without Hands* (1961) over a ten-year period, beginning in 1951. She published excerpts in the periodical *Botteghe Oscure* and in *Mademoiselle* in 1953. In the last of the ten available Dictaphone transcripts, McCullers describes the plot of *Clock Without Hands*, and Mercer replies, "If you went back to work on that [novel], it might be as close to what we are trying to do here as anything that you might do" ("10th Experiment" 8). I refer to the transcripts by experiment and page number, all of which are found in Box 1 Series 5 of the Dr. Mary E. Mercer/Carson McCullers Collection (MC 296) at Columbus State University.

2. Biographer Josyane Savigneau cites McCullers' 1963 correspondence with biographer Oliver Evans, in which McCullers describes a "book of memories" she intends to write, entitled *The Flowering Dream* (313). Though McCullers did publish an essay about writing in *Esquire* by the same name, "The Flowering Dream" (1959), *Illumination and Night Glare* is presumably the memory text she envisioned and worked on just before her death.

3. Reeves and Carson McCullers divorced before World War II and remarried at its end.

4. In light of the toll that editing *The Mortgaged Heart* took on her, McCullers' sister, Rita Smith, wrote to McCullers' lawyer, Floria Lasky, regarding the prospect of editing McCullers' autobiography into a book that, "no matter the outcome of [*The Mortgaged Heart*], [she] did not want to work on any other book of Carson's" (qtd. in Dews, *Illumination and Night Glare* 20).

5. See Gussow's *NY Times* review.

6. There is no 4th Experiment. The 7th Experiment ends abruptly with an incomplete sentence.

7. Carlos Dews also gifted his papers related to his McCullers research to the CSU archive.

8. The Dictaphone transcripts are typed in all caps, but after this first quotation, I use standard typing; I have preserved the original number and placement of ellipses from the transcripts.

9. See, for instance, Experiment 7.

10. See MC 296, Box 14, Folder 6-C-1970, 4.10.

11. See MC 296, Box 13, Folder 6-B.1, 19.

12. See MC 296 Box 13, Folder 6-C, 4.10.

13. For readings of McCullers' sexuality and its relation to her fiction, see, among others, Adams, Kenschaft, Gleeson-White, and Segrest.

14. A Nov. 29, 1967 letter from Mercer mentions correspondence from Reeves McCullers *and* Annemarie Schwarzenbach among McCullers' collected letters (MC 296, Box 14, Folder 6-C).

15. See Stuart Sherman's profile "Carson McCullers" in *BOMB* 33 (Fall 1990). Sherman read to McCullers in her last year. He notes that McCullers was at work on a life writing text entitled, "In Spite Of," about famous figures overcoming physical challenges. Dews notes that some of this material appears in *Illumination and Night Glare* (xv–xvi).

WORKS CITED

Adams, Rachel. "'A Mixture of Delicious and Freak': The Queer Fiction of Carson McCullers." *Carson McCullers.* Ed. Harold Bloom. NY: Infobase Pub., 2009. 17–43. Print.

Carr, Virginia Spencer. *The Lonely Hunter: A Biography of Carson McCullers.* Athens, GA: U of Georgia P, 1976. Print.

Derrida, Jacques. "...*That Dangerous Supplement.*" *Of Grammatology.* Trans. Gayatri Chakravorty Spivak. 1974. Baltimore: Johns Hopkins P, 1997. 141–156. Print.

The Carlos L. Dews Collection (MC 175). Columbus State University Archives, Columbus, Georgia. Feb. 2015. Print.

Dews, Carlos E. *Illumination and Night Glare: The Unfinished Autobiography of Carson McCullers (Volumes I and II).* Diss. U of Minnesota, 1995. Minneapolis: UMI, 1995. Print.

Evans, Oliver. *The Ballad of Carson McCullers: A Biography.* NY: Coward-McCann, 1966. Print.

Gilmore, Leigh. *Autobiographics: A Feminist Theory of Women's Self-Representation.* Ithaca, NY: Cornell UP, 1994. Print.

Gleeson-White, Sarah. *Strange Bodies: Gender and Identity in the Novels of Carson McCullers.* Tuscaloosa, AL: U of Alabama P, 2003. Print.

Gusdorf, Georges. "Conditions and Limits of Autobiography." Ed. and Trans. James Olney. *Autobiography: Essays Theoretical and Critical.* Princeton, NJ: Princeton UP, 1980. 28–48. Print.

Gussow, Mel. "In Unfinished Memoirs, Carson McCullers Recalls a Struggle to Write." *New York Times,* 15 Apr. 2000. Web. 23 Mar. 2015.

Kenschaft, Lori J. "Homoerotics and Human Connections: Reading Carson McCullers 'As a Lesbian.'" *Critical Essays on Carson McCullers.* Eds. Beverly Lyon Clark and Melvin J. Friedman. NY: G.L. Hall, 1996. 220–233. Print.

LeJeune, Philippe. "The Autobiographical Pact." *On Autobiography.* Ed. Paul John Eakin. Minneapolis: U of Minnesota P, 1989. 3–30. Print.

McCullers, Carson. *Clock Without Hands.* 1961. NY: Houghton Mifflin, 1998. Print.

——. "The Flowering Dream: Notes on Writing." *Esquire,* Dec. 1959. 162–64. Print.

——. *The Heart is a Lonely Hunter.* 1940. NY: Houghton Mifflin, 1998. Print.

——. *Illumination and Night Glare: The Unfinished Autobiography of Carson McCullers.* Ed. Carlos L. Dews. Madison: U of Wisconsin P, 1999. Print.

——. *The Member of the Wedding.* 1946. NY: Houghton Mifflin, 2004. Print.

——. *The Member of the Wedding: The Play.* 1950. NY: New Directions, 2006. Print.

——. *The Mortgaged Heart.* 1971. NY: Houghton Mifflin, 2005. Print.

——. *The Square Root of Wonderful.* 1957. Cherokee, NC: Cherokee Publications, 1990. Print.

The Dr. Mary E. Mercer/Carson McCullers Collection (MC 296). Columbus State University Archives, Columbus, Georgia. February 2015.

——. "1st Experiment." 11 April 1958. MS. Dr. Mary E. Mercer/Carson McCullers Collection (MC 296). Columbus State University Archives, Columbus, Georgia. Print.

——. "2nd Experiment." 14 April 1958. MS. Dr. Mary E. Mercer/Carson McCullers Collection (MC 296). Columbus State University Archives, Columbus, Georgia. Print.

——. "3rd Experiment." 21 April 1958. MS. Dr. Mary E. Mercer/Carson McCullers Collection (MC 296). Columbus State University Archives, Columbus, Georgia. Print.

——. "8th Experiment." 9 May 1958. MS. Dr. Mary E. Mercer/Carson McCullers Collection (MC 296). Columbus State University Archives, Columbus, Georgia. Print.

——. "10th Experiment." 12 May 1958. MS. Dr. Mary E. Mercer/Carson McCullers Collection (MC 296). Columbus State University Archives, Columbus, Georgia. Print.

Reed, Rex. "Frankie Addams at 50." *New York Times*, 16 Apr. 1967. 15. Print.

Savigneau, Josyane. *Carson McCullers: A Life.* NY: Houghton Mifflin, 2001. Print.

Segrest, Mab. "'Lines I Dare Draw.'" *Out in the South.* Eds. C.L. Barney Dews and Carolyn Leste Law. Philadelphia: Temple UP, 2001. 204–228. Print.

Sherman, Stuart. "Carson McCullers." *BOMB Magazine.* (Fall 1990). Web. 23 Mar. 2015.

Watson, Julia and Sidonie Smith. *Reading Autobiography: A Guide of Interpreting Life Narratives.* 2nd ed. Minneapolis: U of Minnesota P, 2010. Print.

Whitt, Jan. "Introduction." *Reflections in a Critical Eye: Essays on Carson McCullers.* Lanham, Maryland: UP of America, 2008. Print.

Telling It "Slant": Carson McCullers, Harper Lee, and the Veil of Memory

Jan Whitt

Literary works lie on a continuum—somewhere between "just-the-facts-ma'am" reporting and fantasy or science fiction. Authors of creative non-fiction produce newsworthy information, avoiding embellishment and inaccuracy, while telling a compelling story. Novelists and short story writers draw primarily from their own imaginations but often depend on experiences located in time and place, always vulnerable to questions from readers about what "really" occurred and what they "made up."

Contemporary studies about the borderland between fiction and non-fiction both complicate and enrich the conversation about what is real and what is imagined:

- Is Truman Capote's *In Cold Blood* (1966) truly what he called a "nonfiction novel"? If so, how does a reader account for invented scenes? In one of them, investigator Alvin Dewey meets a friend of the murdered Herbert Clutter family in a graveyard—and Capote provides dialogue and a detailed setting. However, it turns out, Capote was not present (neither was anyone else).

J. Whitt (✉)
College of Media, Communication and Information, University of Colorado,
478 UCB, Boulder, CO 80309, USA

© The Author(s) 2016   67
A. Graham-Bertolini, C. Kayser (eds.), *Carson McCullers in the Twenty-First Century*, DOI 10.1007/978-3-319-40292-5_4

- Is *Midnight in the Garden of Good and Evil* (1994) a travelogue, a novel, or a murder mystery? How does one account for John Berendt's "Author's Note" at the end of the novel? In his message to the reader, Berendt explains that he has altered chronology and changed names of characters (what he describes as taking "certain storytelling liberties") but that he has remained "faithful to the characters and to the essential drift of events as they really happened" (n.p.). But what constitutes an "essential drift of events," and does it matter?
- Finally, is Jon Krakauer wise when he injects himself into a tale about Chris McCandless and a sojourn into the Alaska wilderness? Is the author's presence in the story a distraction? Does Krakauer's personal point of view disrupt or enhance *Into the Wild* (1996)? Does the reader care what the author thinks of McCandless, or is it more informative and pleasurable if readers come to their own conclusions about a character's life experiences?

Of course, deciding where to place a book in a library or bookstore is not the only catalyst for discussions about authorial intent, genre distinctions, or textual integrity. Examples of the slippery slope between fiction and nonfiction proliferate, and not all case studies are as clear as *A Million Little Pieces* (2006) in which author James Frey lied about several events in an otherwise factual and compelling memoir, sparking a national conversation about memoir and its discontents. Traditionally, literary scholars consider the role of creative writing; the writer's obligation to her or his readers; the place of memoir in nonfiction studies; the purposes and contributions of journalistic inquiry; the difficulty of determining what is true; and other topics. "Tell all the truth, but tell it slant/Success in Circuit lies," writes Emily Dickinson, reminding readers several lines later that "The Truth must dazzle gradually/Or every man be blind" (506–507). How much is too much manipulation of dialogue, alteration of plot, and creative invention? Is full disclosure the answer? Even if we were to address these and similar issues adequately, how might we best account for both the wonders and pitfalls of memory?

One way out of the conundrum might be to embrace a new way of understanding autobiography, personal essay, and memoir by focusing upon autobiographical novels such as Carson McCullers' *The Heart Is a Lonely Hunter* (1940) and *The Member of the Wedding* (1946) and Harper Lee's *To Kill a Mockingbird* (1960). All three beloved coming-of-age novels with female protagonists have escaped the kind of scrutiny that

Capote, Berendt, Krakauer, and others have faced (and continue to face). Under the cover of fiction, McCullers and Lee created mythopoetic universes in which Mick Kelly, Frances (Frankie) Addams, and Jean Louise (Scout) Finch face a maze of adolescent challenges. Occasionally, their confusion provides moments of comic relief; most often, though, there is nothing amusing about a world in which girls are afraid, demeaned, ignored, manipulated, and ostracized.

Did McCullers and Lee find solace in detaching themselves from their young heroines, or did they confront their dislocation by creating characters in their own image? How much of their narratives directly reflect their lives and the time periods during which they themselves were learning about gender roles and sexuality? How much in their autobiographical novels is truth told "slant"? Further, in the cases of female writers such as Lula Carson McCullers and Nelle Harper Lee—who used their middle, more masculine names professionally—how do readers account for artistic deflection? For example, were the authors "tomboys," or were they bisexual, lesbian, or simply uninterested in submitting themselves to prevalent gender expectations? Do answers to these questions matter, and, if so, why?

At first glance, memoir and autobiographical novels might not appear to have much in common; in fact, the assumption may be that memoir is factual but autobiographical novels allow the author to manipulate chronology, change names, invent dialogue, and violate other tenets of nonfiction. One of literary journalist Sara Davidson's essays, "The Gray Zone," addresses directly the role of memoir, a particularly rich and problematic category of nonfiction, and provides a worthy introduction to a discussion of authorial identity and authentic experience in both fiction and nonfiction. Davidson authored bestsellers *Loose Change: Three Women of the Sixties* (1977) and *Cowboy: A Novel* (1999). In both, she protects the identities of her sources—often family members, friends, or partners—to a limited extent, but she also deals with the theoretical underpinnings of memoir itself. In "The Gray Zone," Davidson engages generally with the complexity of nonfiction and in particular with the difficulties she has encountered in writing memoir.

Beginning with a reference to Patrick Hemingway, editor of his father Ernest Hemingway's *True at First Light*, and with Patrick Hemingway's decision to publish the work as "fictionalized memoir," Davidson asks the question that drives this study: "When a story has its wellspring in life—in actual events and real people—what constitutes a fictional rendering and what constitutes memoir?" In journalism, she suggests, the answer matters "absolutely" because reporters have a responsibility not to "invent, change or embellish the smallest detail." In the "gray zone" where she writes, however, the answer for her (and, presumably, for us) is not so clear:

> When a writer sets out to tell a true story, he immediately finds himself constrained by the fallibility of memory. No one can recall the exact words of a conversation that took place a few days ago, let alone years, even if the writer attempts to recreate the conversation faithfully. In addition, the very process of translating mood, nonverbal signals and emotions into words creates a reality on the page that does not exactly mirror the event in life. But beyond this, the writer makes a deliberate choice as to how much he will permit himself to take liberties. (49)

Ultimately, Davidson argues for what she calls "not a better system of classification" for nonfiction but "full disclosure" (50) by the authors themselves. Dealing with the difference between fiction and nonfiction and between the novel and memoir, Davidson writes in her introduction to *Cowboy* that "at one end of the spectrum are works that are entirely imagined, and at the other end, works that purport to be fact. Most, however, are a blend of fact and imagination, and yet a line has been drawn to separate one from the other" (xi).

AUTOBIOGRAPHY IN NOVELS BY HARPER LEE AND CARSON MCCULLERS

Harper Lee and Carson McCullers join Sara Davidson and other writers who operate most comfortably in the "gray zone" between fiction and nonfiction. Although McCullers and Lee are not known as journalists (McCullers worked for only a short time for her hometown newspaper), they depend on their life experiences in ways not so dissimilar from Davidson. In *Scout, Atticus and Boo: A Celebration of Fifty Years of* To Kill a Mockingbird, author Wally Lamb discusses his approach to writing and suggests that his experience might be similar to Harper Lee's:

> You start with who and what you know. You take a survey of the lay of that land that formed you and shaped you, and then you begin to lie about it. You tell one lie that turns into a different lie, and after a while those models

sort of lift off and become their own people rather than the people you originally thought of. And when you weave an entire network of lies, what you're really doing, if you're aiming to write literary fiction, is, by telling lies, you're trying to arrive at a deeper truth. (38)

Lamb is not the only person to note the wisdom of relying upon the geography and the people one knows best. Rick Bragg, whose work also often lies on the continuum between fact and fiction, praises *To Kill a Mockingbird*, both for its truthfulness and its artistry:

> It was so real, it was so true to the dirt and the trees and the houses and the dusty streets and the mad dogs, and the sheriff who wants to do right if he can just figure out how, and the mean-spirited neighbor and the kind people in town, and the racial prejudice and the handful of people who just didn't fall in step. All that, it wasn't just true; it was beautifully, beautifully done. (qtd. in Murphy 59)

Like Lamb and Bragg, the Rev. Thomas Lane Butts, pastor of the First Methodist Church that Harper Lee and her family attended, confirms the veracity of Lee's memory of Monroeville, Alabama, called "Maycomb" in *To Kill a Mockingbird*: "The book is not supposed to be autobiographical," Butts said, "but all novels have some autobiography in them, and all autobiographies have some fiction in them too" (qtd. in Murphy 68). Specifically, Butts remembers the fictional universe Lee created—the "rural, poverty-stricken" residents, the "hardscrabble" life the townspeople led, the institutionalized racism, and the "muddy" streets filled with "people coming to town with their mules and wagons" (68–69).

One of the most compelling sources in the conversation about Lee and novels that are based on actual acquaintances, events, and locales is Mark Childress. He argues that the "parts" of novels that are "physically real" seem to fascinate readers—although he fails to understand the devotion to actual people and places: "I've never quite understood that. To me, everything in a novel's real, and I really don't care where the author got it. But for readers that is important. They love to know how much of it was autobiographical" (qtd. in Murphy *Scout, Atticus and Boo* 81). Referring to *To Kill a Mockingbird*, Childress adds:

> Any writer who says he doesn't write out of his own life is lying. Of course he does—all your writing is based on your own life. But it's "Do you transform

the material?" And I think that's what she did, and put such magic on it. But, yeah, her life was probably something like the life in there, but it wasn't so beautifully dramatically shaped, and there wasn't one moment that pulled it all together. That's the beauty of fiction, that's what fiction can do: give shape to narrative. (81)

"Telling It 'Slant': Harper Lee, Carson McCullers, and the Veil of Memory" explores the often arbitrary boundaries between fiction and nonfiction, between the autobiographical novel and the memoir. Both Lee and McCullers grew up in the Deep South, living periodically in New York City. They published autobiographical novels that include *To Kill a Mockingbird*, *The Heart Is a Lonely Hunter*, and *The Member of the Wedding*. Lee's novel *Go Set a Watchman* (2015) reintroduces the reader to her beloved protagonist and explains what happened to Atticus Finch, Jean Louise (Scout) Finch, Jeremy Atticus (Jem) Finch, and Charles Baker (Dill) Harris. Calpurnia essentially disappears from *Go Set a Watchman*, and Aunt Alexandra, Atticus's stern sister, returns. Like *To Kill a Mockingbird*, *Go Set a Watchman* is also partially autobiographical.

Some similarities between the two authors are familiar to readers and scholars. Lee (1926–the present) grew up in Monroeville, the daughter of an attorney. The youngest of four children, she was a tomboy in a small, quiet town, and she converted her childhood memories into fiction. McCullers (1917–1967) grew up in Columbus, Georgia, and, like Lee, spent much of her life in New York. Unlike Lee, however, McCullers did not seek the anonymity that a bustling city provides; instead, she sought new, exciting, and highly public relationships. In *The Heart Is a Lonely Hunter* and *The Member of the Wedding*, McCullers relates narratives drawn from memory as she creates protagonists Mick Kelly and Frankie Addams. Like Lee, McCullers grew up as a tomboy in a small Southern town, immersed herself in books, moved to New York City for extended periods of time, and interacted with emerging and established artists, musicians, and writers.

What can autobiographical novels by Lee, McCullers, and others tell us about the veil of memory? What can we learn about the tenuous boundaries that separate a novel that is based on fact from a memoir? Why are these categories institutionalized and too often uninvestigated, and, more importantly, why might literature in the "gray zone" affect a reader's impressions about what is true and what is truth told "slant"?

The Heart Is a Lonely Hunter *and* The Member
of the Wedding

Carson McCullers both loved and hated the Deep South, a land of magnolias and verbena, restored historic homes, and plush countrysides graced with sunshine. When she writes about "orchard blossoms in gray rain" in the poem "The Mortgaged Heart" (*Mortgaged* 286), McCullers describes a familiar sight in Georgia, but the juxtaposition of images also symbolizes the stark contrasts and paradoxes that characterized her life. McCullers learned to live with complexity and contradiction, and she developed a highly sophisticated sense of irony. In everything, from McCullers' bisexuality, to her often confused longings for a personal as well as a fictional Messiah, to her contradictory feelings about the South itself, the author of *The Heart Is a Lonely Hunter* and *The Member of the Wedding* sought to make peace with the paradoxes of life.

Georgia is a region that McCullers both longed for and avoided. She was born in Columbus on February 19, 1917, the daughter of Lamar and Marguerite Smith. The ambivalence she felt toward her homeland is revealed in "The Flowering Dream: Notes on Writing": "People ask me why I don't go back to the South more often. But the South is a very emotional experience for me, fraught with all the memories of my childhood. When I go back South I always get into arguments, so that a visit to Columbus in Georgia is a stirring up of love and antagonism" (*Mortgaged* 279). McCullers once told a friend that she needed to "go home periodically to renew [her] sense of horror" (*Collected Stories* viii).

Yet McCullers often spoke lovingly and tenderly of Georgia summers and childhood Christmas seasons, and she was heir to a rich and dramatic regional history that enlivened her fiction. "Down in the South it will be early evening," she reminisced during a New Year's Eve in London. "Quiet, orange firelight will flicker on kitchen walls, and in the cupboards there will be the hog-jowl and the black-eyed peas to bring good fortune in the coming year" (*Mortgaged* 215). In "How I Began to Write," McCullers describes the sitting-rooms of her "old Georgia home" in which she and her brother and sister performed homemade dramatic productions: "In summertime the rooms were stifling until the time for curtain, and the clock was silenced by sounds of yard-boy whistling and distant radios" (*Mortgaged* 249). McCullers may often have fled the South, but as she wrote, "the voices reheard from childhood have a truer pitch" (*Mortgaged* 279), and as a child she explored the Georgia woods and imagined stories while sitting under an awning of trees beside her home. Although McCullers was quick to remember the "vacant, broiling" afternoons of August and quick to describe the "heat-shimmered air" (*Mortgaged* 233), she drew on locale in all her novels. "When I work from within a different locale from the South," McCullers wrote, "I have to wonder what time the flowers are in bloom—and what flowers?" (*Mortgaged* 279).

Because she was conflicted about the South, New York City provided an adolescent McCullers with an escape from the dreary dullness of her early Georgia days. "I longed for wanderings," McCullers wrote. "I longed especially for New York. The firelight on the walnut folding doors would sadden me, and the tedious sound of the old swan clock. I dreamed of the distant city of skyscrapers and snow" (*Mortgaged* 251). Descriptions of small-town Southern life appear in much of McCullers' fiction, including *The Ballad of the Sad Café* and *The Member of the Wedding*. "There's absolutely nothing to do in the town," writes McCullers in *The Ballad of the Sad Café*. "Walk around the millpond, stand kicking at a rotten stump, and figure out what you can do with the old wagon wheel by the side of the road near the church. The soul rots with boredom" (71).

McCullers loved the cold and snow of the North; no wonder, then, that she describes Southern cotton mill towns as "dreary," their "summers white with glare and fiery hot" (*Ballad* 3). In *The Member of the Wedding*, McCullers records the thoughts of her young protagonist, Frankie: "The long and flowering spring was over and the summer in the town was ugly and lonesome and very hot. Every day she wanted more and more to leave the town: to light out for South America or Hollywood or New York City" (23). Even though twelve-year-old Frankie wants to "tear down this whole town" (23), ultimately, she cannot escape it. When McCullers describes Frankie's longings, she, of course, reveals her own: "But although she packed her suitcases many times," McCullers writes, "she could never decide to which of these places she ought to go, or how she would get there by herself" (*Member* 23).

The poverty and racism of Georgia during McCullers' youth seemed to her incongruous with the affluence of many white town leaders and with the prevalent religious beliefs of the region, respectively, and McCullers battled many of the attitudes that were a part of the fabric of Columbus life. Christian ministers proclaimed human equality and the unmerited love of God, but the founding families of Columbus too often upheld a class system and promoted racial hatred. In her essay "The Russian Realists and

Southern Literature," McCullers analyzes Southern society and its "spiritual inconsistencies":

> The "cruelty" of which the Southerners have been accused is at bottom only a sort of naiveté, an acceptance of spiritual inconsistencies without asking the reason why, without attempting to propose an answer. Undeniably, there is an infantile quality about this clarity of vision and rejection of responsibility. (*Mortgaged* 258)

What the reader of McCullers' work remembers is a region characterized by belief in the heterosexual nuclear family, a reliance on religion, the rugged individuality born of an agrarian economy, and the memory of the Civil War and the end of slavery. Although to live in the South for McCullers and her characters might be to "rot in boredom," there was "ever an ambivalent pull, for home was also a balm that soothed, healed, enveloped, protected" (56), writes McCullers' biographer Virginia Spencer Carr.

McCullers never entirely left the people and the locale she knew best. Whether she described the terrain; the soldiers of nearby Fort Benning, Georgia, or the mind of an adolescent, McCullers relied on what she knew. She exchanged the provincial people with whom she grew up for the cosmopolitan, artistic people of New York; she traded the anonymity of Columbus for the excitement of friendships with the famous. She associated with Edward Albee, W. H. Auden, Leonard Bernstein, Elizabeth Bowen, Truman Capote, Aaron Copeland, Salvador Dali, Isak Dinesen, Gypsy Rose Lee, Marilyn Monroe, Edith Sitwell, Tennessee Williams, and others.

However, in spite of the New York life she made for herself, McCullers remained a native of Columbus, married twice to a southerner, Reeves McCullers of Alabama. She wrote about the climate, the attitudes of the residents, and the landmarks (for example, the bridge between Columbus and Phenix City, Alabama; the First Baptist Church; Wynnton School; Columbus High School; the W. C. Bradley Memorial Library, which became the Columbus Public Library; the First National Bank; the *Columbus Ledger-Enquirer*; and 1519 Stark Avenue, her home). McCullers' sympathetic treatment of adolescents in works such as *The Member of the Wedding* and *The Heart Is a Lonely Hunter* originated during the early years McCullers spent in school. Feelings of isolation and of existing as an outcast plagued her and led to her later search for what she described several times in *The Member of the Wedding* as the "we of me." The "we of me" may be understood as a sense of belonging, of acceptance, which so often eluded McCullers herself. Carr describes McCullers' high school years by saying:

> Most of Carson's high school classmates thought her eccentric. She usually stood out in a crowd because she dared to be different. Her skirts and dresses were always a little longer than those worn by the popular girls whose clubs and cliques gave them prestige among their peers. She also wore dirty tennis shoes or brown Girl Scout oxfords when the other girls were wearing hose and shoes with dainty heels. (29)

In *The Member of the Wedding*, Frankie watches her peers as they form clubs and make plans and ostracize her from the activities for which she longs. In *The Heart Is a Lonely Hunter*, McCullers similarly reveals her own adolescent feelings when describing Mick Kelly:

> In the halls the people would walk up and down together and everybody seemed to belong to some special bunch. Within a week or two she knew people in the halls and in classes to speak to them—but that was all. She wasn't a member of any bunch. In Grammar School she would have just gone up to any crowd she wanted to belong with and that would have been the end of the matter. Here it was different. (88)

References to people and places in McCullers' life punctuate *The Heart Is a Lonely Hunter* and other novels, although McCullers rarely addresses directly the autobiographical nature of her work. Like McCullers, Harper Lee is subtle; however, Lee's sister Alice Finch Lee (1911–2014) is quick to share her perspective on her younger sister, their tight-knit family, and their hometown.

To Kill a Mockingbird

Alice Finch Lee said with some passion that *To Kill a Mockingbird* is not based on their lives. Perhaps irritated by those who repeatedly questioned the family on the matter, Alice Lee said, "Despite people wanting to make *To Kill a Mockingbird* a biography or an autobiography or a true story, we had a mother. We loved both parents" (qtd. in Murphy 121). Although it is true that Lee's mother was present, she suffered from what physicians might now call bipolar disorder and was unable to care adequately for her children. In the novel, Atticus Finch's wife dies when Scout is two.

Similarities between Lee's life and Scout's experiences are numerous. Lee was born April 28, 1926, the child of Amasa Coleman (A.C.) Lee and Frances Cunningham Finch, and both "Cunningham" and "Finch" are familiar names to readers of *To Kill a Mockingbird*. For example, Atticus Finch tells his son: "The Cunninghams are country folks, farmers, and the crash hit them hardest" (21). Lee was raised as a Methodist, the Protestant denomination mentioned in the novel. According to Harper Lee biographer Charles J. Shields, the Lees descended from ancestors whose "upbringing was Methodist, with a stringent dose of Calvinism" and who "frowned on drinking, card playing, and other time-wasting behavior" (36). When the Lees moved to Monroeville in 1912, it had a population of 750, which certainly supports Lee's memory of a small town with dirt streets. Shields makes clear how much Maycomb resembled Monroeville:

To populate the streets of Maycomb, Lee thought back on the inhabitants of Monroeville in the early 1930s: its officials, merchants, churchgoers, and even the local ne'er-do-wells. After the novel was published, some Monroeville folks believed they recognized themselves and neighbors. (127)

One of the most often-quoted descriptions in *To Kill a Mockingbird*—repeated nearly verbatim in the film—is of the town; in fact, the setting becomes as real as any character in the novel:

Maycomb was an old town, but it was a tired old town when I first knew it. In rainy weather the streets turned to red slop; grass grew on the sidewalks, the courthouse sagged in the square. Somehow, it was hotter then: a black dog suffered on a summer's day; bony mules hitched to Hoover carts flicked flies in the sweltering shade of the live oaks on the square. Men's stiff collars wilted by nine in the morning. Ladies bathed before noon, after their three o'clock naps, and by nightfall were like soft teacakes with frostings of sweat and sweet talcum.

People moved slowly then. They ambled across the square, shuffled in and out of the stores around it, took their time about everything. A day was twenty-four hours long but seemed longer. There was no hurry, for there was nowhere to go, nothing to buy and no money to buy it with, nothing to see outside the boundaries of Maycomb County. But it was a time of vague

optimism for some of the people: Maycomb County had recently been told
that it had nothing to fear but fear itself. (5–6)

Similarly, there is little doubt that Scout is modeled on Lee herself: she
dreaded school, fought with other children, and preferred the company of
boys. Ironically, Alice Lee does support many of the comparisons between
the author and her protagonist. "Nelle Harper grew up quite the little
tomboy" (121), Alice Lee said, adding, "Nelle Harper was very athletic.
She liked to play with the little boys more than the little girls because she
liked to play ball" (qtd. in Murphy122). Harper Lee could fight, too, as
did Scout in *To Kill a Mockingbird*. "Scout here, she's crazy—she won't
fight you any more" (23), Jem tells Walter Cunningham in the novel.
Later, though, Scout tackles Cecil Jacobs anyway: "My fists were clenched
and I was ready to let fly. Atticus had promised me he would wear me out
if he ever heard of me fighting any more; I was far too old and too big
for such childish things, and the sooner I learned to hold in, the better
off everybody would be. I soon forgot" (74). Shields relates a story about
Lee's protecting her childhood friend Truman Capote:

> "Get *offa* him!" Nelle roared. "Get off now!" She peeled the older boys
> from on top of their prey, uncovering beneath flailing elbows and knees her
> friend Truman Capote, lying on his back, red-faced and tearful, in the sand-
> pit of the Monroeville Elementary School playground ... Nelle hauled him
> to his feet and escorted him away from his antagonists, glancing backward
> as if daring any of the others to pursue ... Though she was only seven years
> old, Nelle Harper Lee was a fearsome stomach-puncher, foot-stomper, and
> hair-puller, who "could talk mean like a boy." Once, three boys tried to
> challenge her. Each ended up facedown, spitting gravel and crying "Uncle!"
> within moments. (31–32)

Capote later would base Ann (Jumbo) Finchburg in "The Thanksgiving
Visitor" (1967) on his friend Nelle Harper Lee. Shields calls Jumbo a
"sawed-off but solid tomboy" (32). For her part, Lee loved Capote,
describing him poetically through Scout's eyes and referring in the following excerpt both to Capote's darker self and to the Radley house of *To
Kill a Mockingbird*:

> Dill was off again. Beautiful things floated around in his dreamy head.
> He could read two books to my one, but he preferred the magic of his
> own inventions. He could add and subtract faster than lightning, but he

preferred his own twilight world, a world where babies slept, waiting to be
gathered like morning lilies. He was slowly talking himself to sleep and taking me with him, but in the quietness of his foggy island there rose the faded
image of a gray house with sad brown doors. (144)

Lee and Capote—like Scout and Dill in the novel—were devoted to one
another, as Shields documents: "Yet despite their spats, separations, and
grudging reconciliations, the two friends remained inseparable. They
swam in the pond ... and if nothing else, they could always walk to the
town square" (47–48). Lee and Capote maintained a generally support-
ive and affectionate relationship into adulthood, and Lee accompanied
her friend to Holcomb and Garden City, Kansas, to help him conduct
interviews for *In Cold Blood* (1965), a literary accomplishment that followed closely on the heels of Lee's *To Kill a Mockingbird* and the Academy
Award-winning film by the same name. Shields writes:

> Nelle presented him with a steadfast friendship. Her faithfulness was some-
> thing she never hesitated to prove. Truman touched in her a desire to see
> underdogs treated "fair and square"—a sentiment that would be important
> to her throughout her life. Because of her loyalty, some of Truman's loneli-
> ness gradually abated: he had a good friend and didn't feel so alone. (50)

Other similarities between Harper Lee and Scout Finch emerge during a
study of the novel and of nonfiction accounts about Monroeville and the
Lee family. For example, the Alfred R. Boleware family lived in a house
described as "dark, ramshackle ... with all the paint fallen off," a reference,
of course, to the Radley home. Dressing up as a ham on Halloween also
originated in Monroeville, where one of Lee's classmates wore a fertil-
izer sack and another dressed as a ham (Shields 33). In addition, Lee
had a brother named Edwin, who was six years older than she (instead
of the four years that separate Jem and Scout), and Mrs. Henry Lafayette
Dubose is drawn from an ex-Confederate captain and his wife who scared
the children: the woman was "an invalid in a wheelchair," said Shields,
adding, "Children passing by were not exempt from her imprecations"
(35). Although there was no Calpurnia, Hattie Belle Clausell tended the
Lee home: "When Nelle barged through the screen door after a day of
play," writes Shields, it was usually Clausell who took off the child's overalls and prepared her "to be scrubbed in the tub, combed, and given sup-
per in the kitchen" (41). Shields even reveals that a neighbor of the Lees
fired a shotgun at someone "prowling in his collard patch" , just as Nathan

Radley did, and in 1934, a rabid dog attacked two adults and two children in Monroeville, "prefiguring the scene in the novel of Atticus shooting a mad dog" (127).

The most significant example of a character drawn from Lee's life is Atticus Finch himself. Interestingly, the novel was originally entitled *Atticus*. A. C. Lee became an attorney in 1915 and is no doubt the inspiration for Atticus Finch. Although Finch loves his children, one cannot imagine him rolling around on the living room floor with them, and A. C. Lee was not the type of father who played with his children or tousled their hair either: "His mannerisms were those of someone always preoccupied with his thoughts" (56), Shields writes, although one source told the biographer that A. C. Lee "encouraged Nelle to clamber up on his lap to 'help' him read the newspaper or complete the crossword puzzle" (58).As in the novel and film, Harper Lee played with her father's pocket watch. In addition, A. C. Lee spoke in a "precise and deliberate" way (Shields 56), as does Atticus Finch, and he was fearless, according to one source who remembers how A. C. Lee confronted the local grand dragon of the Ku Klux Klan from his porch in 1934 and threatened him with a "drubbing" in an editorial (Shields 57). Also, as in the novel, Harper Lee called her father by his first name.

Like McCullers' thematic focus in *The Heart Is a Lonely Hunter* and *The Member of the Wedding*, Lee, too, explores gender roles and race and ethnicity in *To Kill a Mockingbird* and *Go Set a Watchman*. In *Go Set a Watchman*, one of these issues takes precedence when an older Jean Louise Finch returns home for a visit. As Lee writes:

> It had never fully occurred to Jean Louise that she was a girl: her life had been one of reckless, pummeling activity; fighting, football, climbing, keeping up with Jem ... she must now go into a world of femininity, a world she despised, could not comprehend nor defend herself against. (116)

Further, she realizes that she differs significantly from the father she once adored, who—much to the surprise of many readers—is a racist in *Go Set a Watchman*: "But a man who has lived by truth—and you have believed in what he has lived—he does not leave you merely wary when he fails you, he leaves you with nothing. I think that is why I'm nearly out of my mind" (179), said Scout Finch, whom Lee describes as "color blind" (122). Unfortunately, *Go Set a Watchman* often descends into polemic, undercutting the poignancy of the child's perspective in *To Kill a Mockingbird.* One excerpt reflects a mature Scout's perspective on the townspeople, whom she now sees more clearly:

> Why doesn't their flesh creep? How can they devoutly believe everything they hear in church and then say the things they do and listen to the things they hear without throwing up? I thought I was a Christian but I'm not. I'm something else and I don't know what. Everything I have ever taken for right and wrong these people have taught me—these same, these very people. So it's me, it's not them. Something has happened to me. (167)

Given the themes that McCullers and Lee address, it seems clear that autobiographical novels are in the same category as what literary critics call "true stories" and "stories based on fact." Authors write about what they know, perhaps especially when they are young (McCullers wrote and published *The Heart Is a Lonely Hunter* when she was in her early twenties; Lee wrote and published *To Kill a Mockingbird* in her early thirties). As Jean-Paul Sartre writes in *Nausea,* "A man is always a teller of tales, he lives surrounded by his stories and the stories of others, he sees everything that happens to him through them; and he tries to live his own life as if he were telling a story" (39).

Davidson describes memoir as a hybrid form, as a disguised narrative, as a text that emerges from what she calls the "gray zone." As she suggests, literary works such as nonfiction novels and imagined autobiography defy labels. Perhaps surprisingly, autobiographical novels and memoirs have a great deal in common and provide context for conversations about the borderland between fiction and nonfiction. Both literary approaches depend on characters seen through a veil of memory, voices heard as an echo. Time slips past: Mick Kelly finds herself working at Woolworth's, Frankie continues her search for the "we of me," and Scout meets Boo Radley and slides almost imperceptibly from innocence into experience. Like McCullers and Lee, we tell ourselves about ourselves in fiction, in nonfiction—and in everything in between.

WORKS CITED

Berendt, John. *Midnight in the Garden of Good and Evil.* New York: Vintage, 1994. Print.

Carr, Virginia Spencer. *The Lonely Hunter: A Biography of Carson McCullers.* New York: Carroll and Graf, 1975. Print.

Davidson, Sara. *Cowboy: A Novel.* New York: HarperCollins, 1999. Print.
——. "The First Day of the Rest of My Life." *Newsweek* 22 Jan. 2007: 55–58. Print.
——. "The Gray Zone." *Book* July/August 1999: 49–50. Print.
——. *Leap!: What Will We Do with the Rest of Our Lives?* New York: Random House, 2007. Print.
——. *Loose Change: Three Women of the Sixties.* Berkeley: U of California P, 1977. Print.
Dickinson, Emily. *The Complete Poems of Emily Dickinson.* Ed. Thomas H. Johnson. Boston: Little, Brown, 1960. Print.
Lamb, Wally. "Foreword." *Scout, Atticus and Boo: In Celebration of Fifty Years of To Kill a Mockingbird.* Ed. Mary McDonagh Murphy. New York: HarperCollins, 2010. Print.
Lee, Harper. *Go Set a Watchman.* New York: HarperCollins, 2015. Print.
——. *To Kill a Mockingbird.* New York: J.B. Lippincott, 1960. Print.
McCullers, Carson. *The Ballad of the Sad Café.* Boston: Houghton Mifflin, 1971. Print.
——. *Collected Stories of Carson McCullers.* Boston: Houghton Mifflin, 1987. Print.
——. *The Heart Is a Lonely Hunter.* Boston: Houghton Mifflin, 1940. Print.
——. *The Member of the Wedding.* New York: Bantam, 1983. Print.
——. *The Mortgaged Heart.* Ed. Margarita G. Smith. Boston: Houghton Mifflin, 1971. Print.
Murphy, Mary McDonagh. *Scout, Atticus and Boo: In Celebration of Fifty Years of To Kill a Mockingbird.* New York: HarperCollins, 2010. Print.
Sartre, Jean-Paul. *Nausea.* New York: New Directions, 2007. Print.
Shields, Charles J. *Mockingbird: A Portrait of Harper Lee.* New York: Henry Holt, 2006. Print.
Sims, Norman, ed. *The Literary Journalists: The New Art of Personal Reportage.* New York: Ballantine Books, 1984. Print.

Musings between the Marvelous and Strange: New Contexts and Correspondence about Carson McCullers and Mary Tucker

Carmen Trammell Skaggs

"Everything significant that has happened in my fiction has also happened to me," Carson McCullers once claimed (qtd. in Carr 107). Perhaps one of the most significant relationships of McCullers' life began several years before she knew that any of her life experiences would be recorded in fiction—the relationship between McCullers and Mary Tucker, her piano teacher in Columbus, Georgia. Formerly a concert pianist, Mary Tucker was the wife of Lieutenant Colonel Albert Sydney Johnston Tucker, the commanding officer assigned to Fort Benning in 1930. Acknowledged by her parents as an accomplished pianist at age thirteen, Carson McCullers auditioned with Columbus' newest esteemed pianist, earning the prized position as her student. Only four years later, however, Lieutenant Colonel Tucker was reassigned by the military, ending McCullers' apprenticeship with her beloved teacher. In the bloom of her adolescence and during her own soul-searching for an artistic identity, McCullers lost the mentor

C. Trammell Skaggs (✉)
Kennesaw State University, Kennesaw, GA, USA

© The Author(s) 2016   83
A. Graham-Bertolini, C. Kayser (eds.), *Carson McCullers in the Twenty-First Century*, DOI 10.1007/978-3-319-40292-5_5

she describes in a letter addressed to Tucker and dated February 1950 (Mary Sames Tucker Papers) as her Beethoven and Mozart, the marvelous and strange. In the same letter, she suggests that *The Member of the Wedding* (1946) owed its origins to time spent with the Tucker family. As these two acknowledgements suggest, McCullers simultaneously felt an intimate kinship with and a distant awe of her teacher. Tucker embodied musical genius—replacing McCullers' need for the more traditional male musical models of Beethoven and Mozart—but she remained as mysterious and strange to the young protégé as these historical figures. Even so, McCullers felt an intimate connection to Tucker and her family.

As numerous critics have noted, McCullers' "Wunderkind," first published in *Story* in December of 1936, contains strong autobiographical elements of her relationship with Mary Tucker. From the early work of researchers and biographers like Margaret Sullivan and Virginia Carr, McCullers scholars have attempted to quantify the importance of her musical training and background on her fiction. Perhaps equally—if not more—important, however, is the personal relationship that McCullers forged with Mary Tucker and her family. In a June 1950 letter, McCullers described the Tuckers as second parents, the ones she had chosen out of mutual affinities and tastes. Despite the temporary severing of this relationship for the fifteen years following Tucker's 1934 relocation, these two women lingered in one another's thoughts and dreams. Throughout their lifetimes, both of them would continually reflect upon their relationship and parting of ways in letters and conversations. The two eventually reconciled; ironically, a letter from Tucker to McCullers, congratulating her on the success of *The Member of the Wedding*, prompted the rekindling of their friendship.

As McCullers herself explains in "The Flowering Dream: Notes on Writing," published in *Esquire*, December 1959:

> Spiritual isolation is the basis of most of my themes. My first book was concerned with this, almost entirely, and all of my books since, in one way or another. Love, and especially love of a person who is incapable of returning or receiving it, is at the heart of my selection of grotesque figures to write about—people whose physical incapacity is a symbol of their spiritual incapacity to love or receive love—their spiritual isolation. (274)

As someone who acknowledged her own inward craving and need for intimacy, acceptance, and kinship, McCullers found these coveted qualities

more often than not with men and women who—for various reasons—
were separated from her geographically. The most intimate of her relationships were often kindled, recollected, and even recreated through
correspondence. Recognizing the centrality of this communication,
McCullers acknowledges:

> In any communication, a thing says to one person quite a different thing
> from what it says to another, but writing, in essence, is communication;
> and communication is the only access to love—to love, to conscience, to
> nature, to God, and to the dream. For myself, the further I go into my own
> work and the more I read of those I love, the more aware I am of the dream
> and the logic of God, which indeed is a Divine collusion. ("The Flowering
> Dream" 281–82)

While Carson McCullers' correspondence with Mary Tucker, collected in the Mary Sames Tucker Papers, 1936–1967, and other letters
in the Mary E. Mercer Collection of Carson McCullers-Mary Tucker
Correspondence 1959–1976, both housed in the David M. Rubinstein
Rare Book and Manuscript Library at Duke University, offers scholars
important insights into their relationship, recently acquired collections
in both the Margaret S. Sullivan Papers and the Dr. Mary E. Mercer/
Carson McCullers Collection at Columbus State University offer additional context and background for understanding the complexity and
importance of this friendship. Some of the most interesting correspondence about the relationship between Mary Tucker and Carson
McCullers appears in the Margaret S. Sullivan papers. Like McCullers,
Margaret Sullivan graduated from Columbus High School in Columbus,
Georgia. Sullivan described her affinity with McCullers to Mary Mercer
in a letter dated August 15, 1971: "Columbus had not changed very
much when I came along after Carson and I think I shared the ambivalent feelings she had about the place and the people; I had also studied piano 13 yrs. and loved writing so a surface, emotional identification
came easy" (Margaret S. Sullivan Papers). Before the end of her life, she
would share even more in common with McCullers, including suffering
from a debilitating illness. During the research for her doctoral dissertation, "Carson McCullers 1917–1947: The Conversion of Experience,"
to complete the requirements for the PhD in English Literature from
Duke University, she cultivated a relationship with friends and associates
of Carson McCullers, including Mary Tucker, initially by correspondence

and then later in person. Sullivan and Tucker's correspondence spans the remainder of Tucker's life. Both share an admiration of McCullers. In Sullivan's search to understand the intimacy of Tucker and McCullers, she becomes a surrogate devotee for the aging pianist. Through Sullivan, Tucker reclaimed her opportunity to build a lasting relationship with a younger, talented admirer. Sullivan, in turn, developed her understanding and awe of McCullers through the lens of Tucker's memories. The transformation of Margaret Sullivan and Mary Tucker's relationship is apparent by the gradual change of salutation and tone in their letters. Mary Tucker begins by formally addressing her as Miss Sullivan, but the later correspondence begins affectionately with Margaret—dear.

While the Sullivan papers illuminate Mary Tucker's perspective on the significance of her relationship with McCullers, The Dr. Mary E. Mercer/Carson McCullers Collection at Columbus State University provides further insight on how McCullers described her relationship with her childhood piano teacher. The collection contains transcriptions of therapy sessions conducted between April and May of 1958. Formerly a Commonwealth Fellow in Psychiatry at Payne Whitney-Cornell Medical Center, Dr. Mercer was practicing psychiatry privately in 1958 from her home in Nyack, New York. At the time, Carson McCullers was one of her patients. As experiments intended to help McCullers overcome writer's block, the dictaphone sessions included material that she originally intended to publish in an autobiography. Interestingly enough, the sessions were not reproduced in that form, but poor health forced McCullers to rely later upon dictation to compose the material that was posthumously published as her unfinished autobiography, *Illumination and Night Glare.* Not long after the recording of the 1958 dictaphone sessions, Mercer and McCullers severed their official doctor/patient relationship, allowing them to maintain a lifelong, intimate friendship for the remainder of McCullers' life.

Although the dictaphone sessions are now available for scholarly use in the Dr. Mary E. Mercer/Carson McCullers Collection, scholars must consider whether McCullers or Mercer ever intended these to be part of the public discourse about the author. In the first experiment with the dictaphone, dated April 11, 1958, McCullers remarks, "It would certainly cramp a patient's style if they thought you were playing it back to other people .... I don't mind ... it is not a secret at all, ... it is a secret and not a secret, both ...." Even in the safe confines of the initial recording, McCullers seemed both aware of and conflicted about the fragile divide between public and private that every well-known author faces. Following these initial comments, she goes on to say that "the energy in life is in sharing and the wealth ... our wealth is in throwing away ... our wealth is in waste ...." (Mercer/McCullers Collection). Her story, she seems to recognize, belonged both to her and to her audience. Interestingly enough, during the same session McCullers tells Mercer that she "want[s] to name these letters between us ... our flowering dream ...." Just a year and a half later, she uses this same phrase again as the title of her essay published in *Esquire*: "The Flowering Dream: Notes on Writing." McCullers' repetition of the phrase suggests that the experiments with Dr. Mercer—initially undertaken to overcome writer's block—focused her attention on her craft.

In response to numerous written requests from Margaret Sullivan (as with Virginia Spencer Carr), Mary Mercer repeatedly rejected the invitation to talk openly of her relationship with Carson McCullers. In a letter dated August 28, 1977, she explained to Sullivan, "I must tell you that I do not feel that I can talk to you or anyone else about Carson. Time has made it abundantly clear that my public role in Carson's life was that of a physician. I do not believe that a physician has the right to talk about her patients" (Margaret S. Sullivan Papers). Six years earlier, in a letter dated October 2, 1971, Mercer told Sullivan, "I doubt if I shall be able to talk to you or anyone about Carson now or perhaps ever." Instead, she suggested that Sullivan had "learned a great deal by [her] own meditations, and also, of course, in being able to read Carson's own words directly. She [Carson] always knew her own words spoke for her best" (Margaret S. Sullivan Papers). Ironically, access to the transcriptions of McCullers' therapy sessions provides scholars with the writer's own words about her most deeply held feelings and intimate relationships. We scholars, however, bear a responsibility to acknowledge McCullers' own misgivings about revealing the secrets of the sessions. As McCullers acknowledged in the initial session, "You would tremble ... more than ... you would be convulsed with trembling the first time, you know, thinking that ... of it being read back to his friends ... and enemies ... a real betrayer ...." ("1st Experiment," Mercer/McCullers Collection).

Although initially not successful in penetrating Mary Mercer's private recollections of McCullers, Sullivan forged an intimate friendship of her own with Mary Tucker. In many ways, Mary Tucker served as Margaret Sullivan's muse for writing about Carson McCullers. In a letter to Mary Mercer dated September 29, 1973, Sullivan recalls her first visit with Mary

Tucker at Tuckaway, the Tuckers' home in Lexington, Virginia: "I took a walk down a road in front of Tuckaway, filled with Mary's recollections of Carson and happy in feeling the presence of Carson through memories—albeit a younger Carson—despite distance and time" (Margaret S. Sullivan Papers). In some of their early exchanges, Margaret Sullivan asks Mary Tucker to think about what she calls the "music time" and the "peer factor" with Carson. Tucker responded in a letter dated November 18, 1965, with the following:

> Please give me a little more time to think about the 'music time' with Carson. I still believe any competent piano teacher would have given her all her cup would hold. What was the peer factor was the entire family of Tuckers, especially Gin [Mary's daughter, Virginia]. We brought some of the outside Columbus world to her. She met people who had lived in China, in Alaska, in the Philippines. Tuck [Colonel Tucker] had been practically everywhere, had his Passport stolen in Moscow. We all loved to tell stories & she was eager to listen to them. It was [a] fine four years for all of us as we were very proud of her, and she quite naturally enjoyed us for a number of plausible reasons—(I hope this doesn't sound stuffy and complacent!). (Margaret S. Sullivan Papers)

Carson McCullers recalls her first introduction to Virginia Tucker and Colonel Tucker—affectionately referred to as "Gin" and "Tuck"—in therapy sessions with Dr. Mary Mercer. In a transcription dated May 16, 1958, McCullers recalls these memories:

> Virginia Tucker and I were always very close friends as children. We met when I was playing piano for Mary Tucker, the first time. She came in from the swimming pool and I had just finished playing the Hungarian Rhapsody with lots of fireworks and also Paganini, just playing all this flamboyant music, you know. She just stood in the doorway and when I finished playing she came in the room with her slicker on over her bathing suit. Mrs. Tucker introduced us. She excused herself to get dressed. This was the first time I met the Tuckers. And then Tuck came in, too, Colonel Tucker.
>
> And Mary, the first thing she said to me was, "Do you know what repertoire is?" I said, "no." She said, "Let's make repertoire." And she started with Bach. I played nothing, Dr. Mercer, except Liszt, Paganini, all these things which appeal to a 12 year old child. And she said, "Do you play the Harmonious Blacksmith?" and I said, "no." "No Handel, no Bach?" I said, "nothing." And so she took my hand and said, "Look, that is a very good

Bach hand." I had very well-articulated hands. So she said, "Let's make a tentative repertoire." And she started with some Bach Inventions and we went on to that Third Fugue. Also Scarlatti. Oh, she was a magnificent teacher. And I had never heard Bach. And she played for me ... Bach ... Ravel. ("10th Experiment," Mercer/McCullers Collection)

Margaret Sullivan includes in her dissertation Gin Tucker's memory of this same first encounter between the Tuckers and McCullers, recorded in a letter dated October 1, 1965:

> My first recollection of Carson concerns her first visit to us in our house at Benning where she arrived, accompanied by a "large Wagnerian mother" in an enormous hat, and sat down and played the Hungarian Rhapsody (Second)—what else? It was not that she played it well but that she played it at all. Loud and fast. At this time she was thirteen. It was apparent at once that here was a very considerable talent. In a reasonably short time, my mother was aware she had a prodigy on her hands. She took this responsibility very serious indeed. I don't think any of us doubted that Carson had the prospects of a great career as a pianist. (qtd. in Sullivan, "Carson McCullers 1917–1947" 105)

When attempting to articulate to Sullivan her tangible contribution to McCullers' formation as an artist, Tucker identifies the instilling of discipline in a letter dated November 18, 1965: "It is possible that the discipline of her piano work was very good for her and that she was able later on to use this discipline in her writing. All the experiences of genius are formative, or so I believe" (Margaret S. Sullivan Papers). McCullers also agrees with Mary Tucker's claim that she introduced her to artistic discipline. In the 10th dictaphone experiment, Dr. Mercer asks McCullers, "Is Mrs. Tucker the first person in your life who introduced you to the form of discipline? You cannot play well or do anything else really well without discipline." McCullers responds:

> Yes, and I worked like a field hand I must say. She would give me two lines for a fugue and I would do two pages. She would tell my mother, she is just a glutton for work. I don't want her to work that hard. They were good pages, too. But she didn't realize that I had to go to school too (who didn't realize) ... I practiced four hours a day. I just barely did my homework for school. I just always passed, see, because I was practicing. ("10th Experiment," Mercer/McCullers Collection)

Mary Tucker's letters repeatedly describe McCullers as a "genius"—a designation that Tucker establishes as a given. In several of the letters, she repeatedly diminishes her own role in McCullers' subsequent success. As she explains in correspondence with Sullivan on December 11, 1965: "the child was a genius, and it seems, from the distance of 31 years since her piano lessons ended, all in the world I did was to introduce her to the discipline, guide her taste, help her with some knotty problems, teach her to think out her own fingering (after months of scales and arpeggio practice) & stick to it if it was sensible fingering, change it if it was not" (Margaret S. Sullivan Papers).

More than guiding McCullers' mastery of the piano, Mary Tucker unknowingly shepherded her through the awakening of her identity as a writer. During that time, McCullers craved the affirmation, tenderness, and intimacy of a relationship with her teacher. From a distance of more than 15–30 years after they parted ways, however, McCullers and Tucker remained inextricably linked. Tucker describes their relationship in a letter to Margaret Sullivan dated March 12, 1966:

> I am sure she already told you that I kept a sort of facade of formality, quite deliberately, & perhaps instinctively also, in order to keep as much authoritative control & guidance of that extraordinary talent as possible. I recognized in her even as an early teenager, a very formidable will & temperament. I feel entirely certain I was never sarcastic or cutting or unkind to the child because I've never been that way with any one, but I needed the proper perspective with her if this makes any sense to you. I didn't want to be mistaken or unobservant, or careless about anything to do with that child's playing. Very naturally, Carson must have sensed this aloofness if it amounted to that, and matched it with a reserve of her own. (Margaret S. Sullivan Papers)

In her therapy session with Dr. Mercer, transcribed on May 20, 1958, McCullers recounts her own inability to diminish this distance between them. She explains:

> I'm so afraid that someone will turn me down ... I'll just have to turn them down, but real hard, real hard, yeh ... but Mary Tucker, I should never have acted like I did ... she would try to caress me. I would just duck out of her hands. Run away, you see? The last time we were together ... she would say something, I would say something ... play something, or she would play something and just burst into tears. I would. And she would cry too. She

loved me also. I was too afraid. Afraid of exposing myself. I never told her I loved her. She just knew it, but I never told her in words. I would have died rather than ... yeh ... and then when they left ... yeh ... they left me. It was that tension of knowing they were going to leave that made me so ornery and peculiar, see? Yeh ... I knew they were going to leave me. ("10th Experiment," Mercer/ McCullers Collection)

While McCullers claims that she was anticipating the abandonment that would come in the spring of 1934, Mary Tucker seems to never have considered an alternative artistic path for her young protégé than Julliard and a profession as a concert pianist. As she explains to Margaret Sullivan in a letter dated September 30, 1965:

I do know, I believe, the complete story, as far as anyone can know with a person so complex as Carson, just how she decided to write instead of play. One thing can be said here & now & that is I did not discourage her from going away for further study, nor did I ever say she was not talented enough. It was contrariwise! I was so convinced (and still am) of the musical genius that the shock of her sudden announcement that she was giving up music for writing did a lot of damage to me emotionally, since I could attribute it only to my having fallen short in my 'management' of her.

Tucker continues her recollection of this period in another letter to Sullivan on March 12, 1966:

Back to Carson, in the months since writing & meeting you I've thought a lot, & realize how much I neglected that poor child. ... Because of recognizing her quality which was plainly genius, I was too zeroed into the business of getting her into professional habits of work and being convinced about it. It seems to me now that she must have realized her physical strength was not enough for the demands of a professional career. Perhaps this was intuition also. But she concealed it from me. (Margaret S. Sullivan Papers)

As much as McCullers viewed the Tuckers' departure from Columbus as abandonment, Mary Tucker viewed Carson's changed professional ambitions as a betrayal of their years of work together. Although Tucker claims that "it is silly to dream over what we might or might not have done during that last year," she confesses that she has "theorize[d] about that, (I've been doing it for 32 years) and come up again and again with the bitter disappointment Carson suffered over our departure, leaving

her behind." As she explains to Sullivan in a letter, Tucker viewed Carson
McCullers as

> genuinely devoted to her adopted family, she was also aware—is this again
> intuitively? that she wanted to write as keenly as she wanted to play piano,
> and this was her coup de grace for me who was betraying her & for herself
> too—a quick blow and a hard one, "Member of the Wedding" came of it,
> as Carson told me, so it was not a total loss. It took me an unreasonable
> time to accept all this—16 years. I never once thought it as Carson's fault
> or that she reacted in that way out of pique or disappointment but I did
> think something in my behavior with her was at fault—and for quite a long
> while this was a serious affliction. What did I do wrong to make Carson turn
> against her music?? (12 March 1966, Margaret S. Sullivan Papers)

As Mary Tucker's letters indicate, Carson McCullers' decision to pursue the artistic path of writing instead of music filled her with what she
describes as both "a sense of failure" and "perhaps even guilt" (Letter
to Sullivan, 17 September 1965, Margaret S. Sullivan Papers). Likewise,
Carson McCullers suffered tremendously from the rejection she felt when
the Tuckers left Columbus.

McCullers confirms these sentiments in the first letter she writes to
Mary Tucker in 1950 after their long separation, responding to Tucker's
note of congratulations on the success of *The Member of the Wedding*:

> My dear, long-silent friend, I am happy to hear from you. You and your fam-
> ily are the most cherished memory of my early youth... To me you were the
> descendant of Bach and his solitary, appointed votive. I remember every-
> thing about those years, all about you and Colonel Tucker and Ginny and
> Buddy.
>   I did not realize that you were upset with me. I thought that only I was
> upset and had a sense of shame and failure. The truth is that I loved you far
> too much and could not comprehend these mysterious emotions, you were
> Beethoven, Mozart, the strange and marvelous, the artichokes, too. And I
> love your family, your house. With Ginny and Buddy, I could express my
> love—but with you I could only give back the music you had taught me. So
> in the last year when I had that pneumonia, when I felt I had failed, I knew
> an inexpressible shame and sorrow. And then you all went away. I don't like
> to think of that year.
>   When you see *The Member of the Wedding*, it should speak to you. If it
> had not been for the Tuckers, I doubt if that particular work would have
> been done. (Mary Sames Tucker Papers)

Perhaps the best description of the complex and interwoven relationships between McCullers, Tucker, Sullivan, and Mercer may be described in McCullers' own words, recorded in the transcription of a therapy session dated April 21, 1958: "Do you understand that pattern in love? People who love one person, loves another person, they are very much alike and loved each other. Do you understand?" ("3rd Experiment," Mercer/ McCullers Collection). Mary Tucker continued to ponder her friendship with McCullers in letters written to both Mercer and Sullivan. The mutual love for McCullers shared by these women provided the basis for their acquaintances; shared affinities extended these relationships throughout Tucker's lifetime. Just as it took years of distance and time for Mary Tucker and Carson McCullers to finally rekindle their friendship, it took over ten years for Mary Mercer to agree to speak openly with Margaret Sullivan about Carson McCullers. For many years following the completion of her dissertation, Margaret Sullivan pursued her ambition of publishing the definitive McCullers biography. If her dissertation provides any clues, she certainly intended to identify Mary Tucker as one of the most significant influences on McCullers' development and work. In the Preface to her dissertation, Margaret Sullivan asserts the "three experiences which have had the most profound impact on her [Carson McCullers's] writing: her relationship to Columbus, to her family, and to Mary Tucker, her piano teacher." Sullivan credits these three influences with generating McCullers' dominant themes of the quest for identity, "the need to belong, the relationship between the lover and the beloved, the dual nature of man, and the conflict between truth and illusion" ("Carson McCullers 1917–1947," viii).

Serving as her mentor, mother-figure, muse—even a Mozart, Mary Tucker's influence on Carson McCullers appears not only in the autobiographical strains of her fiction but throughout the lifetime of correspondence between and about these women. When Frances, the young prodigy of "Wunderkind," confesses her inability to live up to her piano teacher's ambitions for her, she "hurries past him," out the door that "shut to firmly" behind her, "stumbling down the stone steps" (*Collected Stories* 70). Real life, however, could not afford the closure—metaphorical or literal—that the fictitious account supplies. Instead, the stumbling journey of McCullers would be intertwined with her teacher's until her death. After Carson McCullers' death in 1967, Mary Tucker identified "blazing courage" as one of her former pupil's greatest qualities (Letter to Sullivan, 29 September 1967, Margaret S. Sullivan Papers). Perhaps this blazing courage is exemplified by McCullers' unwillingness to run away from the music or the musician of her youth. In an undated letter to Tucker, McCullers writes, "Sometimes I think I love music more intensely every day that I live. But writing so much—(And I get a kick out of that, too) I don't have much time for practice" (N.d., Tucker indicates late 1935 or early 1936, Mary Sames Tucker Papers). Like Mary Tucker, we will never know what might have emerged from the musical genius of McCullers, but we remain grateful for the marvelous and strange musings revealed in her words.

WORKS CITED

Carr, Virginia. *The Lonely Hunter: A Biography of Carson McCullers.* Garden City: Doubleday, 1975. Print.

McCullers, Carson. *Collected Stories.* Boston: Houghton Mifflin Company, 1998. Print.

——. "1st Experiment." 11 April 1958. TS. Dr. Mary E. Mercer/Carson McCullers Collection (MC 296). Columbus State University Archives, Columbus, Georgia. Print.

——. "3rd Experiment." 21 April 1958. TS. Dr. Mary E. Mercer/Carson McCullers Collection (MC 296). Columbus State University Archives, Columbus, Georgia. Print.

——. "10th Experiment." 16 May 1958 and 20 May 1958. TS. Dr. Mary E. Mercer/Carson McCullers Collection (MC 296). Columbus State University Archives, Columbus, Georgia. Print.

——. "The Flowering Dream: Notes on Writing." *The Mortgaged Heart.* Ed. Margarita G. Smith. Boston: Houghton Mifflin, 1971. 274–282. Print.

——. Letter to Mary Tucker. February 1950. MS. Mary Sames Tucker Papers. David M. Rubenstein Rare Book & Manuscript Library, Duke University, Durham, North Carolina. Print.

——. Letter to Mary Tucker. June 1950. MS. Mary Sames Tucker Papers. David M. Rubenstein Rare Book & Manuscript Library, Duke University,Durham, North Carolina. Print.

——. Letter to Mary Tucker. N.d. MS. Mary Sames Tucker Papers. David M. Rubenstein Rare Book & Manuscript Library, Duke University, Durham, North Carolina. Print.

Mercer, Mary. Letter to Margaret Sullivan. 2 October 1971. MS. Margaret S. Sullivan Papers (MC 298). Columbus State University Archives, Columbus, Georgia. Print.

Sullivan, Margaret. "Carson McCullers 1917–1947: The Conversion of Experience." Diss. Duke University, 1966. Print.

——. Letter to Mary Mercer. 15 August 1971. MS. Margaret S. Sullivan Papers (MC 298). Columbus State University Archives, Columbus, Georgia. Print.

——. Letter to Mary Mercer. 29 September 1973. MS. Margaret S. Sullivan Papers (MC 298). Columbus State University Archives, Columbus, Georgia. Print.

Tucker, Mary. Letter to Margaret Sullivan. 28 August 1977. MS. Margaret S. Sullivan Papers (MC 298). Columbus State University Archives. Columbus, Georgia. Print.

——. Letter to Margaret Sullivan. 11 December 1965. MS. Margaret S. Sullivan Papers (MC 298). Columbus State University Archives. Columbus, Georgia. Print.

——. Letter to Margaret Sullivan. 12 March 1966. MS. Margaret S. Sullivan Papers (MC 298). Columbus State University Archives. Columbus, Georgia. Print.

——. Letter to Margaret Sullivan. 18 November 1965. MS. Margaret S. Sullivan Papers (MC 298). Columbus State University Archives. Columbus, Georgia. Print.

——. Letter to Margaret Sullivan. 17 September 1965. MS. Margaret S. Sullivan Papers (MC 298). Columbus State University Archives. Columbus, Georgia. Print.

——. Letter to Margaret Sullivan. 29 September 1967. MS. Margaret S. Sullivan Papers (MC 298). Columbus State University Archives. Columbus, Georgia. Print.

——. Letter to Margaret Sullivan. 30 September 1965. MS. Margaret S. Sullivan Papers (MC 298). Columbus State University Archives. Columbus, Georgia. Print.

The Image of the String Quartet Lurking in *The Heart Is a Lonely Hunter*

Kiyoko Magome

As a teenager, Carson McCullers was serious about becoming a concert pianist, and her practical experience and profound knowledge of music are evident in many of her literary works. For example, in the outline of her first novel, *The Heart Is a Lonely Hunter* (1940), submitted to Houghton Mifflin in 1938, she clearly stated that it would be based on a "contrapuntal" structure like "a fugue" ("Author's Outline" 148). The musical components of this novel have been analyzed persuasively in such articles as C. Michael Smith's "'A Voice in a Fugue': Characters and Musical Structure in Carson McCullers' *The Heart Is a Lonely Hunter*," Janice Fuller's "The Conventions of Counterpoint and Fugue in *The Heart Is a Lonely Hunter*," and my own "Two Years of Counterpoint."[1] However, I argue that there is another musical image lurking beneath the fugal structure of *The Heart Is a Lonely Hunter*, that of a string quartet. Though evidence of McCullers' special interest in the string quartet cannot be found in her biographies, it is possible that the musical image crept into the novel almost unconsciously at the moment of writing that she calls "illumination" (*Illumination and Night Glare* 3–4, 32).[2] In fact, the novel has resulted in critics like Margaret B. McDowell choosing the

K. Magome (✉)
Modern Languages and Cultures, University of Tsukuba, 1-1-1 Tennodai, Tsukuba, Ibaraki 305-8571, Japan

© The Author(s) 2016   97
A. Graham-Bertolini, C. Kayser (eds.), *Carson McCullers in the Twenty-First Century*, DOI 10.1007/978-3-319-40292-5_6

word "quartet" to express the relationship between the four lonely characters who congregate around the deaf-mute John Singer (35, 37), which seems to indicate the possibility that on another level, the word can also be regarded as a musical term and thus bring about a new interpretation of the novel. In addition, a close reading of McCullers' early short story "Court in the West Eighties" reveals that the image of a string quartet existed in her imagination as early as 1934. Further, a comparison between McCullers' and other modernist writers' musico-literary works written between the mid-1930s and the mid-1940s demonstrates the importance of the image of a string quartet not just in McCullers' early works but in a much larger musico-literary, socio-historical context.

The string quartet represents a small, highly democratic structure, evoking in the composer, the performer, and the audience the image of a unique, ideal discourse. Christina Bashford explains its history and characteristics:

> The story of the string quartet begins in the second half of the eighteenth century, with the newly emerging body of works composed for two violins, viola and cello ... and intended as 'real' chamber music: that is, music to be performed for its own sake and the enjoyment of its players, in private residences (usually in rooms of limited size), perhaps in the presence of a few listeners, perhaps not. ... [The string quartet] was the quintessential 'music of friends', an intimate and tightly constructed dialogue among equals, at once subtle and serious, challenging to play, and with direct appeal to the earnest enthusiast. 'Four rational people conversing' was how Goethe would later see it. (3–4)

While the close, dynamic interactions among the four independent string players were "intended as 'real' chamber music" in Europe in the mid-eighteenth century, the string quartet is still "widely regarded as the supreme form of chamber music" ("String Quartet"). In fact, in a conversation with the novelist Haruki Murakami, the world-famous conductor Seiji Ozawa repeatedly emphasizes the importance of the string quartet, pointing out that musicians need to experience it to learn the fundamentals of effective ensembles (346, 349, 367–68). Another marked characteristic of the string quartet is that unlike members of an orchestra, the four musicians play without a conductor. The structure of a string quartet, which traditionally doesn't have a conductor, or a visible center controlling the whole discourse, has often been considered a symbolic microcosm similar to the Empedoclean universe based on the interactions among the four elements.[3] Thus, the string quartet evokes the image of a well-balanced, dynamic world with no center, where four independent members keep communicating closely with each other in the passage of time. This discursive image often appeared in literature during the modernist period and played various roles in such works as Virginia Woolf's "The String Quartet" (1921), Aldous Huxley's *Point Counter Point* (1928), T. S. Eliot's four poems published between 1935 and 1942 and collected as *Four Quartets* (1943), Thomas Mann's *Doctor Faustus* (1947), and McCullers' "Court in the West Eighties" and *The Heart Is a Lonely Hunter.*

McCullers' "Court in the West Eighties," written around 1934 but published posthumously, has attracted little critical attention but is worth examining because it gives us the opportunity to notice the image of a string quartet in her literary imagination and to read *The Heart Is a Lonely Hunter* from a new perspective. The short story begins as follows:

> It was not until spring that I began to think about the man who lived in the room directly opposite to mine. All during the winter months the court between us was dark and there was a feeling of privacy about the four walls of little rooms that looked out on each other. Sounds were muffled and far away as they always seem when it is cold and windows everywhere are shut. (11)

Like McCullers, the young female narrator-protagonist came to New York City probably in the mid-1930s, during the decade of the Great Depression, and is struggling to survive her first year at university. The "court" she can see from her room is surrounded by "four walls" with closed windows. In the "dark," "cold" space, sounds are "muffled and far away," evoking "a feeling of privacy" or even isolation. As the title and the opening scene show, the court exists at the center of the story and of the residents, but it is like a deserted blank space drawing nobody's attention at least "[a]ll during the winter months."

The warm spring weather brings change, and the narrator-protagonist sees "through the open window" the man with the red hair living on the opposite side of the court plainly for the first time (12–13). She also hears his "humming" and feels "his nearness to" her (13). In addition, such residents around the court as "the [female] cellist whose room [is] at a right angle with" the narrator-protagonist's and "the young couple living above" the cellist can finally be seen and heard (13). These are the five main characters of this story, and their relationships begin to change gradually. For example, the cellist "annoy[s] everybody" by "facing the court with her cello" and practicing "lazily" (14–15). Meanwhile, the narrator-protagonist keeps watching the man with the red hair without talking to him and assumes that "this man across from [her understands] the cellist and everyone else on the court as well" and that he is "the one person able to straighten … out [troubles around the court]" (14–15). In other words, the narrator-protagonist "imagine[s] about him" as she wants to (14). She herself admits: "It is not easy to explain about this faith I had in him. I don't know what I could have expected him to do, but the feeling was there just the same" (16). Thus, in her imagination, he has changed into someone God-like who can control the small world around the court perfectly.

The irony is that even in summer the five characters still "[act] as strangers" without communicating directly with each other, and the young couple and finally the man with the red hair leave the place toward the end of the summer (16). This narrative structure implies that even though the four seasons rotate, the court remains basically the same, existing at the center of the place but having no centripetal, unifying power at all. Similarly, ignoring the narrator-protagonist's expectation, the mysterious God-like man has disappeared without jumping into the center of the discourse to activate the relationships among the residents. In short, the end of the story highlights the reality that there is no reliable center in terms of both place and person, suggesting that the two remaining characters, the narrator-protagonist and the cellist, will live in a new structural image around the court. This is the moment in the story that the image of a string quartet quietly emerges. One important key is that toward the end of the story, the cellist has started "practic[ing] fiercely, jabbing her bow across the strings" (18). It is true that her lazy "practicing annoyed everybody" around the court in the past, but her hard practice suggests that she is trying to do something new through her performance. In addition, throughout the story, the number "four"—the court surrounded by "the four walls," the rotation of the "four" seasons, and the "four" ordinary residents watched by the mysterious man—and the image of a discourse with no center have been emphasized. Therefore, it seems natural that we, stimulated by these several elements, imagine that the cellist is trying to play a string quartet, or to create the well-balanced, dynamic musical microcosm consisting of four players and functioning perfectly together with no powerful center like a conductor.

However, the story also implies that realizing an active discourse like a string quartet in the small world around the court is extremely difficult. First of all, the cellist cannot create harmony by herself. The narrator-protagonist will never join the musical microcosm on a symbolic level to enjoy close interactions with the cellist and the other residents, for even at the very end of the story, she is still obsessed with the idea that the man with the red hair is the powerful, possible center of the world around the court. In fact, she sees "a sort of halo" around his red hair when he moves out, and remembering him she says: "But no matter how peculiar it sounds I still have this feeling that there is something in him that could change a lot of situations and straighten them out" (19). Another important point related to the narrator-protagonist's obsession is that she juxtaposes her daily life around the court with the larger world of the 1930s. She writes her thoughts randomly on a typewriter: "*fascism and war cannot exist for long because they are death and death is the only evil in the world*" (13–14; emphasis original). While the man with the red hair is regarded as the God-like center of the courtyard by the narrator-protagonist who doesn't really know anything about him, we know that in Europe the mysterious center of *fascism and war*, or Hitler, actually fascinated many people, was worshiped enthusiastically by them, and brought about "the only evil in the world" on a massive scale. The juxtaposition reveals how attractive mysterious God-like men look in different situations and how danger-ous it can be to believe them blindly as reliable centers of any discourse. Thus, "Court in the West Eighties" inspires us to imagine a democratic discourse like a string quartet as an ideal microcosm, but at the same time, it reminds us that such a construction cannot be easily realized in the real world.

The image of a string quartet in "Court in the West Eighties" remains deep below the surface and only emerges through a careful reading, but a comparison between the short story and *The Heart Is a Lonely Hunter* makes it much more visible, for the two works are like musical variations. In fact, Virginia Spencer Carr points out that "[t]he young girl and the redheaded man [in 'Court in the West Eighties'] proved to be sensitively drawn prototypes of Mick Kelly and John Singer [in *The Heart Is a Lonely Hunter*], who were germinating even then" (44). The structure of *The Heart Is a Lonely Hunter* is similar to that of "Court in the West Eighties." In a nameless town "in the middle of the deep South" (3), four lonely persons—Mick Kelly, a poor adolescent girl who loves European classical music; Doctor Benedict Copeland, an African-American physician who helps the black community; Jake Blount, a frustrated radical who wanders in the South; and Biff Brannon, a café owner who calmly observes people around him—are drawn to John Singer, the deaf- mute. As Jennifer Murray writes, on one level, "the characters are representative of various social, sexual, and racial positions" (110). The end of Part One describes their relationships in this microcosmic world:

> By midsummer Singer had visitors more often than any other person in the [boarding] house ... Mick loved to go up to Mister Singer's room ... [Doctor Copeland] made another visit. Jake Blount came every week ... Even Biff Brannon came to the mute's room one night ... Singer was always the same to everyone ... [He] nodded or smiled to show his guests that he understood. (77–79)

Singer is the center of the four characters as well as of the novel. However, like the man with the red hair and the courtyard in "Court in the West Eighties," Singer and his room do not have enough power to unify these individuals, which causes the following situation: "The four people had been coming to his [Singer's] rooms now for more than seven months. They never came together—always alone" (174). By the end of Part Two, Singer fails in entertaining the four people at the same time, his mute friend Spiros Antonapoulos dies in a distant insane asylum, and these depressing incidents trigger his suicide. Part Three focuses exclusively on one day, August 21, 1939, depicting the fragmenting world after the death of the symbolic center. At this moment, the image of a string quartet, or the well-balanced, dynamic musical structure with no center, appears as a possible model for a better society.

John Singer, the symbolic center of the novel, is the most significant key to exploring how and why the image of a string quartet appears. McCullers writes about how he was created:

> It [the illumination] always comes from the subconscious and cannot be controlled. For a whole year I worked on *The Heart Is a Lonely Hunter* without understanding it at all. Each character was talking to a central character, but why, I didn't know ... I had been working for five hours and I went outside. Suddenly, as I walked across a road, it occurred to me that Harry Minowitz, the character all the other characters were talking to, was a different man, a deaf mute, and immediately the name was changed to John Singer. The whole focus of the novel was fixed and I was for the first time committed with my whole soul to *The Heart Is a Lonely Hunter*. ("The Flowering Dream" 275)

The uncontrollable power of McCullers' "subconscious" suddenly changed the central character's name from "Harry Minowitz" to "John Singer," which decided the novel. This fact indicates how important the name "John Singer" is. The name "John" probably suggests highly religious images related to God, whereas "Singer" almost certainly evokes the image of a person who sings. However, these images are ironic. "John" in this novel, set in the late 1930s, is worshiped fairly easily, which confuses us when we think about the skeptical, unstable Western world after the death of God.[4] In addition, this character named "Singer" is "a deaf mute." McCullers shows this highly ironic name "John Singer" at the beginning of the novel and gradually reveals its profound, complex meanings by describing how the other characters react to him. For example, Biff points out that "[o]wing to the fact he [Singer] was a mute they [Jake and Mick] were able to give him all the qualities they wanted him to have" (198). In other words, the more they visit Singer, the more complex and God-like his image becomes. In fact, Mick begins to imagine the music not Singer's "ears" but "his mind" can hear and feels that "[i]t was funny, but Mister Singer reminded her of this [Mozart's] music" (44–45). Doctor Copeland looks at Singer's face and juxtaposes him with Spinoza, his favorite Jewish philosopher (159). Thus, Singer gradually changes into what Biff calls "a sort of home-made God" full of the four characters' various—often unrealistic—expectations (198).

Each character visits the "home-made God" and feels comfortable, but they cannot create a comfortable community. The following scene discloses this fact dramatically in the image of a musical performance:

> One night soon after Christmas all four of the people chanced to visit him at the same time. This had never happened before. Singer moved about the room with smiles and refreshments and did his best in the way of politeness to make his guests comfortable. But something was wrong ...
> Singer was bewildered. Always each of them had so much to say. Yet now that they were together they were silent ... [I]n the room there was only a feeling of strain. His hands worked nervously as though they were pulling things unseen from the air and binding them together.
> Jake Blount stood beside Doctor Copeland. 'I know your face. We run into each other once before—on the steps outside.'
> Doctor Copeland moved his tongue ...
> Each one of them looked at Singer as though in expectation. He was puzzled. He offered refreshments and smiled ...
> Each person addressed his words mainly to the mute. Their thoughts seemed to converge in him as the spokes of a wheel lead to the center hub ...

> They discussed the weather some more. Each one seemed to be waiting
> for the others to go. Then on an impulse they all rose to leave at the same
> time. (178–80)

Nobody speaks at first, and "a feeling of strain" fills the room. However, there is another important element to this scene—"the music from the radio" Singer bought "[f]or all of them [the four guests] together" (178–79). In this situation, Singer begins to move "[h]is hands ... nervously." Of course, he may be encouraging his quiet guests to talk to each other by gesture, but on another level, the scene also looks like that of a musical performance, where a conductor stands at the center of the musicians, making them play according to the movement of his hands. Interestingly, just after the descriptions of Singer's hands, Jake finally speaks to Doctor Copeland as if following the conductor's instructions. However, the conversation doesn't develop among the four guests, which reveals that Singer is not much of a conductor. He is unable to bring about effective communication among the musicians themselves. What exists in this room is thus only one kind of relationship between Singer and each guest, or the structural image of "the spokes of a wheel [led] to the center hub" separately. In fact, each guest "look[s] at Singer" and "addresse[s] his words mainly to the mute." The ironic conclusion of this scene is that the four isolated guests act together only when they leave the room.

While it becomes clear that Singer, unlike a good conductor, cannot play the role of an effective center to organize the other four main characters as a community, they keep projecting unrealistic expectations and images onto him. As in "Court in the West Eighties," the actual communication among the five main characters remains basically the same throughout the novel, but on a symbolic level, Singer, unlike the man with the red hair, is connected to not one person's but the four widely different characters' expectations and imaginations. It is natural that Singer does "not seem quite human" (20) but changes into someone God-like or monstrous in terms of his highly complex image. The direct cause of his suicide appears on the surface to be the result of the shock of Antonapoulos' death, but on another level, we find that "[b]y making Singer divine, the townspeople depersonalize and, in effect, murder him" (Whitt 146). In fact, on his way to the distant asylum near the end of Part Two, Singer is happy because he doesn't yet know of Antonapoulos' death. However, upon remembering the four characters, he feels suffocated and finally sleeps, as if foreshadowing his own impending death: "For a while his thoughts lingered in the town he was leaving behind him. He saw Mick and Doctor Copeland and Jake Blount and Biff Brannon. The faces crowded in on him out of the darkness so that he felt smothered … The train rocked with a smooth, easy motion … [A]nd for a short while he slept" (274–75). Thus, Singer as a God-like image at the center of the narrative disappears from the town as well as the novel.

As analyzed above, the highly ironic name "John Singer" presented at the beginning of the novel keeps stimulating us to explore the God-like image projected onto the deaf-mute character and his relationship with music. The four lonely characters almost unconsciously expect "John" to be a God-like person, but he cannot endure the role of the "home-made God" for long. His extremely complex image finally bursts, killing him. However, it turns out that the name "Singer" is not as ironic as it seems, for there are various interactions between the deaf-mute character and music. For example, Mick imagines the music in Singer's mind and juxtaposes him with Mozart. In addition, the music on the radio in his room—probably the European classical music Mick loves—influences the atmosphere of the scene with his four guests, where the image of Singer as an inept conductor appears. Thus, the novel implies that the four characters who revolve around Singer in the microcosmic world desire a social structure with a mysterious "home-made God" conducting at its center, but they cannot realize it successfully. In fact, after describing the five main characters' characteristic communication patterns throughout Parts One and Two, McCullers suddenly destroys the discourse by killing the symbolic center of her story and dramatically accelerates the process of painful fragmentation toward the novel's end. Since it becomes clear that such a discourse doesn't function, a better alternative needs to be considered. The novel does cope with this difficult situation by quietly suggesting the structural image of a string quartet, where the four independent elements interact with each other dynamically in balanced ways with no controlling, unifying center.

As in "Court in the West Eighties," we actually come across elements associated with the image of a string quartet throughout *The Heart Is a Lonely Hunter*. For example, after Singer disappears at the end of Part Two, Part Three breaks up into four sections—"Morning," "Afternoon," "Evening," and "Night"—dealing with the other four characters, respectively. The four lonely characters placed in the four separate sections highlight the importance of the number "four" even more effectively than before. After the death of the symbolic center, Doctor Copeland remains

physically weak and moves out, Jake joins a riot and "get[s] out of town
before dark" (298), Mick works hard for her family and cannot concen-
trate on music, and Biff in his café is "suspended" between "the past ...
and a future of blackness, error, and ruin" (306). Ihab Hassan understands that in Part Three "[t]he center, as Yeats would say, can no longer
hold and things fall apart in four distinct scenes ... But no Second Coming
is foreseen in the novel, nor do the characters hope to resolve their pre-
dicament" (215). It is true that "no Second Coming is foreseen in this
novel," but it conveys at least the image of a string quartet as a possible
social structure in the future. This image becomes more visible when we
focus on the similarities between "Court in the West Eighties" and *The
Heart Is a Lonely Hunter*. At the end of the short story, the narrator-
protagonist and the cellist are left around the court, whereas in Part Three
of the novel, Biff as the observer-character and Mick remain in the town.
While the cellist starts practicing fiercely, Mick has been "making herself a
violin"; more precisely, she has been struggling to change "a cracked uku-
lele" into a violin (37). Even though Mick's special interest in the piano
and musical composition is obvious, the expression that "the thought of
the violin [keeps] worrying her" makes us imagine her obsession with it as
well as her strong desire to complete and play it (43). If we relate the two
similar works to each other as musico-literary variations on the theme of
the number "four" and regard them as a larger musico-literary discourse,
it suggests that the two characters, the cellist and Mick as a violinist, are
looking for two more string players and preparing for a performance in a
string quartet.

   The image of a string quartet in McCullers' early works interacts with
her famous technique of counterpoint, functioning not just in America
but also in Europe simultaneously. Just as "Court in the West Eighties"
set in New York City stimulates us to imagine the larger relationship
between America and Europe through such expressions as *fascism and
war*, the American South in *The Heart Is a Lonely Hunter* keeps reminding us of the European situation through contrapuntal techniques. For
example, in one scene, Mick's friend Harry Minowitz asks, "I say is that
Mozart a Fascist or a Nazi?" (95). In another scene, Jake and Doctor
Copeland argue "Fascism" by comparing "[t]he Nazis [and] the Jews"
with "the South" and "the Negro" (256–57). In addition, "one full-
page manifesto" in Jake's room is entitled "The Affinity Between Our
Democracy and Fascism" (292). The radio also relates the two worlds
effectively. While sophisticated European classical music is introduced

to the nameless town in the American South, especially Mick, through the radio (29, 86, 99–102), it also informs what is happening in Europe vividly to the town at the end of the novel: "The radio [in Biff's café] was on and there was talk about the crisis Hitler had cooked up over Danzig" (303).[5] The contrapuntal juxtaposition between the American South and Europe in the late 1930s helps us realize that in the Western world after the death of God, the person filling in the absent center could have been someone like Singer, the considerate "home-made God," not a monster like Hitler. Either way, as we know from the fragmenting world at the end of the novel and the historical fact, a discourse depending heavily on a God-like or monstrous person at its center is so unstable and/or dangerous that people need a better discursive model sooner or later. This is where the image of a possible social discourse based on the elaborate structure of a string quartet appears. As explained earlier, since the string quartet was born in Europe and has represented a highly democratic microcosm with no center, it is quite natural and effective to encourage us to juxtapose the American South contrapuntally with Europe through its image and to imagine a better social discourse in the future on a larger scale.

A close reading of "Court in the West Eighties" and *The Heart Is a Lonely Hunter* reveals that between 1934 and 1939, McCullers almost unconsciously clung to a discursive image similar to that of a string quartet. While there is no clear evidence that she was especially interested in the string quartet, the musical form/structure strongly attracted talented writers at that time and had a great influence on literature during the modernist period. As pointed out earlier, Virginia Woolf wrote an experimental short story entitled "The String Quartet" in 1921, making the so-called stream of consciousness intertwine with a vivid musical performance (69–72). Several years later, Aldous Huxley used various musical structures and techniques throughout the novel *Point Counter Point* but focused exclusively on Beethoven's String Quartet no. 15 in A, op. 132 in the last scene (425–32). However, the string quartet plays important roles most actively in literature between the mid-1930s and the mid-1940s. During this period, such music lovers as Eliot and Mann, like McCullers, wrote musico-literary works reflecting the European situation concerning World War II. In their works, the image of a string quartet functions in different ways. Therefore, through a comparison among the three writers' musico-literary works related to string quartets, we can explore McCullers' characteristic way of dealing with it more closely.

Eliot's four poems published between 1935 and 1942—"Burnt Norton," "East Coker," "The Dry Salvages," and "Little Gidding"—were collected as *Four Quartets* in 1943. Unlike McCullers, Eliot "had no technical training, [but] music was the art that personally affected [him] most deeply" (D. Fuller 134). While working on the four independent poems, he gave a lecture entitled "The Music of Poetry" in 1942 and pointed out that though he understood his lack of musical knowledge, "a poet may gain much from the study of music," including "a quartet" (*The Music of Poetry* 27–28). In other words, we can see how his theory in this lecture was put into practice in *Four Quartets*. Another point is that "it was only in writing 'East Coker' that I [Eliot] began to see the Quartets as a set of four" ("The Genesis of *Four Quartets*" 23), which means that the strategy of quartets, especially string quartets, appeared in Eliot's mind in the middle of writing the four independent poems.[6] Mann started writing *Doctor Faustus* in 1943 and used a string quartet in a totally different way in the novel. This is largely because Mann, unlike Eliot, created his musico-literary work in collaboration with Theodor W. Adorno, the famous German philosopher, sociologist, and, most importantly, musicologist.[7] In fact, Adorno argues "[t]hat Schönberg's roots lay in the polyphony of the string quartet has never been doubted" (*Introduction* 97), and the string quartet composed by Mann's protagonist Adrian Leverkühn, the talented composer reflecting the image of Schönberg on one level, represents an important turning point in his life as well as the novel (458). The image of a string quartet in McCullers' early works emerges differently mainly because she understood the musical structure profoundly but perhaps didn't use it intentionally as a literary device. Therefore, as noted previously, only fragmentary elements of the string quartet, such as a cellist, an obsession with a violin, and discourses consisting of four people with no center, can be found in her works. However, this is not a weak point but rather a great stimulus for us to read the texts closely, use our imaginations fully, and relate the fragments to each other to reveal what is hidden deep beneath the surface.

When we read McCullers' "Court in the West Eighties" and *The Heart Is a Lonely Hunter* carefully as musico-literary variations, fragmentary elements of the image of a string quartet begin to emerge and prompt us to notice new aspects of her famous first novel. The image is well worth examining especially because the short story and the novel are McCullers' early works. A close analysis of the image will move the study of her later works in a new direction. In addition, we can also read "Court in the West Eighties" and *The Heart Is a Lonely Hunter* in a much larger musico-literary, socio-historical context by relating the image of a string quartet in them to that in Eliot's and Mann's works. In so doing, her experiences in the American South and New York City until 1939 become significant, for they had a great influence on her two early works. Similarly, between the mid-1930s and the mid-1940s, Eliot and Mann in Europe and America made their works like *Four Quartets* and *Doctor Faustus* elaborately reflect their personal experiences and social situations in both worlds. Since all three of them wrote musico-literary works dealing with the image of a string quartet almost at the same time in different ways, we can compare them with each other and analyze the musico-literary, socio-historical image of a string quartet around World War II. In this sense, McCullers' two early works greatly help us understand not just the American South and New York City but also a much more complex discursive image that talented Western writers of the time were obsessed with and/or longed for. We haven't fully examined the image of a string quartet appearing in McCullers' early works and modernist literature in terms of its influence on the creation of our present world since the end of World War II. It is time for us to explore more closely how and to what degree musical structures can affect literary and/or social ones and how we can use the image of a string quartet to make our present world better toward the future.

Notes

1. In "Two Years of Counterpoint," I examine *The Heart Is a Lonely Hunter*, "Madame Zilensky and the King of Finland," and *The Ballad of the Sad Café*. For a closer analysis of them in a larger context, see *The Influence of Music on American Literature since 1890*.
2. McCullers taught at least "chamber music" by using an old gramophone in "a lecture-study course in music appreciation for a dozen culture-loving Columbus ladies" during the summer of 1937 (Carr 71). As for "illuminations," she explains: "What are the sources of an illumination? To me, they come after hours of searching and keeping my soul ready. Yet they come in a flash, as a religious phenomenon" (*Illumination and Night Glare* 32).
3. Empedocles, the pre-Socratic philosopher and poet, claimed that four elements—earth, water, air, and fire—constructed the universe and that they kept mingling and separating eternally by two powers, Love and Strife. Philip Ball emphasizes that "[t]he four elements of antiquity perfuse the history of Western culture," analyzes Shakespeare's works as examples, and points out that "[l]iterary tradition has continued to uphold the four ancient elements, which supply the organizing principle of T. S. Eliot's *Quartets*" (10). Northrop

Frye also writes: "The four elements are not a conception of much use to modern chemistry—that is, they are not the elements of nature. But, as [Gaston] Bachelard's book and its companion works show, and as an abundance of literature down to Eliot's *Quartets* also shows, earth, air, water and fire are still the four elements of imaginative experience, and always will be" (vii).

4. In fact, Mick thinks about the relationship between the absence of God in society and the existence of Singer: "Everybody in the past few years knew there wasn't any real God. When she thought of what she used to imagine was God she could only see Mister Singer with a long, white sheet around him. God was silent—maybe that was why she was reminded" (101–02).

5. McCullers, working on the novel, had "global as well as local concerns in mind" (Boddy xxiv). For detailed information, see Carr 84 and Savigneau 60.

6. As David Fuller and many other critics have argued, "it has often been supposed that he [Eliot] had specifically in mind the late [string] quartets of Beethoven, [especially op. 132]," and "[i]t has also been claimed that Eliot reported having in mind Béla Bartók's [String] Quartets numbers 2–6" (139–40).

7. For the process of their collaboration, see Adorno, "Toward a Portrait of Thomas Mann"; Mann, *The Story of a Novel.*

WORKS CITED

Adorno, Theodor W. *Introduction to the Sociology of Music.* Trans. E. B. Ashton. New York: Seabury P, 1976. Print.

——. "Toward a Portrait of Thomas Mann." *Notes to Literature.* Trans. Shierry Weber Nicholsen. Vol. 2. New York: Columbia UP, 1992. 12–19. Print.

Ball, Philip. *The Elements.* Oxford: Oxford UP, 2002. Print.

Bashford, Christina. "The String Quartet and Society." *The Cambridge Companion to the String Quartet.* 2003. Ed. Robin Stowell. Cambridge: Cambridge UP, 2005. 3–18. Print.

Boddy, Kasia. "Introduction." *The Heart Is a Lonely Hunter.* By Carson McCullers. 1940. London: Penguin, 2008. xi–xxviii. Print.

Carr, Virginia Spencer. *The Lonely Hunter: A Biography of Carson McCullers.* 1975. Athens: U of Georgia P, 2003. Print.

Eliot, T. S. *Four Quartets.* 1943. Orlando: Harvest, 1971. Print.

——. "The Genesis of *Four Quartets.*" 1953. *T. S. Eliot: Four Quartets.* 1969. Ed. Bernard Bergonzi. London: Macmillan, 1987. 23. Print.

——. *The Music of Poetry.* Glasgow: Glasgow UP, 1942. Print.

Frye, Northrop. "Preface." *The Psychoanalysis of Fire.* By Gaston Bachelard. Trans. Alan C. M. Ross. 1964. Boston: Beacon, 1968. v–viii. Print.

Fuller, David. "Music." *T. S. Eliot in Context.* 2011. Ed. Jason Harding. Cambridge: Cambridge UP, 2012. 134–44. Print.

Fuller, Janice. "The Conventions of Counterpoint and Fugue in *The Heart Is a Lonely Hunter.*" *Mississippi Quarterly* 41.1 (1987): 55–67. Print.

Hassan, Ihab. *Radical Innocence: Studies in the Contemporary American Novel.* Princeton: Princeton UP, 1961. Print.

Huxley, Aldous. *Point Counter Point.* 1928. Normal: Dalkey Archive P, 2004. Print.

Magome, Kiyoko. *The Influence of Music on American Literature since 1890: A History of Aesthetic Counterpoint.* Lewiston: Edwin Mellen, 2008. Print.

——. "Two Years of Counterpoint: Carson McCullers' Musico-Literary, Socio-Aesthetic Discourse." *Southern Studies* 11 (2004): 67–86. Print.

Mann, Thomas. *Doctor Faustus: The Life of the German Composer Adrian Leverkühn as Told by a Friend.* 1947. Trans. H. T. Lowe-Porter. New York: Alfred A. Knopf, 1948. Print.

——. *The Story of a Novel: The Genesis of Doctor Faustus.* 1949. Trans. Richard and Clara Winston. New York: Alfred A. Knopf, 1961. Print.

McCullers, Carson. "Author's Outline of 'The Mute.'" *The Mortgaged Heart.* 124–49.

——. "Court in the West Eighties." *Collected Stories of Carson McCullers.* 1987. Boston: Houghton Mifflin, 1998. 11–19. Print.

——. "The Flowering Dream: Notes on Writing." *The Mortgaged Heart.* 274–82. Print.

——. *The Heart Is a Lonely Hunter.* 1940. New York: Bantam, 1983. Print.

——. *Illumination and Night Glare: The Unfinished Autobiography of Carson McCullers.* Ed. and introd. Carlos L. Dews. Madison: U of Wisconsin P, 1999. Print.

——. *The Mortgaged Heart.* 1940. Ed. Margarita G. Smith. Boston: Houghton Mifflin, 1971. Print.

McDowell, Margaret B. *Carson McCullers.* Boston: Twayne, 1980. Print.

Murakami, Haruki, and Seiji Ozawa. *Conversations with Seiji Ozawa about Music.* Tokyo: Shinchosha, 2011. Print.

Murray, Jennifer. "Approaching Community in Carson McCullers' *The Heart Is a Lonely Hunter.*" *Southern Quarterly* 42.4 (2004): 107–14. Print.

Savigneau, Josyane. *Carson McCullers: A Life.* Trans. Joan E. Howard. Boston: Houghton Mifflin, 2001. Print.

Smith, C. Michael. "'A Voice in a Fugue': Characters and Musical Structure in Carson McCullers' *The Heart Is a Lonely Hunter.*" *Modern Fiction Studies* 25 (1979): 258–63. Print.

String Quartet. *The New Grove Dictionary of Music and Musicians.* 2nd ed. 2001. Print.

Whitt, Jan, ed. *Reflections in a Critical Eye: Essays on Carson McCullers.* Lanham: UP of America, 2008. Print.

Woolf, Virginia. "The String Quartet." 1921. *Monday or Tuesday.* Doylestown: Wildside P, 2003. 65–72. Print.

Entering the Compound: Becoming with Carson Mccullers' Freaks

renée c. hoogland

Characters can only exist, and the author can only create them, because they do not perceive but have passed into the landscape and are themselves part of the compound of sensations.

Gilles Deleuze & Félix Guattari, *What Is Philosophy?*

Carson McCullers' "freakish" characters, hovering uncomfortably between the normal and the abnormal, the human and the monster, the readable and the unreadable, have been recuperated by literary critics for various psychosocial boundary positions. In line with more overall concerns with difference, diversity, and the power relations subtending them, the grotesque figures populating the author's literary landscape have been aligned with disabled and transgendered people, with the deviant and the queer, as well as identified as the crippled and debilitated offshoot of the oppressive sociopolitical structures of the postwar period in which they find their origins.

Valid and valuable as such readings of McCullers' freaks may be (and I count my own reading of her tomboy figure among such politicized appreciations of her work),[1] forging a direct connection between sociopolitical

r. c. hoogland (✉)
Wayne State University, Detroit, MI, USA

© The Author(s) 2016
A. Graham-Bertolini, C. Kayser (eds.), *Carson McCullers in the Twenty-First Century*, DOI 10.1007/978-3-319-40292-5_7

frameworks and the operations of textual configurations does not actually address what makes these freakish figures interesting and worthy of critical attention to begin with, i.e., their function and effect as literary, hence as aesthetic rather than human beings—or, indeed, as nonhuman becomings.

In this essay, I address the inscription of freakishness in McCullers' *The Member of the Wedding* (1946) on a functional-material level (more about this in a moment) in order to argue against hermeneutical procedures that offer a symptomatology of either psycho-political systems or of the inner struggle of a writer or character. Hence, I foreground the liminal figure of the novel's protagonist as an aesthetic creation, which functions as a space of energetic possibilities that underlies and generates radical arrangements of language and life that cannot be reduced to the disciplinary operations of established forms of literary criticism. Several key concepts from Gilles Deleuze's writing, and from his collaborative work with Félix Guattari, will, I believe, be helpful in unraveling the textual knot at the heart of McCullers' short novel, which took her five years to finish, and about which she wrote in a letter to her husband Reeves that it was "one of those works that the least slip can ruin. It must be beautifully done. For like a poem there is not much excuse for it otherwise."[2]

The Member of the Wedding is divided into three parts in which the protagonist appears—significantly—under three different names: Frankie, F. Jasmine, and Frances, respectively. The novel relates the events taking place in the course of slightly more than a week in the life of a twelve-year-old tomboyish girl, Frankie, whose mother has died in childbirth and who spends the long, hot summer days talking to and playing cards with black housekeeper Berenice Sadie Brown and her six-year-old cousin, John Henry West, while her father is out to work. Throughout that last week of August in 1944, the Second World War figures ominously in the background and, if not directly affecting the course of narrative events, provides a specific historical setting that adds to the tense atmosphere permeating the text. Like most of her novels and short stories, McCullers situates the narrative in a provincial town in the Deep South, an at once real and imaginary realm that is usually peopled with eccentric, lonely, and dislocated characters, who are depicted in rather grotesque terms. Frankie is no exception, as is clear from the novel's opening sentences:

> It happened that green and crazy summer when Frankie was twelve years old. This was the summer when for a long time she had not been a member. She belonged to no club and was a member of nothing in the world. Frankie had become an unjoined person who hung around in doorways, and she was afraid.[3]

The novel thus opens with some kind of happening or an event and the inscription of a mood. What "happened," however, is never exactly described or defined, and it is therefore not an ordinary event, identifiable in time and space, nor is it exactly part of the narrative events proper. Though crucial to its operations, what happens that summer is an intensity of feeling, a current of perception and sensation, an aesthetic event whose nature and effects reverberate throughout the text, as a movement, an energy, as, in Deleuzian terms, its underlying diagram.

Diagrams, or thinking diagrammatically, is a key aspect of Deleuze's thought on form and matter. Diagrams, in his philosophy, have no necessary relation to visual representation, nor do they serve—as they do in several different scientific disciplines—as problem-solvers. A diagram, instead, has "neither substance nor form, neither content nor expression" but constitutes an "abstract machine" of "pure matter-function," a space of energetic possibilities capable of generating form on its own.[4] Deleuze thus argues against essentialist notions of form, which project matter as the inert receptacle of forms imposed from the outside, as much as against a phenomenological (or Kantian) approach of reality, which posits matter as real on the condition that it is being given form and meaning in and through our experience of it: the appearance of things in our experience of them realizes them as objects. Thinking diagrammatically, in contrast, entails that the real is not so much a question of realization—e.g., the future being merely a modality of time in which past possibilities are realized—but a question of the actualization of virtualities. The abstract machine is the "aspect or moment at which nothing but functions and matters remain" (*TP* 141):

> Defined diagrammatically in this way, an abstract machine is neither an infrastructure that is determining in the last instance nor a transcendental Idea that is determining in the supreme instance. Rather, it plays a piloting role. The diagrammatic or abstract machine does not function to represent, even something real, but rather constructs a real that is yet to come, a new type of reality. (*TP* 143)

The distinction between the possible and the virtual (at the core of diagrammatic thought) is precisely so crucial because it allows for the emergence of the novel, of the genuinely new. After all, the realization of a possibility adds nothing more to a predefined form but reality. The virtual becoming actual, in contrast, points to the morphogenetic capabilities of matter:

Actualisation breaks with resemblance as a process no less than it does with identity as a principle. Actual terms never resemble the singularities they incarnate. In this sense, actualisation or differenciation is always a genuine creation. It does not result from any limitation of a pre-existing possibility.[5]

Approaching a novel—or any work of artistic creation, for that matter—from a diagrammatical perspective, encourages us to look, not so much for the meaning behind the words, for the operations of the sign (signifier/signified), in order to establish the relations between the content and its form, but rather to attend to the matter-content and the function-expression of the text as a space of energetic possibilities. Matter, being unformed substance, in a work for art becomes matter-content, which only has "degrees of intensity, resistance, conductivity, heating, stretching, speed, or tardiness." Function, at the same time, only has "'traits,' of content and of expression, between which it establishes a connection." Seen as abstract machine or diagram, in which matter content and function-expression generate form on their own, a novel is thus not a realization of possibilities (of language, of thought, of meaning) but an abstract machine, truly open-ended, in which virtualities become actual: "Writing now functions on the same level as the real, and the real materially writes" (*TP* 141). The distinction between form of expression and form of content appears only on the level of semiotization: the deeper movement consists in the conjugation of matter and function; in other words, in the virtual diagram, in the novel itself as a cartography of an abstract machine.

Space constraints force me to limit my exploration of this cartography to the first part of McCullers' novel, which is largely concerned with moments leading up to the narrative present, to the "happening" or event with which it opens, and which is therefore, not surprisingly, quite oppressively marked by non-events, by stasis and stagnation: "The summer in the town was ugly and lonesome and very hot," and Frankie "stayed home and hung around the kitchen, and the summer did not end" (*MW* 26).

In this first section, Frankie's overwhelming sense of non-belonging dominates the text, as well as her typically adolescent consciousness. Her masculine appearance and her equally unfeminine pursuits—she sports a close crew cut; usually walks around in a BVD undershirt, shorts, and sneakers; has dirty fingernails; and loves throwing knives—have, up until now, been fully socially acceptable. At the age of twelve, however, she is expected to begin the transformation from tomboy into Southern Lady. On one level, then, Frankie's anxious thoughts about her dislocation in the world, about her non-membership and her fear of eternal exclusion, persistently return her to the uncontrollability of her gendered body:

> She stood before the mirror and she was afraid. It was the summer of fear, for Frankie, and there was one fear that could be figured in arithmetic with paper and a pencil at the table. This August she was twelve and five-sixths years old. She was five feet and three-quarter inches tall, and she wore a number seven shoe. In the past year she had grown four inches, or at least that was what she judged. Already the hateful little summer children hollered to her: "Is it cold up there?" And the comments of grown people made Frankie shrivel on her heels. If she reached her height on her eighteenth birthday, she had five and one-sixth growing years ahead of her. Therefore, according to mathematics and unless she could somehow stop herself, she would grow to be over nine feet tall. And what would be a lady who is over nine feet tall? She would be a Freak. (*MW* 25)

Yet, the precise terms in which Frankie's uncontrollability is cast—form imposed from the outside: mathematics, systems of measurement, the imperialism of language and sociocultural categorization—take the evocation of the forces of growth, movement, and process in this passage beyond those of the stratified stages of traditional psychosexual development. Frankie's embodied anxiety exceeds the regime of the sign so that the form of expression—of her animated being as much as of language itself—is no longer really distinct from the form of the passage's content. Especially in its clash with the paralyzing atmosphere of the swelteringly hot summer kitchen, the excessive adolescent body makes itself felt as a site of becoming, of unruly and untimely differentiation, or, to use another Deleuzian term, of deterritorialization, i.e., any process that decontextualizes a set of relations, rendering them virtual and preparing them for new, more remote actualizations. Hence, just as the spatial/temporal setting of the novel transcends its historical specificity in order to actualize its intensity, makes itself *felt* as mood, so does this passage suggest that Frankie's fears are precisely not rational or calculable, predetermined, or enchained by established systems of stratification—or territorialization—but fully animated and animating, in and of the body.

A body, for Deleuze and Guattari, is "not defined by the form that determines it nor as a determinate substance or subject nor by the organs it possesses." A body, they write, is defined, on one hand, by the "sum total of the material elements belonging to it under given relations of movement and rest, speed and slowness" and, on the other hand, by the sum total of the "intensive affects it is capable of at a given power or degree of potential." Invoking the Spinozan term "longitude" and "latitude" to describe these two dimensions of the body, Deleuze and Guattari thus point to a mode of individuation that is very different from that of a person or a subject. Neither a thing nor a substance, a body is "nothing but affects and local movements, differential speeds"—a *haecceity*, or "thisness"—whose two dimensions are the "two elements of a cartography" (*TP* 260-1). Both the overall mood of the novel's fictional world and Frankie's fears are thus neither individual nor historical, but rather pre- or impersonal, functional-material entities—virtualities—actualized in language, affective creations in an assemblage defined by speeds and affects.

Affect, for Deleuze, is the ability to affect and to be affected. Where feelings can be identified and described in individual terms (my personal preferences, loves, hates, annoyances), and emotions tend to manifest themselves as projections of feelings (orientations, dispositions) toward the world (which need not be genuine), affect is a non-conscious experience of intensity; it is a moment of unformed and unstructured potential. "Of the three terms," writes Eric Shouse, "affect is the most abstract because affect cannot be fully realized in language, and because affect is always prior to and/or outside of consciousness. Affect is the body's way of preparing itself for action in a given circumstance by adding a quantitative dimension of intensity to the quality of an experience. The body has a grammar of its own that cannot be fully captured in language."[6]

Affects cannot be individually labeled; they are intensities. Frankie, in her ability to be profoundly affected—by the world, by the war, by the bewildering experiences of her embodied being—is a creature of affect. The coincidence of affect and the aesthetic is repeatedly textually inscribed by references to music, especially in Frankie's acute response to the lonely horn playing a blues tune—"low and dark and sad"—in the distance: "Frankie stood stiff, her head bent and her eyes closed, listening. There was something about the tune that brought back to her all the spring: flowers, the eyes of strangers, rain." Then, "all at once," the horn "danced into a wild jazz spangle that zigzagged upward," subsequently returns to the first blues song, and, then, "without warning, the thing happened that Frankie could not believe"; the music finishes, the horn breaks off: "For a moment Frankie could not take it in, she felt so lost" (*MW* 44). Her sense of loss of (her) self when it stops indicates that the sound of the horn, the tune, here does not merely serve as a backdrop or a metaphor for the protagonist's mood. Instead, as an element in the cartography of the moment, in its thisness, and its intensity, the music is inseparable from the hour, the season, the air, as much as Frankie herself is. All form part of an entire assemblage (of speeds and affects), a *haecceity*, in its "individuated aggregate," in which Frankie herself ceases to be a subject to become an event.

Deleuze's use of the musical term counterpoint clarifies the pre-personal or even impersonal quality of Frankie's experience: the modulation of her being, being-enfolded-in the sound of the horn, being taken up in the linear combination of the melodic lines of blues and jazz, does not suggest a process of identification but a becoming. Becoming and music can be brought together in such a way that, as Marcel Swiboda suggests, a "becoming is capable of proceeding through music." Counterpoint, or the "interweaving of several different melodic lines horizontally where the harmony is produced through linear combinations," rather than a "vertical chordal structure or setting," he continues, is most usually a term to describe something we hear. However, when counterpoint is used to describe something other than what we can hear, e.g., an interweaving of a different set of lines, it "opens up to a different function,"[7] an interaction of lines of movement, between and across species and their environment, where music enters into a relation of proximity to something else, in this case, to Frankie, in her animated, embodied being, and therewith generates a "becoming," with Frankie becoming music and music becoming something else (e.g., an aesthetic creation in language).

The self, it should be clear, is, for Deleuze, not a stable or rational being that stays the same over time but, instead, a "constantly changing assemblage of forces, an epiphenomenon arising from the chance confluences of languages, organisms, societies, laws, expectations, and so on."[8] In short, it is not a question of being but of becoming.

"Becoming" is, in fact, a cornerstone concept in Deleuze's ontology. In conjunction with the concept of difference, it serves to rectify the limitations of Western philosophy, with its primary focus on being and identity. Becoming is pure movement, a becoming anew in a process of ongoing change and differentiation, and as such, qua concept, does justice to the richness of our experiences in ways that the Platonic notions of being, origin, and essence cannot. Frankie's becoming music, and music becoming something else, captures the complexity and, at the same time, the affirmative potential of the concept of becoming, which is always double:

> A line of becoming is not defined by points that it connects, or by points that compose it; on the contrary, it passes *between* points, it comes up through the middle, it runs perpendicular to the points first perceived, transversally to the localizable relation to distance or contiguous points ... a line of becoming has neither beginning nor end, departure nor arrival, origin nor destination ... a becoming is neither one nor two, nor the relation of the two; it is the in-between, the border or line of flight or descent running perpendicular to both. (*TP* 292)

Becomings need not be pleasant or reassuring. Nowhere is this more poignantly palpable than when Frankie recalls visiting The House of Freaks at the "Chattahoochee Exposition" when it came to town in the Fall. She had seen "all of the members of the Freak House"—The Giant, The Midget, The Wild Nigger, The Pin Head, The Alligator Boy, and The Half Man-Half Woman—and was afraid of all of them, for it had "seemed to her that they had looked at her in a secret way and tried to connect their eyes with hers, as though to say: we know you. She was afraid of their long Freak eyes. And all the year she had remembered them, until this day" (*MW* 27).

Again, this is not an experience of identification but, in its immediacy, singularity, and materiality, a becoming anew, a becoming-Freak. Both Frankie, the adolescent-tomboy, and the freaks are doubly configured as spaces of in-betweenness and are swept up in a non-localizable relation that carries one into proximity of the other, thus forming a "line-block" of becoming, a "zone of proximity and indiscernibility." The fact that this moment of movement, the line of flight, this "no-man's land" of becoming-Freak, continues to haunt and affect Frankie almost a year after the event confirms that becoming is "born in History, and falls back into it, but is not of it."[9] Becoming-Freak constitutes a "border-proximity" that is "indifferent to both contiguity and to distance" (*TP* 292).

Becoming is a process that is essentially affective in nature and hence neither personal nor exclusively human. Indeed, Deleuze suggests, affect is "not the passage from one lived state to another but man's [sic] nonhuman becoming ... it is a zone of indetermination, of indiscernibility, as if things, beasts, and persons ... endlessly reach that point that immediately precedes their natural differentiation" (*WP* 173). This is what links literature to life: "Life alone creates such zones where living beings whirl around, and only art can reach and penetrate them in its enterprise of co-creation" (*WP* 173). The lived (becoming) finds expression in literary composition:

The writer uses words, but by creating a syntax that makes them pass into sensation that makes the standard language stammer, tremble, cry, or even sing: this is the type, the "tone," the language of sensations ... The writer tests language, makes it vibrate, seizes hold of it, and rends it in order to wrest the percept from perceptions, the affect from affections, the sensation from opinion ... (*WP* 176)

By emphasizing the difference between percept and perceptions, affect and affections, sensation from opinions, Deleuze and Guattari foreground the work that a work of art (or literature) does, work that is aesthetic in nature and that is independent of the artist-creator and of the viewer or reader alike. What art does, they maintain, is to "preserve," and it is the "only thing in the world that is preserved" (*WP* 163). What art preserves is not a substance (with more or less longevity) but the "created," which is self-positing and preserved in itself: the work of art is an abstract machine with morphogenetic capabilities. What is preserved—"the thing or the work of art"—is not a monument in the sense of a testament, record, or memorial of something else, however, but, instead, "a bloc of sensations, that is to say, a compound of percepts and affects." In such a monument:

Percepts are no longer perceptions; they are independent of a state of those who experience them. Affects are no longer feelings or affections; they go beyond the strength of those who undergo them. Sensations, percepts, and affects are *beings* whose validity lies in themselves and exceeds any lived. (*WP* 164)

The major event of any great novel is thus not a particular narrative event, or a sequence of narrative events linked in a chain of cause and effect, but an aesthetic event, or a series of such events, that generates affects. The urgency and therewith the impact of great novels derives from the need for the creation of a tone or style, a language of sensation. Language, ordinary language, is no more and, in effect, no less than a mediator in the process of creation, a process that takes flight in a space of tightness, in close passages. Deleuze writes: "We have to see creation as tracing a path between impossibilities ... creation takes place in bottlenecks ... without a set of impossibilities, you won't have the line of flight, the exit that is creation ..."[10] It is precisely such an event, a line of flight emerging from within a set of impossibilities that are affective (rather than rational, calculable, semiotic, comprehensible) in nature, which forms the major event with which *The Member of the Wedding* opens, and which gives the novel its form as well as its title.

The occasion is the visit home of Frankie's brother Jarvis in the company of his fiancée Janice. Although Frankie had known that her brother, a corporal in the army stationed in Alaska, was getting married, she had, up till now, been thinking more about Alaska than about her brother or the wedding per se. Indeed, this was the "year when Frankie thought about the world. And she did not see it as a round school globe, with the countries neat and different-colored. She thought of the world as huge and cracked and loose and turning a thousand miles an hour" (*MW* 23). Thinking about the world makes her "sick and tired of being Frankie. She hated herself, and had become a loafer and a big no-good who hung around the summer kitchen: dirty and greedy and mean and sad" (*MW* 22). The whirlwind of becoming, being enfolded into an ever-widening span of forces, movement and affects that far extend beyond the constricting boundaries of the suffocating kitchen, that exceed the old familiarities of childhood, and that escape all mode of measurement and definition, entails that Frankie ends up with a "queer tightness in her chest," which lasts all summer, and which makes her feel to be trapped in fears of her looseness, worrying "who she was and what she was going to be in the world" (*MW* 32). Whereas the hugeness of these feelings scare her, the line of light that takes her out of her (former) self also promises a range of novel possibilities for being:

> She wanted to be a boy and go to the war as a Marine. She thought about flying aeroplanes and winning gold medals for bravery. She decided to donate blood to the Red Cross; she wanted to donate a quart a week and her blood would be in the veins of Australians and Fighting French and Chinese, all over the world, and it would be as though she were close kin to all of these people. (*MW* 23)

Her dreams—of traveling to South America, Hollywood, or New York City and of becoming the most famous radio reporter of all times—clearly do not meet the requirements of Southern womanhood and clash with the restrictions imposed from the outside: Frankie remains stuck in the endless summer heat and the constricting atmosphere of the kitchen—"The world seemed to die each afternoon and nothing moved any longer. At last the summer was like a green sick dream, or like a silent crazy jungle under glass"—until, "on the last Friday of August, all this was changed: it was so sudden that Frankie puzzled the whole blank afternoon, and still she did not understand" (*MW* 3). What has "happened," the "whole thing," is just as incomprehensible to her kitchen companions Berenice Sadie Brown and John Henry West as it is unnamable, inexpressible in ordinary language for Frankie herself:

> Frankie sat at the table with her eyes half closed, and she thought about a wedding. She saw a silent church, a strange snow slanting down against the colored windows. The groom in this wedding was her brother, and there was a brightness where his face should be. The bride was there in a long white train, and the bride also was faceless. There was something about this wedding that gave Frankie a feeling she could not name. (*MW* 4)

The inexpressible event is an event of experience, affective in nature, and thus beyond words, beyond individuality and identity (the bride and groom are both "faceless"), but not transcendent in the ordinary sense, for it is concrete, material, and singular, and it changes everything: a new cartography. Affect, we recall, is the body's way of preparing itself for action in a given circumstance by adding a quantitative dimension of intensity to the quality of an experience, an experience that cannot be fully captured in language: a feeling that we cannot name.

Whereas before her brother's visit, Frankie had "thought of the world, and it was fast and loose and turning" (*MW* 37), now, whenever the "gladness of the wedding rose up in her," she feels a "new unnameable connection" (*MW* 55). At the same time, when she thinks about her brother and the bride, there is a "tightness in her that would not break" (*MW* 21). It is this tightness, this "bottleneck," that allows her to become differently, to create a new affective assemblage, for which she finds (silent) expression in one of the novel's most memorable phrases: "A thought and explanation suddenly came to her, so that she almost said it aloud: *They are the we of me*" (*MW* 42). Just as Ahab's quest in *Moby-Dick* is a question of becoming-whale, so is Frankie's quest, in my approach, essentially a becoming-wedding. The fact that, on a narrative level, she is ultimately not allowed to accompany her brother and his bride into the world does nothing to detract from this. For Frankie's desire to become a member of her brother's wedding is not the ludicrous or desperate fantasy of an anxious tomboy who fears to be left out, who is stuck in confining and bewildering gender expectations, who cannot fulfill her dreams within the constricting sociocultural context of the postwar South. Instead, it is the actualization of a creative involution, a becoming: "The world seemed no longer separate from herself and … all at once she felt included" (MW 49).

Becomings, Deleuze writes with Guattari, are "neither dreams nor phantasies. They are perfectly real." This realness is neither a social/external nor a psychic/internal reality; the reality of becomings is immanent: "What is real is the becoming itself … Becoming produces nothing but itself." It "lacks a subject distinct from itself" and it has "no term, since its term in turn exists only as taken up in another becoming of which it is the subject, and which coexists, forms a block, with the first" (TP 238). Frankie's becoming-wedding is thus a specific reality, a creative involution, which involves her not as distinct subject but as a creature of affects, as an epiphenomenon.

As a literary creation, Frankie forms a queer textual configuration that affects us, as readers, as a "bloc of sensations." Her becoming-wedding takes the place of language as a semiotic system, a singular movement or energy that we *feel* rather than interpret. A liminal or boundary figure, the freakish tomboy at the heart of the novel does not represent a realistic portrait of a disturbed adolescent, whose irrational dreams come to a tragic ending. "A great novelist," Deleuze posits, is "above all an artist who invents unknown or unrecognized affects and brings them to light as the becoming of his characters" (WP 174). Frankie as becoming-wedding is an artistic creation by means of which possibilities for movement, for becoming, for lines of flight are opened up.

Frankie's dissolution into F. Jasmine and Frances in the novel's second and third parts and, ultimately, into a vaguely suggested future in which none of the "fixtures" of the long hot Summer continue to figure (the text almost casually reveals that John Henry develops meningitis and dies a horrible death, while Berenice Sadie Brown gallivants off with her beau) underlines the process of becoming to be a question of shifting intensities, a quantitative dimension that is added to the quality of an experience, a question of affect. "Artists," Deleuze continues, "are presenters of affects, the inventors and creators of affects. They do not only create them in their work, they give them to us and make us become with them, they draw us into the compound" (WP 175). This, I suggest in conclusion, is why Frankie's figure, especially in the first section of the novel, as well as several of McCullers' other freakish characters, continues to haunt us, to draw us in, to exact our critical and aesthetic involvement—and why they continue to affect us and do not leave us unchanged.

NOTES

1. renée c. hoogland, "The Arena of Sexuality: The Tomboy and Queer Studies," *Doing Gender in Media, Art, and Culture*, ed. Rosemarie Buikema & Iris van der Tuin (New York: Routledge, 2009) 99–114.
2. Ctd. in Josyane Savigneau, *Carson McCullers: A Life* (Boston: Houghton Mifflin, 2001).
3. Carson McCullers, *The Member Of The Wedding* (Boston: Houghton Mifflin Co., 2004) 3. Hereafter *MW*.
4. Gilles Deleuze, and Félix Guattari, *A Thousand Plateaus: Capitalism and Schizophrenia* (Minneapolis: University of Minnesota Press, 1987) 142. Hereafter *TP*.
5. Gilles Deleuze, *Difference And Repetition*, trans. Paul Patton. New York: Columbia University Press, 1994) 212. Hereafter *DR*.
6. Eric Shouse, "Feeling, Emotion, Affect," in *M/C Journal* 8.6 (2005). 17 May, 2014 <http://journal.media-culture.org.au/0512/03-shouse.php>.
7. Marcel Swiboda, "Becoming + Music," in *The Deleuze Dictionary*, ed. Adrian Parr (New York: Columbia University Press, 2005) 23.
8. Cliff Stagoll, "Becoming," in *The Deleuze Dictionary*, ed. Adrian Parr (New York: Columbia University Press, 2005) 22.
9. Gilles Deleuze, & Félix Guattari, *What Is Philosophy?*, trans. Hugh Tomlinson and Graham Burchell (New York: Columbia University Press, 1994) 110. Hereafter *WP*.
10. Gilles Deleuze, "Mediators," in *Negotiations: 1972–1990*, trans. Martin Joughin (New York: Columbia University Press, 1995) 133.

WORKS CITED

Deleuze, Gilles, & Félix Guattari. *What Is Philosophy?* Trans. Hugh Tomlinson and Graham Burchell. New York: Columbia University Press, 1994. Print.

——. *A Thousand Plateaus: Capitalism and Schizophrenia*. Trans. Brian Massumi. Minneapolis: University of Minnesota Press, 1987. Print.

Deleuze, Gilles. "Mediators." *Negotiations: 1972–1990*. Trans. Martin Joughin. New York: Columbia University Press, 1995. 121–34. Print.

——. *Difference And Repetition*. Trans. Paul Patton. New York: Columbia University Press, 1994. Print.

hoogland, renée c. "The Arena of Sexuality: The Tomboy and Queer Studies." *Doing Gender in Media, Art, and Culture*. Ed. Rosemarie Buikema & Iris van der Tuin. New York: Routledge, 2009. 99–114. Print.

McCullers, Carson. *The Member Of The Wedding*. Boston: Houghton Mifflin Co., 2004. Print.

Savigneau, Josyane. *Carson McCullers: A Life*. Boston: Houghton Mifflin, 2001. Print.

Shouse, Eric. "Feeling, Emotion, Affect." *M/C Journal* 8.6 (2005). <http://journal.media-culture.org.au/0512/03-shouse.php>. Accessed 09/13/2015. Web.

Stagoll, Cliff. "Becoming." *The Deleuze Dictionary*. Ed. Adrian Parr. New York: Columbia University Press, 2005. 21–23. Print.

Swiboda, Marcel. "Becoming + Music." *The Deleuze Dictionary*. Ed. Adrian Parr. New York: Columbia University Press, 2005. 23–24. Print.

"To be a Good Animal": Toward a Queer-Posthumanist Reading of *Reflections in a Golden Eye*

Temple Gowan

Carson McCullers' poem "Love and the Rind of Time" reflects on the material history of the planet and the relatively recent evolution of the human species, positing two questions: "Only a flicker of eternity divides us from unknowing beast/And how far are we from the fern, the rose, essential yeast?/Indeed in these light aeons how far/From animal to evening star?"[1] Though the poem references a traditional humanist binary—"us" and "unknowing beast"—it also acknowledges that "only a flicker" of evolutionary time separates humans from other sentient species. In fact, the lines above assert that what separates humans from plants or fungi is an infinitesimal difference and, most strikingly, wonder at the notion that animals, which, in the context of the poem, I take to include human beings, are made of the same matter, the same material substance, as the stars. The poem goes on to assert that in the entire cosmos, "Nothing lapses, no gene is lost." In the last stanza, the poem reflects on how, in the evolutionary process, the "struggling gene[s]" of seaweed "predestine" cells that become fish, that become nonhuman mammals, that become human beings; it thus foregrounds the transimmanence[2] of all matter and beings.

This poem is an example of McCullers' interrogation of the human, and her interest in thinking about not only species, but also materiality,

T. Gowan (✉)
Department of English, University of Mississippi, Oxford, MS, USA

© The Author(s) 2016
A. Graham-Bertolini, C. Kayser (Eds.), *Carson McCullers in the Twenty-First Century*, DOI 10.1007/978-3-319-40292-5_8

in terms of connection and continuum. "Love and the Rind of Time" provides an appropriate entry into understanding how McCullers' novel *Reflections in a Golden Eye* relates to posthumanisms, new materialisms, and animal studies—twenty-first century modes of critique that have turned away from the human and the discursive and toward the other-than-human and the material as their primary areas of focus. "Love and the Rind of Time" imagines corporeality as what Stacy Alaimo has termed "trans-corporeality"—"in which the human is always intermeshed with the more-than-human world." Trans-corporeality, she explains, "underlines the extent to which the substance of the human is ultimately inseparable from 'the environment'" (*Bodily* 2). Critical work that takes into account the other-than-human has become increasingly urgent as we recognize how the human/nonhuman binary has been deployed against members of our own species, as well as how fantasies about our own species have had destructive effects on other species and the planet.

Originally titled *Army Post*, *Reflections* is set on a military base in the South and portrays the convoluted relationships that play out on an army post during peacetime. Its main character, Captain Penderton, becomes obsessed with a young soldier, Private Williams, who in turn becomes obsessed with the Captain's saucy wife Leonora. Leonora herself is having an affair with the Captain's colleague, Major Langdon, who is married to the fragile and disturbed Alison, whose closest friend is her effeminate Filipino "houseboy" Anacleto. Though other critics have observed the presence of numerous nonhuman species in the novel, these readings are mostly anthropocentric. They assume that nonhuman animals in the text are merely symbols or substitutes and ultimately exist to serve human ends, while one of my goals is to take nonhuman animal agency seriously. Drawing from Foucault's analytics of power, I illuminate the ways that McCullers both subverts the discourse of speciesism and queers the human/nonhuman binary, specifically by challenging regimes of biopower.

In discussing queer aspects of McCullers' work, I am not concerned with how the author herself uses the term "queer." Rather, I agree with Rachel Adams that current usages of queer theory "not only allow for a more supple understanding of intimacy but also help to explain how McCullers' fiction resists the regimes of the normal that dominated American culture in her time" (556). *Reflections'* Captain Penderton is arguably the most clearly "queer" character in McCullers' fiction; that is, if we use the term "queer" primarily to denote same-sex object choice. The narrator explains that the Captain had "a sad penchant for becoming enamoured of his wife's lovers" (314). McCullers herself referred to him as "a homosexual" (*Mortgaged* 276). The term "homosexual," however, suggests a fixed identity category that does not adequately reverberate with the wide range of erotic couplings and practices that abound in the novel. Adding the lens of "posthumanist" to a queer reading of *Reflections* foregrounds the important presence of materiality and both human and nonhuman bodies in the novel. As Michael O'Rourke explains, queering the non/human "means that we open ourselves to the sense of the world," that we become "singular plural, not substantial, settled, or stable subjects, but singular beings in a relational regime independent of identitarianism or anthropomorphism. Our transimmanence, or allness, a being-with towards others, all others, brings about new modes of sociability" (xviii). Looking at *Reflections* from not only a queer, but a queer-posthumanist perspective, provides an even greater opportunity for openness.

When McCullers was only a senior in high school, she was stricken with rheumatic fever, an illness that probably contributed to her lifelong struggle with poor health and bouts of mandatory bed rest (Carr 568). She completed *Reflections* in just two months, soon after she had been confined to bed again after physically exhausting herself writing her first novel *The Heart Is a Lonely Hunter* (570). McCullers' struggles with illness must have made her acutely aware of her own body, its limitations and longings, its potentials for pleasures and pains, and her experience as the wife of a soldier must have made her intimately familiar with the disciplinary practices that an institution such as the military imposes on bodies.[3] In paying attention to corporeality in *Reflections*, I join other scholars such as Adams and Sarah Gleeson-White who are concerned with McCullers' deviant bodies or "freaks," but I add to this work a specific attention to biopower, a critique that both seems especially pertinent for a novel set on an army base and that opens up the text to posthumanist potentials.

In *Discipline and Punish*, Foucault argues that discipline produces "docile bodies," bodies that are subjected and practiced. He explains the dual function of discipline as such:

> Discipline increases the forces of the body (in economic terms of utility) and diminishes these same forces (in political terms of obedience). In short, it dissociates power from the body; on the one hand, it turns it into an 'aptitude,' a 'capacity,' which it seeks to increase; on the other hand, it reverses the course of the energy, the power that might result from it, and turns it into a relation of strict subjection. (138)

In Foucault's analytic of power, discipline takes hold of bodies by controlling their energies—by regulating the movements they exercise. This is particularly clear in settings such as factories, schools, and military bases, where the repetition of specific bodily acts is the mechanism by which power functions. He identifies four techniques of discipline: It sometimes requires *enclosure*, "a protected place of disciplinary monotony" that is different from all others and closed in on itself (141). Disciplinary space is divided into sections and thus relies on *partitioning* (143). It requires *functional sites*, or usable space (143). And finally, its units, which exist in the form of individual bodies, are organized by *rank* (145).

While the opening lines of *Reflections* claim to reveal little to nothing of the novel's plot, they accurately demonstrate Foucault's analysis of how a disciplinary system like the military functions, a point on which the remainder of the novel's plot turns: "An army post in peacetime is a dull place. Things happen, but then they happen over and over again. The general plan of a fort in itself adds to the monotony—the huge concrete barracks, the neat rows of officers' homes built one precisely like the other, the gym, the chapel, the golf course and the swimming pools— all is designed according to a certain rigid pattern" (309). McCullers' description of the army base highlights its monotony and insularity, its partitioning of usable space. Especially interesting is the mention of spaces that are meant for recreation—even these cannot exist outside of the disciplinary organization of space and, thus, seem incapable of fulfilling their promise of pleasure, opening a gap or, rather, presenting a question of where, when, and how pleasures might be experienced. I emphasize the question of *pleasures* because, while Foucault's perspective on the potential for resistance to power in *Discipline and Punish* has been regarded as quite bleak, he later contends in the first volume of *The History of Sexuality*, "The rallying point for the counterattack against the deployment of sexuality ought not to be sex-desire, but bodies and pleasures" (157). "Bodies and pleasures" are key to McCullers' queer-posthumanist resistance to the normalizing effects of biopower, a point to which I will return.

Foucault's fourth technique of discipline, rank, is crucial to my reading of *Reflections*. Early in the novel, the narrator lists the "participants" of the tragedy as "two officers, a soldier, two women, a Filipino, and a horse" (309). As Robert K. Martin points out, "The sequence can hardly be accidental: first the White men, by rank; then the women, unranked; then the 'Oriental,' sex not indicated; then the horse. The men are situated by their military ranks, the women by their gender; the Filipino has neither rank nor gender" (2). Rank, however, is not fixed; it exists only within a network of relations. Foucault observes that discipline itself is an "art of rank, a technique for the transformation of arrangements" (*Discipline* 146). Counterintuitively, the "difference" of rank is achieved through perceived sameness—the individual who is most like the one "above" him will rise in rank—a point that the narrator of *Reflections* reiterates by explaining that part of the "dullness" of life on an army base can be attributed to the fact that "once a man enters the army he is expected only to follow the heels ahead of him" (309). In other words, the "art of rank" is based on norms, whether they function as genders, sexualities, races, bodies, or species.

In a telling conversation with the Captain, Major Langdon, undoubtedly the most normatively masculine character in the novel, expresses how he believes military discipline functions when he imagines if Anacleto, rather than "dancing around to music and messing with water-colors," had joined the army: "Anacleto wouldn't have been happy in the army, no, but it might have *made a man of him*. Would have *knocked all the nonsense out of him* anyway ... In the army they would have run him ragged and he would have been miserable, but even that seems to me better than *the other*" (384, emphasis added). Thus, at least one of the goals of the military's regulatory power is normative gender expression, which it achieves at least in part through the perpetual threat of physical violence to the body. Further, achieving that goal is more important than being happy, or, to put it another way, being queer is worse than being unhappy.

Later, the Major shares with Captain Penderton his philosophy of "the good life": "Only two things matter to me now—to be a good animal and to serve my country. A healthy body and patriotism" (386). Assuming that "good animal" and "healthy body" are meant to relate as do the concepts of "serving one's country" and "patriotism," Major Langdon's "favorite aphorism" demonstrates a major concern of posthumanist thought, that human beings *are* animals *with* bodies. As Cary Wolfe points out, far from suggesting a period "after" the human, posthumanist perspectives require that we "attend to that thing called 'the human' with greater specificity, greater attention to its embodiment, embeddedness, and materiality" (*What* 120). In other words, we can no longer set "the human" wholly apart from other species based on concepts such as "mind" or "reason," *especially* if we understand one condition of modernity to be that subjects are governed at the level of the *body*.

The new relevance of corporeality in biopolitical thought, as Sherryl Vint puts it, "forces us to confront our continuity with other animals" (444).[4] Though Foucault does not discuss how biopower functions in relation to nonhuman animals, scholars of critical animal studies have applied his analytics of power to humans' relationships to our fellow species. Chloë Taylor points out that biopower, as regulatory and disciplinary, is not mutually exclusive with Foucault's concept of sovereign power, or the right to kill. Taylor reminds us that this relation of power is typically invisible, because as Foucault points out, sovereign power, which originates with overt war or violence, "continues in the guise of politics and through the exercise of a law that becomes naturalized" (541). Though some laws exist to regulate our relations with nonhuman animals—those that prevent "unnecessary" cruelty or prohibit hunting in certain situations, for example—most of our encounters with other species occur when those animals appear on our *plates*. Meat is a symbol of our sovereign power over other animals, and in modern industrialized societies, it is the point at which humans' "right to kill" other animals is most invisible.[5] Sovereign power, which is actually a self-appointed right, is naturalized through myths of origin and/or difference. We use the concept of difference, along with its counterpart, sameness, to govern our relations with various nonhuman species—whether it is ethical to domesticate them, to confine them to zoos or labs, to save them, or to kill them.

McCullers links the concepts of "rank" and "species" in *Reflections* when the narrative describes the Captain's disdain for unranked men: "He looked on all soldiers with bored contempt. To him officers and men might belong to the same biological genus, but they were of an altogether different species" (314). Later in the text, Private Williams' disregard for ranked men is described in similar terms: "To this young Southern soldier the officers were in the same vague category as negroes— they had a place in his life, but he did not look on them as being human" (390). These examples demonstrate what scholars of critical animal studies have come to call the "institution of speciesism". As Cary Wolfe, drawing from Derrida, explains, the institution of speciesism "relies on the tacit agreement that the full transcendence of the 'human' requires the sacrifice of the 'animal' and the animalistic, which in turn makes possible a symbolic economy in which we can engage in what Derrida will call a 'noncriminal putting to death' of other *humans* as well by marking *them* as animal" (6). In Foucauldian terms, the institution of speciesism is sovereign power become "natural law," governed by regulatory practices of discipline in the form of species difference.

By revealing both the Captain and the Private's attitudes toward their social others, framed in the language of both rank and species, McCullers denaturalizes the supposed hierarchy of both. The similarity of both men's perspectives is unexpected. While it seems typical that the Captain would think of himself as superior to other enlisted men based on the hierarchy of rank, it is rather surprising that the Private would view his superiors in an almost identical fashion. It reveals precisely the problematic consequence of the naturalization of the institution of speciesism that Derrida warns against: As long as violence toward, or the killing of, nonhuman animals based solely on their species remains acceptable, there is always the possibility that the discourse of speciesism will be used to mark *any* social other. Disturbingly, in fact, we eventually learn that in his past, Private Williams murdered a black man in an argument over a wheelbarrow of manure, hid the body, and never thought of himself as a murderer (369).

Turning again to the participants of *Reflections'* tragedy, while the horse, Firebird, is listed last, presumably occupying the very bottom of the hierarchy because he is not "even" human, he nevertheless plays a significant role. A number of critics have paid attention to Firebird's part. For example, Melissa Free constructs an interesting reading of queer birds in the text, citing Lillian Faderman's extensive history of twentieth-century American lesbian life. According to Faderman, "queer bird" was a term popular in the 1930s that was used to refer to lesbians (106). The Major refers to Anacleto as a "rare bird" (333), and the novel's title—*Reflections in a Golden Eye*—refers to a vision of a peacock seen by Anacleto and the Captain, the text's queer male characters. Free points out that the name "Firebird" is constructed with two words that suggest "passion" (fire) and "queer" (bird); therefore, she suggests that Firebird is a substitute for the Private and argues that the Captain's eventual violence toward the horse is "an attempt to destroy desires that are specifically queer" (434). Sarah Gleeson-White similarly asserts that Firebird is a "substitute for more orthodox channels of desire for Penderton" (54), reducing the Captain's experience with the horse to an example of autoeroticism, which ultimately erases the body of the nonhuman.

Much more than a mere symbol or substitute, Firebird is a full character, and McCullers gives him a degree of agency that exceeds that of some of the novel's human characters. The narrative positions Leonora Penderton and her beloved horse Firebird as a young married couple.

The narrator refers to him as "a young husband" and to Leonora as his "beloved and termagant wife" (322). Early in their relationship, when the horse was "ill-trained," the pair struggled for dominance, resulting twice in Leonora being thrown and biting through her bottom lip, leaving blood on her clothing for all the men to see.[6] The sign of Leonora's blood is especially significant in light of the narrator's earlier note that the Captain had been unable to take her virginity on their wedding night, a point that further suggests Firebird's role as "lover."[7]

Despite their earlier struggles, the horse is now "perfectly trained" by his mistress. Fascinatingly, however, the two continue to *act out* their prior skirmishes because it gives them *both* pleasure: "During this struggle between horse and rider, Mrs. Penderton laughed aloud and spoke to Firebird in a voice that was vibrant with passion and excitement: 'You sweet old bastard, you!'" (322). Their erotically charged performance "had a theatrical, affected air—it was a jocular pantomime performed for their own amusement and the benefit of spectators. Even when the froth showed on his mouth, the horse moved with a certain fractious grace *as though aware of being watched*" (322, my emphasis). In this scene, Firebird, though he is perfectly trained, docile, and under the command of his mistress, *chooses* to perform this daily "mock rebellion" that both he and Leonora understand to be a game, a form of play.

In her work on "queer canine literature," Alice Kuzniar asserts that pleasures shared between humans and their pets have the potential to disrupt normative sexual identity categories because these relationships may "redefine where intimacy, even eroticism can lie, and articulate a desire for a different passion, intensity, and tactile knowledge" (206). If asked for an example of "role-play," we might think of an activity that occurs between a therapist and patient, or we may suggest the example of erotic role-play, an activity that occurs between human sexual partners. Most people who have ever had a canine companion will know that in a game of fetch, a dog might pretend that she doesn't *want* to have the object of play taken away, but in fact, this is a mock rebellion. She wants the game to continue; the feigned struggle is a part of the role-play. All of these instances of play, whether they occur between humans or between human and nonhuman, as with Leonora and Firebird, are examples of intimate, though not necessarily sexual, relations. This kind of interaction between the human and nonhuman has queer potentiality. According to Kuzniar, it "transcends the constrictions that gender and sexuality place upon the human body ... not in the banal sense that it offers different forms of genital stimulation";

rather, pleasure shared between human and nonhuman animals "opens up the subject in unique ways that, *precisely because independent of gender and sexuality*, are liberating" (208, emphasis added). Leonora and Firebird's play offers a way to begin to understand McCullers' queer-posthumanist resistance to power, which culminates in Captain Penderton's own experience with Firebird.

As mentioned, the narrative's most straightforward explanation of the Captain's queer desire is that he had a habit of "becoming enamoured with his wife's lovers." This is true of his friend Major Langdon, with whom Leonora has been carrying on a prolonged affair.[8] Since Firebird is figured as one of Leonora's lovers, the text presents two triangulations: Leonora/Langdon/Penderton and Leonora/Firebird/Penderton. Further, the Captain undoubtedly associates his wife's horse with the object of his obsession, Private Williams. The Captain is not a skilled rider, a well-known fact at the stables, and the soldiers call him "Captain Flap-Fanny" behind his back (323). Therefore, his decision to take Firebird out after having suffered over his desire for the Private for some time is a pointed one, whether his motivation is to display his dominance over his wife's beloved horse or to somehow get closer to the Private.

When the Captain mounts Firebird, he expects the horse to rebel as he does on his daily morning rides with Leonora, and he is relieved when the horse seems docile and amenable to his command. Though the Captain takes this as a sign that he is in control, the reader already knows that Firebird is likely performing. At the beginning of their ride, the Captain allows Firebird to gallop as he pleases: "The horse, which had not been exercised that day, seemed to go a little mad from the pleasure of galloping with unchecked freedom" (352). Then suddenly, "with no preliminary tightening of the reigns, the Captain jerked the horse up short" so that "Firebird lost his balance, sidestepped awkwardly and reared" (352). This sadistic procedure, which he repeats twice, "was not new to the Captain. Often in his life he had exacted many strange and secret little penances on himself which he would have found difficult to explain to others" (352). It seems fairly clear that the "strange and secret little penances" that the Captain enacts on himself are sexual, specifically, masturbatory, and he sadistically attempts to reenact these on Firebird.

Initially, the Captain is "exceedingly satisfied" with his game, but he fails to take into account Firebird's own agency. When this becomes clear, the Captain is rightly terrified:

The third time the horse stopped as usual, but at this point something happened which disturbed the Captain so that all of his satisfaction instantly vanished. As they were standing still, alone on the path, the horse slowly turned his head and looked into the Captain's face. Then deliberately he lowered his head to the ground with his ears flattened back. The Captain felt suddenly that he was to be thrown, and not only thrown but killed. (352)

In this second moment of nonverbal communication between nonhuman and human, the Captain panics and braces himself for what is to come, yet, once again, Firebird's actions are deliberate—he delays his rebellion to catch his rider off-guard. After waiting until they reach a steep cliff, the horse abandons the trail and plunges down "with the speed of a demon" (353). As the Captain clings desperately to Firebird's mane, resting his head along the horse's neck, he whispers to himself, "I am lost." The Captain "saw suddenly as he had never seen before. The world was a kaleidoscope" (354). Through the dizzying speed of his movement on the horse, the Captain sees anew the stuff of the world in impossible detail—a tiny flower half-buried in leaves, a pinecone, a bird in the sky, an individual shaft of sunlight.

The Captain becomes aware of his own body as a part of the body of the world: "He was conscious of the pure keen air and he felt the marvel of his own tense body, his laboring heart, and the miracle of blood, muscle, nerves, and bone … he had soared to that rare level of consciousness where the mystic feels that the earth is he and that he is the earth" (354). McCullers' prose here is reminiscent of the concluding question posed by "Love and the Rind of Time": "From weed to dinosaur through the peripheries of stars/From furtherest star imperiled on the rind of time, / How long to core of love in human mind?" In this moment of surrendering selfhood, of abandoning his own subjectivity, the Captain experiences a bliss that he has never known: "And having given up life, the Captain suddenly began to live. A great mad joy surged through him" (354). The joy that the Captain experiences is predicated upon, on one level, relinquishing control, a new experience for the Captain, who has never allowed himself to experience pleasure without self-punishment and, more specifically, who has never been allowed to do so by the disciplinary structures in his life.

The Captain's joy also stems from his "giving up life," his loss of selfhood. Gleeson-White's interpretation of the scene between the Captain and Firebird is that it speaks to the "transformative promise" of "alternative pleasures" (52). She adds, "In creating *metaphoric relations* between the self and an other, the homoerotic body of McCullers' texts swells beyond its limits in a shattering of the self" (58, emphasis added). I agree with Gleeson-White's conclusion; however, the relation that McCullers creates in this case is hardly "metaphoric." Rather, it is the specific relation between man and horse, between human and nonhuman, and it is notably Firebird's own agency that serves as the catalyst for the Captain's transformative experience. As mentioned, the question of the Captain's "desire" for Firebird is irrelevant, for the very *escape* from desire is what makes this scene an example of radical resistance to power. If what the Captain experienced for a moment during his ride with Firebird was, in Gleeson-White's phrase, a "shattering of the self," that shattering must be rooted in his perception of himself as the very stuff of the world. It is not merely the "self" constituted by discourse, but his corporeality—"the miracle of blood, muscle, nerves, and bone"—as co-constituted by the world. The Captain's joy is ultimately predicated upon his glimpse of what I have referred to as both transimmanence and transcorporeality. It is a queer-posthumanist loss of selfhood.

The concepts of transimmanence or trans-corporeality, which McCullers explores in "Love in the Rind of Time" and that resurface in *Reflections*, have important ethical and political consequences, for, as Cecilia Åsberg points out, they are ultimately about "power relations, about who gets to live and who gets to die" (10). McCullers imagines a utopian moment for the Captain, a moment of resistance and liberation, but it is ultimately fleeting. He viciously beats Firebird as soon as the horse comes to a halt. Tellingly, this sadistic behavior toward nonhuman animals does not originate with that moment. Earlier in the novel, the narrator recounts an incident in which the Captain, feeling "restless"—code for his queer desire—happened upon a kitten on a freezing night and shoved it into a mailbox to die (315). By portraying this pattern of violence toward nonhuman animals that manifests when the Captain is faced with his own queer desire, McCullers foregrounds the insidious nature of disciplinary structures that are grounded in species difference and links the oppression of the nonhuman to the oppression of the queer. With his feet back on the ground, the Captain beats Firebird in an attempt to reinstate the condition of sovereign power of the human over the nonhuman, of normative over queer, an ordering that, despite the Captain's fleeting moment of joy, makes sense of his world.

Before concluding, I would like to add one more point about the role of the nonhuman animal gaze in *Reflections*. As its title suggests, seeing, looking, and watching play an important role in the narrative. Before his fateful ride with Firebird, the Captain "looked into the horse's round, purple eyes and saw there a liquid image of his own frightened face" (351). Referring to the power of the animal gaze, trainer and philosopher Vicki Hearne states that "the horse cannot escape knowledge of a certain sort of the rider ... and the rider cannot escape knowing that the horse knows the rider in ways the rider cannot fathom" (109). Relatedly, Stanley Cavell asserts that "The horse ... is a rebuke to our unreadiness to be understood, our will to remain obscure" (qtd. in Wolfe 5). And finally, Wolfe asserts that the traditional humanist subject "finds the animal others' knowing us in ways *we* cannot know and master *simply unnerving*" (4). In other words, the animal gaze exposes us to alternative ways of knowing. We see ourselves in the gaze of the nonhuman animal Other, but this is not the "self" that we have imagined. Rather, it is a reflection of both difference *and* sameness that we are unable to confront.

In his now-famous account of being gazed upon, naked, by his own pet cat in *The Animal That Therefore I Am*, Derrida states:

> As with every bottomless gaze, as with the eyes of the other, the gaze called "animal" offers to my sight the abysmal limit of the human: the inhuman or the ahuman, the ends of man, that is to say, the bordercrossing from which vantage man dares to announce himself to himself, thereby calling himself by the name that he believes his gives himself. (12)

Thus, when Derrida asserts, "The animal looks at me, and I am naked before it. Thinking perhaps begins there" (5), "nakedness" refers to both the cultural standard of feeling shame at one's own nudity *and* with the stripping away of difference in which our own self-definition as *human* is rooted. When the Captain looks into Firebird's eyes, he is confronted with a kind of queer self-knowledge. Not only is he faced with his own nonnormative and culturally maligned desires, he is forced to confront his subjectivity stripped of the normalizing terms of rank, gender, sexuality, and species. The Captain's recognition of both unfathomable difference and radical sameness with the nonhuman Other recalls the wonder expressed in "Love and the Rind of Time" at the notion that "Only a flicker of eternity divides us from unknowing beast."

McCullers' very portrayal of Firebird as a character with agency—that he actively engages in a shared dramatic performance with Leonora, that he is aware of being observed by an audience, and that he derives pleasure from this as well as from the repetition of the act itself—is notable in and of itself. Even more striking, however, is the queer-posthumanist potentiality of human and nonhuman relations in the novel. It is pertinent to recall Foucault's insistence that bodies and pleasures, not desire or object-choice, offer the *only* real challenge to discourses of normalization. Ladelle McWhorter reminds us that, according to Foucault, sex was invented, and thus, "There is no naturally existing single thing that every instance of the word *sex* actually names. Once it emerges as an epistemic object, sex can be used to explain all kinds of things about people's behavior. Eventually, it becomes the explanatory principle par excellence, used to explain virtually everything about most of us" (124). Individuals who are deemed sexually deviant are, of course, particularly at the mercy of the disciplines. Desires, then, even in the plural, can always be used in disciplinary regimes to create and control subjects. Pleasures, on the other hand, are productive and can therefore resist normalizing discourses. In *Reflections*, such pleasures manifest as queer-posthumanist experiences shared by human and nonhuman, which produce new spaces for unexpected experiences that defy conventional or expected categorization, if only for a moment.

NOTES

1. Printed in *The Mortgaged Heart*, p. 290–1.
2. I take the term "transimmanence" from O'Rourke's paraphrase in "The Open" of Jean-Luc Nancy's philosophy.
3. Although the term "the body" may sometimes seem to flow more efficiently and is the term Foucault himself often uses, I will attempt to avoid it because I feel that it implies an abstraction, when what I mean to emphasize is actually the *particularity* of individual bodies, human, or otherwise.
4. Similarly, in *What Is Posthumanism?* Wolfe asserts, "For biopolitical theory, the animality of the human becomes a central problem—perhaps *the* central problem—to be produced, controlled, or regulated for politics in its distinctly modern form" (100).
5. Carol Adams explains that animals become "absent referents" through meat eating: "Animals' lives precede and enable the existence of meat. If animals are alive they cannot be meat. Thus a dead body replaces the live animal. Without animals there would be no meat eating, yet they are absent [invisible] from the act of eating meat because they have been transformed into food" (51).

6. "Twice Mrs. Penderton was badly thrown, and once when she returned from her ride the soldiers saw that she had bitten her lower lip quite through so that there was blood on her sweater and shirt" (322).

7. "When she married the Captain she had been a virgin. Four nights after her wedding, she was still a virgin, and on the fifth night her status was changed only enough to leave her somewhat puzzled" (322).

8. "And although the affair between his wife and Major Langdon had been a torment to him, he could not think of any likely change without dread. Indeed his torment had been a rather special one, as he was just as jealous of his wife as he was of her lover. In the last year he had come to feel an emotional regard for the Major that was the nearest thing to love that he had ever known" (327).

WORKS CITED

Adams, Carol J. *The Sexual Politics of Meat: A Feminist-Vegetarian Critical Theory.* New York: Continuum, 2006. Print.

Adams, Rachel. "'A Mixture of Delicious and Freak': The Queer Fiction of Carson McCullers." *American Literature* 71.3 (1999): 551–83. Print.

Alaimo, Stacy. *Bodily Natures: Science, Environment, and the Material Self.* Bloomington: Indiana UP, 2010. Print.

——. "Thinking as the Stuff of the World." *O-Zone: A Journal of Object-Oriented Studies* 1.1 (2014): 13–21. Print.

Åsberg, Cecilia. "The Timely Ethics of Posthumanist Gender Studies." *Feministische Studien* 31.1 (2013): 7–12. *SocINDEX with Full Text.* Web. 14 Sept. 2015.

Carr, Virginia Spencer. *The Lonely Hunter: A Biography of Carson McCullers.* New York: Doubleday, 1975. Print.

Derrida, Jacques. *The Animal That Therefore I Am.* Trans. David Wills. Ed. Marie-Louise Mallet. New York: Fordham UP, 2008. Print.

Faderman, Lillian. *Odd Girls and Twilight Lovers: A History of Lesbian Life in Twentieth-Century America.* New York: Penguin Books, 1991. Print.

Foucault, Michel. *Discipline and Punish: The Birth of the Prison.* 1975. Trans. Alan Sheridan. New York: Vintage Books, 1995. Print.

——. *The History of Sexuality. Vol. I: An Introduction.* 1978. New York: Vintage Books, 1990. Print.

Free, Melissa. "Relegation And Rebellion: The Queer, the Grotesque, and the Silent in the Fiction of Carson McCullers." *Studies In The Novel* 40.4 (2008): 426–446. *Literary Reference Center.* 4 Nov. 2013. Web.

Gleeson-White, Susan. *Strange Bodies: Gender and Identity in the Novels of Carson McCullers.* Tuscaloosa: U of Alabama P, 2003. Print.

Kuzniar, Alice. "'I Married My Dog': On Queer Canine Literature." *Queering the Non/Human*. Eds. Noreen Giffney and Myra J. Hird. Burlington: Ashgate, 2008. 205–226. Print.

Martin, Robert K. "Gender, Race, and the Colonial Body: Carson McCullers' Filipino Boy, and David Henry Hwang's Chinese Woman." *Canadian Review of American Studies* 23.1 (1992): 95. Humanities International Complete. Web. 14 Sept. 2015.

McCullers, Carson. *The Mortgaged Heart*. London: Penguin, 1975. Print.

——. *Reflections in a Golden Eye*. 1941. *Complete Novels*. New York: Literary Classics of the United States, 2001: 309–93. Print.

McWhorter, Ladelle. *Bodies and Pleasures: Foucault and the Politics of Sexual Normalization*. Bloomington: Indiana UP, 1999. Print.

O'Rourke, Michael. "The Open." *Queering the Non/Human*. Eds. Noreen Giffney and Myra J. Hird. Burlington: Ashgate, 2008. xvii–xxi. Print.

Taylor, Chloë. "Foucault and Critical Animal Studies: Genealogies of Agricultural Power." *Philosophy Compass* 8.6 (2013): 539–51. EBSCO. Web. 15 Sept. 2015.

Vint, Sherryl. "Animal Studies in the Era of Biopower." *Science Fiction Studies* 37.3 (2010): 444–55. JSTOR. Web. 16 Sept. 2015.

Wolfe, Cary. *Animal Rites: American Culture, the Discourse of Species, and Posthumanist Theory*. Chicago: U of Chicago P, 2003. Print.

——. *What Is Posthumanism?* Minneapolis: U of Minnesota P, 2010. Print.

Coming of Age in the Queer South: Friendship and Social Difference in *The Heart Is a Lonely Hunter*

Kristen Proehl

In 1946, shortly after the publication of *The Member of the Wedding*, a coming-of-age novella featuring an unruly, twelve-year-old tomboy protagonist in Jim Crow Georgia, Carson McCullers was invited by Tennessee Williams, the now-iconic Southern playwright, to spend the summer at his house in Nantucket, Massachusetts, along with his domestic partner, Pancho Rodriguez. Williams had not met McCullers but greatly admired *The Member of the Wedding* and offered to help her adapt it for the stage. Many of McCullers' contemporaries found her to be a rather exhausting friend: playwright Lillian Hellman, for instance, claimed, "Carson burdened everyone who got close to her. If you wanted burdens, liked burdens, you accepted Carson and her affection" (Qtd in Carr 374). But Williams, for his part, took an almost immediate liking to her: "The minute I met her," he said, "she seemed like one of my oldest and best friends" (qtd. in Lahr 206). McCullers quickly reciprocated the affection and later referred to this period in her life as a "magnificent" summer of "sun and friendship" (*Illumination* 24).

The two friends worked at opposite ends of a long table for most of the summer as she adapted her book for the stage and he finished his play, *Summer and Smoke* (Lahr 108). McCullers described him as a "true collabo-

K. Proehl (✉)
SUNY-Brockport, Brockport, NY, USA

© The Author(s) 2016
A. Graham-Bertolini, C. Kayser (Eds.), *Carson McCullers in the Twenty-First Century*, DOI 10.1007/978-3-319-40292-5_9

143

rator," and he noted that she was the only person he could stand to work in the same room with (108). In the afternoons, they would often go swimming and return home to eat her special potato recipe, Spuds Carson (Carr 273). She brought flowers into the house daily and in the evenings played Bach, Schubert, and other favorite composers (274). Initially, Pancho appreciated McCullers' domestic attention (273–4). The emotional and intellectual intimacy of Williams and McCullers' friendship, however, eventually generated tensions in Williams' already tempestuous relationship with Pancho, who at one point grew so jealous that he packed a trunk of belongings and threatened to leave for Mexico (Lahr 109). Williams said that McCullers seemed oblivious that their friendship was the source of romantic conflict (109). Domestic tensions aside, the summer proved a creatively generative one for both authors and likely influenced McCullers' renderings of queer friendship in her play version of *The Member of the Wedding*.

When McCullers' adaptation of *The Member of the Wedding* opened several years later at the Empire Theater in New York City, it was a Broadway hit and, in many ways, the height of her professional career. Her friendship with Williams continued for many years and generated a rich correspondence. Their highly affectionate letters reveal a remarkable openness about their personal lives: Williams shares intimate details about his relationship with Pancho; McCullers shares information about her turmoiled relationship with her husband Reeves, including details of their polyamorous relationship and love triangle with another man, as well as her own affairs with and attractions to women. They also traded gossip about other writers, such as Truman Capote, and occasionally discussed social issues.[1]

McCullers' intimate friendship and correspondence with Williams was one of many such relationships that she maintained throughout her life, particularly with gay men. One of the most important of which was her friendship with Jordan Massee, a distant cousin, and his partner, Paul Bigelow, both of whom were also friends with Williams. In the early twentieth century, Massee's wealthy family was, some might argue, the literary hub of Macon, Georgia, as they often hosted sophisticated parties for well-known authors (Hutton ix). As McCullers' biographer Virginia Carr notes, McCullers' relationship with Massee was arguably one of the most loyal and constant of her life (163). But she met Massee, like Williams, long after her writing career was underway. Therefore, I am not so much interested in the influence of these queer friendships upon her writing, but rather in the ways in which these relationships are anticipated by the non-normative models of friendship that proliferate in her novels and, in particular, in *The Heart Is a Lonely Hunter*. McCullers' portrayals of friendships between gender non-conforming or queer adolescents and children have long been a source of critical interest. Literary scholars such as Gary Richards, Rachel Adams, Patricia Yaeger, Michelle Abate, and others have focused especially upon the friendship between the tomboy protagonist of *The Member of the Wedding*, Frankie Addams, and her queer cousin, John Henry West, which is a type of relationship that Abate refers to as the tomboy/sissy dyad (xvii). There are numerous other similar pairings throughout American literature, such as Scout Finch and Dill Harris of *To Kill a Mockingbird* or Jo March and Laurie Laurence of *Little Women*. Scholars have called attention to the ways in which tomboys and sissy figures discipline one another to conform to gender norms.[2] As I have argued elsewhere, queer children in these relationships seem to recognize something of themselves in one another and, in so doing, form a sympathetic bond (Proehl 128). Intimate yet volatile, these relationships destabilize the boundaries of romantic and platonic love, challenge institutions of heterosexuality, and ask us to reconsider the very nature of friendship itself (128). In McCullers' fiction, friendship often has the intimacy, emotional turbulence, and imbalanced power dynamics that we have come to associate, albeit stereotypically, with romantic relationships. As McCullers portrays Frankie's and Mick's identifications with male characters who transgress gender norms—including gender nonconforming boys, such as Bubber and John Henry, and queer men, such as Singer—she signals the tomboy figure's potential queer sexuality in adulthood. In both *The Member of the Wedding* and *The Heart Is a Lonely Hunter*, queer friendship is a vehicle through which McCullers suggests a relationship between gender nonconformity in childhood and adult homosexuality.

In 1940, at the age of twenty-three, McCullers garnered the attention of the American reading public with the publication of her first novel, *The Heart Is a Lonely Hunter*. The text's opening scenes feature Mick Kelly, whom another character describes as a "gangling, towheaded youngster [who] looks like a boy" (18). Like Frankie Addams, Mick forms a close friendship with a younger, gender-bending relative, her brother, Bubber, who is called a "sissy" by the other children when he expresses his desire for a "real pretty" costume with colors like a "butterfly" (166). In contrast to *The Member of the Wedding*, however, the dynamics of this dyad remain largely on the periphery of the novel's plot. But queer friendship—and, a more expansive vision of it, at that—remains central to *The Heart Is a Lonely Hunter*. The novel focuses primarily on Singer and Antonapoulos' relationship and Mick's friendship with Singer. Numerous other forms of queer friendship appear throughout the novel, however, particularly in other characters' relationships with Singer. McCullers not only speaks to the ways in which friendship often serves as a guise for romantic relationships but also to the "queer potential" of all friendships.[3] As I will show later on, McCullers' portrayal of the queer possibility of friendship includes relationships that transgress gender and sexual norms, as well as ones that bridge differences in race, age, and disability. She also explores how same-sex and cross-gender friendships have the potential to acquire some of the traits and characteristics that are more commonly associated with romantic relationships. Her expansive use of the term queer, which includes relationships that are non-normative in ways that extend beyond sexuality, anticipates the rise of queer theory. Her specific interest in the relationship between friendship and queerness anticipates the groundbreaking scholarship of Michel Foucault and Lillian Faderman, as well as more recent studies of queer friendship across the disciplines such as those of John S. Garrison, Tom Roach, Anna Muraco, and others.

Ivy Schweitzer notes that since the classical era, friendship has been idealized as a private, sympathetic exchange between two individuals who not only share similar values and ideas but also a sense of equality (28). Prior to the nineteenth century, friendship was at times even classified as the most "important and ennobling" forms of human relationships but has since been persistently and progressively devalued in favor of familial and romantic bonds (9). As a site of sympathetic attachment, Schweitzer notes, friendship has been "increasingly feminized, privatized, and removed from the public sphere of democratic politics" (10). In recent years, prominent literary critics and philosophers have endeavored to expose the political nature of friendship. Jacques Derrida's *The Politics of Friendship* argues that friendship is never outside of the realm of politics and is in fact vital to structures of democracy and political community. Foucault, Carroll Smith-Rosenberg, Schweitzer, and others have revealed how friendship may disrupt binary understandings of gender and sexuality, as well as social hierarchies of race, gender, and class. In his oft-cited interview, "Friendship as a Way of Life" (1981), Foucault argued for the potentially subversive nature of queer friendship when he emphasized its centrality to the future of queer politics.

Given that friendship and identity development are two of the most persistent themes in adolescent literature, it is perhaps unsurprising that this genre features a proliferation of queer friendships. Situated at the margins of childhood and adulthood, adolescence is a liminal developmental period; authors, therefore, often turn to adolescence to explore the experiences of marginalized individuals and groups. Adolescence is also a period that is marked with intense identification with others, as young adults search for models, both within and beyond the home, of who and what they might become. By integrating representations of sympathy and identification, queer friendship becomes a vehicle through which authors meditate on issues of social equality, citizenship, and the bonds that form the body politic.

Historically, friendship has played a vital role in LGBT communities, particularly in the mid- to late twentieth century, when by necessity or choice, friend networks often served as surrogates for unsupportive familial ones. Although McCullers composed *The Heart Is a Lonely Hunter* at an earlier historical moment, her writing suggests an interest in the ways in which the term "friend" was often invoked as a substitute for words that might indicate a romantic relationship. One finds evidence of this tendency even in the letters and correspondences of McCullers' contemporaries, including Tennessee Williams. In many ways, for a gay man living in the mid-twentieth century, Williams was remarkably open about his sexuality with his peers; in his letters and correspondences, however, he nevertheless sometimes refers to his partner, Pancho, as his "Mexican friend."[4] As scholars such as Lillian Faderman and Carroll Smith-Rosenberg have noted, the complex intersection of friendship and queerness also extends back to the eighteenth and nineteenth centuries with the presence of "romantic friendships." Before homosexuality existed as a social category, a higher degree of affection and even passion was permissible in same-sex friendships (Farr 103). Moreover, other forms of nonnormative relationships, such as "Boston marriages," in which two women established a household in the absence of men, were also common at this time and complicated categories of romantic and platonic love (103). Tellingly, as the term "queer" evolved into a derogatory euphemism for homosexuality in the late nineteenth century, romantic expressions of same-sex friendship, as well as the Boston marriage, began to decline (103).

McCullers opens *The Heart Is a Lonely Hunter* with a representation of queer friendship. She describes the relationship between Singer and Antonapoulos: "two mutes," she calls them, who were "always together" in their small, Georgia mill-town. "Early every morning," McCullers writes, "they would come out of the house where they lived and walk arm in arm down the street to work. The two friends were very different" (3). The next paragraph begins, "every morning the two friends walked silently together" (3), and the third paragraph, "in the late afternoon the two friends would meet again" (3). McCullers' use of the term "friend" is similar to her treatment of the term queer in both *The Member of the Wedding* and *The Heart Is a Lonely Hunter*. She repeats both terms with such frequency that they begin to acquire new layers of meaning. Her repetition of "two friends" calls the very meaning of the phrase into question. Throughout this section, she also uses the phrase "two mutes" interchangeably with "two friends." She begins the fourth paragraph with a line that echoes the first: "in the dusk the two mutes walked slowly home together" (4). By using these two phrases repeatedly and interchangeably, McCullers suggests a parallel relationship between the marginalization that Singer and Antonapoulos experience because of both their queerness and disability in the late 1930s.

From the vantage point of normative society, Singer and Antonapoulos may be simply perceived as "two mutes" or "two friends," but in private these two labels quickly unravel and appear insufficient and inaccurate. Singer provides abundant care and compassion for Antonapoulos when he becomes physically ill despite the fact that he persistently mistreats him. Antonapoulos is "fretful," restless, and "irritable," finds fault with the food and drink that Singer brings to him, and communicates with a "bland smile" rather than sign language (7). Nevertheless, when Antonapoulos is hospitalized because of his mental illness, the separation proves unbearable for Singer. As McCullers writes, "within Singer there was always the memory of his friend. At night when he closed his eyes the Greek's face was there in the darkness—round and oily, with a wise and gentle smile. In his dreams they were always together. It was more than a year now since his friend had gone away" (201). The absence of Antonapoulos affects Singer so deeply that it begins to disrupt his sense of time: "This year seemed neither long nor short," he reflects. "Rather it was removed from the ordinary sense of time—as when one is drunk or asleep. Behind each hour there was always his friend" (201). As Singer becomes increasingly distraught over the loss of his queer relationship, he develops a nonnormative sense of time. His experience resonates with Halberstam's observation that "queer uses of time and space develop, at least in part, in opposition to the institutions of family, heterosexuality, and reproduction" (1). In the absence of Antonapoulos, queerness seems to persist for Singer in other kinds of ways, even affecting his perception of the world around him. McCullers' portrayal of Singer and Antonapoulos not only reveals her interest in relationships that subvert classifications of romantic and platonic love but also characters who complicate binary understandings of gender and sexuality. While Antonapoulos does not appear to reciprocate Singer's affection, this very imbalance of reciprocity marks it as a nonplatonic relationship—or, at the very least, one that is experienced as such by Singer, even if unknowingly. Their relationship defies modern classifications of heterosexual and homosexual love, as the precise nature of how each of them experiences the relationship is marked with ambiguity. It reflects McCullers' famous claim in *The Ballad of the Sad Café* that in all relationships, including romantic, platonic, or even parent/child relationships, there is a "lover and beloved," and no one wants to be the beloved (25–26). As time passes during their separation, Singer's feelings for him become even more imbalanced: "his thoughts of his friend spiraled deeper until he dwelt only with the Antonapoulos whom he alone could know" (204). He writes letters to Antonapoulos, and, as he does so, his longings become so intense that he holds his breath (216). Singer, whom McCullers clearly constructs as the lover in this relationship, not only cares for Antonapoulos unconditionally but also idealizes him: "all the times that they had been unhappy were forgotten" (204). As Singer's thoughts "spiral" in intensity and obsessiveness, they seem increasingly at odds with dominant understandings of friendship, which have tended to emphasize equality and equanimity (204). From our twenty-first-century perspective, it is hard not to interpret Singer's feelings for Antonapoulos as unrealized romantic affection. Regardless of the precise nature of the relationship, it certainly functions as a critique, at some level, of the ways in which friendship has often served as a guise for gay relationships. At the same time, the ambiguity of the relationship also simultaneously works to expand our understanding of friendship to include relationships that exist in between and across the boundaries of romantic, platonic, and familial love.

The exclusivity of Singer and Antonapoulos' friendship also marks it as queer. As McCullers states, "they never had no friends" (201). They try to develop a friendship with someone named Carl, who is also deaf. They bring him over for a dinner and initially they have a good time. But Antonapoulos, in the process of serving up copious amounts of liquor to all of them, becomes convinced that Carl has stolen all of the liquor: he becomes enraged and his grimaces and obscene gestures frighten Carl, who never returns again. This scene underscores the queerness of Singer and Antonapoulos' friendship, as Antonapoulos clearly responds to Carl as if he were a romantic threat. While the novel focuses predominately on Singer's perspective and behavior, this scene reveals how Antonapoulos also contributes to the queerness of this relationship. McCullers introduces the hopeful possibility that individuals who are marginalized due to disability may form alliances with one another, but then proceeds to reveal the limitations and challenges of such friendships.

McCullers' representations of queer friendship extend in important ways beyond Singer's relationship with Antonapoulos. For instance, McCullers explores the queerness of friendships that exist across differences in age. Notably, Mick's social relationships seem limited to individuals who are either much older or younger than she is. As Biff describes, she was always "pulling a couple of snotty babies in a wagon … if she wasn't nursing or trying to keep up with the bigger ones, she was by herself " (18). Additionally, individuals who are much older than Mick, such as Biff, appear drawn to her as well. Biff wants to reach out and touch her "sunburned, tousled hair," but not in a way that he has ever wanted to touch a woman before (121). In other words, he feels an intense sense of connection to Mick, but it is not one that conforms in any kind of coherent way to categories of romantic, platonic, and familial love.

While Mick's queerness may attract Biff's attentions, it seems to have the opposite effect upon her peers, with whom she struggles to form relationships. For her part, however, Mick herself seems primarily drawn to Singer. She understands herself as an individual who is divided into two rooms: an "outside" and an "inside room" (244). The former encompasses her responsibilities to others and society's gendered expectations for her future, whereas the latter includes her musical creativity, her plans to travel the world, and Singer. As an economically underprivileged girl in the small-town South, Mick's "inside room" and the desires that she associates with it mark her as queer. Her travel plans and artistic dreams, in particular, transgress social expectations for other young women of her class background. Mick feels that she and Singer have a kind of "secret together" (241): the inner room thus becomes a symbolic representation of closeted queer identities as well as a site of friendship. The symbolism of the room also gestures to their physical meeting place: a room in her parents' house, which Singer rents out as a long-term boarder. Finally, the room is also a site where many of the novel's other characters, such as Biff

Brannon and Jake Blount, meet with Singer and the space therefore offers continuity across many of the novel's queer friendships.

Long before Singer's arrival, however, Mick expresses queer sentiments about other boarders within the Kelly household. For instance, Mick recalls a girl named Celeste in vivid detail: she remembers how she pulled the crust off of her sandwiches, wore red-wool jumpers, and ate hardboiled eggs (242). Mick fantasizes about becoming her "best friend" and how they would spend the night together, but her feelings also prevent her from approaching her as she might another person. Eventually, Celeste moves away and this friendship remains unrealized. Nevertheless, Mick's fantasies about Celeste hint at her own queer identity and also set the stage for her queer friendship with Singer. After Celeste, a boy named Buck moves into the room. By contrast, he is described in fairly grotesque terms: he is "big," has "pimples on his face," and smells bad (242). Mick nevertheless develops invasive thoughts about him, just like Celeste. The fluidity of Mick's desires and obsessions, which drift across gender and sexual orientations and defy categorizations of romantic and platonic love, is a key component of her queer identity.

As McCullers portrays the visits of other characters to Singer's room, she continues to develop an association between the "inner room" and queer friendship. It is important to the novel's social criticism that Mick is not the only character to feel an intense attraction to Singer. Other characters, all of whom feel marginalized or disconnected in some way, seem intensely drawn to his quiet presence—they include Dr. Copeland, an African American doctor who has devoted his life to racial progress; Biff Brannon, an unhappily married man who runs the local café; and Jake Blount, a wandering, alcoholic socialist. Singer, McCullers writes, "was never busy or in a hurry. And always he met his guests at the door with a welcome smile" (91). He was also "always the same to everyone" (92). While all of these characters feel as though they benefit from their visits with Singer and believe that he understands them completely, Singer himself does not appear to benefit from these relationships in any meaningful way. He becomes so popular that there is always the sound of a voice emanating from the room, but this sound itself becomes a symbol of the lack of reciprocity in human relationships. They communicate with Singer in a way that *they* can understand, but they seem unconcerned about whether he understands them and fail to make any attempt to learn about his own problems and concerns. Moreover, they make no adjustments to their mode of communication for his disability and thus seem generally unconcerned with reciprocity.

The imbalances in Singer's friendships become particularly apparent when he goes to visit Antonapoulos in the hospital. None of his friends know where he is or why he has left; rather than responding with a sense of concern, they instead feel a "hurt surprise" in his absence (92). They cannot fully understand why Singer would leave—and they do not take into consideration the fact that they know very little about him. The "quietness" of the room in his absence troubles them, which is ironic given that the only sounds in the room are their own voices. McCullers implies that our desire to be heard by others often masquerades for real connection and intimacy.

In the opening paragraph, McCullers notes that the two friends, Singer and Antonapoulos, were "very different" (3), a characterization that could be applied to most of the other relationships in the novel as well. These queer friendships exist across social divisions of the segregated, Jim Crow South, and between individuals who share little common ground. Jake Blount, who is perpetually loud and belligerent, seems mismatched for friendship with Singer, who is uncannily serene. But these differences only heighten Jake's attraction to him. As McCullers writes, Blount "wanted to return to the mute's room and tell him of the thoughts that were on his mind. It was a queer thing to want to talk to the deaf-mute. But he was lonesome" (64). Here, as in *The Member of the Wedding*, McCullers rather playfully gestures to the multiple meanings of the term queer at this historical moment as both unusual and strange and as a derogatory euphemism for homosexuality.[5] She also again points to a parallel relationship between disability and queerness. Part of what makes it a "queer thing," in Blount's mind, is not only that Singer is a man but a deaf man. Even Blount seems aware that Singer's inability to communicate with him equally queers their friendship. As the queer friendships of *The Heart Is a Lonely Hunter* transgress differences in race, gender, age, and sexuality, they raise questions about the capacity for individuals, particularly those from marginalized groups, to forge bonds across social differences and meditate on the potential (or lack thereof) for equality in human relationships.

Of all of the novel's queer friendships, Mick's relationship with Singer is particularly intense and even verges on obsessive. This is perhaps because their friendship is intertwined with her coming of age as a queer, adolescent girl. "Just Mr. Singer," Mick reflects, "She wanted to follow him everywhere. In the morning she would watch him go down to the front steps to work and then follow along a half a block behind him. Every afternoon as soon as school was over she hung around at the corner near the store where he worked" (306). Later on, she waits for him to come home and feels a "desperate desire to see him" (318). For her part, Mick seems somewhat cognizant of the nonnormative dynamics of their relationship: she starts to visit him only twice a week because she worries that he will grow tired of her, even though she always finds him sitting pleasantly over a "queer, pretty chess game" (306). She continues to follow him, even though she does not really want to, and, sometimes, a "queer feeling" comes over her and she feels as though what she is doing is wrong (310). While she seems to have little conscious understanding of their shared queer identities, she nevertheless recognizes that their sense of connection may violate several social taboos.

When Antonapoulos dies, Singer commits suicide by shooting himself in the chest (326)—or, as we might imagine, the heart. His suicide makes visible the queerness of his relationship with Antonapoulos, as his response seems more characteristic of what one might expect from a romantic relationship. The lack of reciprocity that Singer experiences in all of his relationships by this point in the novel also seems a contributing factor to his death. Mick discovers his body after he has committed suicide, which further underscores her sense of connection to him. She finds him after she goes into his *room* to play the radio, which is significant because both the room and her interest in music are associated with her queerness. Mick's father, who in many ways symbolizes the external forces that repress queer identity, pushes her out of the room when he views the body. At Singer's funeral, she finds it impossible to stay in the same room with the casket; this gestures symbolically to the closure of her own "inside room" or the queer part of herself. Singer's death also anticipates the conclusion of *The Member of the Wedding*, which likewise portrays the dissolution of a tomboy figure's queer, cross-gender friendship because of death. John Henry's death is, in some ways, quite different from Singer's because it occurs not from suicide but rather results from a sudden illness. In both cases, however, these two deaths are associated with a lack of reciprocity, as Frankie shows a persistent inability to reciprocate John Henry's affections. Kathryn Bond Stockton has argued that the queer child is always growing "toward a question mark" (3), and these texts certainly reflect that observation. In both texts, as tomboys witness the loss of queer friends, they are reminded that, particularly in the mid-twentieth century Deep South, one's future as a queer child is always in peril and deeply uncertain.

Toward the end of the novel, Mick says that there are two things that she cannot wrap her head around: the death of Singer and the fact that she now works at a Woolworth's to support her family. Earlier in the novel, she laments the fact that girls do not, typically, have the option to get a part-time job, which means that they have to drop out of school to earn money. "A boy has a better advantage," she reflects, "... a boy can usually get some part-time job that don't take him out of school and leaves him time for other things. But there's not jobs like that for girls. When a girl wants a job she has to quit school and work fulltime. I'd sure like to earn a couple of bucks a week like you do, but there's just not any way" (246). While Mick's lament about employment seems in some ways to trivialize Singer's death, these two events are certainly connected symbolically for Mick. Her dreams for the future transgress social norms and expectations for young women, and they are a key part of her queer identity. By associating Singer's death with her employment at Woolworth's, she gestures to the ways in which both of their futures are truncated.

Queer friendships in *The Heart Is a Lonely Hunter*, much like her portrayals of non-normative families in *The Member of the Wedding*, become a vehicle through which McCullers imagines the possibilities, as well as the limitations, of political alliances across social differences.[6] They point to intersectional relationships between different identity categories, including race, gender, sexuality, and disability. But if McCullers' representations of friendship are meant to serve as a model for the potential for human connection across difference, they offer a rather pessimistic one. Although the socially marginalized individuals of this novel do forge relationships with one another, they typically fail to demonstrate any meaningful reciprocity or equality of connection across social differences. Marginalized in multiple ways, Singer is a source of quiet strength for others, but when he finds himself suffering, he does so alone, in spite of his multiple queer friendships. The future for each of the novel's characters—and, in particular, that of the gender non-conforming, adolescent girl—is marked with uncertainty and solitude. Thankfully for McCullers, the demise of queer friendships in this novel run contrary to the queer friendships in her own life, which seem remarkable in their degree of reciprocity and endurance. Even after her death, Massee continued to play an important role in managing her legacy, and both Williams and Massee fondly shared biographical insights about McCullers in interviews. Carr consulted Williams for her biography on McCullers, *The Lonely Hunter*, published in 1975, which arguably remains the most authoritative biography on her life. Williams followed up with Carr when he felt that she presented inaccurate information about McCullers' romantic experiences, which speaks to his investment in how her story was narrated after her death ("Exotic Birds").

As McCullers portrays friendships that display the intensity that we tend to associate with romantic love, she challenges society's devaluation of friendship in favor of romantic and familial relationships. She also reveals the multiplicity of relationships that exist across and between the conventional social categorization of human relationships. Although McCullers' portrayal of queer friendship is infused with a degree of pessimism, it nevertheless complicates our understanding of friendship and reveals its subversive potential. Considering *The Heart Is a Lonely Hunter* was published in 1940—long before the Civil Rights movement, and certainly the LGBT rights movement, had gained momentum—McCullers' pessimism might be better understood as appropriately grounded in the realities of Jim Crow era Georgia. *The Heart Is a Lonely Hunter* reveals how queer friendship might serve as a vehicle for social transformation, even as it warns of its fragility and potential for inequality.

NOTES

1. See *The Selected Letters of Tennessee Williams, Volume II: 1945–1957.*
2. For more on the tomboy/sissy dyad, see also Abate, Richards, and Adams.
3. This terminology   draws from Eric Tribunella's "Refusing the Queer Potential: John Knowles' *A Separate Peace.*"
4. See *Selected Letters*, II, 51, 57.
5. See the Oxford English Dictionary for more on the evolution of this term. In some ways, McCullers' use of the term often seems to anticipate LGBT activists' reclamation of the term as a signifier of non-normative gender and sexual identities.
6. For more on McCullers and her representation of the nonnormative family, see Proehl, "Tomboyism and Familial Belonging."

WORKS CITED

Abate, Michele Ann. *Tomboys: A Literary and Cultural History.* Philadelphia: Temple UP, 2008. Print.

Adams, Rachel. "A Mixture of Delicious and Freak: The Queer Fiction of Carson McCullers." *American Literature* 71.3 (1999): 551–583. Print.

Carr, Spencer. *The Lonely Hunter: A Biography of Carson McCullers.* Athens: U of Georgia P, 1975. Print.

Derrida, Jacques. *The Politics of Friendship.* New York: Verso, 2005. Print.

Ewell, Barbara, Carlos Dews, Virginia Spencer Carr, and Will Brantley. "Exotic Birds of a Feather: Carson McCullers and Tennessee Williams." *The Tennessee Williams Annual Review.* Murfeesboro, TN: Middle Tennessee University, 2000. Web.

Farr, Daniel. Boston Marriages. *American Countercultures: An Encyclopedia of Nonconformists, Alternative Lifestyles, and Radical Ideas in U.S. History.* Ed. Gina Misiroglu. Armonk, NY: Sharpe Reference, 2009. Print.

Faderman, Lillian. *Surpassing the Love of Men: Romantic Friendship and Love Between Women from the Renaissance to the Present.* New York: Morrow, 1981. Print.

Foucault, Michel. "Friendship as a Way of Life." *Ethics: Subjectivity and Truth (Essential Works of Foucault, 1954–1984, Vol. 1).* Ed. Paul Rabinow. New York: New Press, 2006. Print.

Garrison, John S. *Friendship and Queer Theory in the Renaissance Gender and Sexuality in Early Modern England.* Florence: Taylor and Francis, 2014. Print.

Halberstam, Judith. *In a Queer Time and Place: Transgender Bodies, Subcultural Lives.* New York: New York UP, 2005. Print.

Hutto, Richard Jay. *A Peculiar Tribe of People: Murder and Madness in the Heart of Georgia.* Guilford, CT: Lyons, 2011. Print.

Lahr, John. *Tennessee Williams: Mad Pilgrimage of the Flesh.* New York: W.W. Norton & Company, 2014. Print.

McCullers, Carson and Carlos Dews. *Illumination and Night Glare: The Unfinished Autobiography of Carson McCullers.* Madison: University of Wisconsin P, 2002. Print.

McCullers, Carson. *The Ballad of the Sad Café.* New York: Houghton Mifflin, 2005. Print.

——. *The Heart Is a Lonely Hunter.* New York: Houghton Mifflin, 2000. Print.

——. *The Member of the Wedding.* New York: Houghton Mifflin, 1946. Print.

Proehl, Kristen B. "Sympathetic Alliances: Tomboys, Sissy Boys, and Queer Friendship in *The Member of the Wedding* and *To Kill a Mockingbird.*" *ANQ: A Quarterly Journal of Short Articles, Notes and Reviews* 26.2 (2013): 128–33. Print.

——. "Tomboyism and Familial Belonging in Carson McCullers's *The Member of the Wedding*: Queer Sentiments." *Jeunesse: Young People, Texts, Cultures* 7.1 (2015): 87–109. Web.

Muraco, Ann. *Odd Couples: Friendships at the Intersection of Gender and Sexual Orientation.* Durham: Duke UP, 2012. Print.

Richards, Gary. *Lovers and Beloveds: Sexual Otherness in Southern Fiction, 1936–1961.* Baton Rouge: Louisiana State UP, 2005. Print.

Roach, Tom. *Friendship as a Way of Life: Foucault, AIDS, and the Politics of Shared Estrangement.* Albany: SUNY P, 2012. Print.

Schweitzer, Ivy. *Perfecting Friendship: Politics and Affiliation in Early American Literature.* Chapel Hill: The U of North Carolina P, 2006. Print.

Smith-Rosenberg, Carroll. "The Female World of Love and Ritual: Relations Between Women in Nineteenth-Century America." *Signs* 1.1 (1975): 1–29. Print.

Tribunella, Eric L. "Refusing the Queer Potential: John Knowles's *A Separate Peace.*" *Children's Literature* 30.1 (2002): 81–95. Web.

Williams, Tennessee . *The Selected Letters of Tennessee Williams, Vol. II: 1945-1957.* Eds. Albert Devlin and Nancy Marie Patterson Tischler. New York: New Directions, 2004.

Queer Eyes: Cross-Gendering, Cross-Dressing, and Cross-Racing Miss Amelia

Miho Matsui

The Ballad of the Sad Café (1951) is considered representative of the southern gothic, and because of this it has some marked similarities with William Faulkner's "A Rose for Emily" (1930). They are both stories about eccentric spinsters in the South, though the former belongs to the New South, and the latter to the Old South. Both protagonists are motherless and raised by their fathers; both, after their fathers die, live alone with a black male cook. Living their lives as spinsters, the two women cannot avoid attracting the attention of the townspeople who are very curious, in particular, about their sexuality. They are eccentric women in southern society, finally rejecting their relationship with the townspeople and—as if to avoid being looked at by the voyeuristic eyes of the townspeople—locking themselves within their own houses.

Despite the similarities between the two characters, Carson McCullers' spinster, Miss Amelia Evans, who lives around the middle of the twentieth century, has a more ambiguous identity in terms of gender, sex, and race. In fact, Amelia is an extremely subversive southern white lady. Her appearance and conduct definitely deviate from the norm of southern womanhood, which defines ladies as being "beautiful, fragile, good"

M. Matsui (✉)
School of Design, Sapporo City University, Art Park 1, Minami-ku, Sapporo-shi, Hokkaido 005-0864, Japan

A. Graham-Bertolini, C. Kayser (eds.), *Carson McCullers in the Twenty-First Century*, DOI 10.1007/978-3-319-40292-5_10

157

(Jones, *Tomorrow* 356). In the myth of southern womanhood, as Jones points out, "ladies [don't] labor; they [don't] dress like men, and they [don't] act like men" (Jones, "Women Writers" 277). McCullers also depicts Amelia with racial ambiguity, at least on the surface. Amelia is born "dark and somewhat queer of face" (*Collected* 206), and she is "a dark, tall woman with bones and muscles like a man" as an adult (198). Her sunburned face has "a tense, haggard quality," and she is slightly "cross-eyed" (198). After her father's death, she runs the store she inherits from him, but she also "[operates] a still three miles back in the swamp" (198); namely, she is a moonshiner and bootlegger, jobs that are usually associated not with middle-class white women but rather with lower class white or black people.

Amelia transgresses from white femininity to black masculinity, and in addition, her sexuality is also ambiguous. The narrator reports that Amelia "cared nothing for the love of men" and that her marriage was a "queer marriage" lasting only for ten days (198). She resists the masculinity and heterosexuality of her husband Marvin Macy. She refuses to go to bed with him on their wedding night; after that, she hits hard "whenever he [comes] within arm's reach of her;" and finally "[turns] him off the premises altogether" (221). Ten days after the marriage, he left the town with no one to see him go, and her resistance seems successful until Macy returns home and fascinates hunchbacked Cousin Lymon, who has been living with Amelia and helping her run a café. At the end of the story, Amelia is beaten by the vengeful Macy and his partner Lymon and is forced to shut herself inside her house where she becomes "sexless and white" (197).

This ending can be interpreted as Amelia being punished by the patriarchy because of her transgressive gender, sexuality, and racial codes. However, the story can also be interpreted as a white woman resisting white male dominance by affiliating with blackness and cross-dressing. It is important to explore the meaning of the word "queer" that McCullers uses and to focus on Amelia's crossed eyes, which the narrator sometimes calls "queer" eyes (228, 236).[1] In the South, white men in the dominant upper class are given privilege. Women and black people, as the others of the dominant white male, are observed and controlled by this white male gaze and are expected not to transgress beyond their category. This gaze is what Michel Foucault calls "a normalizing gaze, a surveillance that makes it possible to qualify, to classify and to punish" (184). Amelia's queer eyes, and also the narrator's eyes—the narrator also queers the narrated object, as will be argued later—subvert the authoritative, normalizing gaze and they show that McCullers, by deconstructing the politics of looking and being looked at, seeks an alternative context regarding gender, sexuality, and race. McCullers resists the normalizing gaze by making "the surface" subversive, or by subverting via the surface, namely, by having her protagonist cross-dress and "wear" her blackness.

Critical theories of vision and visuality reveal that looking is not a neutral act, and in the relation between "seeing" and "being seen," the viewer and the viewed form a hierarchal power relationship. Feminist critics argue that vision is patriarchal, and they refute the idea of making vision privileged. Laura Mulvey, in her groundbreaking paper "Visual Pleasure and Narrative Cinema" (1975), analyzes the structure of looking in mainstream Hollywood cinema. She maintains:

> In a world ordered by sexual imbalance, pleasure in looking has been split between active/male and passive/female. The determining male gaze projects its fantasy onto the female figure, which is styled accordingly. In their traditional exhibitionist role women are simultaneously looked at and displayed, with their appearance coded for strong visual and erotic impact so that they can be said to connote *to-be-looked-at-ness*. (19; italics original)

In classical Hollywood movies, males are positioned as gazing subjects, while females are objects of the male gaze, objects to be surveyed by the male's active and voyeuristic gaze, and thus deprived of subjectivity. A female body is a fetish object of the male gaze, and audiences see the movie while assimilating their gaze with the male voyeuristic gaze. Meanwhile, women can be the "gazing subjects"; however, as Susan Wolstenholme argues in regard to Freud's reading of E. T. A. Hoffman's "The Sandman" (1817) in "The Uncanny" (1919), the female gaze is to be repressed in a male-dominated society:

> In Freud's reading of E. T. A. Hoffmann's story "The Sandman," while the eyes of the castrating father are of central importance, Freud also characterizes women to be not only the object of a gaze but gazing subjects; and the gaze of women and girls evidently threatens him. Evidently the female gaze, as well as the woman's body that forms the object of the man's gaze, is frightening, something to be avoided, perhaps disallowed or repressed. To relieve the anxiety it creates in men, the woman's gaze must be sacrificed to the woman's role as object and to the man's gaze. (9)

Thus, the hierarchal dichotomy between male and female, looking and being looked, subject and object constructs the position of women in patriarchal culture.

If "seeing" includes power relationships between those who see and those who are seen, it also relates to racial hierarchies. Because racial segregation is based on the color of the skin, the white gaze is repressive to black people, as Frantz Fanon describes:

> I arrive slowly in the world; sudden emergences are no longer my habit. I crawl along. The white gaze, the only valid one, is already dissecting me. I am *fixed*. Once their microtomes are sharpened, the Whites objectively cut sections of my reality. I have been betrayed. I sense, I see in this white gaze that it's the arrival not of a new man, but of a new type of man, a new species. A Negro, in fact! (95; italics original)

Black people are forced to form their consciousness or subjectivity "through the eyes of others," specifically through the eyes of the whites (Du Bois 8). Regarding women in the male dominant society, women's subjectivity is constructed through the male gaze, as John Berger explains as follows:

> Men look at women. Women watch themselves being looked at. This determines not only most relations between men and women but also the relation of women to themselves. The surveyor of woman in herself is male: the surveyed female. Thus she turns herself into an object—and most particularly an object of vision: a sight. (47)

Under the patriarchal visionary system, the female gaze through which women look at themselves as a subject is the others'/male gaze, which means that what constructs female identity is not the female gaze but the male gaze. Similarly, black people and white women are both located as an object of the dominant white male gaze and are both observed and controlled by it. It seems natural that McCullers, born in the South where the white-male centered way of looking is dominant, explores the relation between the gaze and gender/racial identity in her work.

MISS AMELIA AND THE GAZE

Amelia is a grown-up tomboy, a woman who has grown up without sloughing off her masculine traits. Besides being dark, tall, and muscular like a (black) man, she is familiar with the world of men, such as those in medicine, commerce, law, and even with the world of bootlegging or moonshining. Amelia is biologically female, while her conduct and role in society resemble those of not only white but also black men. She is a phallic woman transgressing the racial boundary.[2] Also, Amelia is cross-eyed. Psychoanalytically, there is the substitutive relation between the eye and the male organ (Freud 231); therefore, Amelia, who loses normal vision, is figuratively emasculated. Moreover, it is significant that after losing the final boxing battle against Macy, Amelia's body loses its masculinity—"the great muscles of her body shrank until she was thin as old maids are thin when they go crazy" and her eyes become "more crossed" (252). Thus, to be cross-eyed is closely related to being emasculated and this emasculation seemingly shows Amelia's defeat in the battle against masculine force; however, as it will be argued later, her defeat is subversive.

The story unfolds over the triangular relationship among a masculine woman, Amelia; a masculine white man, Marvin Macy; and a feminine dwarf, Cousin Lymon. The story ends when Macy and Lymon defeat Amelia and leave the town after they destroy the café. Their battles are related to gaze. During their "queer marriage," which was prompted by Macy's one-sided courting, Amelia is less cross-eyed and has the power to resist forced heterosexual sex with Macy. However, after Amelia becomes somewhat feminized by being fascinated with Lymon and assuming the role of his mother, it is Macy who has an advantage in the battle of the gaze.

Macy is sent to a penitentiary for committing repeated crimes after Amelia kicks him out of her house. When he returns to the town, Macy regains the masculine and active gaze/power, which he lost during his marriage to Amelia. As soon as he returns to the town, the narrator describes Macy wandering and looking around everywhere: "First, he went to the mill ... and looked inside" (233). Then, his gaze is related to a phallic image: "Marvin Macy folded the knife he had been honing, and after looking about him fearlessly he swaggered out of the yard" (236). Macy is "one of seven unwanted children whose parents could hardly be called parents at all," "an evil character," and a womanizer (217). His savageness and immorality almost make him lose his whiteness, but he still benefits from the privilege of being white. When he is abandoned by his parents, the town saves him because they do not let "white orphans perish in the road" (218). It is also suggested that he is a member of the KKK—"that spring she [Amelia] cut up his Klansman's robe to cover her tobacco plants" (222). As Suzanne Morrow Paulson argues, "Marvin represents the brute masculine force of a misogynist and racist community" (194). Macy comes back to resume a position to repress woman and racial others.

In this regard, the fact that the color of Amelia changes when she hears about Macy should be examined. When Amelia and Macy went to the room to sleep on the first day of their marriage, "[w]ithin half an hour Miss Amelia had stomped down the stairs in breeches and a khaki jacket" with her face "darkened so that it looked quite black" (220). Then, when "[s]he read the Farmer's Almanac, drank coffee, and had a smoke with her father's pipe," her face "had now whitened to its natural color" (220). Subsequently, whenever Amelia hears about Macy, her face becomes darkened. When Amelia hears of Macy's return, "[t]he face of Miss Amelia was very dark, and she shivered although the night was warm" (230). When she hears about a letter from Macy, "her face was still hardened and very dark" (231). When she hears Lymon groan "Oh, Marvin Macy," "her face was dark and hardened" (238). These changes in facial color suggest that Amelia is upset by the references to Macy, and repressed by his presence; however, if the white male oppression makes Amelia darken, this hardened black Amelia can, in the context of southern racism and sexism, evoke the image of the black people who are in imminent danger of white men's violence. In the figure of Amelia who changes color, McCullers surely carves the meaning of white male repression in southern society.

In contrast to Amelia, Lymon is fascinated with Macy's gaze from the moment he meets Macy, and they see each other as two criminals: "It was a peculiar stare they exchanged between them, like the look of two criminals who recognize each other" (233). Moreover, Lymon goes so far as to "wiggle his large pale ears with marvelous quickness and ease," flutter "his eyelids" so that they look like "pale, trapped moths in his sockets" (235), and perform a little trot-like dance in order to get Macy's attention. Lymon is "a sight to see" (235). Amelia only watches Lymon doing these things "with her crossed, gray eyes, and her fists closed tight" (238).

Amelia's eyes cannot exchange a stare with other people's eyes. Even if someone looks at Amelia's eyes, her eyes seem to be staring at each other, since they are crossed inwardly. In fact, there are few scenes in which Amelia exchanges a stare with someone, which contrasts with the mutual gaze relationship of Lymon and Macy. It is more important to notice that, even if the female gaze is threatening to the men, Amelia cannot return a stare when she is the object of the gaze. In the dichotomy between the one who sees and the one seen, Amelia has the disadvantaged position within the dynamics of gaze. Therefore, when Macy approaches Amelia and Lymon, "[s]he locked the doors and all the windows very carefully," so that "nothing was seen of her and Cousin Lymon" (236–37).

We can find an asymmetry between Amelia, who is passive about the act of looking, and Macy, who is active. At the end of the story, Amelia decides to have a fight with Macy only to lose it because of Lymon's collusion with Macy. Then after Macy and Lymon leave the town together, Amelia becomes more cross-eyed and loses her muscle, with her appearance being like that of an old crazy maid. Ultimately she stays in her house, which is "bound to collapse at any minute" (197).

There is another gaze that is focused on Amelia that needs to be examined closely: the gaze of the townspeople, most of whom are white male laborers in a small southern town. Amelia, as a spinster, is always an object of their curious gaze: Amelia is a freakish spectacle to the townspeople, who are tired of the drudgery of daily life. For example, on the night after the wedding, the young boys in the town peep inside of Amelia's house through the window and report what really happened between the bride and groom to the whole town: "A groom is in a sorry fix when he is unable to bring his well-beloved bride to bed with him" (220). Likewise, the relationship between Amelia and Lymon, as well as the triangular relation between Amelia, Lymon, and Macy draw curious stares from the townspeople. The highlight of the spectacle is a boxing match between Macy and Amelia, which can be interpreted as a pornographic scene, as will be discussed later.

The narrator relates that the townspeople are obsessed with a desire to see Amelia. Moreover, the narrator also demands that we as readers also see her:

So for the moment regard these years from random and disjointed views. See the hunchback marching in Miss Amelia's footsteps when on a red winter morning they set out for the pinewoods to hunt. See them working on her properties. (214)

Here, the reader is supposed to assume the role of a voyeur who peeps at Amelia through the eyes of the narrator, in the same way as the townspeople watch her. Thus, the greater the number of subjects who see Amelia, the more Amelia becomes firmly fixed as a spectacle in the text.

In terms of a spectacle, Lymon, who is a "dwarf," is vulnerable to becoming an object in the eyes of "normal" people. However, it is significant to notice the difference between Amelia and Lymon in terms of their being objects of the others' gaze. Lymon seems to be willing to be an object of the gaze and takes pleasure in it, while Amelia rejects being an object beyond necessity. For example, she sells the expensive accessories that Macy presented her with. Meanwhile, Lymon, who does not appear in public for a few days after visiting Amelia's house, and is believed to have been murdered, reappears before the townspeople as follows:

> The hunchback came down slowly with the proudness of one who owns every plank of the floor beneath his feet. In the past days he had greatly changed ... Beneath this [his coat] was a fresh red and black checkered shirt belonging to Miss Amelia. He did not wear trousers such as ordinary men are meant to wear, but a pair of tight-fitting little knee-length breeches. On his skinny legs he wore black stockings, and his shoes were of a special kind, being queerly shaped, laced up over the ankles, and newly cleaned and polished with wax. Around his neck, so that his large, pale ears were almost completely covered, he wore a shawl of lime-green wool, the fringes of which almost touched the floor. (209)

His appearance makes the men present dumb with shock. Because femininity, as Sarah Gleeson-White claims, is a more spectacular gender than masculinity (86), then, it can be said that Lymon represents femininity—in this instance, exaggerated femininity. Lymon is a caricature of a woman as the object of the gaze. If, as Gleeson-White also notes, Macy in a red shirt, and a wide belt of tooled leather carrying a tin suitcase and a guitar, is a "hyper-masculine image of the cowboy" (81) or a caricature of ideal American masculinity,[3] then a coalition between Macy and Lymon seems to be one between hyper-masculinity as a subject of the gaze and hyper-femininity as an object of the gaze. In other words, the Macy-Lymon pair represents a caricature of a heterosexual couple, and Amelia, who denies a heterosexual relationship with Macy, is finally avenged by this mock-heterosexual couple. We might infer here that Lymon's self-spectacularization is a way of turning his objective position into a subjective one by actively making himself an object and catching others' eyes. However, there is a rumor that after Macy and Lymon leave town, Macy sells Lymon into a sideshow; therefore, being an object of the gaze can lead to objectification. It is a dangerous world in which "looking at" or "being looked at" constructs the power relationship, and one thus becomes the object of the gaze.

CROSS-DRESSING MISS AMELIA/CROSS-DRESSING NARRATOR

Amelia does not always appear dressed as a man. When she is required to fit into the gender code, or when it gives her advantage to dress like a woman, she wears feminine attire. During her wedding ceremony, she wears a wedding dress, which was passed down by her mother. After she is mesmerized by Lymon, she sometimes wears a red dress, for example, on Sundays. Then after Macy comes to town, Amelia puts aside her overalls and "[wears] always the red dress" (238). However, we must closely examine what Amelia's dressing according to the code of femininity really represents.

Here, it is necessary to consider how the clothes a woman wears function in relation to the gaze of others. Clothing is a sign of what those who wear it are. When a woman wears a feminine dress, it means that she may be an object of the male gaze; that is, an object of male sexual desire. For example, when Frankie Addams in *The Member of the Wedding*, who first appears as a tomboy in the story, dresses like an adult woman—she wears a pink organdie dress and black pumps, and puts on lipstick and Sweet Serenade—she comes close to being raped by a soldier who sees Frankie, in her dress, as sexually mature: "He [the soldier] was looking at F. Jasmine from the top of her head, down the organdie best dress, and to the black pumps she was wearing" (81). Likewise, when Amelia appears in a wedding dress, it indicates to Macy that she accepts being his object of heterosexual desire. In both cases, Frankie and Amelia do not intend to draw attention from the male gaze. They only intend to adjust themselves to the gender code. However, to the male gaze, Frankie's dress means that she is a prostitute and Amelia's dress means that she is a bride. Thus, the men interpret the women's feminine appearance, whether it is adult or virginal, as acquiescence to a sexual relationship and try to have sex with them.

In contrast, when a woman dresses like a man, she becomes an object of the gaze because of her deviance from the normative code. This gaze is meant to surveil and normalize them, and it functions as a punishment. Frankie fears that if she grows up to be an extraordinarily tall woman, she will be "a Freak" (25), which means that she has internalized this normalizing gaze. As for the gaze focused on Amelia, it is the gaze of curiosity, the desire to see or peep at a freak who deviates from the norms of the society. This gaze also includes the gaze of normalization because the townspeople expect that Amelia will be "a calculable woman," when they see her in a wedding dress (219). On the surface, Amelia in a feminine dress seems to adjust herself to the gaze, which makes her an object of desire or an object of the gaze itself.

However, it should be noted that the more the narrator describes Amelia in a feminine dress, the more it is revealed that there is inconsistency between her feminine appearance and her real self, as evident in the scene of the wedding ceremony:

> Anyway, she strode with great steps down the aisle of the church wearing her dead mother's bridal gown, which was of yellow satin and at least twelve inches too short for her ... As the marriage lines were read Miss Amelia kept making an odd gesture—she would rub the palm of her right hand down the side of her satin wedding gown. She was reaching for the pocket of her overalls, and being unable to find it her face became impatient, bored, and exasperated. (219)

Here, Amelia looks like a caricature of an ordinary bride. Moreover, the discord between her real self and her appearance shows itself in the form of a physical sign, "an odd gesture." To the townspeople, a wedding dress should be a sign of an exemplary female figure in patriarchal society. However, when the wedding dress, a sign of femininity, is put on the body of Amelia, its meaning deviates from the expected.[4]

Moreover, when Amelia wears a red dress, she reveals that her surface is inconsistent with her reality. For example, the narrator reports that she wears swamp boots and overalls during the week, but on Sunday, she puts on a dark red dress that hangs on her "in a most peculiar fashion" (214). Likewise, when Macy shows a threatening attitude toward Lymon, she comes out from behind her counter and approaches Marvin Macy very slowly, with her fists clenched and "her peculiar red dress hanging awkwardly around her bony knees" (241). Here, Amelia wears a red dress to draw the attention of Lymon, whom she loves. "A red dress" is one that makes female sexuality visible, and in this sense, it is correct to wear a red dress. However, she fails to draw Lymon's attention. Instead, this red dress reveals her lack of femininity. Whether it is a wedding dress that symbolizes the purity of a woman, or a red dress that accentuates a woman's sexuality, Amelia's feminine way of dressing is always cross-dressing.[5]

When Amelia constructs herself according to the male-oriented/patriarchal gaze, the reader can recognize a contradiction between her inside and her outside. It is difficult to determine by her outward appearance if

Amelia is cross-dressing when she wears male clothes or female clothes. Paulson sees the red dress as "a symbol of feminine weakness" (194). However, Amelia's feminine dressing as cross-dressing seems to subvert the woman's position as an object of the gaze. Amelia, who is made an object of the gaze by the townspeople, especially the men, rebels by being an object of the gaze as a parody. Amelia, who is "cross-eyed," and therefore weak in terms of the dynamics of the gaze, subverts the desire of the gaze by "cross-dressing." This subversion is in contrast to Lymon, who attempts to subvert the dichotomy between subject and object but falls into a trap.

In terms of subverting the desire of the gaze, the narrator tells the story in such a way that the voyeuristic desire of the gaze, which includes that of the readers, fails to be fulfilled. For example, in the following scene, the gaze or camera eye of the narrator focuses on Amelia's thigh, which is revealed via her tucking up her red dress:

> She did not warm her backside modestly, lifting her skirt only an inch or so, as do most women when in public. There was not a grain of modesty about Miss Amelia, and she frequently seemed to forget altogether that there were men in the room. Now as she stood warming herself, her red dress was pulled up quite high in the back so that a piece of her strong, hairy thigh could be seen by anyone who cared to look at it. (243)

This gaze intends to normalize her conduct from the patriarchal point of view, suggesting that to do such a thing in front of men is immoral. Meanwhile, it can also be interpreted as a form of the male voyeuristic gaze that peeps at women's bodies: that is, the pornographic gaze. However, at the same time, the narrator also frustrates male desire because Amelia's thigh is "a strong, hairy thigh." Clair Kahane notes that this strong, hairy thigh signifies "male power" (348) and that Amelia's body is thus masculinized. In this way, the narrator's eye focuses on the confused gender identity of its object.

In the same way, during the fight between Amelia and Macy, which is the largest spectacle in the story, the eyes of the narrator, the readers, and the townspeople who see this event create a voyeuristic gaze. Sandra M. Gilbert and Susan Gubar argue that this fight is a "primal scene of the sexual consummation which did not take place on their wedding night" (109). In fact, in the narrator's description there are more than a few words that imply that this "battle *is* sex" (109; italics original).[6]

According to Joyce Carol Oates, boxing is a "mimicry of a species of erotic love in which one man overcomes the other in an exhibition of superior strength and will" (30), and is "akin to pornography" in that "in each case the spectator is made a voyeur, distanced, yet presumably intimately involved" (105–06). The reader must be careful regarding the gaze that witnesses this battle. What is significant here is a difference in the structure of visuality between this battle scene involving Amelia and Macy and the scenes of ordinary pornography. The visual structure of this battle deviates from the ordinary gender construction of viewing pornography. Generally, when watching a pornographic film, the audience obtains pleasure when a man takes on an active role and a woman takes on a passive role, while in this scene involving Amelia and Macy, the audience (most of whom are male) cannot obtain pleasure from seeing Amelia finally conquered by Macy. This lack of fulfillment occurs because the audience expects to watch Amelia conquer Macy; therefore, the male gaze fails to satisfy their desires even though the man subdues the woman. The narrator, in describing the scene as pornographic, offers it up to the male/voyeuristic gaze, but the desire of that gaze is frustrated. Thus, this fight is a parody of a pornographic scene and the male gaze.

Mulvey points out that the gaze that views mainstream Hollywood movies is masculinized and that the gaze that views films is also gendered. Thus, some questions arise: What is the gender of this narrator who functions as a camera eye via which to see Amelia? Can we say that because the author is female, then the narrator is also female? Does the reader unconsciously behold the narrator's story from the townspeople's point of view, that is, from a southern male-oriented view? Many critics describe the narrator as a "he," but some consider the narrator to be female.[7] Paulson points out that "the fact that the narrator is an ambiguous figure—conforming to patriarchal views at times and at other times demonstrating feminine compassion—implies how difficult it is for anyone to overcome conditioning determined by gender" (193). However, as mentioned above, the narrator sees Amelia with an active male gaze, and at the same time, reflects the image that subverts the male desire. This gaze intends to frustrate or distract the desire to determine his/her gender. While the narrator apparently views Amelia with the male gaze, he/she also describes what frustrates male desire. Thus it is crucial to consider that the gender of the narrator is not ambiguous but that the narrator sees Amelia through a female gaze pretending to be male. Therefore, it can be said that the narrator is also cross-dressing and this cross-dressed narrator destabilizes the male-oriented gender code and visual structure.

RETURN OF THE CROSSED/QUEER EYES

Many critics interpret the defeat of Amelia as a form of retaliation or pun-ishment because she transgresses the gender code of patriarchal southern society, and they argue that she is finally confined to a state of femininity.[8] To be sure, Amelia, as the southern white woman who crosses the bound-aries of gender and race and attempts to subvert the white-male dominion, could not avoid being punished in southern society. However, consider-ing that the narrator—pretending to see Amelia through the lens of white masculine desire—also reveals a viewpoint that frustrates this desire, it is questionable whether we can call the outcome of the story simply a "defeat." After she loses the battle with Macy, her body is feminized and finally becomes like a crazy old maid, as cited above. However, it would be fairer to say that her body, which is masculine by its nature, becomes androgynous or cross-gendered. Meanwhile, though the narrator reports that her face finally becomes white, the house, a metaphor for Amelia's body, finally shows itself to be partially blackened: "the painting was left unfinished and one portion of the house is darker and dingier than the other" (197). Amelia, though forced into whiteness by the white man, is still metaphorically cross-racial.

Amelia finally boards up the house, confines herself inside, and blocks the gaze of others. Meanwhile, she keeps one window upstairs unboarded, and according to the narrator, she looks down on the town from behind this window. Her confinement means that eventually Amelia herself becomes invisible, and at the same time, she morphs into a large (crossed) eye that looks at the others. This eye reflects a futile world in which the people lose their café and have nothing to do except listen to the songs sung by the chain gang:

> Yes, the town is dreary. On August afternoons the road is empty, white with dust, and the sky above is bright as glass. Nothing moves—there are no chil-dren's voices, only the hum of the mill. The peach trees seem to grow more crooked every summer, and the leaves are dull gray and of a sickly delicacy ... There is absolutely nothing to do in the town ... The soul rots with boredom. You might as well go down to the Forks Falls highway and listen to the chain gang. (252–53)

This "chain gang" is variously read by critics, because in spite of the racial distinction (the chain gang consists of seven black men and five white men), the voices that sing together achieve harmony—"The voices are dark in the golden glare, the music intricately blended, both somber and joyful" (253). The gang is often interpreted as a symbol of "harmony in human relationships" (Paulson 187). Meanwhile, Paulson simultaneously argues that the chain gang "represents a destructive force in an American society grounded in misogyny and the acceptance, indeed the celebration, of homosocial groups, masculine aggression, and criminality" (189). She also notes that the chain gang, even though composed of criminals, can enjoy some freedom outside the prison, while "the defeated Amelia" is completely boarded up inside the house (188). However, here, Paulson seems to miss the fact that the gang is also watched by a phallic gaze of the guard. As the narrator says, "[t]here is a guard, with a gun, his eyes drawn to red slits by the glare" (253). Foucault points out that public penalties include "two things: the collective interest in the punishment of the con-demend [sic] man and the visible, verifiable character of the punishment" (109). In this way, though the chain gangs seem to enjoy their freedom, we must not forget that they labor under the repression of the surveillance gaze. It can even be said this condition is an allegory for southern society itself. By revealing that white and black people can both be surveyed by the normalizing gaze, the chain gang shows the sterile condition brought about by the binary opposition of black and white, "the subject that sees" and "the object that is seen."[9]

Amelia is oppressed by the dominant white gaze based on sexism and racism and the gender-coded eyes of the innocent townspeople, who impose gender norms on Amelia and desire to make her "a calculable woman" (219). Lymon is said to be sold into "a side-show" by Macy at the end of the story (252), and Macy, who continues stealing, may be imprisoned again and therefore become an object of the surveillance gaze. In the binary opposition of the gaze, the subject and the object are easily exchangeable. After describing the townspeople's voyeuristic way of seeing, the narrator goes on to describe the surveillance of the criminals because he or she intends to show that there is no difference between the voyeuristic gaze and the surveillance gaze. In either case, the exchange of the subject and the object only brings about another form of oppression.

Amelia resists the repressive gaze with her subversive surface. And seemingly, she loses the battle. However, the repressed "queer" eyes of Amelia, after being defeated once, return as eyes that are even more crossed and deflected than before. The gaze of Amelia, whose inside and outside are incongruous, cannot be exchangeable with the linear gaze that exists between those who see and those who are seen; in other words, the gaze of the binary opposition in which the subject and the object can always be exchanged. The queer gaze of Amelia does not intend to subvert this opposition, but to deflect or cross its linear quality to reveal the sterility of this binary opposition. These queer/crossed eyes that see the townspeople through the window appear at the beginning of the story. Thus, it can be said that the narrator intends to construct the story as it develops, as shown by this queer gaze in the opening. In sum, cross-eyed, cross-dressed, cross-gendered, cross-racial Amelia looks at the small southern town askew and attempts to deconstruct the patriarchal code of its society. In the battle of the gaze, Amelia is determined to be defeated but her defeat deconstructs oppression.[10]

NOTES

1. The etymology of "queer" is thought to be traceable to the German word *quer*, which means perverse and oblique ("Queer," *Oxford*), or the Low German word *queer*, which means "oblique, off-center" ("Queer," *Online*).
2. Regarding Amelia as a phallic woman, see Gleeson-White 101–02. Gleeson-White argues that "the phallic/uncastrated/masculine Miss Amelia becomes the castrator of Marvin Macy: she denies him the position of having the phallus in order to save her own phallic position" (102).
3. Michael Kimmel explains how the traits of the mythic cowboy figure are regarded as "manly" (150). "He is a natural aristocrat" (150) and "is free in a free country, embodying republican virtue and autonomy" (151). Also, Kimmel points out that "he is white" (151).
4. Clare Whatling points out that "Amelia's physical strangeness is exaggerated only when she attempts to conform to feminine norms" (239).
5. Gleeson-White also argues that Amelia's wedding dress and red dress show that she is cross-dressed. See Gleeson-White 92–94.
6. Gilbert and Gubar cite the following passages: "For a while the fighters grappled muscle to muscle, their hipbones braced against each other. Backward and forward, from side to side, they swayed in this way" (*Collected* 249).
7. As Paulson points out (203, n.12), Lawrence Graver sees the narrator as being female (25). However, it seems that Graver identifies the author with the narrator, or simply thinks that if the author is female, the narrator is female.
8. For example, Kahane argues that Amelia is "left a woman, gender-locked in a decaying house" (348). Paulson says that "[l]ike blacks in the Southern

community, Amelia is victimized by white males" (194). See also Carvill
38–39; Gleeson-White 110; Westling 126.
  9. By this ending, McCullers might also desire to show that in a world in which
visionary discrimination is dominant, gaze functions as a form of repression,
but voice and sound function as a form of liberation.
 10. Permission to reprint this essay from the original Japanese version has been
granted by *Studies in American Literature* 41 (2005): 37–52. Copyright©
2005 by The American Literature Society of Japan.

WORKS CITED

Berger, John. *Ways of Seeing.* London: Penguin, 1972. Print.
Carvill, Caroline. "You Might as Well Listen to the Chain Gang: *The Ballad of the
Sad Café.*" *Reflections in a Critical Eye: Essays on Carson McCullers.* Ed.
Jan Whitt. Lanham: UP of America, 2008. 33–45. Print.
Du Bois, W.E.B. *The Souls of Black Folk.* 1903. Oxford: Oxford UP, 2007. Print.
Fanon, Frantz. *Black Skin, White Masks.* Trans. Richard Philcox. 1952. New York:
Grove P, 2008. Print.
Foucault, Michel. *Discipline and Punish: The Birth of the Prison.* Trans. Alan
Sheridan. London: Penguin, 1977. Print.
Freud, Sigmund. "The 'Uncanny.'" *The Standard Edition of the Complete
Psychological Works of Sigmund Freud.* Ed. James Strachey. Vol. 17. 1955.
London: Vintage, 2001. 217–56. Print.
Gilbert, Sandra M. and Susan Gubar. *No Man's Land: The Place of the Woman
Writer in the Twentieth Century. Volume 1: The War of the Words.* New Haven:
Yale UP, 1988. Print.
Gleeson-White, Sarah. *Strange Bodies: Gender and Identity in the Novels of Carson
McCullers.* Tuscaloosa: U of Alabama P, 2003. Print.
Graver, Lawrence. "Carson McCullers." *University of Minnesota Pamphlets on
American Writers* no. 84. Minneapolis: U of Minnesota P, 1969. Print.
Jones, Anne Goodwyn. *Tomorrow Is Another Day: The Woman Writer in the South,
1859–1936.* Baton Rouge: Louisiana State UP, 1981. Print.
——. "Women Writers and the Myths of Southern Womanhood." *The History of
Southern Women's Literature.* Eds. Carolyn Perry and Mary Louise Weaks.
Baton Rouge: Louisiana State UP, 2002. 275–89. Print.
Kahane, Claire. "The Gothic Mirror." *The (M)other Tongue: Essays in Feminist
Psychoanalytic Interpretation.* Eds. Shirley Nelson Garner, Claire Kahane, and
Madelon Sprengnether. Ithaca: Cornell UP, 1985. 334–51. Print.
Kimmel, Michael. *Manhood in America: A Cultural History.* New York: Free P,
1996. Print.
McCullers, Carson. *Collected Stories of Carson McCullers.* Boston: Houghton,
1987. Print.

——. *The Member of the Wedding*. 1946. London: Penguin, 1987. Print.

Mulvey, Laura. *Visual and Other Pleasures*. New York: Palgrave, 1989. Print.

Oates, Joyce Carol. *On Boxing*. 1987. New York: Harper, 2006. Print.

Paulson, Suzanne Morrow. "Carson McCullers's *The Ballad of the Sad Café*: A Song Half Sung, Misogyny, and 'Ganging Up.'" *Critical Essays on Carson McCullers*. Eds. Beverly Lyon Clark and Melvin J. Friedman. New York: Hall, 1996. 187–205. Print.

"Queer." *Online Etymology Dictionary*. Ed. Douglas Harper. 2013. Web. 28 September 2013.

——. *Oxford Dictionary of Word Origins*. 2nd ed. 2002. Print.

Westling, Louise. *Sacred Groves and Ravaged Gardens: The Fiction of Eudora Welty, Carson McCullers, and Flannery O'Connor*. Athens: U of Georgia P, 1985. Print.

Whatling, Clare. "Reading Miss Amelia: Critical Strategies in the Construction of Sex, Gender, Sexuality, the Gothic and the Grotesque." *Modernist Sexualities*. Eds. Hugh Stevens and Caroline Howlett. Manchester: Manchester UP, 2000. 239–50. Print.

Wolstenholme, Susan. *Gothic (Re)Visions: Writing Women as Readers*. Albany: State U of New York P, 1993. Print.

"Nature is Not Abnormal; Only Lifelessness is Abnormal": Paradigms of the In-valid in *Reflections in a Golden Eye*

Alison Graham-Bertolini

In 1939, Carson McCullers began outlining a story that she initially titled "Army Post." The genesis of the story came from a remark made to her by her husband, James Reeves McCullers, about "a voyeur who had been arrested at Fort Bragg, a young soldier who had been caught peeping inside the married officers' quarters" (Carr, *Lonely* 89). In 1941, "Army Post" was first published, renamed *Reflections in a Golden Eye*. The novel is set on an army base in a nameless southern town. The story features an army Captain, Captain Penderton, who hides his homosexuality from the world because of pressure to be "normal." The Captain's standing in the military makes this pressure all the more violent; to be a nonconformist means risking his rank and career. Yet, the Captain's stunted sexual desires lead him to experience a number of pathological conditions, such as kleptomania and voyeurism, which completely disrupt his life. At the novel's conclusion, Captain Penderton commits murder, killing Private Ellgee Williams, who is stalking his wife. I argue that the system-shattering act of murder is a metaphor, a gesture that depicts Captain Penderton "killing" his restrictive hyper-hetero-shroud to suggest that he may live a life free from culturally constructed heteronormative constraints. McCullers deliberately undermines conceptions of "normality" in Captain Penderton,

A. Graham-Bertolini (✉)
North Dakota State University, Fargo, ND, USA

© The Author(s) 2016
A. Graham-Bertolini, C. Kayser (Eds.), *Carson McCullers in the Twenty-First Century*, DOI 10.1007/978-3-319-40292-5_11

Alison Langdon, and her Filipino servant Anacleto, by demonstrating how performances of "the normal" lead them to great unhappiness and tragedy. Moreover, I demonstrate that the atypical attributes of these characters ultimately allow them to resist and challenge a social order that denies equal treatment to all.

The 1940s was a period in history when the systematic murder of individuals with cognitive and physical disabilities was occurring at the hands of the Nazis, resulting in a heightened awareness of the pathology of bodily incoherence the world over. But as noted by Lennard J. Davis, "While we tend to associate eugenics with a Nazi-like racial supremacy, it is important to realize that eugenics was not the trade of a fringe group of right-wing fascist maniacs. Rather, it became the common belief and practice of many, if not most, European and American citizens" (6). Such focus was evident in the heightened emphasis on the anomalous body within the military system in the United States—a scar, disfigurement, mental illness, disease, and/or nonconforming sexual orientation were seen as symptoms of one's incommensurability with normative social prescripts and not appropriate for the disciplined uniformed body and its environs. As argued by Davis,

> The emphasis on nation and national fitness obviously plays into the metaphor of the body. If individual citizens are not fit, if they do not fit into the nation, then the national body will not be fit. Of course—such arguments are based on a false idea of the body politic … Nevertheless, the eugenic "logic" that individual variations would accumulate into a composite national identity was a powerful one. (6)

The concern was that anomalous bodies would result in an anomalous nation, so those with overt physical and mental differences were stigmatized by being rejected from service, or were shunned, shamed, and even physically punished by the larger population. Davis suggests that the mentality of the time sought to create a universal worker, one whose physical characteristics would be uniform, as well as the result of their labors—they were to provide a "uniform product" (6). Similarly, enlisted men and women were mobilized into a disciplined fighting force wherein uniformity was a key goal and individuals were expected to act as a unit. In *Reflections*, such uniformity is evident from the very first lines of the text:

> An Army post in peacetime is a dull place. Things happen, but then they happen over and over again. The general plan of a fort in itself adds to the monotony—the huge concrete barracks, the neat rows of officers' homes

built precisely like the other, the gym, the chapel, the golf course and the swimming pools—all is designed according to a rigid pattern ... once a man enters the army he is expected only to follow the heels ahead of him. (309)

Conditioning recruits to "follow the heels ahead" presumably alleviated the nation's fears that young people might fall prey to sexual perversion, delinquency, or worse, by fostering in them a healthy respect for law and order and enforcing "proper" gender roles.

Near the conclusion of *Reflections in a Golden Eye*, Captain Penderton and his neighbor, Major Morris Langdon, have the following conversation, which questions the convention of homogeneity:

'You mean,' Captain Penderton said, 'that any fulfillment obtained at the expense of normalcy is wrong, and should not be allowed to bring happiness. In short, it is better, because it is morally honorable, for the square peg to keep scraping the round hole rather than to discover and use the unorthodox square that would fit it?'

'Why you put it exactly right,' the Major said. 'Don't you agree with me?'

'No,' said the Captain, after a short pause. (384)

Major Langdon insists to Captain Penderton that we all must strive to adhere to cultural constructions of normality. Yet, the entire novel demonstrates the fallacy of this way of thinking.

Homosexuality was classified as a mental illness in the *Diagnostic and Statistical Manual of Mental Disorders* until 1973, when the American Psychiatric Association finally voted to replace the diagnosis with the classification of "sexual orientation disturbance."[1] Sarah Gleeson-White observes, "In the America of McCullers' time, homosexuals, ostracized as some kind of defiling force, faced the real risk of social punishment: Harassment and arrest, for example" (61). Homosexuality then, functioned like other forms of illness and disability in the 1940s, placing queer individuals in opposition to normative categories of identification. McCullers, who referred to herself as an "invert" and at times believed herself to be a man (Carr, *Lonely* 167, 159), was well aware of the discrimination one might encounter by refusing to conform to expected gender norms. Rachel Adams explains that "the invocation of the term queer" in McCullers' work is "frequently associated with her characters' receptiveness to otherwise unthinkable permutations of sex and gender, which are defined in opposition to normative categories of identification and desire" (554). Moreover, writes Adams, "Such a veiled deployment of the queer is unsurprising at a historical moment when it regularly functioned as a shaming mechanism to legitimate discrimination and physical violence against homosexuals" (554).

Carson McCullers states in "The Flowering Dream: Notes on Writing," that "the fact that Captain Penderton ... is homosexual, is also a symbol, of handicap and impotence" (1). Captain Penderton is described as "a delicate balance between the male and female elements, with the susceptibilities of both the sexes and the active powers of neither" (314). The Captain's lack of "active powers" indicates his repressed essence. Captain Penderton perceives one of the other enlisted men on the base, Private Williams, as utterly masculine and soldierly; in many ways, he believes Private Williams to be all that he is not. He admires the soldier's "dumb eyes, heavy sensual lips that were always wet" (370), and his "deft, brown hands" (373). Where he once scorned the barracks and the mess hall, he now finds he has a sudden urge to belong to them (387). The sudden physical longing he harbors for Private Williams is a problem for Captain Penderton, not because of his homosexuality, which he does not acknowledge, but because he can't come to terms with the fact that he is attracted to a private, a person who wields no power or authority in the military social system and is thus "beneath" him; and also because when Williams does not return his interest, Captain Penderton must accept that he has feelings for a person who does not reciprocate his love.

The Captain grows more and more "obsessed" (381) with Williams until he eventually stops trying "to find the justification for the emotion that had so taken possession of him. He thought of the soldier in terms neither of love nor hate; he was conscious only of the irresistible yearning to break down the barrier between them" (388). If we believe that the Private (with his able-bodied, emotionless, hyper-masculine exterior) represents heteronormativity for the Captain, then his desire to "break down the barriers between them" indicates that at some level he wants not only to break down the barriers between himself and the Private, but to also break down the barriers that classify sexual desire as homosexual versus heterosexual. His inability to do so infuriates the Captain, whose anger is directed both toward the Private (further fueling his obsession), but more so toward himself, because he is obsessed with a man who he thinks is unworthy of his attention. The Captain's anger with himself is intensified further by the fact that his voluptuous and beautiful wife, Leonora Penderton, openly scorns her husband's lack of authority. By performing the hyper-aggressive act of slaying Private Williams, Captain Penderton is succumbing to his desire for conformity by doing what he is expected to do as the protector of his wife; but importantly, he is also metaphorically killing his obsession with heteronormativity. His obsession with the Private comes to an end when he literally kills it—suggesting that he must move on to live a life free of conformity. The murder then can be understood as a truly heroic act because it implies that the Captain has become a figure of possibility in an otherwise stagnant binary world.

The text thus tells two stories; the first is the obvious story about relationships on an army base in the 1940s, while the parallel narrative is metaphoric, wherein the Captain and the Private appear as almost two versions of the same man. Both men live in a world of sexual repression, and for both characters, this subjugation of the self leads to disaster. Private Williams is heterosexual, but represses his desire for women because he has been taught that all women are diseased. Captain Penderton represses his attraction to Private Williams because at this point in American history, there was no legitimate space for homosexuality to exist. Both men reduce their sexual activity to stalking and watching the target of their affection: Private Williams stalks Leonora Penderton, who is married to the Captain, while Captain Penderton stalks the Private.

Private Ellgee Williams is described as a series of contradictions. He seems "a bit heavy and awkward" at first glance, but this is belied by an agility, which is compared to that of "a wild creature" (309). His hands are described as "small and delicate" like a woman's but also "very strong" (309). His behavior too, is either that of a seemingly upstanding enlisted man, or much like a wild creature. He spends his free time "in the woods surrounding the post" in the "wild unspoiled country" (310) and he is largely emotionless—as Margaret McDowell writes about Private Williams, "So completely does he avoid extremes of feeling that no one has seen him laugh, become angry, or suffer during the time that he has been in the army" (56). In fact, McDowell continues, "He never becomes ... a truly developed human being capable of relating to other human beings or capable of forming even the most elementary moral discriminations" (57). Perhaps in crafting this character McCullers was conscious of the idea that "to have a disability is to be an animal, to be part of the Other" (Davis 9). Douglas C. Baynton explains this way of thinking further, observing that from the mid-nineteenth century on, "the opposite of the normal person was the defective ... the *sub*normal ... that which pulled humanity back toward ... its animal origins" (19). Even more worrisome is that Private Williams engages in activities that jeopardize the safety of others; from his voyeuristic behavior and stalking of Leonora Penderton, to picking fights, to committing murder, Private Williams has no sense of right and wrong.

Private Williams first encounters Captain Penderton when he is assigned to clear a wooded area behind the Captain's home. This scene can be read as analogous to the barriers of self: Captain Penderton is secretly undisciplined and wild, with an unkempt ego; he is a man who is attracted to pleasure rather than military order. In clearing the "wilderness" around his home he is trying to clear what is wild and unkempt from his mind, including anxiety surrounding his masculinity. Judith Butler has written most notably of the extent of gendered anxiety, claiming that men often perform masculinity to an extreme to assuage their knowledge that gender is a performance, something that they *do* but do not *feel*. For Captain Penderton, who is gay, this is especially true. Unfortunately, his attempts to impose order on the wilderness go very wrong when Williams clears away too much brush, angering the Captain for the first time. Using metaphor and symbol, McCullers foreshadows the way that Captain Penderton's true nature will be exposed, as the Private clears the "brush" hiding his identity over the course of the story.

At the outset of the narrative, we learn that Captain Penderton suffers from a number of "basic lacks" (McCullers 314). He is a coward (315), a thief (340), and a sadist who once took pleasure from killing a kitten (315). The suggestion is that these problematic aspects of his character are the result of his repressed sexuality. No matter how hard he works to conform, there are aspects of himself that resist the conventional. Subverting these essential parts of himself leads to erratic and troubled behavior, including a dysfunctional relationship with his wife, Leonora. When early in the novel Leonora strips naked after the Captain urges her to dress properly for dinner, he overreacts, threatening, "I will kill you! ... I will do it! I will do it!" (317). The Captain is trying desperately to perform the role of dominant patriarch because of his anxiety regarding his own gender. When Leonora is unaffected by his threats, he is sickened, not by the reality of their relationship, but because he realizes that the scene might have been witnessed through the curtainless window, that his humiliation might have been public, and his lack of control exposed.

The army encourages enlisted men and women to depend passively on authority to direct and dictate their lives by making enlisted personnel act without critical thinking. For example, enlisted men and women are expected to follow orders; they must get over the taboo of killing by treating the enemy as an object rather than as a human; and they must eliminate a sense of self-preservation by conditioning themselves to go into battle knowing they risk bodily injury or death. Such "docile bodies" find themselves "in the grip of very strict powers that impose on [them] a variety of constraints, prohibitions or obligations" (Foucault *D & P* 136). In *The History of Sexuality*, Foucault writes about ways in which the body began to be treated as a political machine:

> Its disciplining, the optimization of its capabilities, the extortion of its forces, the parallel increase of its usefulness and its docility, its integration into systems of efficient and economic controls, all this was ensured by the procedures of power that characterized the disciplines: an *anatomo-politics of the human body*. (139)

This quote explains to some degree the Captain's obsession with regulating himself—in the Captain's case, his rank in the military and the corresponding power he wields as a Captain are directly related to his ability to model a useful and disciplined body.

All of the characters in *Reflections* are regulated by the constraints and obligations of their environment, but not all of the characters blindly accept such regulation. Alison Langdon is ill with a heart condition, an ailment that denotes both her physical illness and the symbolic "broken heart" she suffered at the death of her eleven-month-old daughter. The narrator explains, "She was very ill and she looked it. Not only was this illness physical, but she had been tortured to the bone by grief and anxiety so that now she was on the verge of actual lunacy" (319). Alison has additionally discovered that her husband, Major Langdon, is having an affair with Leonora Penderton, a betrayal that contributes to her "obvious unhappiness" (330). Her knowledge of the affair unwittingly pushes her toward the singular symbolic gesture of suicide. She tries to stab and kill herself with a pair of garden shears, but finding them "too blunt," cuts her nipples off instead (327, 338), leaving her physical body as scarred and partial as her mental state. Major Langdon sees Alison's act of self-mutilation as "something morbid and female, [something] altogether out of his control" (330), but the act is emblematic of Alison's loss, first the loss of her daughter and second the loss of her husband. The violent removal of her nipples indicates her scarred maternal capacity, especially her inability to nurse the missing child. Simultaneously, this act reflects the harm done to her sexuality; her scarred breasts reveal the way her sexuality has been damaged as the result of her husband's betrayal.

Alison Langdon's self-effacement might be understood either as an act of resistance or as an act of complicity with oppression. According to Ehrenreich and English,

> Women use sickness as an escape from their oppression as workers and wives. They are not being dishonest, or faking. Our culture encourages people to express resistance as 'illness,' just as it encourages us to view overt rebellion as 'sick.' The oppression is real; the resistance is real; but the sickness is manufactured. (160)

Ehrenreich and English explain that illness became a tool for women in oppressive environments to resist social artifice. Thus the "hysteria" exhibited by Alison Langdon is a critical tool for destabilizing oppressive normative behaviors. As noted by Elaine Showalter, the "feminist understanding of hysteria has been influenced by work in semiotics and discourse theory, seeing hysteria as a specifically feminine protolanguage, communicating through the body messages that cannot be verbalized" (286). For example, when early in their marriage Alison cries when the Major shoots a quail, the Major understands her response as "female" and "morbid" (330) though she is simply communicating her sorrow at the bird's death in a nonverbal way. Alison's physical and mental instabilities allow her to avoid many restrictive social rituals and behaviors in which she might otherwise be expected to take part. She is excused from "the routine of sports and parties that her husband thought suitable" (362) for reasons that are chalked up to her seemingly inferior biology. Her illness is considered a feminine condition, a condition suffered by the weaker sex, and so is accepted as an excuse to bypass social functions by her husband and neighbors. Her disintegrating body provides her with the framework to avoid tasks and expectations that she despises while simultaneously allowing her to unleash emotions that might otherwise be considered wholly impolite—according to her husband, for example, she is often "bitter," "cold," and "finicky" (332). Similarly, Leonora Penderton excuses Alison's odd mannerisms and comments because she considers Alison "to be quite off her head, and did not believe even the simplest remark she made" (349). Alison thus uses her invalid status to resist social norms.

Alternately however, Alison's disfigurement can be understood as a corporeal marker of her physical and mental difference from other, more typical, army wives. Many people, including her own husband, believe she is "a hyperchondriacal fake" (362), and so her bodily dysfunction invalidates her entirely in the eyes of the world. Being an invalid certainly contributes to the perception that Alison is "not valid," a long-standing cultural interpretation of feminine illness that situates women's physical suffering as manipulative, sentimental, or a joke (Herndl xii). Thus, despite the fact that she is the only person in the novel who recognizes, for example, that Captain Penderton is a thief and that Private Williams is sneaking up to Leonora's bedroom at night, her opinions are largely ignored and discounted. Ultimately, Alison is committed to a sanatorium by her husband for suggesting that Leonora might be having an affair with "an enlisted man" (378) and for demanding a divorce (378). Major Langdon calls in an array of doctors to examine Alison before making this decision—the doctors "struck matches in front of her nose and asked her various questions" (379), an "examination" that reveals McCullers' disdain of reigning medical techniques. Alison is moved to the insane asylum where she dies of a heart attack. Thus, the most reasonable character in the story is rendered permanently voiceless.

Unable to leave her husband because she has no financial means of support, Alison Langdon is complicit in acceding to her "place" in a patriarchal system but also, to some degree, successful in controlling that place. She uses what limited agency she has to belie social expectations and behaviors. The only character who recognizes the worth of Alison Langdon is Anacleto, the Langdon's effeminate Filipino servant. Anacleto is a foreigner, a colonized subject. He is effeminate, and he is entirely dependent on the Langdons for his livelihood, conditions that situate him on the margins of society and make him a target for bullies like Major Langdon. Yet, by portraying himself as just slightly incompetent, Anacleto is able to temporarily disrupt the imbalance of power between himself and his superiors. Anacleto defies Major Langdon in a variety of ways, including using broken English to "addle the Major" (333), following the Major's orders at a frustratingly slow pace, intentionally doing a poor job at the tasks he has been assigned, or by conveniently forgetting to complete the tasks he has been assigned. On one occasion, Anacleto takes 38 minutes to mix the Major a drink, and on another occasion, he neglects to properly polish the Major's boots, so that they "looked as though they had been rubbed over with flour and water" (345). His buffoonery thus becomes a way to avoid a prescripted world in which he would be wholly powerless. The techniques that Anacleto uses to defy obsessive social conventions are similar to ways in which Alison Langdon uses her physical and emotional instability as tools to avoid enacting oppressive normative behaviors.

Unlike Alison and Anacleto, Captain Penderton fears losing authority in the military community where he holds rank, so he performs "normalcy" to an extreme. Yet, Captain Penderton's physical body reveals that he is not entirely contained by the restrictions he places on himself. He is literally oozing out around the edges of his constraints, as noted by the other enlisted men. When he rides a horse, for example, "his buttocks spread and jounced flabbily in the saddle. For this reason he was known to the soldiers as Captain Flap-Fanny" (323). Other telltale marks on the Captain's body point to his inability to mask his difference; for example, we learn that although he is only 35 years old, his face and body appear older, showing "the strain of his long efforts ... there were bruise-like circles beneath his eyes and his complexion was of a yellow, mottled color" (380). His body is so marked by his struggle to conform that the strain is actually visible to the human eye. Psychologically, Captain Penderton

is in a constant state of repressed agitation. His preoccupation with the soldier grows in him like a disease ... As in cancer, when the cells unaccountably rebel and begin an insidious self-multiplication that can ultimately destroy the body, so in his mind did the thoughts of the soldier grow out of all proportion to their normal sphere. (380)

His thoughts become a "diseased obsession" (381), so much so that he must resort to taking Seconal, a type of sleeping pill, to be at all functional. Thus, again we see the physical and pathological implications for restricting and containing his sexuality. In other words, his obsession with heteronormativity is manifesting as physical bodily damage.

The zenith of the Captain's self-destruction occurs one afternoon when he takes his wife's horse, Firebird, for a ride. Three times, while the horse gallops, he tightens the reins and jerks the horse up short:

The horse, which had not been exercised that day, seemed to go a little mad from the pleasure of galloping with unchecked freedom ... They had galloped rhythmically for perhaps three quarters of a mile when suddenly with no preliminary tightening of the reins, the Captain jerked the horse up short. He pulled the reins with such unexpected sharpness that Firebird lost his balance, sidestepped awkwardly and reared ... This procedure was repeated twice. The Captain gave Firebird his head just long enough for the joy of freedom to be aroused and then checked him without warning. (352)

Checking the horse's freedom replicates what he is doing to himself. He controls his own sexual urges, denying himself the freedom to be who he is. Yet, instead of succumbing to the sadistic discipline imposed on him by the Captain, the horse gallops away with Captain Penderton on his back. As the horse races through the wilderness, Captain Penderton experiences a complete loss of control, which (interestingly) leads him to euphoria. At the moment he believes that his life is over, he "suddenly began to live" (354). He is happy for the first time in the novel.

When the horse finally stops, the Captain ties him to a tree and beats him "savagely" (355). The anger he is experiencing is again misplaced. He is not angry with the horse for running away, but rather he is angry with himself for allowing himself to experience the euphoria of freedom as a result of loss of control. This is disturbing because it is only by relinquishing self-control that the Captain finds temporary happiness. As soon as a modicum of self-possession returns to him he masochistically beats the horse. He is so regulated by ideological systems that he is unable to be true to his own nature.

Minutes later, as the Captain lays sobbing on the ground, he sees Private Williams "looking down on him," from a position that might mistakenly be read as one of higher ethical or moral good. Private Williams is completely naked in this scene, and his body glistens in the sun (356). He ignores the Captain, unties the horse, strokes its muzzle, and leads it gently away. Here, we see Private Williams physically releasing what has been contained, freeing the oppressed, at least this is how it appears to the Captain. Captain Penderton, the oppressor, is unable to allow himself such freedom. When he believed his life was over, he experienced relief but cannot sustain such happiness in his daily life because he has been so conditioned to conform. What the Captain does not realize is that Private Williams is as equally obsessed with Leonora Penderton as he himself is with the Private. Neither man is in fact happy or fulfilled.

To Captain Penderton, Private Williams appears to be the model of masculine detachment. But as always with McCullers' characters, circumstances are not always as they first appear. Private Williams is, like the Captain, indisputably disturbed, a condition that seems to arise from his own sexual repression. Before spying on Leonora Penderton, Private Williams had "never seen a woman naked" (320); moreover,

He had grown up in a household exclusively male. From his father ... he had learned that women carried in them a deadly and catching disease which made men blind, crippled, and doomed to hell. In the army he also heard much talk of this bad sickness and was even himself examined once a month by the doctor to see if he had touched a woman. Private Williams had never willingly touched, or looked at, or spoken to a female since he was eight years old. (320)

Not only has Private Williams never acknowledged his own sexuality, he actually fears it. Sexual repression in the Private has manifested itself in a number of ways, including the murder of another man, and more recently, picking fights with other soldiers to release his pent up energy (389). Private Williams becomes obsessed with Leonora Penderton after accidentally seeing her naked. He stalks her, then repeatedly breaks into her home and her bedroom where he watches her for hours while she sleeps. The narrator observes, "He dreamed of the Lady every night ... to him she was always in the room where he had watched her in the night with such absorption. His memory of these times were wholly sensual ... once having known this he could not let it go; in him was engendered a dark, drugged craving as certain of fulfillment as death" (391). His behavior is intrusive, obsessive, and clearly disturbed.

When Captain Penderton finally catches Private Williams in his wife's room, he shoots him. In *Understanding Carson McCullers*, Virginia Carr notes that this act "had been determined for him, first by his family, then by the Major Langdons in his career. The self-estranged Captain is fated to die the isolate, having severed his one tenuous grasp at communion with another human being" (*Understanding* 50). In other words, Carr believes that the Captain has killed his only chance at finding love with another human being. Hugo McPherson similarly argues that Captain Penderton has annihilated "the force that he has both loved and feared—the "natural" man" (145). While symbolically it might appear as though Captain Penderton is attempting to eradicate the object of his desire so that he can *return* to a condition of self-estranged isolation, I read this scene differently. He kills Private Williams because heterosexuality alone does not a docile body make. In other words, Private Williams at this moment is exposed as deviant to the Captain. The Captain realizes that the Private is not the ideal embodiment of manly independence that he had imagined; in fact, he realizes that the Private is just as flawed and disturbed as he himself. The Private has stalked and obsessed over Leonora just as the Captain has stalked and obsessed over the Private. For the Captain, admitting that socially acceptable heterosexuality can manifest itself in deviant or aberrant ways interrupts and ends his obsession with heterosexuality, which is what the Private has represented to him until this moment.

The Captain shoots Private Williams, telling himself that in this moment "he knew all" (393). Yet, the narrator corrects this assumption, noting, "What it was that he knew he could not have expressed. He was only certain that this was the end" (393). I believe that this moment marks "the end" of the Captain's struggle to repress his homosexuality. Sarah Gleeson-White likewise observes that the murder, done with a "phallus-pistol," is "an act of penetration" (60). Captain Penderton's homogenous mindset is disrupted when he catches Private Williams in the unconscionable act of voyeurism, so that he finally realizes that the idea of the normal is a fallacy. After killing the Private, the Captain is described as "A broken and dissipated monk" shrouded in a "queer, coarse wrapper" (393). McCullers uses the word "queer" very deliberately at this moment, to emphasize the homosexual identity that the Captain is unable to escape. Moreover, the metaphor of the "broken dissipated monk" is appropriate for a man who has led an isolated and sexless life. The Captain, in essence, has murdered his desire to conform and in doing so has freed himself from a shroud of desolation.

The climax of this story suggests that "normality" is an illusion; that the only thing that is abnormal is normalness (Carr, *Lonely* 2). McCullers demonstrates that it is not abnormality that is dangerous to our society but trying repeatedly to reconcile what makes us unique, by struggling to fit the "square peg into the round hole" (384). McCullers understands that our fears of difference, of hierarchy, and loss of power, leave us unable to break free of the assumptions and prejudices that legitimate exclusion and impede our quest for full personhood.

NOTE

1. "In sexual orientation disturbance it is only diagnostically valid to classify an individual as having pathological behavior if the individual is in some way harmed from normal functioning as a result of their sexual orientation" (Kularski 1).

WORKS CITED

Adams, Rachel. "The Queer Fiction of Carson McCullers." *American Literature*. 71.3. (1999). 551–83. Print.

Baynton, Douglas C. "Disability and the Justification of Inequality in American History." *The Disability Studies Reader*. Ed. Davis, Lennard J. New York: Routledge. 2013. Print.

Carr, Virginia Spencer. *The Lonely Hunter: A Biography of Carson McCullers.* Garden City, New York: Doubleday, 1975. Print.

Carr, Virginia Spencer. "Reflections in a Golden Eye." *Understanding Carson McCullers.* Columbia: U of South Carolina P, 1990. 37–52. Print.

Davis, Lennard J. "Introduction: Normality, Power, Culture." *The Disability Studies Reader.* Ed. Davis, Lennard J. New York: Routledge. 2013. Print.

Ehrenreich, Barbara and Deirdre English. *Complaints and Disorders: The Sexual Politics of Sickness,* Second Ed. New York: Feminist Press, 2011. Print.

Foucault, Michel. *Discipline and Punish: The Birth of the Prison.* New York: Random House, 1995. Print.

——. *The History of Sexuality: An Introduction.* New York: Vintage Books, 1990. Print.

Free, Melissa Relegation and Rebellion: "The Queer, the Grotesque, and the Silent in the Fiction of Carson McCullers." *Studies in the Novel* 40.4 (Winter 2009): 426–46. Print.

Gleeson-White, Sarah. *Strange Bodies: Gender and Identity in the Novels of Carson McCullers.* Alabama: UP of Alabama, 2003. Print.

Kularski, Curtis M. "Changes in the Classification of Homosexual Behavior in the Diagnostic and Statistical Manual of Mental Disorders." *Academia.edu.* Web. Accessed: Nov. 1, 2014, http://www.academia.edu/1154979/.

McCullers, Carson. *Reflections in a Golden Eye. Complete Novels.* New York: Library of America, 2001. 307–93. Print.

——. "The Flowering Dream: Notes on Writing." *Esquire,* 1959.

McDowell, Margaret B. *Carson McCullers.* Boston: Twayne Publishers, 1980. Print.

McPherson, Hugo. "Carson McCullers, Lonely Huntress: *Reflections in a Golden Eye.*" *Critical Essays on Carson McCullers.* Eds. Beverly Lyon Clark and Melvin J. Friedman. New York: G.K. Hall and Co. 1996. 143–46. Print.

Savigneau, Josyane. *Carson McCullers: A Life.* Trans: Joan E. Howard. New York. Houghton Mifflin. 2001. Print.

Showalter, Elaine. "Hysteria, Feminism, and Gender." *Hysteria beyond Freud.* Eds. Gilman, Sander L., Helen King, Roy Porter, G. S. Rousseau, and Elaine Showalter. Berkeley: U of California P, 1993. Web.<http://ark.cdlib.org/ark:/13030/ft0p3003d3/>.

An "archaeology of [narrative] silence": Cognitive Segregation and Productive Citizenship in McCullers' *The Heart Is a Lonely Hunter*

Stephanie Rountree

The constitution of madness as a mental illness [...] thrusts into oblivion all those stammered, imperfect words without fixed syntax in which the exchange between madness and reason was made. The language of psychiatry, which is a monologue of reason about madness, has been established only on the basis of such a silence.

I have not tried to write the history of that language, but rather the archaeology of that silence.
—Michel Foucault, *Madness and Civilization*, 1965

When Carson McCullers published *The Heart Is a Lonely Hunter* in 1940, she unknowingly composed a literary capstone to the forty-year growth of mental institutions in the U.S. South. This regional increase in state-controlled mental institutions coincided with the national proliferation of such facilities, but, for the South, it offered the region its first expansive opportunity to institutionalize feebleminded[1] persons close to home.[2] As Steven Noll reports in *Feeble-Minded in Our Midst*, the rate of institutionalization in the South nearly tripled during the 1900–1940

S. Rountree (✉)
Georgia State University, Atlanta, GA, USA

© The Author(s) 2016   189
A. Graham-Bertolini, C. Kayser (eds.), *Carson McCullers in the Twenty-First Century*, DOI 10.1007/978-3-319-40292-5_12

boom (4): "[b]y the mid-1920s, each southern state had initiated an institutional program for the care and control of its feeble-minded population" (12). Noll attributes this rise in institutionalization to three key factors: "better medical and scientific detection" of mental deficiencies, "an increasing societal awareness" of mentally disabled persons, and mostly, the South's notorious ability to "segregate and control a portion of the population labeled as deviant" (4).

Two of these three factors—social awareness through circulating rhetorics and the South's historical penchant for "solving" social unease with segregation—manifest in Carson McCullers' *The Heart Is a Lonely Hunter* in ways that expose national and liberal ideals of U.S. citizenship while simultaneously organizing the narrative. McCullers' novel features John Singer, a peaceful and noble deaf-mute, at the center of a collection of characters from a Georgia mill town—Biff Brannon, Jake Blount, Dr. Benedict Copeland, and Mick Kelly. Singer's relationships with these divergent personalities foster the novel's modernist themes of community, compassion, loss, and the barriers that divide humanity. While many scholars have privileged Singer's character in scholarship, often asserting as Emily Russell does in *Reading Embodied Citizenship* that his "physical difference" provides the remaining characters with "a blank slate upon which to project their fantasies of being understood" (75), I focus on a lesser-discussed[3] character—Singer's dear friend, the Greek, deaf-mute, and mentally deviant Spiros Antonapoulos who is sent to a mental institution at the novel's opening. By reading Antonapoulos's institutionalization as manifest of national politics regarding mental deviants in the early twentieth century, I ultimately map how the same logic that compels cognitive segregation as a liberal technology also underwrites the narratological structure of *Lonely Hunter*. Just as the practice of mental institutionalization segregated cognitively unproductive citizens from mainstream society—thereby unburdening normative citizens and enabling their productivity, so is Antonapoulos removed to the margins of the narrative—thereby rendering Singer eligible to serve as the narrative fulcrum by befriending the other four prominent characters.

"Menacing" the Feebleminded

Antonapoulos's removal to the mental institution would not have seemed extreme to an American reader in the 1940s, as cognitive segregation had grown tremendously in the previous four decades, both regionally and nationally. Between 1903 and 1940, growth of feebleminded institutionalization dramatically outpaced total population growth: whereas the U.S. population expanded by 64 percent during this era, the mentally institutionalized population increased at an astonishing 743 percent, from approximately 14,000 to 118,000 patients (Trent 166; Noll 38; U.S. Census). As Noll highlights, much of this growth can be attributed to the new ability to diagnose feeblemindedness through the Binet-Simon IQ test, which was first introduced by French psychologist Alfred Binet in 1906 (30). Nationally, IQ testing fostered a rise in social awareness of feeblemindedness, particularly as the U.S. entered World War I. Noll reports that these tests "revealed an astounding number of feeble-minded people ... The results proved especially disheartening in the South, where the average white male scored in the imbecile range" (9). The rising awareness of the prevalence of feebleminded persons among the white South spurred a growing sense of public unrest. Educators and medical professionals termed this troubling phenomenon "the menace of the feebleminded"[4] (Trent 165). Studies that emerged amidst the feebleminded menace sought two primary aims: to determine the cause of mental defects and to establish the most optimal response (e.g. treatment, institutionalization).

One of the most influential teacher-researchers working during the era of the feebleminded menace was Henry H. Goddard. As one of the first U.S. researchers to adopt the Binet-Simon IQ test, he became a vociferous advocate of both IQ testing and hereditary psychiatry. Goddard staked much of his psychological research upon the use of IQ testing, whether for the scholastic placement of feebleminded students at his school in Westchester or for the testing of immigrants as they passed through Ellis Island (Noll 30; Trent 168). With the 1912 publication of his generational case study, *The Kallikak Family: A Study in the Heredity of Feeble-Mindedness*, Goddard emerged as a leading public figure supporting national efforts to expand mental institutions.

Goddard's *Kallikak* study traced the ancestry of one of his feebleminded students, "Deborah Kallikak's,"[5] back to a great-grandfather who had procreated with a feebleminded woman out of wedlock. Her same great-grandfather later married an "upstanding Quaker" and had additional children (Trent 164). Profiling the divergent generations of offspring between the illegitimate, feebleminded branch and the legitimate, cognitively normative branch, Goddard concluded a "causal link between vice and retardation," claiming that the feebleminded lineage was prone to "a variety of social vices," while the normative lineage "produced a line of respectable, law-abiding, and successful citizens" (164). Compounding

Goddard's riling conclusion was his assertion that, not only were such feebleminded persons the cause of social depravity, but also, they were "multiplying at twice the rate of the general population" (164). Goddard's *Kallikak* study circulated widely among professional and mainstream audiences after its U.S. publication. His conclusions spurred the already existing paranoia over the menace of the feebleminded and the seeming lack of organized response. Trent explains the phenomenon of this menace:

> The menace of the feebleminded was principally the threat of millions of morons, most of whom were *not in the institution*. These members of the higher grade of feebleminded individuals made up a sizable part of the *lower-class population*. At the same time, they were increasing because of their *sexual fecundity* and because of *immigration*. Accordingly, morons were becoming more and more of a drain on society because of their propensity toward *social vice*. They were out there among us, and they were doing bad things. (165, emphasis added)

As Trent's account illustrates, Goddard's *Kallikak* study riled national anxiety by organizing mental deficiency within a series of extant social rhetorics, particularly those that pertained to the South during this era. The study rose to mainstream awareness just as progressive southerners were calling for social reform in the "class- and caste-based southern culture," though the struggle to "reconcile 'progress and tradition'" proved especially difficult (Noll 12, 13). Meanwhile, Goddard's study both linked feeblemindedness to "the lower-class population" and underscored that these persons "were not in the institution," disrupting progressive efforts by bearing upon longstanding anxieties over class distinction and activating the "traditional" southern impulse toward segregation.

Reinforcing the classist undertones of early-twentieth-century mental pathology, Noll explains that early IQ tests "reflect[ed] middle-class value systems"; "early intelligence tests notoriously underscored those groups that did not share middle-class patterns of thought and behavior. The lower classes, minority groups, and immigrants constituted significant percentages of those classified as mentally defective on the basis of these tests" (2). Given the South's considerably impoverished population and subsequent lack of access to quality education, the fact that these tests deemed the average white male southerner an "imbecile" comes as no surprise. These results were frequently indications of external social factors, not necessarily or exclusively of mental competence as an empirical fact.[6]

Nevertheless, the influence of these early, classist IQ tests, combined with Goddard's asserted causal link between feeblemindedness and low-class debauchery, demonstrates how mental deficiency in the early-twentieth century reinforced extant constructs of class-normative U.S. citizenship by pathologizing poverty. Goddard's study only further exploited social anxieties regarding class politics.

Compounding his classist approach, Goddard also emphasized the propagation of the feebleminded population, especially through "sexual fecundity" of these so-called menacing persons. He claimed that "[t]here are Kallikak families all about us. They are multiplying at twice the rate of the general population" (qtd. in Trent 164). By asserting feebleminded promiscuity, Goddard tapped into concerns over the nation's efforts to control reproductive behavior, especially in the wake of first-wave feminism. Therefore, it logically follows that, "[t]o solve the problem of the Kallikaks, Goddard turned to familiar solutions: marriage restriction, segregation, and sterilization" (Trent 165). Feebleminded procreation spurred social and administrative fears over proliferation of non-normative citizens, threatening the cognitively normative ideal of U.S. citizenship.

Likewise, U.S. citizenship was also under attack by a third form of propaganda activated by Goddard's study: the immigrant threat. Goddard's selection of an immigrant child, especially a *Greek* immigrant, hearkened contemporaneous anxiety resulting from the late-nineteenth- and early-twentieth-century immigration boom; "nearly 12 million immigrants arrived in the United States between 1870 and 1900" ("Immigration"). This number grew to twenty-five million in the early decades of the twentieth century, while "Italians, Greeks, Hungarians, Poles, and others speaking Slavic languages constituted the bulk of this migration" (Diner). Trent reports, "[b]y 1900, one out of every seven Americans was foreign born" (138). As with the fear of sexual fecundity, the influx of foreigners threatened "racial and cultural impurity," lest immigrants procreate with "American blue bloods" (138). Exacerbating this fear of racial impurity was immigration's impact on the labor market. The U.S. State Department reports that immigrants during this period "flocked to urban destinations and made up the bulk of the U.S. industrial labor pool," threatening the livelihood of American-born laborers (Diner). Their competition in the labor pool, coupled with national anxieties over racial purity, "led to the emergence of a second wave of organized xenophobia. By the 1890s, many Americans, particularly from the ranks of the well-off, white, native-born, considered immigration to pose a serious danger to the nation's health and security" (Diner).

Further aggravating Americans' already tenuous anti-immigration sentiment, Goddard's *The Kallikak Family* "scientifically" diagnosed immigrants as feebleminded. But, his conclusion was not without evidence, however correlative. The same year that he published *The Kallikak Family*, "Goddard began giving Binet [IQ] tests to immigrants on Ellis Island," and by 1917, he reported that "as many as 40 percent to 50 percent of immigrants were feebleminded" (Trent 168). Together with these "conclusive" IQ test results, Goddard's *The Kallikak Family* fueled national paranoia over the influx of foreigners, especially eastern Europeans, on American soil (168). Immigrants, like impoverished citizens, were pathologized as mentally defective.

Engaging classism, segregation, sexuality, and immigration, Goddard's *The Kallikak Family* consolidated medical research with the national zeitgeist, exemplifying a propaganda par excellence that fueled unprecedented expansion of mental institutions between 1900 and 1940. In the wake of *The Kallikak Family*'s success, other studies emerged and found similar praxis by confirming extant social anxieties (Trent 177–178). For example, Arthur H. Eastbrook held a special exhibit in 1921 "at the American Museum of Natural History" that welcomed "nearly ten thousand visitors" (178). In fact, mainstream dissemination of studies in feeblemindedness was so rampant that Trent characterizes this phenomenon as a "national pastime" (178).

Menacing Rhetorics in *Lonely Hunter*

As these studies figured a "national pastime," we can explore how McCullers' 1940 novel featuring a deaf and mute character with a mentally deficient friend at the heart of its plot bears up the genealogy of such feebleminded rhetoric. Jake Blount's Marxist proselytizing and proletarian unrest demonstrates the era's anxiety regarding class instability. Dr. Benedict Copeland's Marxist indictment of the racialized flow of capital and opportunity characterizes the African American's destitute condition during this segregated Jim Crow era. Meanwhile, both Biff Brannon's gender-curious behavior and Mick Kelly's burgeoning sexuality evoke the era's vigorous preoccupation with gender and sexuality in the wake of first-wave feminism. *Lonely Hunter*'s ethos and much of its resultant scholarship are characterized by these social rhetorics that activated Goddard's *Kallikak* study—class instability, segregation, and sexuality.

Antonapoulos's and Singer's sexualities, like Brannon's and Kelly's, also evoke the sexual anxiety inherent in the feebleminded menace. The narrated affection between the two deaf-mute characters has also received much scholarly attention, as most notably explored by Gayatri Chakravorty Spivak in her chapter "A Feminist Reading: McCullers's *Heart Is A Lonely Hunter.*" Spivak argues that Singer and Antonapoulos share "a human relationship of love and sexuality at furthest remove from so-called 'normal' relationships. ... It is an unconsummated and, indeed, sexually unacknowledged relationship between two deaf-mute male homosexuals of completely incompatible personalities" (133). Citing the novel's opening line—"In the town, there were two mutes, and they were always together" (McCullers 3)—Spivak argues how the narrative can be read as "coupling" the two in a romantic sense (134). Tracing the trajectory of Singer and Antonapoulos's proposed love story, Spivak asserts that Antonapoulos is "indefinitely displaced through mutism, homosexuality, and idiocy" (134). Similarly, in *Strange Bodies: Gender and Identity in the Novels of Carson McCullers*, Sarah Gleeson-White reads Singer and Antonapoulos's relationship as homosexual, and she situates their sexuality in threatening alterity to normative, "ideal" subjectivity. She explains, "If the human body and its discursive representations are analogous to the workings and conceptions of the social body, it follows that homoerotic desire ... is thus a polluting threat to the fiction of heterosexual social harmony" (61). Taking McCullers's literary depiction of Singer's and Antonapoulos's bodies as correlative to social dynamics, Gleeson-White argues that their implied homosexuality menaces the novel's heteronormative community. In this way, the two mutes' sexuality further hearkens contemporaneous anxiety over sexuality that reinforced the menace of the feebleminded; their deviant sexuality, as Gleeson-White asserts, poses a "threat" to "heterosexual social harmony."

The last of the four rhetorics that fueled the feebleminded menace—the immigrant threat—manifests in *Lonely Hunter* through Antonapoulos's Greek identity. Antonapoulos's character falls clearly into a genealogy of literature inspired by Goddard's *Kallikak* study of a Greek moron. As Trent accounts, "Goddard's moron would live on in popular literature and in the public's conscience for at least four decades ... 'little moron' jokes would (along with Polack jokes, both of which had their origins in Goddard's testings) become all the rage" (165). Moronic indictments of immigrants, especially eastern Europeans like Greeks and Polacks, followed both Goddard's *Kallikak* study and the results of his IQ testing at

Ellis Island. Given the social perception of eastern Europeans at the time, one might argue that naming Antonapoulos a "Greek idiot" would have been, in colloquial terms, redundant. As such, McCullers as narrator only calls Antonapoulos by a feebleminded moniker once in the novel, when Biff recalls Singer's former friend, "[t]he big deaf-mute moron," and in that sole instance, she does not employ the adjective "Greek" ahead of the noun (321).

Instead, throughout the novel, McCullers references Antonapoulos by his ethnicity, calling him "the Greek" (4, 6, 7, 231), "the big Greek" (5, 8, 92, 200, 202, 203, 220, 221), and "the obese and dreamy Greek" (3). In context of the "raging" ubiquity of Polack jokes, we can read McCullers' extensive use of "Greek" through its moronic connotation. In the same vein, one might even interpret the conspicuous scarcity of feebleminded monikers as avoiding colloquial redundancy. By reinforcing this nominal stereotyping, McCullers' illustrations of Antonapoulos evoke denigrating caricatures of overweight, swarthy Greek immigrants. Antonapoulos is described as "big" (5, 6, 7, 8, 92, 200, 202, 203, 220, 221), "fat" (4, 6, 219, 220, 221), "oily" (3, 6, 93, 200), and "round" (3, 200, 203). McCullers spends paragraphs narrating the Greek's bodily excess.[7] Such narrative indulgence in Greek stereotyping is evidence of the last of the four contemporaneous rhetorics that animated the menace of the feeble-minded—the immigrant threat—and it activated well-known stereotypes of feebleminded immigrants. Both characterizations work together to signify Antonapoulos's mental deviance, justifying his segregation.

Ultimately, Antonapoulos's sexual, mental, and ethnic deviances manifest in ways that justify his institutionalization. To understand the weight of this term *deviance*, Noll's engagement with sociologist Bernard Farber proves most useful. Noll employs Farber's work to delineate how a subject's mental identification is determined in two ways: by his relationship with society and by society's response to him. Those who are incognizant of social decorum, who are entirely unable "to attain the level of conduct necessary for the continuation of an existing social organization," are considered "incompeten[t]" (Farber qtd. in Noll 3). Meanwhile, those who are higher functioning, yet who are associated with social vices such as "poverty, alcoholism, [or] crime" are considered "deviant" (Farber qtd. in Noll 3). Noll cautions us that "[s]ociety can ignore, pity, or help those viewed as incompetent. Conversely, it can punish or isolate those seen as deviant" (Noll 3). Farber's "incompetence vs. deviance" dichotomy found especial utility in the South, where the regional "tradition" of racial segregation reinforced support for cognitive segregation as a viable solution. And, as with Jim Crow segregation, institutionalization of cognitive deviants did more to protect normative society and preserve ableist constructs of citizenship than it necessarily did to benefit those who were segregated.[8]

Underwriting Antonapoulos's cognitive segregation are several layers of deviancies that weave nearly interchangeably throughout McCullers' characterizations of him, explaining precisely why society isolates the mute, feebleminded, and potentially homosexual Greek. As we have already seen, his Greek ethnicity aligns Antonapoulos with the moronic connotation of eastern Europeans during this era. But, even more explicitly, McCullers clearly, though often indirectly, characterizes Antonapoulos as feebleminded. In his first description of the novel, he wears a "stupid smile" (3), and unlike Singer, he hardly employs sign language, aside from a few "vague, fumbling" signals "to say that he want[s] to eat or to sleep or to drink" (4). Antonapoulos often does not understand events in which he participates. For example, when he and Singer seem to make another deaf-mute friend in Carl, Antonapoulos sabotages the relationship because he believes that Carl "had ... drunk up all the gin," when really "it was he himself who had finished the bottle" (203). Repeatedly, Antonapoulos is described as having a "bland" expression (7, 8, 10) or observing his surroundings "drowsily" (5, 10, 94), where both terms indicate a low level of cognition. Most bluntly, as mentioned, Biff Brannon calls Antonapoulos "the big deaf-mute moron whom Singer used to walk with" (231).

Furthermore, tracing Farber's definition of mental deviance as those who are associated with "alcoholism" and "crime," we see repeated depictions of Antonapoulos's love of drink, whether he is resenting Singer for enforcing a teetotaler lifestyle (6–7), sabotaging a new friendship because Carl allegedly consumes all of his gin (203), or only consenting to return to the asylum when "Singer [buys] a bottle of whiskey ... and lure[s] him into the taxi" (94). Antonapoulos's love of alcohol is one of his more prominent qualities, aligning him with the mentally deviant alcoholic Farber describes. Not to mention, his forays into "theft, committing public indecencies, and assault and battery" (8) at the novel's beginning signify the "crime" Farber underscores. As such, Antonapoulos's cousin enacts social "isolat[ion]" to control his mental deviance. Here again, the narrative conspicuously characterizes the Greek's mental state; he is sent to the very bluntly named "state insane asylum" (9).

Taken together, Antonapoulos's homosexuality, Greek ethnicity, and outright depiction of mental deficiency in the novel justify his cognitive segregation to the insane asylum. Such "evidence" of his deviance illustrates the logic that led families and communities to institutionalize their own. Investigating this practice in context of American capitalism, institutionalization did not merely function as an altruistic provision of sanctuary or rehabilitation but, rather, as a liberal technology upholding ideals of "productive citizenship" (Trent 3).

COGNITIVE SEGREGATION AND PRODUCTIVE CITIZENSHIP

In his historical analysis of this rise in mental institutions, James Trent considers a community's feebleminded presence in relation to the decidedly American imperative of capitalist productivity. He first highlights this imperative when exploring perceptions of feeblemindedness in the late nineteenth century, just prior to the "menace" described above. At that time, researchers and teachers simply considered the mentally deviant population a "burden" (23). Speaking of one such teacher, Samuel Gridley Howe, Trent explains:

> Typical of progressives of his generation, Howe acknowledged the burden of feeblemindedness to the family, community, and *state*, but claimed that the responsibility for the burden rested with a public indifferent to laws of heredity, to the loss of productivity caused by untrained defectives, and to the expense of caring for pauper idiots ... Burdensome idiots, he stressed, were *unproductive citizens*. ... It was in the self-interest of all citizens, he claimed, to train idiots not only to relieve them of their unproductive inactivity but also to relieve *productive citizens* of one more social burden. (Trent 24, emphasis added)

Eerily foreshadowing eugenically motivated sterilization and prohibitions against feebleminded marriage, Howe lamented "public indifferen[ce] to laws of heredity." Though, the greatest repercussion of such growth in the feebleminded population, he argued, would be the drain on economic productivity, the "burden" on "family, community, *and state*." The feebleminded were both "unproductive" by their inability to labor effectively, and they also encumbered otherwise "productive citizens" for their care. It was the responsibility of the state to free normative citizens of the feebleminded burden. Eschewing the civil freedom of mentally deviant citizens, the state sought to uphold normative citizens' ability to labor within a capitalist economy.

By reading capitalist logic through the ensuing boom in state-implemented mental institutions, the liberal function of institutionalization becomes clear: national expansion of mental institutions enabled productive citizens to labor effectively by segregating cognitively unproductive persons. Indeed, the economic boon of institutionalization was widely acknowledged. One nineteenth-century teacher, when advocating the construction of a new asylum in his state, characterized its benefit: "being consumers and not producers they are a great pecuniary burden to the state" (Knight qtd. in Trent 25). Even more insidiously, another teacher, Edouard Seguine, "in his *Idiocy* [1866] devoted a lengthy appendix to cases of idiots who after receiving proper physiological education became productive citizens, some even giving their lives in service to the Union army" (Trent 25). As early as the Civil War, it seems, the management of feebleminded persons toward a capitalist imperative required productivity through both bodily labor and sacrifice. The repackaging of this *burden* into a *menace* only further advanced the financial aim by mobilizing social and financial support to institutionalize feebleminded bodies by the thousands. Through the vilifying shift in rhetoric at the turn of the century, the original liberal imperative endured: cognitive segregation emerged as a technology used to stimulate and activate productive citizenship.

Just as we saw with the rhetorics of the feebleminded menace, the logic of using cognitive segregation in support of productive citizenship likewise permeates *Lonely Hunter*. From the beginning of the novel, Singer and Antonapoulos are characterized in opposition to one another, where Singer represents the productive citizen, and Antonapoulos, the unproductive one. In the opening paragraph, the characters are contrasted by their "very different" cognitive and hygienic abilities (McCullers 3). Antonapoulos dresses "sloppily" and wears "a gentle, stupid smile" (3). Singer, on the other hand, is "always immaculate and very soberly dressed," and he has "a quick, intelligent expression" (3). Antonapoulos "work[s] for his cousin," Charles Parker, at a "fruit and candy store" cooking foods and providing unskilled labor (3), and Charles Parker maintains his employment ostensibly out of familial obligation. Meanwhile, Singer works as a "silverware engraver" (4), decidedly not out of charity.

Singer's industry is also evident when "one day the Greek bec[omes] ill" (6). Singer takes charge of Antonapoulos's care, "rigidly enforce[ing] the doctor's orders" (6–7); "Singer nurse[s] his friend so carefully that after a week Antonapoulos [is] able to return to his work" (7). During this week, though, Antonapoulos sulks around the apartment, resentful of Singer's efforts, and despite his friend's attempts to cheer up "the big Greek," "a change" overcomes him (7). Still resentful of Singer, Antonapoulos starts acting out. He begins stealing minor items from restaurants they visit (7). Later, he "urinate[s] in public," accosts strangers on the sidewalk, and steals larger, more expensive items far more flagrantly (8). McCullers narrates, "[Singer] was continually marching Antonapoulos down to the courthouse during lunch hour to settle these infringements of the law ... All of his efforts and money were used to keep his friend out of jail" (8). As Antonapoulos continues his downward spiral into unproductive, deviant behavior, Singer's productivity increases, as does the burden he bears.

Three important points underscore the significance of the two friends' life together before the asylum. First, Antonapoulos poses a relatively innocuous burden upon his cousin and Singer before his illness. It is not until he falls ill and Singer begins regulating his diet that Antonapoulos lashes out in lewd and illegal fashion. One might consider Antonapoulos's behavior as representative of the rhetorical shift from the *burden* of the feebleminded to a *menace*. The regulation of his food and drink was particular offense to Antonapoulos, "[f]or, excepting drinking and a certain solitary secret pleasure, Antonapoulos loved to eat more than anything else in the world" (4). He rebels against this infringement upon his personal liberty. Even Singer seems to notice the shift in his friend's demeanor: "In all the years before it had seemed to Singer that there was something very subtle and wise in this smile of his friend ... Now in the big Greek's expression Singer thought that he could detect something sly and joking" (8). By Singer's observation, we can read Antonapoulos's behavior as both intentional and recalcitrant. He deliberately devolves from a social burden to a social menace in direct protest of the doctor's and Singer's encroachment upon his (dietary) freedom.

Second, just before Antonapoulos is institutionalized, Singer serves as the liaison between his friend and the law, interceding on the Greek's behalf. For a long time, Singer is able to financially and legally reconcile the gulf between his friend's deviance and society's laws. Singer's intercessory function is the same role that he will come to play during the bulk of the novel. As scholars often cite, Biff Brannon claims that he, Jake, Dr. Copeland, and Mick "ma[k]e of him a sort of home-made God" (232). Singer represents a kind of authority for the other characters, while at the same time, by his mutism, he takes on "all the qualities they want[] him to have" (232). In this way, Singer serves as an intercessor for the other four characters, too. He is both deity and representative of their own personal projections; he reconciles for them a higher power and individual subjectivity just as he first does for Antonapoulos.

Third, and most significantly, Singer's "burden" manifests on two registers: first, in context of the plot and, second, relative to the narrative structure. Within the plot, Antonapoulos burdens Singer's time, effort, and finances as his friend must continually bail him out of jail. Relative to the narrative structure, however, Antonapoulos burdens Singer's availability to serve as the novel's pivotal character. As McCullers explains, before Antonapoulos is sent away, "[t]he two mutes had no other friends, and except when they worked, they were alone together" (5–6). Singer's capacity to serve as an effective intermediary among the other four characters is encumbered by his exclusive devotion to Antonapoulos. When Charles Parker ships Antonapoulos off to a mental institution, Singer is suddenly "unburdened" by his friend, and he becomes available to the remaining four characters. In this way, Singer's productivity is "liberated," but freed in service of cognitively normative characters who are more "worthy" of his attention, narratologically speaking.[9] Just as Howe championed, segregating the mentally deviant character "relieved productive citizens of one more social burden" (Trent 24).

Deviance and Death: "conditions of citizenship"

Deviance—in general, and particularly here in Antonapoulos's case—indicates contrast against a normative ideal. Relative to U.S. liberalism and its capitalist imperative, we can understand Antonapoulos's deviancies as diverging from notions of citizenship that privilege productivity, as outlined through Trent's analysis earlier. Persons who deviate from the normative citizenship compromise the capitalist system. Russell emphasizes this point, arguing that "one's ownership of one's body—and one's capacity, or ability, to labor—stands as a founding concept in the construction of U.S. citizenship" (4). In *Crip Theory*, Robert McRuer pushes Russell's "founding concept" one step further, positing that within U.S. liberalism, "compulsory heterosexuality is contingent on compulsory able-bodiedness, and vice versa" (2). Here, McRuer links together two defining parameters of U.S. citizenship: capitalist production via able-bodiedness and normative reproduction via heterosexuality. Taking his assertion that disability and homosexuality are invariably linked in service of a capitalist imperative, as they are equally "embodied, visible, pathologized, and policed" (2), we can further understand Antonapoulos's cognitive deviance and sexual deviance as conceptually intertwined.[10] In terms of disability and sexual deviance, Antonapoulos and Singer facilitate the normative subjectivity of the four other prominent characters. And in the logic of cognitive segregation, he deviates from the norm so severely that his expulsion to the margins of society, and indeed to the margins of the narrative, are justified.

As the queer and cognitively disabled Other, Antonapoulos is relegated from the primary narrative at the beginning of the novel, and through McRuer, we can read his deviance as reinforcing the normativity of other characters from the "visible" yet "pathologized and policed" margins of the narrative. Indeed, McCullers structures the novel through third-person limited narrations from each of the five main characters' points of view—Singer, Biff, Jake, Dr. Copeland, and Mick. Organizing these perspectives by chapter, McCullers is able to express interior subjectivity of each of these characters; however, Antonapoulos's voice is conspicuously absent. The Greek is only ever represented through another character's perspective, mostly Singer's, despite his three-part service to the novel: his deviance inaugurates the plot's motion; he serves as the "home-made God" for Singer; and, his death instigates Singer's suicide, thereby ushering in the novel's moral exigence. That the denouement of the novel is prompted by the death of, first, Antonapoulos and, later, Singer, underscores their Othering. As sexually and physically deviant characters, the two mutes are denied futurity in the narrative logic of the text. In their absence, the narrative produces the subjectivity of the remaining four characters toward the modernist theme of the novel—"social ... disintegrat[ion]" (Russell 75).

Considering the literary depiction of disability in a broader context, Russell offers that these representations can "create a point of friction in national logic that may not enact revolution, but can momentarily make strange America's familiar categories of citizenship" (22). It is my goal that this investigation into Antonapoulos's character has "made strange" the liberal logic that organized the forty-year growth in mental institutions just prior to *Lonely Hunter*'s publication. Antonapoulos's various deviancies, all organized around mental deficiency, reveal the exploitative treatment of feebleminded persons, both in the narrative and more broadly in U.S. history. As with racial segregation, cognitive segregation worked to reinforce cognitively normative ideals of U.S. citizenship by removing feebleminded persons from mainstream society, and the same liberal logic that organized these real-life violences also organizes the narrative of *Lonely Hunter*. Antonapoulos's cognitive segregation serves as a narrative linchpin; the entire plot depends upon his cognitive segregation at the start of the novel. Once Singer is unburdened by the Greek's mentally deviant menace, he becomes a socially productive agent in the community dynamics of the plot, fostering Biff's, Jake's, Dr. Copeland's, and Mick's personal evolutions. And yet, Singer cannot serve the other four until Antonapoulos is institutionalized.

The fact that cognitive segregation organizes *Lonely Hunter*'s exigency and that the narrative reinforces productive citizenship reveals the insidious mechanics of liberal ideology, influencing not just social and economic structures, but also narrative composition. And, we can trace the pervasive influence of liberal logic in cognitive segregation as it manifests on three registers: first, in reality, as manifested by the 1900–1940 boom in U.S. mental institutionalization; second, in the novel's plot, as traced through the logics that justify and enforce Antonapoulos's institutionalization; third, and perhaps most insidiously, in the narrative structure that removes Antonapoulos to the margins of the text. Narratologically, Antonapoulos is segregated, and such segregation enables production of the *Lonely Hunter*'s ethos.

An "archaeology of [narrative] silence

In this chapter's epigraph, I quote from the Preface of Michel Foucault's *Madness and Civilization* as he situates his scholarship on the evolution of madness-as-pathology, contrasting it against a simple history of psychiatry. Foucault insists, "*I have not tried to write the history of* [psychiatric] *language, but rather the archaeology of* [madness's] *silence*" (xi). Foucault declares that madness as subjectivity has been muted by medicalized pathology, and this concept of muted madness within a structure of hegemonic power resonates deeply in McCullers' tale of a mad, deaf-mute who is removed to the margins of the narrative. Antonapoulos's mutism evokes the liberal process of silencing citizens of non-normative cognition, segregating them from mainstream society in support of idealized productive citizenship. Narratologically, such silencing reinforces McRuer's assertion that queer/disabled characters, whose presence underwrites constructs of normative citizenship, have long been rendered "invisible" through liberal mechanisms that seek to naturalize able-bodied, cognitively normative, and heteronormative ideals of citizenship.

Following Foucault, I have sought to render visible an "archaeology of [narrative] silence" in *Lonely Hunter* that has both rendered

Antonapoulos's institutionalization the impetus of the plot and simultaneously enforced his character's isolation from the narrative. Importantly, this
term *archaeology* denotes more than a mere history: Foucault later articu-
lates its definition as "a history of discursive objects that does not plunge
them into the common depth of a primal soil, but deploys the nexus of
regularities that govern their dispersion" (*Archaeology of Knowledge* 48).
Mapping *archaeology* as a discursive history obliges "[a] task that consists
of not—of no longer—treating discourses as groups of signs ... but as
practices that systemically form the objects of which they speak" (49). In
this way, we might consider the weight of McCullers' literary construction not simply as it *was influenced by* its literary moment, but as *it helped
to shape* the American imagination at a key moment in U.S. history. Her
deployment of a silently mad character not only hearkens rhetorics of the
feebleminded menace, but it also engages in a "nexus of regularities" that
renders the able-bodied, productive citizen a normative ideal. Her novel
participates in a broader ontological process that "systemically form[s] the
object" of the mad-yet-silent immigrant in the national imagination at the
same time that it hearkens an anterior occurrence of this national foil to
productive citizenship.[11]

Ultimately, my archaeology of McCullers' narrative returns us to
Russell's inspiration for her work in *Reading Embodied Citizenship*: just
as her literary analysis encourages interrogation of idealized citizenship in
the "national imaginary" that impacts real-life "conditions of citizenship"
(22), I offer my analysis of *The Heart Is a Lonely Hunter* as a challenge to
the ongoing reality of cognitive segregation in the U.S., despite extensive
psychological and behavioral research that advocates integrating persons
with cognitive differences into mainstream society in earnest.[12] For example, cognitive segregation still plagues public schools in McCullers' home
state: as recently as August 2015, *The Washington Post* reported that "[t]
he Justice Department has accused Georgia of segregating thousands of
students with behavior-related disabilities, shunting them into a program
that denies them access to their non-disabled peers and to extracurricu-
lar activities and other basic amenities" (Brown). In an eerie nod to the
region's history of racial segregation, many of these "centers" run by the
Georgia Network for Educational and Therapeutic Support (GNETS)
"are housed in poor-quality facilities once used as schools for black children during the days of Jim Crow. GNETS students report feeling as if
they are in prison, separate from their peers and without access to athlet-
ics or clubs" (Brown). Practically speaking, cognitive segregation such as

that practiced by GNETS in Georgia Public Schools is often a logisti-cal "solution" to help overstretched public educators and administrators relieve "normal" classrooms from the "burden" of students with disabili-ties. Public educators are already overtaxed by large student-to-teacher ratios, limited funds for resources, and unrealistic expectations mandated by Common Core curriculum and standardized testing; in light of these burdens, compounding a classroom's already overwrought responsibilities by accommodating the unique needs of students with disabilities is simply too much to ensure the *productivity* of the classroom.

In the context of this study, however, we must ask: what is at stake when success is measured by standards of *productivity*, as determined by liberal ideals of citizenship? And further, how might we reject these latent forms of liberal segregation without imposing neoliberal incarnations of the same old injustices? How can we develop opportunities to incorporate citizens into mainstream U.S. society in ways that genuinely benefit per-sons with non-normative cognition? Such incorporation must not include, as David Mitchell and Sharon Snyder warn us, broad-stroke initiatives under a rubric of "diversity" (4). Such efforts, Mitchell and Snyder assert, have characterized the late-twentieth-century, neoliberal turn toward "inclusionism" as a series of "diversity-based integration practices" that render "difference" so universal that disabled persons become, once again, "invisible" (4). Rather, an ethical approach must direct resources in ways that "explore how disability subjectivities are not just characterized by socially imposed restrictions, but, in fact, productively create new forms of embodied knowledge and collective consciousness" (2). What alter-nate modes of embodied subjectivity might GNETS students teach us? What alternate frameworks for identity might Spiros Antonapoulos and John Singer's relationship have taught us within a narrative structure that eschewed liberal cognitive segregation? We must work to improve social infrastructures to benefit the quality of life for cognitively different per-sons. Such efforts would serve disabled citizenry and, at the same time, ethically complicate the landscape of U.S. citizenship.

NOTES

1. I use this and other historical terms (e.g. *moron, mental defectives*) in this chapter to engage the contemporaneous denotations of the term.
2. The regional "lag" behind national facilities holds true, even for the infa-mous Central State Mental Hospital in Milledgeville, GA, established in

1842. Central State's enrollment trailed far behind northern institutions until the 1900–1940 boom. In Peter G. Cranford's history of the hospital, he reports its population growth: from thirty-three patients in 1842, to "well-over 2000" in 1898, to "upward past the 9000 mark" by 1940 (7, 49, 85). These figures indicate that Central State's average annual growth rate increased by 467 percent during 1900–1940. As a Georgian, McCullers was keenly aware of this hospital's looming presence in the American imagination, and it was perhaps an inspiration for Antonapoulos's institutionalization in *Lonely Hunter*.

3. An important exception to the dearth of critical engagement with Antonapoulos's disability is Heidi Krumland's 2008 essay "'A big deaf-mute moron': Eugenic Traces in Carson McCullers's *The Heart Is a Lonely Hunter.*" Krumland explores how the eugenics movement impacted McCullers' "one-dimensional rendering of Antonapoulos in either comic, negative, or mystic terms" in such a way that the author fails to "grant[ ] him human status" (40). Krumland concludes that "[r]epresenting a cognitively impaired man realistically was a challenge that McCullers could not meet due to the typical preconceptions about cognitive impairment in her time" (40). Krumland's work is foundational in establishing scholarly discussion about the representation of Antonapoulos's cognitive disability in context of the novel's historical moment. However, this chapter diverges from Krumland's consideration of authorial capacity for "authentic" literary representation and, instead, engages the novel as a cultural artifact, dynamically engaged in a social discursive project that works to constitute ideal US citizenship within its historical moment.

4. In *Inventing the Feeble Mind*, James W. Trent, Jr. offers an instructive summary of this shift toward the feebleminded menace: "the new term suggested new meaning and the necessity for a new social response. The pitiable, but potentially productive, antebellum idiot and the burdensome imbecile of the postwar years gave way to the menacing and increasingly well-known defective of the teens. What made this new image so threatening and ensured acute concerns and shrill warnings was the increasing insistence in the first and second decades of the new century that mental defectives, in their amorality and fecundity, were not only linked with social vices but indeed were the most prominent and persistent cause of those vices" (141).

5. The student's pseudonym was "a combination of the Greek words *kallos*, 'good,' and *kakos*, 'bad,'" emphasizing the morality inherent in generational feeblemindedness (Trent 163).

6. It is important to note that the bias of early IQ tests did not go unchallenged; for example, "In 1922–23, Walter Lippmann, the social critic and newspaper editor, wrote a series of articles in the *New Republic* attacking the whole moral and intellectual basis of the intelligence-testing movement" (Noll 32).

7. Krumland also highlights McCullers' pervasive characterizations of Antonapoulos's size; "[i]n making Antonapoulos obese, McCullers employs another negatively connoted trait that has traditionally been used by artists to symbolize dullness, passiveness, and stupidity" (37).

8. Though the late-nineteenth-century impulse toward mental institutionalization was spurred by rehabilitative ambitions, "after 1890," Trent reports, "[c]are, not education or treatment, had become the central focus of institutions" (129). He is quick to clarify that "[t]his institutionalization, of course, did not ensure that all care was good care. Much of it was; some of it clearly was not" (128–129).

9. Krumland emphasizes how McCullers' use of cognitive disability "sets [Antonapoulos] apart from the other characters ... by inventing him as devoid of an essential human attribute: the capacity to love and care" (40). Her interpretation underscores Antonapoulos's relative narrative "worth" because, unlike the cognitively normative characters, he cannot "love and care."

10. The conflation of mental illness with homosexuality is not a new one. Until 1974, the American Psychiatric Association's *Diagnostic and Statistical Manual of Mental Disorders* (DSM) listed homosexuality as a mental disorder (Minton 260–261).

11. At the beginning of this chapter, I claim that McCullers "unknowingly composed" *Lonely Hunter* as a "literary capstone" to the 1900–1940 boom in US mental institutionalization. While we cannot know for certain whether McCullers was aware of her novel's timeliness, we do know that she would likely have been critical of such inhuman treatment of cognitively deviant persons, as evidenced by her compassionate characterization of marginalized figures throughout her literary oeuvre. My reading of the novel as participating in the ontological formation of able-bodied citizenship does not seek to implicate McCullers as consciously writing with such intent. Instead, I contend that liberal American logic *so insidiously pervades* our culture that, even without conscious awareness, it nevertheless seeped into and indeed shaped the fiction of a well-known humanitarian author.

12. For a thorough, accessible discussion of cognitive integration, Steve Silberman's *NeuroTribes: The Legacy of Autism and the Future of Neurodiversity* (Avery, an imprint of Penguin Random House, 2015) offers a robust constellation of recent medical research.

Works Cited

Cranford, Peter G. *But for the Grace of God: The Inside Story of the World's Largest Insane Asylum MILLEDGEVLLE!* Augusta, GA: Great Pyramid Press. 1981. Print.

Diner, Hasia. "Immigration and U.S. History." *IIP Digital. U.S. Dept. of State.* 13 Feb. 2008. Web. 28 Jul. 2015.

Foucault, Michel. *The Archaeology of Knowledge and the Discourse on Language.* 1971. Trans. A. M. Sheridan Smith. New York, NY: Vintage Books, 2010. Print.

——. *Madness and Civilization: A History of Insanity in the Age of Reason.* New York, NY: Vintage Books, 1965. Print.

Gleeson-White, Sarah. *Strange Bodies: Gender and Identity in the Novels of Carson McCullers.* Tuscaloosa, AL: The U of Alabama P, 2003. Print.

"Immigration to the United States, 1851–1900." *Rise of Industrial America. Lib. of Cong.* N.p., n.d. Web. 28 Jul. 2015.

Krumland, Heidi. "'A big deaf-mute moron': Eugenic Traces in Carson McCullers's *The Heart Is a Lonely Hunter.*" *Journal of Literary Disability* 2.1 (2008): 32.43. Print.

McCullers, Carson. *The Heart is a Lonely Hunter.* 1940. Boston: Mariner Books, 2000. Print.

McRuer, Robert. *Crip Theory: Cultural Signs of Queerness and Disability.* New York: New York UP, 2006. Print.

Minton, Henry L. *Departing from Deviance: A History of Homosexual Rights and Emancipatory Science in America.* Chicago, IL: The U of Chicago P, 2002. Print.

Mitchell, David, with Sharon Snyder. *The Biopolitics of Disability: Neoliberalism, Ablenationalism, and Peripheral Embodiment.* Ann Arbor, MI: U of Michigan P, 2015. Print.

Monroe, Doug. "Asylum: Inside Central State Hospital, Once the World's Largest Mental Institution." *Atlanta.* Atlanta magazine, 18 Feb. 2015. Web. 5 Feb. 2016.

Noll, Steven. *Feeble-Minded in our Midst: Institutions for the Mentally Retarded in the South, 1900–1940.* Chapel Hill, NC: The U of North Carolina P, 1995. Print.

Russell, Emily. *Reading Embodied Citizenship: Disability, Narrative, and the Body Politic.* New Brunswick, NJ: Rutgers UP, 2011. Print.

Silberman, Steve. *NeuroTribes: The Legacy of Autism and the Future of Neurodiversity.* New York: Avery, 2015. Print.

Spivak, Gayatri Chakravorty. "A Feminist Reading: McCullers's *Heart is a Lonely Hunter.*" *Critical Essays on Carson McCullers.* Eds. Beverly Lyon Clark and Melvin J. Friedman. New York: Hall, 1996. 129–142. Print.

Trent, Jr., James W. *Inventing the Feeble Mind: A History of Mental Retardation in the United States.* Berkley, CA: U of California P, 1994. Print.

United States Census Bureau. "Historical National Population Estimates: July 1, 1900 to July 1, 1999." *Population Estimates Program, Population Division, U.S. Census Bureau.* 28 Jun. 2000. Web. 25 Oct. 2015.

Seeking the Meaning of Loneliness: Carson McCullers in China

Lin Bin

INTRODUCTION

Carson McCullers (1917–1967) is a phenomenon in China, where she has been twice introduced to the reading public and aroused two waves of "McCullers craze" since the early 1980s. She has had a long-standing influence on Chinese readers of two successive generations. What strikes Chinese readers most about McCullers' fictional work is her scathing representation of loneliness. McCullers scholars in China have thus been engaged in seeking the meaning of loneliness in her works over the past thirty years or so. In my opinion, McCullers' "loneliness" has different meanings to the two generations of Chinese readers: for the first, it signifies isolation within a community, and for the other, it is more closely aligned with the concept of alienation in a crowd.

McCullers was first introduced to China in 1979 through the translation of her novella *The Ballad of the Sad Café* by Li Wenjun, which was followed in 1983 by the publication of the Chinese version of her short story "A Domestic Dilemma" by the same translator. These two translated works were part of the very first mass effort in China to introduce American

L. Bin (✉)
Nanguang #3-520 College of Foreign Languages and Cultures, Xiamen University, No. 422, Siming South Road, Siming District, Xiamen City, Fujian Province 361005, People's Republic of China

© The Author(s) 2016
A. Graham-Bertolini, C. Kayser (eds.), *Carson McCullers in the Twenty-First Century*, DOI 10.1007/978-3-319-40292-5_13

literature to the public upon the official establishment of *Sino-US* diplomatic relations, two years after the Great Cultural Revolution was proclaimed to be formally ended with the downfall of the "Gang of Four."[1] At this point, the Chinese, newly emerged from the suffocating cultural void of the previous decade, were recovering from their shock at the human capacity for cruelty and nursing their wounds from the wreckage of interpersonal relationships damaged by the Revolution. Their encounter with McCullers, and *The Ballad of the Sad Café* in particular, struck a chord of empathy in their hearts as the profundity of loneliness by betrayal and social exclusion was driven home in such a heartrending tone.

After a lapse of about twenty years, the second wave of the "McCullers craze" was initiated by Shanghai "Life, Reading, New Knowledge" Sanlian Bookstore Publishing House (to be shortened to "Shanghai Sanlian Bookstore" hereafter) in 2005, when almost all of the writer's major fictional works were translated and successively published, in addition to her weighty biography *The Lonely Hunter* by Virginia Spencer Carr. The McCullers series quickly became top best sellers nationwide, attracting a new generation of readers while refreshing the older generation's bittersweet memories concerning their first reading of *The Ballad of the Sad Café*. Once again, the readers became mesmerized by McCullers' depiction of loneliness, which I believe has acquired a new meaning for Chinese readers in the contemporary context of China's crisis of modernity, especially in terms of human alienation as closely associated with market economy and globalization.

Owing to the fact that the Chinese culture traditionally promotes the value of community over that of the individual, the conflict between individual and community, which is partially responsible for the current dilemma of modernity in China, remains the topmost concern in the Chinese mind. In this sense, McCullers, with her own crushing anxiety over isolation by community and also over alienation in a crowd, is culturally very Chinese at heart, which seems to me the very reason for her popularity with Chinese readers. With a sense of communal belonging always figuring as the essential element of Chinese identity, Chinese readers and scholars, including me, have been devoted to deconstructing McCullers' loneliness by retrieving some redeeming hope in it; for instance, the critical revelation on the textual transgression of isolating boundaries sheds light on the very nature of the Chinese perspective in McCullers studies. This essay aims to resolve the myth of the "McCullers complex" among Chinese readers and to elaborate upon the "Chinese perspective" of McCullers' reception and research in China by exploring the different social contexts of the two waves of the "McCullers craze," which occurred in the early 1980s and the late 2000s respectively.

THE FIRST "MCCULLERS CRAZE" IN THE 1980S: ISOLATION BY COMMUNITY

Chinese readers' first impression of Carson McCullers was invariably shaped by Li Wenjun's translation of *The Ballad of the Sad Café*. The translated work was first published in the epoch-making[2] inaugural issue of *Foreign Literature and Art* in July 1978 but reached only a small audience because of its limited circulation. Soon after, it gained a much enlarged scope of influence when included in *Collected Contemporary American Short Stories* produced by Shanghai Yiwen Press in April 1979, which served to bring into the Chinese public view quite a few names already prominent on the American literary scene. The collection covers Jewish writers such as Isaac Bashevis Singer, Bernard Malamud, Saul Bellow, and Philip Roth; Norman Mailer as a representative of New Journalism; Kurt Vonnegut, Jr. and Donald Barthelme as representatives of the school of Black Humor; postmodernist writers such as John Cheever, John Updike, and Joyce Carol Oates; African American writer James Baldwin; and also Carson McCullers as one of the major Southern school of writers along with Eudora Welty, Truman Capote, and Flannery O'Connor. With even a short story written by the dramatist Arthur Miller included ("The Misfit"), it practically represents the most brilliant achievements of American literature in the first half of the twentieth century. Among these authors, McCullers made one of the most successful debuts; with Chinese readers deeply impressed by her mesmerizing and heartrending narration of love and loneliness, she became an idol of a whole generation who developed a close affinity with the characters of her creation.

As the longest piece among the nineteen short stories incorporated into the collection, *The Ballad of the Sad Café* was highly recommended in the preface by Tang Yongkuan, late deputy editor-in-chief of Shanghai Yiwen Press and pioneer publisher of translated fictional works from the western world. As he aptly observes,

Amelia and Cousin Lymon in *The Ballad of the Sad Café* seem to have an inner world of mystery; in particular, Cousin Lymon the hunchback's last-moment betrayal at the duel [with Marvin Macy] of Amelia, who has lavished her love on him, abruptly turns the joyful and prosperous café into a heart-breaking scene and reduces lively Amelia from then on into a ghostly presence among the ruins of a demolished mansion so that the story appears shrouded in an atmosphere of grimness. But then, aren't there people in real life whom we cannot see through at first sight? At the ending, the author describes a chain gang singing loudly in chorus while working away at the highway, whose voice seems to be "from the earth itself, or the wide sky … that causes the heart to broaden" (McCullers, *Ballad* 71). Hereby the author must intentionally imply that life and struggle will last forever and are bound to bring hope. (Tang 3–4)

Mr. Tang calls for an understanding of human nature through an analogy between the fictional figures and people in real life. Moreover, what he highlights is not the grim atmosphere itself but the cheerful chorus, not the despair of a lover's betrayal or the tension between the victim and the victimizer, but a broad heart that can readily make peace with all the grievances held against fellow human beings. No doubt, his critical standpoint was determined by the drastic change of political climate in China, when the country started to recover from the ills of the Cultural Revolution marked with a ghastly distorted domestic value system and a relentlessly implemented policy of cultural isolation from the outside world.

In the wake of the landmark downfall of the "Gang of Four" in 1976, Chinese publishers, cautious in their newly acquired freedom and emboldened by a burning sense of mission, set about breaking new ground by publishing a series of American short story collections,[3] which served to fill in the gap left by the decade-long ban on all intellectual products of any foreign culture and were hence voraciously devoured by the intellectually and culturally starved Chinese readers. Scholars generally divide the translation history of British and American literature (1976–2008) into the following three stages: the post-Cultural-Revolution ice-out stage (October 1976–November 1978), the revisionist stage of renaissance in circles of literature and arts (November 1978–June 1989), and the developing stage of prosperity driven by market economy and globalization (Sun and Qingzhu 73). It was during the first stage that McCullers made her debut, together with quite a few other "politically correct" literary classics like Nikolai Gogol's *Dead Souls* (translated by Lu Xun), William Shakespeare's plays (translated by Zhu Shenghao), as well as the first volume of *A Survey of American Literary History* written by Dong Hengxun in January 1978, which marked the official induction of American literature into the country (Sun, H. 73–74). Because Western literature was previously condemned as "bourgeoisie literature" (as opposed to its proletarian counterpart) that seemed to be an "alien and formidable territory" to Chinese readers, the first translated works offered them quite a refreshing reading experience with an almost shocking impact (74), so it is no wonder that along with *The Ballad of the Sad Café*, McCullers' name left an indelible initial impression on the memories of a whole generation of Chinese readers.

According to statistics, "Priced at 1.5 yuan RMB,[4] 230,000 copies of the book were sold then, which shows how many people became acquainted with McCullers, not to mention the additional readers who got to know her through borrowed and used copies of the book. Over the years to follow they would frequently think of Miss Amelia and Cousin Lymon" (Zhang 9). Among these early readers is Su Tong, one of China's top modernist writers who has been regarded as "McCullers' hardcore follower" since he confessed in an essay of the late 1980s that as a senior high school student he "bought with his pocket money the very first book of literature in his life ... through which he got his very first taste of American literature and of *The Ballad of the Sad Café*"; the influence of this novella on his own narrative style in his portrayal of the Chinese South he later duly acknowledged after he made fame as an established writer and pillar of modernist literature in China (qtd. in Li 3). The historical significance of the collection was revealed by Yang Yi when she pointed out the special role the text played in updating the Chinese readers' understanding of contemporary American life and literature, because the stories "not only basically represent the styles and features of the literary schools currently in fashion in the US, but also reflect from various angles the American social life and mindset" (56). Yang believes the Southern school of writing "tends to be enveloped in a gloomy, mysterious and sentimental atmosphere, and though generally focused on analysis of the characters' psychological activities, it tackles themes of gravity," and she goes on to point out that "the human psyche in all its inscrutable morbidity that McCullers painstakingly delineates in *The Ballad of the Sad Café* is nothing but an intricate sign of the 'lonely heart'" (57).

Another collection that helped bring McCullers into the limelight in China is *Selected Short Stories by American Women Writers* published by China Social Sciences Press in 1983. This text includes McCullers' short story "A Domestic Dilemma" translated by Li Wenjun, along with works by women writers who each have an established reputation of distinction in American literary history, such as Kate Chopin, Edith Wharton,

Willa Cather, Katherine Anne Porter, Eudora Welty, Flannery O'Connor, Sylvia Plath, and Joyce Carol Oates. With Charlotte Perkins Gilman's "The Yellow Wallpaper" and Tillie Olson's "I Stand Here Ironing" taken into account, this collection displays a feminist agenda, which is clearly defined in the editor Zhu Hong's detailed introduction that was published in *World Literature* about two years before the collection itself came out. When it comes to Southern women writers, Zhu particularly draws attention to gender-related thematic concerns, declaring that "this collection makes it a point to include the works related to the subject of family and woman issues" and that McCullers' selected piece "describes the commonplace scene in modern American family life with full sympathy and understanding: while the husband is working outside to make a living, the equally educated wife must stay at home, getting drunk in low spirits; and her spiritual crisis is also created by people's indifference in big cities" (19). The theme of loneliness is stressed here by the critic in a culture- and gender-specific context, marked with inequality in separate spheres, as well as estrangement between individuals in urban life.

    When Li Wenjun, McCullers' first Chinese translator, was later interviewed about his early experience with McCullers' translation, he unexpectedly disclosed the fact that Qian Zhongshu,[5] a renowned Chinese writer and scholar, turned out to be an even earlier reader of *The Ballad of the Sad Café*: "As I saw McCullers' name in America's literary journals time and again in 1967, I went to the library of the Institute of Literature [in Chinese Academy of Social Sciences] in search of her books and found *The Ballad of the Sad Café*, with only Qian's signature on the check-out card" (qtd. in Cao, "August Afternoon"). Yet in reply to Li's inquiry about the reason for his interest in McCullers, Qian simply said, "She's fairly good." Nevertheless, his favorable first impression prompted him to check out the book as soon as the library was allowed to re-open in the 1970s, and upon re-reading he decided to translate it for Chinese readers because he believed that its attraction lies in "her exceptional point of view and narrative style of ballad that effectively convey her understanding of the complexities of life." Li elaborated on his point in 1990, promoting the novella once again by ranking it among such classics as Henry James's *Daisy Miller*, William Faulkner's *The Bear*, and Ernest Hemingway's *The Old Man and the Sea* in an article with a title that lays bare the authorial intention—"The Call for Love and Understanding," which is reinforced by his lengthy quote of McCullers' well-known soliloquy about "the lover and the beloved … [who] come from different countries" (*Ballad* 26).

However, he poses a challenge against the then prevailing Western interpretation of McCullers' theme of love to the effect that love is proved incapable of altering the eternal state of lonely human existence.[6] From his point of view,

> It is no doubt logically legitimate for the critics to come to this conclusion through an analysis of characters and plot and on the basis of the author's own comments. But does it stop at that? I could always sense a heart of tenderness throbbing beneath the cold words when I was translating this novella. (Li 6)

He then goes further to infer from Miss Amelia's kind act of doctoring for her townsfolk that

> I feel, and also firmly believe, that this is the author's affection for Miss Amelia, and for all mortal beings at that. While she expresses her doubt about the possibility of their love and happiness, which in itself is also an indictment of the morbid capitalist society that makes it difficult for people to express their affection for each other,[7] in the depth of her heart she still hopes that they could shake off their loneliness and attain mutual understanding, especially for people like Miss Amelia who are not readily understood by others. If she had given up hope, McCullers would have abandoned her faith in the role of literature as vehicle of social and aesthetic values; in that case, why did she bother to make such painstaking efforts to produce one work after another while her body was plagued by illness? (7)

Further, he makes full use of the biographical description of McCullers' marital frustrations to justify a positive answer to his own question: "this woman writer still cherished love in spite of all the bitterness she tasted in her own life. So to speak, although *The Ballad of the Sad Café* declares love's labor lost, it still calls for love and understanding" (8).

As can be seen from the scanty critical reviews of the late 1970s and early 1980s, the keynote of early McCullers' criticism in China is quite different from that in the USA because of the different political and cultural contexts, though at this stage both the Chinese critics and their American counterparts almost unanimously put emphasis on the writer's hallmark theme of loneliness. As far as McCullers' thematic representation of loneliness is concerned, the above-mentioned cases seem to reveal at least two points in common. For one thing, because of their own traumatic experience of interpersonal relations that went wrong for political reasons during the Cultural Revolution, the loneliness about which the Chinese critics are deeply concerned is that of an individual isolated by a community that fails to understand him and consequently excludes him willfully, Miss Amelia in particular. For another, while they try to salvage positive values from the ruins of disillusionment and despair, the Chinese critics are quick to catch, in the story of doom and gloom, some sign of hope to focus on.

THE SECOND "MCCULLERS CRAZE" IN 2000S: ALIENATION IN A CROWD

It is ironic that parallel to the fate of her fictional characters, Carson McCullers lapsed into obscurity soon after the successful debut of *The Ballad of the Sad Café* in China and was neglected for over twenty years by Chinese readers. As a matter of fact, the Chinese reading public was at that time overwhelmed by an unprecedented influx of translated foreign literature covering avant-garde works of such modernist schools of writing as symbolism, expressionism, futurism, stream of consciousness, surrealism, existentialism, New Novel, Beat Generation, absurdism, black humor, and magic realism, to name just a few, in addition to the canonized classical works previously banned and now reprinted in large quantities. McCullers, with her seemingly plain and simple, or rather conservative, writing style was lost in the technically innovative and even stylistically flamboyant type of writings that were mostly products of the modernist scheme of arts to "make it new." Around 1990, Su Tong, having just won early fame as a burgeoning avant-garde writer and attracting a large flock of followers, mentioned McCullers' indispensable influence on his early writing career in an interview, and Li Wenjun, still at the start of his later fruitful and prominent translation career as one of China's leading translators (especially of William Faulkner), related in detail his experience of translating McCullers in the above-mentioned essay "The Call for Love and Understanding," though their attempts failed to bring about any renewed public interest in their own favorite woman writer of all time.

However, the first decade of the twenty-first century saw the second "McCullers craze" in China: a series of McCullers' works were launched into the literary market by Shanghai Sanlian Bookstore, mostly within a span of two years. In August 2005, *The Member of the Wedding* translated by Zhou Yujun came out first, and in April 2007, Li Wenjun's translation of the complete edition of *The Ballad of the Sad Café: and Other Stories*, came out last. In between was *The Heart Is a Lonely Hunter* (translated by

Chen Xiaoli) published in November 2005, followed by *Reflections in a Golden Eye* (translated by Chen Li) and *Clock Without Hands* (translated by Jin Shaoyu), both in December 2007; moreover, the Chinese version of *The Lonely Hunter*, Virginia Spencer Carr's biography, was also released by the same publisher in January 2006. The whole series sold so well that they ranked high on various best seller lists for a time, and *The Heart Is a Lonely Hunter* was said to have been reprinted nine times in less than two years time ("Complete Follow-up"). With the publication of part of *The Mortgaged Heart* (translated by Wen Ze'er) by People's Literature Press in August 2012,[8] almost all of McCullers' major works became known and accessible to Chinese readers.

The root cause of this new wave of the "McCullers craze" is worth examining. As a reporter from *Beijing News* speculated in August 2005, "It can be attributed to the 'McCullers complex' deep-rooted in the heart of the importer," a woman who was an early McCullers fan and is now determined to get her back twenty years later (Cao, "August Afternoon"). Xu Dong, the one responsible for bringing in the McCullers series, claims that she had several negotiations over the copyright issue with McCullers' former literary agents and publishers in the spring of 2004. Zhou Yujun, a friend of Xu's and translator of *The Member of the Wedding*, recalls that Xu, upon learning that most of McCullers' works had not been translated into Chinese yet, proposed the project to Shanghai Sanlian Bookstore and contacted the agents for copyright permission. At Xu's invitation Zhou chose the "thinnest one" of McCullers' books and thus became one of her Chinese translators.[9] Actually McCullers' re-emergence in China is by no means accidental or random; rather, the publishers' renewed interest in McCullers must also be viewed in the context of the developed literary market at home and abroad at the turn of the century. According to scholars of translation history, following a brief decline of the translation of British and American literature in late 1980s, China's publishing industry was generally incorporated into the system of market economy in the 1990s, which, combined with the intellectual property right limits incurred by China's new memberships of the Berne Convention and the Universal Copyright Convention (both acquired in 1992), led to fluctuations of quality and quantity of translated works during the transitional period until 2003. Since 2003, the translation of British and American literary works has finally caught up and kept pace with their publication and promotion in their country of origin (Sun and Qingzhu 77). Under these circumstances, the following two major factors play a significant part. First, the publishers, driven by market forces, have to take profit into serious account and hence come to rely more on common readers' tastes and demands than scholars' recommendations alone, so that common readers are more likely to be considered in the process of selecting which works to translate, as illustrated by the launch of the McCullers series project. Second, with the globalization of the news media, public reading trends in the country of origin and also elsewhere in the world start to exert an increasingly important influence on the publishers' choices. Take, for example, *The Heart Is a Lonely Hunter*, which happened to be the Oprah's Book Club selection in April 2004. As mentioned in the same *Beijing News* article, "when Xu Dong was on the point of reaching an agreement in her negotiation with McCullers' agents, *The Heart Is a Lonely Hunter* hit the headline on all fronts of media book selling including Amazon.com, and it turned out to be Oprah Winfrey's recommendation at work, resulting in its reprint of 600,000 copies" (Cao, "August Afternoon"). *Beijing Evening News* also offered a timely report on October 21, 2005, stressing that "Oprah has recently turned her attention to the literary classics" and that "her recommendation of this particular novel succeeded in helping the sales promotion of the Southern woman writer whose works had practically faded out of public sight" (Sun). In this way, the promotion of the McCullers series in China was reinforced by its synchronization with that in America, and the integration with the world market guaranteed its commercial success to some extent.

The second wave of the "McCullers craze" in the latter half of the first decade of the twenty-first century elicited numerous responses from both old and new fans spanning at least two generations, some of whom even named themselves "Mc-fans" and formed a community by setting up a website devoted to the reading and criticism of her works.[10] To the older generation, McCullers instantly evoked a nostalgic feeling about their previous reading experience of *The Ballad of the Sad Café*. Su Tong, in his essay collection entitled *The Literary Treasure of a Lifetime: Twenty Stories that Have Influenced Me*, mentions his seemingly "inscrutable preference" for McCullers, stating that

> I have not been able to explain whether my preference for this novel could be attributed to certain aesthetic criteria or some other plausible ones, but then preference may not be based on reasoning ... There is no murder in it but disgrace and betrayal that are more cruel than murder; there is no bloodshed but an ending that is more heart-broken than dying. (Su 168)

Besides these classical themes, what held more attraction for the future modernist writer in his impressionable youthful state of development was McCullers' unique style of narration, as he states in an interview that "her story seems to be about love, and also about grief or despair, and between the lines permeates McCullers' unique temperament while beneath the verbal surface the story is sad in itself" (qtd. in Cao, "Su Tong"). Critics recognize McCullers' influence on his writing in the blood-thirsty mob of young boys of *Young Blood* and also in the secretively eerie atmosphere of *The Fair Sex* and *Wives and Concubines*. Both writers "display a strong Southern complex in their works, construct a literary world of their own, and embody some isomorphic features of literature" (C. Chen 62). Indeed, their common obsession with bleak views of desolation, under-currents of violence, and psychological impacts of social transformation in their portrayals of the South—the American South and the Chinese South respectively—gives their works a distinct dimension of intertextuality from the perspective of comparative studies. Therefore, his second encounter with McCullers after twenty years brought him a pleasant surprise, like a reunion with a long-lost friend and mentor.

Meanwhile, the new generation of McCullers fans pinpoints McCullers' so-called "fatal"[11] attraction more clearly on her exquisite depiction of loneliness, as exemplified by the cases of Shu Yu, a rising young poetess born in late 1970s, and A Kang, a renowned professional book collec-tor. While both claim to regard McCullers as one of his or her favorite writers, the former describes her reading experience in terms of sensory aesthetics from a poetic point of view, and the latter discusses McCullers' thematic representation in terms of rational thinking from a philosophic point of view. Shu Yu expresses her feeling about the "magnetic" power of *The Ballad of the Sad Café* as "an unraveled sense of centennial wil-derness, like the scattered pains of one trapped in a sack and pounded by numerous fists in darkness" (302). To be more specific, she discerns in McCullers' novel "a grief of silence and vastness," "an abrupt and funny treacherousness like sailors' posters nailed on the walls of a bar," "an absurd and innocent sense of existence, motionless there forever, which, due to the visual quality of the sense of absurdity of her making, is transformed into a series of vibrating scenes like those in early movies to give people an illusion of reality being identical with on absurdity itself in a matter-of-fact manner." To her, "such biting sense of existence casts doubt on whether this life is worth living," which is exactly the feeling that McCullers intends us to feel—ultimately "the inborn and ingrained loneliness that an individual feels from the moment of his birth" (302). Likewise, the critic laments over the tragic fate of the characters in *The Heart Is a Lonely Hunter*, who "seek in a crowd in vain for a specific and appropriate love, only to be drowned in the even more profound loneliness afterwards" (301); in her eyes, "McCullers' loneliness is a cameo ready to come to life at one's call, where a deaf mute is woken up from his dream to see in shock his own hands madly making signs up in the air" (300). She compares McCullers' "clear and plain" language to the "sunlight on the coast of the Aegean Sea," and the "pause-laden and affirmative sentence patterns that reduce cruelty to the mundane dimension of daily life" to "a dagger-carrying killer on foot who, in his unpretentious profundity, is all the more cruel and merciless in a mood of calmness" (298). In Shu Yu's view, McCullers "stubbornly held on to an adolescent obsession with incompleteness to fend off the sense of alienation brought by civilization" (302).

Compared with the woman poet's sensual experience of McCullers reading, A Kang's observations and meditations seem more inclined to the rational and philosophical, as he sees *The Ballad of the Sad Café*

> enveloped in a dark blue aura of dampness where everyone is struggling deep down in his heart with the doomed fate of being rejected by his beloved while coming to terms with the human instinct for solitude that craves for communication ... In a manner marked with eeriness, mystery and absurdity McCullers conveys a theme of humanity equally eternal as love—loneliness, whose inevitability is in turn confirmed by the absurdity of love. (qtd. in Cao, "August Afternoon")

Indeed, he unveils the paradoxical truth at the core of McCullers' loneliness with great insight. Just as Shu Yu and A Kang's responses reveal, McCullers' poignant perception of love and loneliness in her fictional works penetrates into the hearts of Chinese readers of the new generation and once again strike a sympathetic chord there.

In the words of Cao Xueping, the afore-quoted *Beijing News* reporter, in China

> McCullers has a big influence as many people are captivated by her, but the community who names itself 'Mc-fans' forms a relatively small circle after all. Although McCullers' loneliness is not so widely known as that of Garcia Marquez,[12] it is a continuous flow like a small stream, especially for the reading public and the literary circle. (Cao, "August Afternoon")

However, apparently what strikes Shu Yu and A Kang is the sense of loss and alienation brought by the vast unknown in McCullers' representation of the subtleties of human relationship rather than the sense of "disgrace and betrayal" brought by the known and familiar that is highlighted in Su Tong's works. In a nutshell, the previous interpretation of McCullers' loneliness as an individual's sense of isolation or exclusion by his community has been replaced by an updated version of it as a sense of alienation in a crowd, just like what McCullers expresses as that felt by lovers from different countries,[13] which seems to be the very feeling bred in the soil of modernity.

THE MYTH OF THE "MCCULLERS COMPLEX": DOUBLE MEANING OF LONELINESS

Carson McCullers' Chinese readers have always been impressed by her description of lonely people who suffer from isolation, alienation, and estrangement, and that loneliness is acknowledged as the Southern woman writer's hallmark theme. Her family name, acquired from the ill-fated marriage with Reeves McCullers, has nearly become a synonym of the word "loneliness." What is more, to the Chinese readers over the past thirty-five years, McCullers remains the very embodiment of loneliness of all time: the lonely McCullers is endowed with undercurrents of dangerous charm, and her loneliness appears to be enchantingly mysterious. As Shu Yu points out, McCullers "forces her readers to reflect on the question: what is loneliness?" (300). It is this vicarious and private individual experience of loneliness that collectively creates the myth of the "McCullers complex" in numerous Chinese readers.

McCullers was obsessed with loneliness both in life and in writing. The term "spiritual isolation" strikes the keynote of McCullers criticism over half a century both in China and in the West. In 1957, McCullers wrote: "I suppose my central theme is the theme of spiritual isolation" (qtd. in Carr, "Carson McCullers" 305), and again, in 1959, she claims in her essay "The Flowering Dream: Notes on Writing" that "Spiritual isolation is the basis of most of my themes. My first book was concerned with this, almost entirely, and all of my books since, in one way or another" (280). These statements partly justified and, to a large extent, promoted the initial critical consensus of McCullers' fiction in the 1950s and 1960s, for which "Dayton Kohler's and Oliver Evans's thematic studies served as the impetus," according to Carr ("Carson McCullers" 308). Dayton's essay entitled "Carson McCullers: Variations on a Theme" in 1951 deals with the relationship of McCullers' theme of loneliness to the grotesque and establishes the idea of thematic "unity" in McCullers' work—"her prevailing theme of loneliness and desire" (1). In a similar vein, Evans, in "The Theme of Spiritual Isolation in Carson McCullers" (1952), directs critical attention to the connection between love and "spiritual isolation" by positing the argument that the theme evolving throughout McCullers' major prose works is that love is unable to liberate man from his doomed fate of spiritual isolation. Ihab H. Hassan's 1959 article "Carson McCullers: The Alchemy of Love and Aesthetics of Pain" (1959), which presents a discussion of McCullers' Gothic use of the grotesque in the context of the tradition of Southern literature, contends that while the Gothic qualities of her works "stand in a necessary and paradoxical relation to the facts of Southern life which emphasize the power of tradition and pull of community," her Gothic imagination "derives its peculiar force from a transcendental idea of spiritual isolation" (207). These preliminary studies not only set the tone for subsequent McCullers' evaluations, but they also anticipate impatient dismissals of McCullers as a "simple" author with little variety in her themes.

However, this "loneliness" is contextually contingent and hence much richer in connotation, though McCullers does not bother to make the distinction herself. In real life, her own experience of loneliness is actually marked with duality. That is to say, she puts up a lifelong struggle in the middle ground between individual and community: on the one hand, she longs to break away from the communal bondage, while on the other, she craves for a sense of belonging with the community, which may even give a false impression of a split personality. It seems that the dilemma is paradoxically echoed in the double meaning of her loneliness: she managed to flee her Southern town, and when casting a backward glance at her hometown she was seized with the loneliness of being excluded by her townsfolk, which is a sense of isolation by community. On the other hand, while her move to New York brought her new freedom, she was plunged into another kind of loneliness typical of city life, which is a sense of alienation in crowd. In McCullers' own words, "It has been said that loneliness is the great American malady. What is the nature of this loneliness? It would seem essentially to be a quest for identity" ("Loneliness" 265). Indeed, the two dimensions of McCullers' loneliness both contribute to an individual's identity crisis in the transformed social context.

As Shu Yu observes, McCullers "handles expertly the themes of loneliness and isolation in every story" (297), and her works each embody a superb literary representation of the themes of loneliness. Yet the signifier "loneliness" as McCullers defines it in "Loneliness ... An American Malady" appears a shifting "signified" between two dimensions: on a metaphysically broad scale, "no motive among the complex ricochets of our desires and rejections seems stronger or more enduring than the will of the individual to claim his identity and belong"; on a culturally specific scale, "The European, secure in his family ties and rigid class loyalties, knows little of the moral loneliness[14] that is native to us Americans" (266). From the spontaneous development of an individual self-consciousness, to the establishment of a love relationship that breaks the state of isolation, and to the voluntary pursuit of independence and solitude, her construction of the American identity is centered on the word "loneliness": "Whether in the pastoral joys of country life or in the labyrinthine city, we Americans are always seeking. We wander, question. But the answer waits in each separate heart—the answer of our own identity and the way by which we can master loneliness and feel that at last we belong" (267). Yet the concept of "loneliness," or "spiritual isolation," does not confine itself to American culture alone, but acquires universality in the context of globalization. To a great extent, it transcends the contextual qualifier set specifically by McCullers to refer to New York or America and relates to the general condition of modernity, which makes sense, especially in a Chinese society undergoing transition. At this point, one cannot help asking: if literary taste is both individually and culturally specific, how could it be possible for the two waves of the "McCullers craze" to occur in China following the concentrated translation of McCullers' works in the 1980s and in 2000s respectively? The answer may well lie in the fact that McCullers' experience of loneliness not only possesses qualities in conformity with mainstream Chinese values, but also resonates with the vibrations of social transformation during the two specific historical periods in China. The thematic representation of loneliness in McCullers' works is an in-depth examination of mainstream American values, and the loneliness that she regards as "an American malady" involves a matter of individual and community, which happens to be the crucial factor that determines the Chinese mode of interpersonal relationships and that has faced grave challenges in the social transformation of the latter half of the twentieth century toward modernity.

On the one hand, around 1980, while the reading public's unprecedented enthusiasm in China about foreign literature was a sort of compensation for the cultural void created by the Cultural Revolution, the first wave of the "McCullers craze" could be traced to the post-Revolution mentality of Chinese society in transition. Before the Revolution, Chinese society, basically dominated by the traditional mode of self-sufficient agricultural economy, was a close-knit social network, which typically remained stable with a fixed hierarchy under the reign of Confucian family ethics. Looking back on the condition of social life during the Revolution, contemporary scholars point out that "distorted social culture bred a distorted social life, which in turn reinforced distortions of the culture. Many phenomena that emerged in the Cultural Revolution seem incredibly absurd, such as lack of love and affection, irrational military and ideological wars, educated urban youths' exile to the countryside and mountain areas" (Liu and Guozhong 94). All this has brought about a hazardous collapse of the traditional network of human relations in the Chinese society, which is considered "the greatest disaster of the Cultural Revolution" by Chen Daoming, the famous Chinese actor who said so in an interview by Phoenix News Media concerning *Coming Home*, the latest Zhang Yimou movie released in 2014 (Nian). Speaking of his memories about the persecution his family suffered in the Revolution, Chen was quoted to say that "what makes the Cultural Revolution a holocaust is not how many cultural relics were destroyed, or how long the economic stagnation lasted, but what damage was done to human relationships: you would be enemy of your parents, and husband and wife would antagonize each other, which is so horrifying." His comments are echoed by other witnesses, who generally believe that the Cultural Revolution gave everyone such a sense of insecurity that they did not dare to expose themselves, or lay bare their hearts. Naturally, when the Holocaust was eventually over, the Chinese people were still plagued by multiple crises of belief, faith, and trust, so that they started to reflect on the values of the past decade and call for the recovery of human nature as well as the establishment of a new value system. For that purpose, the translated works of foreign literature, like *The Ballad of the Sad Café*, opened up a whole new window on the dark mysteries of human nature from a refreshed perspective. More important, the Chinese people, newly emerged from their trauma-laden nightmare, could conveniently relate to McCullers' novella, which presents a highly relevant description of a distorted society that suppresses human nature and an individual's intense experience of loneliness in its extreme. In this sense, this particular book, similar to the so-called "scar literature" popular in China at that time, fulfilled the Chinese intellectuals' spiritual needs for an honest probe into the depth of human nature and for a brave pursuit of the truth of human life.

On the other hand, in 2005, McCullers re-emerged from the dust that had started to gather around her and once again struck a chord in the heart of Chinese readers. To a great extent, this new wave of the "McCullers craze" in China seems a fateful encounter in the post-industrial era of globalization, which is termed "the re-reading of McCullers' fatal loneliness" (Cao, "August Afternoon"). Currently China is undergoing a crucial stage of social transformation toward modernity that exerts a great impact on social life, especially communal culture. Indeed, since its planned economy was replaced by market economy, the Chinese society has faced a rising crisis of faith in interpersonal relationships; meanwhile, the alienation of human nature by capital in the process of modernization has led to increasing estrangement and apathy among individuals. For the Chinese people who have always relied on their communal belongingness for the construction of individual identity, this drastic change inevitably brings about an identity crisis. When it comes to the inevitability of such a crisis in a period of social transformation, according to sociologists, modernity tends to cause "the re-adjustment of the human knowledge system and the establishment of new paradigms of social value system, mode of living, and cultural institution," which in its Western version specifically covers

... democratization, liberalization, decentralized power and regularization in politics; marketization, industrialization and urbanization in economy; confirmation of freedom for independent and autonomous individuals; respect for plural lifestyle and multicultural society; highly developed science and technology and material civilization. (Shen 56)

Yet, judging from the experience of modernity in the West, "the greatest perplexity" lies in "what Karl Marx reveals as alienation," for "in a society whose nature of social life is determined by market forces, such symptoms as mutual deception, hedonism, avarice, technolatry and materialism, neurosis, delinquency, heresy, terrorism, and war provide evidence for human irrationality, the greatest shock to humankind itself being human perplexity over its own existence, i.e., the crisis of faith over its own rationality" (Shen 57). While Western intellectuals reflect on the consequences of modernity, China relives the crisis that the West has survived. In this context of social transformation, McCullers' loneliness is endowed with new meaning by a new generation of Chinese readers, and with multiple possibilities of updated interpretation, the previously unique Chinese experience of loneliness eventually becomes part of the global experience in the face of modernity.

It follows that while an older generation of Chinese readers is still indulging in memories of their first taste of McCullers' loneliness conveyed in *The Ballad of the Sad Café*, the new generation is more inclined toward the loneliness represented in *The Heart Is a Lonely Hunter*, whose association with privacy makes it contradictory to the Confucian communal culture where "there is no place for loneliness" (Jiang 22–23). In fact, the latter is "more suitable for an independent expression of 'loneliness,'" as illustrated by the growing pains of thirteen-year-old girl Mick, whose passionate dream of a bright future cools down and eventually fades into nothing but an eternal loneliness that chills the readers to the bone. In the critic's words, "though everyone is lonely, they are not connected by this feeling of loneliness, and they are all doomed to loneliness just as they are mortal beings after all"; "This is a chilling truth, relentlessly true, but McCullers' description is vivid and pungent, and she describes it in such a way that it could be tolerated and must be so" (Cao, "August Afternoon"). Thus, Chinese readers' feedback on McCullers in the 2000s is uniformly much closer to their Western counterparts, because "the violent impact of globalization has enhanced the Chinese people's understanding of the U.S. to an unprecedented level ... and the cultural shock brought by spatial mobility has thus become far less intense and intensive as before" (D. Chen). Moreover, the coincidence of McCullers' second appearance in China and her recommendation by Oprah's Book Club in America provides ample evidence about how effectively globalization as a cultural experience bridges the gap between different nations.

Yet it should be noted that McCullers' loneliness reads differently in different cultural contexts. The difference mainly results from different perspectives informed with different cultural values: whereas in the West McCullers' loneliness may exude an aura of doom in its philosophical profundity concerning the fundamental truth of human existence, Chinese readers tend to willfully focus on the opposite in an effort to retrieve some glimmering hope of salvation from the wreckage of life—especially in the hilarity of the transgression of boundaries drawn between individuals. For instance, Li Wenjun was the first to perceive "a heart of tenderness throbbing beneath the cold words when [he] was translating this novella," and he even inferred from textual evidence and biographical information that the author "still hopes that [the characters] could get rid of loneliness and attain mutual understanding" (8). In my book-length study of McCullers' fiction, I "put forward a model of isolation/transgression, which addresses the long neglected utopian idealism in McCullers' view of social identity" (8). At the bottom of this critical stance must be the "herd mentality" that has been nurtured in the Chinese character by a collective-oriented Confucian culture for thousands of years. As Hu Jian, professor of Peking University, observes in her blog, "There is no denying that the Chinese are a gregarious nation," who have always considered it safe to follow suit and felt solitude rather intimidating from ancient times; further, there is good reason to believe that their fear of loneliness has been culturally and economically institutionalized. In a society where loners may conventionally be despised as social outcasts or eccentric deviants, or even identified with the mentally deranged, it is no wonder that the majority would choose the mainstream to follow either of free will or under pressure. This kind of "herd mentality" faces challenges from the current social transformation and cultural globalization, because paradigms of modernity call for less dependence on collectivity, and hence more individuality. In this sense, McCullers happens to meet the dual psychological demands of Chinese readers, who, torn between individual autonomy and collective belonging, have made a unique contribution to understanding the Southern American woman writer's hallmark theme of loneliness from a typically Chinese perspective.

CONCLUSION

Generally speaking, thanks to the development of mass media, the new wave of the "McCullers craze" in the first decade of the twenty-first century has a more far-reaching influence than the previous one that mainly relied on the circulation of printed books. Different from the previous case, though, the introduction of the McCullers series has not only aroused common readers' enthusiasm, but also caused rising academic interests that incorporate critical views of Western scholars into the Chinese reading experience. According to statistics obtained from China National Knowledge Infrastructure, before 2003 only about ten papers were published in Chinese academic journals on McCullers' two major representative works *The Ballad of the Sad Café* and *The Heart Is a Lonely Hunter*, and they are mostly preliminary studies based on the early "New

Critical Consensus" among the Western critics. However, since 2003, there has emerged a burst of over 250 papers published in various journals, in addition to 120 or more MA theses and PhD dissertations, written from diverse points of view and informed by such critical lenses as feminism, deconstruction, new historicism, and Bakhtinian dialogism, covering themes of love and loneliness, Gothic elements and the grotesque, characters' psychological analysis, gender identity, religious consciousness, and stylistic features.

Yet the burgeoning McCullers' criticism in China seems still lacking in a distinctive Chinese paradigm that can make its own unique contribution to the development of a truly global vision of this particular field of study. In fact, as the foregoing discussion reveals, McCullers' reception in China is context-based and culture-specific in that the two waves of the "McCullers craze" are both products of China's social transformation and value orientation, the first carrying the post-Revolution mentality of the Chinese nation, the second reflecting the turn of modernity, and both capable of being interpreted within the framework of a typically Chinese value system. In the final analysis, the uniqueness of the Chinese perspective resides in its disruption of the reigning order of binary opposition in the Western paradigm of thinking, so that there emerges from McCullers' criticism a heightened sense of reconciliation between individual and community, and for that matter, a consequent hope of salvation from the abyss of loneliness.[15, 16]

NOTES

1. According to historical records, *China and the US formally established diplomatic ties* on Jan. 1, 1979, and the Great Cultural Revolution lasted for ten years between May 1966 and October 1976.
2. The inauguration of this magazine along with *World Literature* is generally acknowledged as "epoch-making" in the sense that it not only marked out the lifting of the decade-long ban on foreign literature and set off the subsequent promotion of a modernist literary revolution in China, but also opened up a whole new window on modern Western schools of literature and thus exerted a shaping influence on a group of leading modern Chinese writers still at their impressionable age then, Mo Yan included (*"Foreign Literature and Art* Lit up the 1980s").
3. The collection under discussion was preceded by *Collected American Short Stories* published by People's Literature Press in September 1978, which mainly includes acknowledged classical works between 1783 and 1913, and

followed by *Selected American Short Stories* in two volumes by China Youth Press in 1980.

4. Cf. The average annual disposable personal income in urban China was 668 yuan RMB in 1979, according to data released by the National Bureau of Statistics of China (http://data.stats.gov.cn/easyquery.htm?cn=C01&zb=A0A03&sj=1979, November 1, 2015).

5. Qian Zhongshu (1910–1998) is regarded as a great master of Chinese studies, "a Chinese literary scholar and writer, known for his burning wit and formidable erudition. Qian is distinguished among other writers and scholars for his broad understanding of both Chinese classics, and Western literary traditions… His satiric novel *Fortress Besieged* became a best seller in the 1970s, and in 1991 it was made into a television drama. Because he was well versed in classic Chinese, his writings often reflect the depth of Chinese literary tradition. His prose is known as one of the most beautiful modern Chinese" (http://www.newworldencyclopedia.org/entry/Qian_Zhongshu).

6. Here Li quotes an unnamed critic who remarks that "even love that is almighty proves powerless in breaking through the eternal human state of loneliness—this is the real intention of this grotesque story… In *The Ballad of the Sad Café*, McCullers reaches the peak of her pessimism, where loneliness becomes an individual's locale of life imprisonment and all attempts to break it down will only lead to deeper seclusion" (qtd. in Li 6).

7. This notion is now considered a prejudice fed by propaganda during the Cultural Revolution, but it may reasonably refer to the alienation widespread in modern society if phrased properly.

8. The translated version of *The Mortgaged Heart* includes six out of the original eleven early stories, three out of the original four later ones, as well as all of the pieces in the two sections of "Essays and Articles" and "Writers and Writing," while poetry as a whole is omitted. "Sucker," "Breath from the Sky," "The Orphanage," "Instant of the Hour After," "Untitled Piece," "Author's Outline of 'The Mute'" and "Who Has Seen the Wind?" are all left out. So are Margarita G. Smith's "Introduction" and "Editor's Note" at the beginning of each section. The translator does not provide any clue as to his principle of selection, and obviously there remains much work for McCullers translators to complete.

9. From interview by personal email correspondence, February 18, 2015.

10. A "McCullers Group" came into being in February 2006 on the virtual intellectual frontier community Douban Website at http://www.douban.com/group/CarsonMcCuller/, whose current 2841 members tellingly choose for themselves a nickname "Lonely Hunter," along with a site named "Carson McCullers Society in China" at http://site.douban.com/140271/, which proclaims itself "the only authoritative organization devoted to the promotion of the American writer McCullers in mainland China."

11. The adjective "fatal" was first used in association with McCullers' loneliness by Cao Xueping in her newspaper article "Su Tong's 'Reunion' with McCullers."

12. Gabriel Jose de la Concordia Garcia Marquez (born March 6, 1927) is a Colombian writer, considered one of the most significant authors of the twentieth century. He was awarded the Nobel Prize in Literature in 1982, and he is well-known in China for his novels *One Hundred Years of Solitude* (1967) and *Love in the Time of Cholera* (1985). Most of his works express the theme of solitude.

13. To quote from *The Ballad of the Sad Café*, "love is a joint experience between two persons—but the fact that it is a joint experience does not mean it is a similar experience to the two people involved. There are the lover and the beloved, but these two come from different countries" (26). This lengthy remark about the loneliness caused by a deep longing for companionship offers a vivid depiction of the sense of alienation typical of modern life.

14. Oliver Evans, the first critic to come up with the phrase "spiritual isolation" as the writer's motif, argues that this "is probably a better term" than McCullers' own term of "moral isolation" on the ground that it is meant to "describe this universal condition of mankind" and "the moral implications are by no means the only ones" (qtd. in Carr, *The Lonely Hunter* 334). However, some recent critics put forward contrary opinions. For example, a Chinese critic contends that the term "moral isolation" implies social causes of human loneliness and identifies McCullers as a moral analyst with a social responsibility to expose "the social evils that isolate the mankind" while the Southern society is shown to be corrupted by forces of industrialization, racism and institutionalized marriage (D. Liu 64–68). Actually, in McCullers' own writings, the two terms are used interchangeably. Besides the above two quotes where McCullers refers to her own theme as "spiritual isolation," "moral isolation" at least appears twice in her essays—once in "Loneliness ... An American Malady" when she says "The sense of moral isolation is intolerable to us" (265) and again in "The Vision Shared" when she claims that "The antagonist [of *The Member of the Wedding*] is not personified, but is a human condition of life; the sense of moral isolation" (270). In either place, the term "moral isolation" has basically the same connotation as "spiritual isolation." Therefore, I adopt the latter for the simple reason that it is the one that more commonly appears in McCullers criticism since Evans's time and therefore forms the common ground of as well as a key word in McCullers studies in the past fifty years.

15. This paper is a product of the research project on "Carson McCullers and Modernity Writing of the American South" (12BWW026), which is supported by the National Social Science Foundation of China

16. All the quotes from Chinese sources in this article are translated by the author.

WORKS CITED

Cao, Xueping. "August Afternoon: McCullers' Loneliness." *The Most Influential Books in China 2003–2005*. Ed. Editorial Board of *Beijing News Book Review Weekly*. Shanghai: Oriental Publishing Center, 2006. Web. http://news.sina.com.cn/o/2005-08-26/09276790255s.shtml. 15 September 2015.

——. "Su Tong's 'Reunion' with McCullers." *Beijing News*. 12 August 2005. Web. http://news.sina.com.cn/o/2005-08-12/10546675330s.shtml. 15 September 2015.

Carr, Virginia Spencer. "Carson McCullers." *Fifty Southern Writers After 1900: A Bio-Bibliographical Sourcebook*. Eds. Joseph M. Flora and Robert Bain. Westport, Connecticut: Greenwood, 1987. 301–12. Print.

——. *The Lonely Hunter: A Biography of Carson McCullers*. New York: Doubleday, 1975. Print.

Chen, Chunxia. "A Brief Discussion of the Southern Complex in the Works of Su Tong and McCullers." *Journal of Hubei Three Gorges Vocational and Technical College* 1 (2010): 62–65. Print.

Chen, Dingjia. "On Globalization and Crisis of Cultural Identification." *Social Science Front Bimonthly* 6 (2003). Web. http://www.literature.org.cn/article.aspx?id=10034. 12 September 2015.

"Complete Follow-up of the Works by Carson McCullers, Representative Figure of Literature of the American South." *Beijing Evening News* 29 June 2007. Web. http://book.sohu.com/20070629/n250832205.shtml. 15 September 2015.

Evans, Oliver. "The Theme of Spiritual Isolation in Carson McCullers." *New World Writing* 1 (April 1952): 297–310. Rptd. in *South: Modern Southern Literature in Its Cultural Setting*. Eds. Louis D. Rubin, Jr. and Robert D. Jacobs. Garden City, N.Y.: Doubleday, 1961. 333–48. Print.

Foreign Literature and Art Lit up the 1980s." 8 May 2009. *Netease News* http://news.163.com/09/0508/10/58PKHLRF00012QEA.html. Web. 1 September 2015.

Hassan, Ihab H. "Carson McCullers: The Alchemy of Love and Aesthetics of Pain." *Modern Fiction Studies* 5.4 (1959/1960: Winter): 311–26. Print.

Hu, Jian. "Why Are the Chinese So Scared of Loneliness." 21 February 2015. Web. http://blog.sina.com.cn/s/blog_6aadcb590102vbs5.html#cre=sinapc&mod=g&loc=40&r=u&rfunc=5. 12 September 2015.

Jiang, Xun. *Six Lectures on Loneliness*. Guilin: Guangxi Normal UP, 2009. Print.

Kohler, Dayton. "Carson McCullers: Variations on a Theme." *College English* 13 (October 1951): 1–8. Print.

Li, Wenjun. "The Call for Love and Understanding." *Free Forum of Literature* 4 (1990): 3–8. Print.

Lin, Bin. *Spiritual Isolation and Textual Transgression: A Post-feminist Study of Gothic Elements in Carson McCullers' Fiction of the 1940s*. Tianjin: Tianjin People's Press, 2006. Print.

Liu, Dangdang. "Be a 'Moral Analyst': Social Criticism in McCullers' Works Drawn from *The Heart Is a Lonely Hunter.*" *Journal of Henan University* 41.5 (September 2001): 64–68. Print.

Liu, Zhong, and Liu Guozhong. "Social Life During the Cultural Revolution and Its Influence on Postmodern Culture." *Journal of Gansu Theory Studies* 6 (2006): 92–96. Print.

McCullers, Carson. *The Ballad of the Sad Café.* New York and London: Bantam, 1971. Print.

——. *The Heart is a Lonely Hunter.* Boston: Houghton Mifflin, 1940. Print.

——. "Loneliness … An American Malady." *The Mortgaged Heart.* Ed. Margarita G. Smith. New York: Penguin, 1981. 265–67. Print.

——. "The Vision Shared." *The Mortgaged Heart.* Ed. Margarita G. Smith. New York: Penguin, 1981. 268–71. Print.

Ni, Jiayuan. *Translation in Foreign Literature and Art and the Reform of Literary Perception, 1978–1980.* MA Thesis. Shanghai International Studies University, 2008. Print.

Nian, Xin. "Chen Daoming Interviewed in Cannes: The Greatest Disaster of the Cultural Revolution Is its Disruption of Interpersonal Relations." 22 May 2014. Web. http://ent.ifeng.com/a/20140522/40078317_0.shtml. 12 September 2015.

Shen, Zili. "Crisis of Faith in Contemporary Chinese Society: Symptoms, Essence and Its Influence." *Truth Seeking* (July 2004): 55–57. Print.

Shu, Yu. "McCullers: Burning Madness into Poetry." *World Literature* 6 (December 2013): 297–305. Print.

Su, Tong. *The Literary Treasure of a Lifetime: Twenty Stories that Have Influenced Me.* Tianjin: Baihua Literature and Art Publishing House, 2005. Print.

Sun, Huijun, and Zheng Qingzhu. "The Translation of British and American Literature in Mainland China in the New Era." *Journal of PLA Foreign Languages University* 33.2 (March 2010): 73–88. Print.

Sun, Xiaoning. "McCullers' Incredible Love." *Beijing Evening News.* 21 October 2005. Web. http://ent.sina.com.cn/x/2005-10-21/1637872445.html. 15 September 2015.

Tang, Yongkuan, ed. *Collected Contemporary American Short Stories.* Shanghai: Shanghai Yiwen Press, 1979. Print.

Zhang, Lili. "Carson McCullers' Novels in China." *Journal of Mudanjiang University* 17.7 (July 2008): 8–10. Print.

Zhu, Hong, ed. *Selected Short Stories of American Women Writers.* Beijing: China Social Sciences Press, 1983. Print.

Yang, Yi. "Review of *Collected Contemporary American Short Stories.*" *Reading* 6 (1979): 56–58. Print.

"The Ballad of Two Sad Cafés": Nicholasa Mohr's Postwar Narrative as 'Writing Back' to Carson Mccullers

Barbara Roche Rico

This essay will use post-colonialism and transatlantic theories to present a new comparative reading of Mccullers' *Ballad of the Sad Café* (1951) and Nicholasa Mohr's *In Nueva York* (1977), a work of the best known female writer of the Puerto Rican Diaspora. The use of such theories can be justified because critics of the Diaspora often use "exile" when describing the displacement experienced by migrants, whom Mohr has herself called "strangers in their own land" (*El Bronx Remembered* ix).

Nicholasa Mohr, the first "Rican" [her term] woman to have her work published in English by a major American publishing house, is also one of the most prolific Rican writers of fiction working today.[1] Her fiction can be read as representing the experience of Puerto Rican migrants during several important historical moments, from the 1940s to the end of the Great Migration later in the twentieth century. To highlight her major contributions: *Nilda* (1973), Mohr's first novel, explores intergroup relations between the Puerto Rican community and the dominant culture, in the period before and during World War II. The short story collections *El Bronx Remembered* (1975) and *In Nueva York* address the Great Migration, the period between 1946 and 1956. The short novels

B.R. Rico (✉)
Department of English, Loyola Marymount University, One LMU Drive, Suite 3800, Los Angeles, CA 90045, USA

© The Author(s) 2016
A. Graham-Bertolini, C. Kayser (eds.), *Carson Mccullers in the Twenty-First Century*, DOI 10.1007/978-3-319-40292-5_14

Felita (1979) and *Going Home* (1986) examine issues prevalent in the period after 1965, among them urban decay, the erosion of barrio institutions, and "revolving-door migration." Later collections of short fiction, especially *Rituals of Survival* (1985) and *A Matter of Pride* (1997), focus more specifically on the role of the female subject in response to some of the social factors mentioned above.

Mohr's writing—including *In Nueva York* (which engages the social imaginary of the post–World War II era)—has been praised critically for what it has included (realistic characters) and what it has lacked (the sensationalism of such earlier writers as Piri Thomas).[2] Until recently, there has been very little criticism addressing Mohr's work as literature.[3] What has emerged instead are either appreciations of the work and its "potential," or criticisms of the work in terms of the horizon of expectations assumed for children's/young adult literature—what the author has termed (in another context), another form of silencing.[4]

Although Mohr has from the outset suggested that her writing was influenced by a short list of novelists, including Carson McCullers, there has heretofore been no comparative examination of the two writers, both of whom address similar historical periods, but from different epistemological perspectives.[5] A list of Mohr's characters in *In Nueva York* not only suggests an influence, but signals a special engagement with McCullers' *Ballad of the Sad Café*.[6] Calling herself "a daughter of the Puerto Rican Diaspora" in her critical writing ("Puerto Rican Writers," 12), Mohr has signaled a connection between her work and those of others "writing back" to the mainstream culture. She asserts that her fiction draws from her own experiences, growing up in what she has termed an internally colonized group. Her work shares a connection with other texts often termed "postcolonial," because of its exploration of identity and affiliation, the need to recover a more authentic view of history and to resist received ones, the challenging of authority relationships, and the negotiation of a bicultural identity.[7] Moreover, in depicting the Puerto Rican neighborhood as a "village within a city," [her term] Mohr's narrative juxtaposes an urban setting and the imagery of small town not unlike that found in McCullers' *Ballad*.

Carson McCullers' *Ballad* will also provide a key subtext for reappraising Mohr's *In Nueva York*. One might start by calling attention to some key similarities between the two narratives: a dwarf with a mysterious history; the owner of a restaurant who is having problems with his marriage; the dwarf's brother who robs both the owner and his wife; and the town itself whose 'small town attitudes' are routinely voiced as a part of the narrative. We see a process of "writing back" in the ways in which Mohr both adopted and re-fashioned key narrative details—to explore the interactions and attachments of characters from a variety of stations in life. The essay will also illustrate how Mohr has adapted some elements in McCullers' work to effect an artful dismantling of clichés often found in the literary representation of the working class. Like McCullers' *Ballad*, Mohr's *In Nueva York* examines how definitions of affiliation and membership are often grounded in the symbolic violence of exclusion.

The Sense of Place: McCullers' Small Town and Mohr's "Village Within a City"

Mohr's narrative engages and refashions key narrative features of McCullers' *Ballad of the Sad Café* as well as its larger representation of the social imaginary of the small town.

> The town itself is dreary ... [T]he town is "lonesome, sad and like a place that is far off and estranged from all other places in the world. The nearest train stop is Society City ... [T]here is nothing whatsoever to do. The largest building, in the center of town, is boarded up completely and leans so far to the right that it seems bound to collapse any moment. The house looks completely deserted ... As likely as not there will not be another soul to be seen along the main street. These August afternoons ... you might as well walk down to the Forks Falls Road and listen to the chain gang." (3)

The passage is highly suggestive. The central building of the town—not only boarded up, but ready to collapse—can be read metonymically. Moreover, the profound sense of isolation is reinforced by the town's distance from Society City, a proverbial 'last stop' for any train. In terms of the symbolic violence of exclusion—there is a way of seeing the world, which involves 'us vs them.' So that the remote community—small town off the beaten path—is a world unto itself. The narrative observer at the beginning asserts, you can study this, or go watch the chain gang. This is important because it suggests an ironic distance. There is almost something philosophical about this, as if the persons in the town are forced together, and like those in a chain gang, are made to engage in a kind of staged activity—a predictable set of moves—beyond which they are unable to venture. Both activities as essentially pointless as they are predictable.

The neighborhood described by Mohr in the opening scene would seem to contrast greatly with that of McCullers' *Ballad*. For Rudi's Luncheonette described in *In Nueva York* is still in operation, if surrounded by urban problems. The story is told from the epistemological position of Old Mary, the dwarf's mother, as she attempts to find a place on the stoop:

> [She] looked up and down the street. It was early afternoon ... Except for a few old people sunning themselves and an occasional drunk slumped against the side of the wall, most of the stoop steps and tenement doorways were empty ... Here and there faces looked out of open windows. (*In Nueva York* 4)

The neighborhood, however quiet, show "signs of life," with men playing dominoes, and a kid standing "on sills against a window guard ... shrieking and bouncing to ... a tune playing on the radio" (4). At the same time, there is a palpable sense of "a decay creeping up," (*Rituals* 78). When Old Mary reflects on the neighborhood, her language reveals the distance between her own experience ("[S]ometimes I'm afraid the building's gonna cave in") and her more recent dreams of a better life: "a clean house in a good neighborhood on a street where they collect garbage, and where you can walk without stepping on them filthy drunken bums. Or be afraid of them dope users" (*In Nueva York* 15). If McCullers' story is set in a "dreary" town, "estranged from all other places in the world," the place in which Old Mary sits is a mockery of what had been advertised— a land of opportunity and great prosperity. Connected with this longing is the metanarrative of the American Dream, whose importance for the migrant experience is outlined in the preface to Mohr's first short story collection:

> These migrants and their children, strangers in their own country, brought with them a different language, culture and racial mixture. Like many before them they hoped for a better life, a new future for their children, and a piece of that good life known as the American dream. (*El Bronx Remembered* ix)

What had been regarded as first of all a destination for many—or in Mary's words "a place where a fortune could be made" (*In Nueva York* 12)—is now seen as an unattainable goal. One becomes resigned to more modest goals—a "fairly clean" spot on her stoop "where she can set down her carseat" (3). Moreover, one becomes used to the weakening of one's identity and familial ties: "People are scattered every place and everything is so far away" (13). Whereas in *Ballad*, Miss Amelia's presence is suggested by a hand at the window of the boarded house, and Old Mary is depicted holding a can of beer.

The relationship between the sense of place and the migrant's double-consciousness also becomes important in contextualizing a) the treatment of Mary's son, the dwarf William, and b) William's own attitude toward the promise of opportunity and prosperity, which other characters (both within and outside his cultural group) typically invoke when addressing the status of the immigrant or migrant.

PATTERNS IN THE REPRESENTATION OF THE DWARF'S ARRIVAL

Among the key narrative elements in both works is the central focus on a dwarf with a mysterious past. Not only is each dwarf's arrival described in some detail, but the dwarf's identity is linked to (real or imagined) genealogical claims, which at least on the surface promise recovery of lost contact. In *Ballad*, Miss Amelia positions herself as resisting any such connections; Old Mary's position is to affirm them.

As Carson McCullers relates, *The Ballad of the Sad Café* began as an image. Her memoir *Illumination and Night Glare* recounts the genesis of the story as a response to what she would later term "an illumination": "It was at a bar [in Sand Street, Brooklyn] ... that I saw and was fascinated by a remarkable couple. Among the customers, there was a woman who was tall and strong as a giantess, and at her heels she had a little hunchback ... [I]t was not until some weeks later that the illumination of 'Ballad of the Sad Café' struck me" (32). Although for many other characters in the story, the arrival of the newcomer becomes a "novelty" or "the cause of amusement," for the main character Miss Amelia, the encounter is life-changing. Indeed, one might trace in the encounters between Miss Amelia and the newcomer a series of meditations on the image, with each event leading toward the woman's dependence on the part of the relationship, despite her more public gestures of self-reliance and invulnerability.

Lymon's arrival is described in the following passage—walking in, one infers, from the last stop at Society City:

[t]he man was a stranger, and it is rare that a stranger enters the town on foot at that hour. Besides, the man was a hunchback. He was scarcely more than four feet tall and he wore a ragged, dusty coat that reached to his

knees. His crooked little legs seemed too thin to carry the weight of his great warped chest and the hump that sat on his shoulders. He had a very large head, with deep-set blue eyes and a sharp little mouth ... He carried a lopsided old suitcase which was tied with a rope. (*Ballad* 6–7)

He is greeted with silence: "They only looked at him" (7). He begins tentatively. Then having realized that his words were failing and his story doubted, the character—like a seasoned performer—makes use of a number of tactics to soften the resistance of his principal audience. The final gesture is the most radical: he cries. (We will explore the reportage of this event further in a subsequent section on the town's values.) For now, let us see this as a kind of performance art, designed to weaken the resistance of his strongest critic, whose attitudes toward hospitality were well known: as the narrator asserts, "It was only with people that Miss Amelia was not at ease," and "the only use Miss Amelia had for people was to make money off them" (5). Lymon's performance for Miss Amelia leads to a gradual softening: from Miss Amelia's "touch [ing] the hump on back" (110), to her trusting him with all that she holds dear.

In his dealing with others, Lymon (often called "the hunchback") continues to be treated as a novelty—or a cause of amusement. In his response to this, however, he first uses a series of aggressive tactics, (in order to intimidate the men of the town), and then uses a well-choreographed performance organized with his accomplice. When a small posse of men ridicules him, Lymon stares at the men's "lower regions" (18). The aggressiveness of this gesture, despite its apparent absurdity, underlines the degree to which the character will go, in order to assert himself, or establish his dominance with those who purport to challenge him. Such gestures, however, are but a preface to the sort of "performance art" we see in his scenes with accomplice Marvin Macy (choreographed in advance)—as if part of a script that was studied some time ago. In this context, the hunchback's frantic painting of the porch fits the notion of Lymon, "who took passionate delight in spectacles" (24), now preparing the stage for the "spectacle" to come.

In contrast to Lymon, William the newcomer in Mohr emerges first as the voice on a page—that of a son whom Old Mary had given up for lost. As the mother learns of the young man's existence and his ambitions for the future, his plans and hers become linked. Whereas Lymon's arrival and his claims to kinship are treated as curiosities, William's letter is immediately shared and celebrated by his mother. Old Mary responds to William's correspondence by expressing a) faith in the supernatural (in a variety of forms):

> After all this time, to receive this [letter] ... it's like a miracle ... I never lost my faith in God. I always prayed for a change of luck. You seen all the novenas and sacrifices I made ... At first I thought it was going to be the lottery ... William is gonna be here with me ... now in my late years when I need this the most. (*In Nueva York* 9, 15–17)

and b) her faith in what Nicholasa Mohr had called, in another context, "the American Dream." It is worth noting that in the preface to her earlier short story collection *El Bronx Remembered*, Mohr linked migrants' aspirations to this ethos. Here, Mohr's text—not without irony—connects the mother's sense of "a promised future" with received notions of opportunity, prosperity, and the comfort.

> He's coming here to be with me and make me happy. He's ... willing to work at anything ... And then, after we save enough money ... we can move out of here ... Yes, we can find another place, because you see, William is white like me. (*In Nueva York* 15)

As in McCullers' narrative, however, the issue of race is never fully absent from the opinions the characters offer.

The scene in which William emerges from the taxi also constitutes a creative "writing back" to McCullers' narrative of Lymon's first appearance. Mohr's narrative focuses on the epistemological position of the viewers who have gathered outside:

> Rudi and several customers came out of the luncheonette to get a better view ... They all stood by the side of the car, waiting. Everyone watched as a large head emerged, covered with thick curly blond hair that shimmered ... The rest of the person had broad shoulders, very short thick arms and legs; he stood no taller than three feet eleven inches. He was neatly dressed in a navy blue suit, white shirt and a tie. He smiled and looked around him and then he saw her. With a swagger to his gait, he rushed up the steps and embraced Old Mary. (24)

What's important here is the process of "writing back." In the case of McCullers, we have an indistinct profile—finally defined as "a traveler"—making its way toward the group. The traveler has only a faded photograph and a long story that no one seems to believe. Here, the car brings William to the curb. As the door opens, the onlookers are represented as if they were putting together William's image as he emerges from the car: they are aware of "his cherubic face, his shimmering golden hair, his strong arms—and then his small size." (It is proleptic that William's features are termed "angelic" and "cherubic," whereas Lymon's descriptions often focus on that which is dirty, evil, or resembling an animal's claw.) As in *Ballad*, the town does not hesitate to express its opinion: pointing and making comments about the "dwarf." Even his mother "trie[s] to pull away" (25). That he is dressed in a suit and tie—and that he embraces her without hesitation—go a long way toward softening the resistance he encounters: "[His mother] looked down and recognized him ... She glanced once more at all the people looking at her. Some of Rudi's customers smiled and nodded" (25). Later, some of those who had been among the onlookers were seen "dressed up for a party and carr[ying] presents of welcome for Old Mary's son" (28).

The Restaurant Owner with Marital Problems

One of the most striking aspects of McCullers' narrative is the conversion of Miss Amelia from someone harsh and litigious, to someone who is capable of (albeit eccentric) gestures of affection. Not only does she trust the hunchback with re-designing her business, but she trusts him with her funds, her keepsakes, and her family history. The narrative notes the change, as if matter-of-factly: "she still loved a fierce lawsuit, but was not so quick to cheat her fellow man and to exact cruel payments" (22). Scenes of tenderness, if not outright physical affection, are reported: "she would bend down and let Lymon scramble on her back and [we would] see them wading forward" (22). The tenderness displayed, beginning with her "touching his hump" and offering him a drink at their first encounter contrasts greatly with her treatment of her earlier suitor Marvin Macy, the groom who had been "treated as a customer."

Miss Amelia's trust is violated in a manner that in retrospect appears quite calculated. The dwarf's involvement in the conspiracy might have to be inferred, but a good deal of inference is encouraged from the outset: from telling the story that no one believes, the wooing of Amelia, to engaging in an affair that the town considered "grotesque." McCullers' text gives the reader a good deal of material here—beginning with Amelia's indifference to and eventual humiliation of Marvin Macy—to suggest a motive for revenge. The sham of a wedding is described in great detail, with the bride refusing the groom the privileges of the bedroom. Taking a longer view, we can see a foster child who had grown into something of a Don Juan, "beloved of many females ... [whom he eventually] degraded and shamed" (28) and then falling for Amelia, perhaps because she was unimpressed, perhaps because she was rich. She treats Macy without respect in several ways, even taking out a court order against him. Whereas Amelia's relationship with Marvin Macy is spelled out, the hunchback's role as a co-conspirator in the revenge plot has to be inferred—most notably through the satisfaction that both seem to take in the destruction of all that Amelia had collected, and all that she had built.

Mohr's narrative, in contrast, dispenses with some of the harsh features we see in Amelia. As we look at the family drama that is implied, we notice interesting adjustments in terms of gender—another form of "writing back." In contrast to the role of Miss Amelia (with her fondness for her desk, her father's memory, and the filing of law suits), the role of the cuckolded lover is played by Rudi Padilla, the owner of the luncheonette. Interestingly, both Miss Amelia and Rudi experience some of the ridicule of the town because of the nature of their attachments, which the gossips consider inappropriate or downright "grotesque." Like Miss Amelia, Rudi embodies a commitment to hard work; at the same time, he fails to understand the ambitions of his spouse. When asked about her ESL courses, for example, Rudi opines, "'What's she have to learn English for? She don't have to talk to nobody'" (49).

It is not without interest that William (like McCullers' hunchback) would both establish his credibility as a character (as he supports the owner's business) and ultimately undermine the family that had given him employment and support. For as in McCullers' narrative, the threat comes not from the dwarf directly, but from someone whom he knows. Exploring the character's emergence in the narrative, we see his rapid transition from being the object of derision, first by the neighbors and then by the customers of the restaurant, to becoming a source of pride. If in the first two stories, we see him treated as the butt of jokes, we see him in the later stories treated by his neighbors as an exemplary worker who can be trusted: he is routinely confided in and asked for advice. That which Lyman purports to be—the trusted confidant—William essentially embodies. Whereas Lymon intimates an attachment to Amelia, William maintains a generally platonic relationship with Rudi's wife. And yet, as the one who is arguably the most innocent in the story, it is the dwarf who inadvertently brings into the marriage the person who does it the greatest harm: William's brother Federico. As the story develops, it becomes clear that there are elements in William's emotional makeup that resemble those of Henry Macy—Marvin's brother—who is kind, worried, and ultimately ineffectual.

Structurally in Mohr's narrative the character of Federico—the confident performer who is able to soften all resistance—could be likened to that of Lymon the hunchback. Interestingly, Federico's past remains a mystery: like Lymon, he "has been traveling" (*In Nueva York* 141). Like that of the hunchback, moreover, his role is to be a confidence man, seducing a woman and taking for himself what she most values. That he is able to play the guitar, that he woos the audience by his performance, and that he exploits the current situation to fund a "promised future" (which does not include the apparent object of his affection) are all critical factors (72). Interestingly, Federico's departure—like William's arrival—is signaled by a note.

The Ironic Representation of the Town, or "Everyone" is Here

Both McCullers and Mohr treat the issue of the collective. In McCullers, it is a given that the town is a character. Clearly it is a force, less of collective understanding than an enforced conformity, with polarizing results. We encounter such judgments early in the story with the reference to the outsider Morris, whose very name is now attached to anything that is seen as womanish; the town's unquestioned anti-Semitism, which has been assessed as a casual occurrence by critics of McCullers since the publication of the work, should be re-evaluated as a representation of the discourse of the time—as unfortunate a part of "the social imaginary" of the town as the Klansman robe mentioned in a later chapter.

McCullers' town delights in creating stories and convincing itself of their veracity. The town—short for rumor/gossip—decides that Miss Amelia has murdered her companion Lymon, and later that she is living in sin. It offers its own advice on a number of issues. By the end of the story, the town for all its bluster, says it would have helped Miss Amelia if it could.

The notion of public opinion is also critical in Mohr, particularly in terms of value judgments that are asserted. From the persons pointing and staring at William from the outset, to Dona Teresa's objections to the same-sex couples in one of the stories, the town (termed "Everyone" in Mohr) is also taken to task for its narrow-mindedness. Characters succeed in Mohr's texts, most often when they ignore or violate the norms established by the town.

The World According to William

In *The Ballad of the Sad Café*, Lymon enters the narrative, recounting a story that no one believes. After a while, however, he enjoys great success because of his ability to perform, to be in fact 'all things to all people.' After "conning" Miss Amelia, he disappears from the town, but not before he has damaged or destroyed all that he has touched. If Lymon's profile from the beginning is represented through recourse to animalistic images, William's image, in contrast, is regarded (by a once skeptical community) in glowing terms.

In an interesting way, William's point of view becomes an epistemological lens through which much of the events of the narrative are not only reported but also commented on. Nowhere is this more important than in the section labeled "The English Lesson," where William's role as adult learner and critic of mainland culture are both in view. As William says of himself, "My ambition is to learn to read and speak English ... and to get a better job" (54). For this reason, it becomes all the more interesting that William's experience becomes a lens through which to judge some elements of the so-called American Dream. In the section describing the night school experience, his epistemological position is the one through which we view the inequities in the educational system—specifically the empty clichés of the ESL teacher "convinced that the small group of people desperately needed her services" (51). William is made to feel uncomfortable, in that he is made to stand rather than sit "and then be at everyone else's level." When he speaks of the geographical features of his homeland, he is silenced before he is finished. After class, he observes the other students in the class debating the value of American citizenship vis-à-vis their own definitions of success. In his conversation with Lali after the class, he provides a needed corrective to his teacher's patronizing—if perhaps well-intentioned—address to the students: "You are now a special member ... of the promised future" (72).

In fact, from early in the narrative, William's earnestness—his sense of authenticity—allows him to be a kind of quiet moral guide. His ethos is such that he is trusted by his family, his employer Rudi, his friend Lali, and even his brother (who would in turn deceive him in the end). Unlike

Lymon who perpetrates the violence—or at least acts as an accomplice in the destruction of Amelia's life—William, however, attempts at each stage to prevent conflicts. A confidant of both Lali and his brother, the dwarf tries to warn them of the reckless nature of their attachment. He acts as an intermediary once the couple's money has been stolen, and Lali has been betrayed. Moreover, later in the story, William tries to thwart two young people in the process of armed robbery, and to help ameliorate the situation at the end. Interestingly, his final words in the narrative are "Bendición"—not a curse but a blessing.

CONCLUSION

Rereading *In Nueva York* through the lens of McCullers' *Ballad* reveals important comparative links, especially in terms of the representation of the marginalized vis-à-vis the predominant "social imaginary" of the time. Several sections of *In Nueva York* call attention to the gap between elements of an official narrative and the experience of a community in diaspora. Such a comparative reading has foregrounded styles of narration that might be called deceptively simple, but whose focus is often on the dignity and the complexity of the person whose social status too often causes him or her to be overlooked.[8]

NOTES

1. When I interviewed her in Brooklyn, New York on 29 July 1996, Ms. Mohr asserted that the term "Rican" is considered preferable to "Neorican or Nuyorican" (seen as passé by her and many other writers in her community.) For further background on Mohr and her motivation to write, see Acosta-Belén, Edna. "Beyond Island Boundaries: Ethnicity, Gender, and Cultural Revitalization in Nuyorican Literature." *Callaloo* 15.4 (Autumn, 1992): 979–998. Print.

2. See AM Flynn, Rev. *El Bronx Remembered*, by Nicholasa Mohr, *Bestsellers* 35 (1975): 266. For reviews focusing on Mohr's "avoidance of stereotyping, trendiness and triteness," see M Sachs, Rev. *Nilda*, by Nicholasa Mohr. *New York Times Book Review*. 7 Nov. 1973: 27–28. Print.; D Gibson, "Fiction, Fantasy, and Ethnic Realities." Rev. *Nilda*, by Nicholasa Mohr. *Children's Literature: Annual of the MLA Seminar on Children's Literature* 3 (1974): 230–234. Print.; AP Nilsen, "Keeping Score on Some Recent Winners." *English Journal* 67.2 (1978): 98–100. Print.; T Slade, "Growing Up Hispanic: Heroines for the 90's." *School Library Journal* 38.12 (1992): 35. Print. For one of the first published academic articles to treat Mohr's fiction,

see J C Miller, "The Emigrant and New York City: A Consideration of Four Puerto Rican Writers." *MELUS* 5.3 (Fall 1978): 82–99. Print., which praises *Nilda's* "portrayal of Barrio life" and *In Nueva York's* representation of the city. And J Flores, "Puerto Rican Literature in the United States: Stages and Perspective." *ADE Bulletin* 91 (1988): 43. Print.

3. Among the articles that stress the importance of Mohr's work within the context of "immigrant" or "migrant" literature are the following: J Flores, "Back Down These Mean Streets: Introducing Nicholasa Mohr and Louis Reyes Rivera." *Revista Chicano-Riqueña* 8.2 (1980): 51–6. Print.; J Miller, "The Concept of Puerto Rico as Paradise Island in the Works of Two Puerto Rican Authors on the Mainland: Nicholasa Mohr and Edward Rivera," *Torre de Papel* 3.2 (1993): 57–64. Print. For discussions of Mohr's work and novels of development, see E McCracken, "Latina Narrative and the Politics of Signification: Articulation, Antagonism, and Populist Rupture," *Critica: A Journal of Critical Essays* 2.2 (1990): 202–07. Print.; M F Olmos, "Growing Up puertoriiqueña: The Feminist *Bildungsroman* and the Novels of Nicholasa Mohr and Magali García Ramis," *Centro: Bulletin of Centro de Estudios Puertorriqueños* 2.7 (1989): 56–73. Print.

4. For interviews in which Mohr cites European and American sources—particularly Chekhov, Maupassant, McCullers, Jackson, and Welty—see interview with the author quoted in *Heath Anthology of American Literature*; Nicholasa Mohr, "Pa'lante," an interview by B Kevane and J Heredia, in *Latina Self-Portraits: Interviews with Contemporary Women Writers*, Albuquerque, Univ, of New Mexico Press, 2000, 83–96. In her essay, "Puerto Rico: A Separation Beyond Language," *Americas Review* 15. 2 (1987): 91.

5. See Mohr, Nicholasa. "Puerto Rican Writers in the U.S., Puerto Rican Writers in Puerto Rico: A Separation Beyond Language," in *Breaking Boundaries: Latina Writing and Critical Reading*, edited by Asunsion Horno-Delgado, Eliana Ortega, Nina M. Scott, Nancy Saporta Sternback. Amherst: Massachusetts UP, 1989. 88.

6. McCullers' text *The Ballad of the Sad Café* will be referred to as *Ballad*.

7. Among the many relevant overviews of the application of postcolonial theories to modern fiction are Bill Ashcroft, *et al.*, *The Empire Writes Back: Theory and Practice in Postcolonial Literatures*, London and New York, Routledge, 1989. Print.; Homi K. Bhabha, *Nation and Narration*, London and New York: Routledge, 1990. Print.; Gustavo Perez-Firmat, *Literature and Liminality*, Durham, Duke, 1986. Print; Gayatri C. Spivak, *The Postcolonial Critic: Interviews, Strategies, Dialogues*, London and New York: Routledge, 1990. Print.

8. The funding for research on this article was provided by a Rains Research Fellowship administered by Loyola Marymount University. I would like to express my thanks to Teah Goldberg, Morika Fields, and Evelyn Hitchcock for their assistance researching material in support of this project.

WORKS CONSULTED

Acosta-Belén, Edna. "Beyond Island Boundaries: Ethnicity, Gender, and Cultural Revitalization in Nuyorican Literature." *Callaloo* 15.4 (Autumn, 1992): 979–998. Print.

——. "Notes on the Evolution of the Puerto Rican Novel." *Latin American Literary Review* 8.16 *Hispanic Caribbean Literature* (Spring 1980): 183–195. Print.

——. "Puerto Rican Literature in the United States." *Redefining American Literary History*. Eds. A. Lavonne Brown Ruoff and Jerry W. Ward. New York: LMA, 1990. Print.

——. "The Literature of the Puerto Rican Migration in the United States: An Annotated Bibliography." *ADE Bulletin* 91 (Winter 1988): 56–62. Print.

Acosta-Belén, Edna and Christine E. Bose, eds. *Researching Women in Latin America\and the Caribbean*. Boulder: Westview Press, 1993. Print.

Acosta-Belén, Edna and Barbara J. Sjostrom, eds. *The Hispanic Experience in the United States: Contemporary Issues and Perspectives*. New York: Praeger, 1988. Print.

Ashcroft, Bill, Gareth Griffiths, and Helen Tiffin. *The Empire Writes Back: Theory and Practice in Postcolonial Literatures*. London and New York: Routledge, 1989. Print.

Bhabha, Homi K. *Nation and Narration*. New York: Routledge, 1990. Print.

Behrman, Christine. Rev. *Going Home*, by Nicholasa Mohr. *School Library Journal* 32.10 (August 1986): 105. Print.

Bercovitch, Sacvan. ed. *Reconstructing American Literary History*. Cambridge: Harvard UP, 1986. Print.

Blicksilver, Edith. "Nicholasa Mohr." *Biographical Directory of Hispanic Literature in the United States*. Ed. Nicolas Kanellas. Greenwood Press, 1989: 199–213. Print.

Burns, Mary M. Rev. *Nilda*, by Nicholasa Mohr. *Contemporary Literary Criticism* 12. 445–48. Print.

Committees of RASD. "Puerto Rican Materials: A Core List of Books for Adults and Young Adults." *RQ* 33.1 (Fall 1993): 50–62. Print.

Cortés, Felix, Angel Falcón, and Juan Flores. "The Cultural Expression of Puerto Ricans in New York City: A Theoretical Perspective and Critical Review." *Latin American Perspectives* 3.3 (1976): 117–50. Print.

DeRonne, Susan. Rev. *Growing Up Inside the Sanctuary of My Imagination*, by Nicholasa Mohr. *Booklist* 90.21 (July 1994): 1934. Print.

Flores, Juan. "Back Down These Mean Streets: Introducing Nicholasa Mohr and Louis Reyes Rivera." *Revista Chicano-Riqueña* 8.2 (1980): 51–6. Print.

——. "Puerto Rican Literature in the United States: Stages and Perspective." *ADE Bulletin* 91 (1988): 43. Print.

Flynn, Anne, M. Rev. *El Bronx Remembered*, by Nicholasa Mohr. *Best Sellers* 35.9 (December 1975): 266. Print.

Forman, Jack. Rev. *El Bronx Remembered*, by Nicholasa Mohr. *School Library Journal* (April 1977): 79. Print.

Garcia, Irma. Rev. *El Bronx Remembered*, by Nicholasa Mohr. *Interracial Books for Children Bulletin* 7.4 (1976): 15–16. Print.

Gibson, Donald B. "Fiction, Fantasy, and Ethnic Realities." Rev. *Nilda*, by Nicholasa Mohr. *Children's Literature: Annual of the MLA Seminar on Children's Literature* 3 (1974): 230–234. Print.

Gonzalez, David. "Puerto Ricans Get Freedom, Culturally." *The New York Times* 26 March, 1996: B.1. Print.

Gordils, Yanis. "Island and Continental Puerto Rican Literature: Cross-Cultural and Intertextual Considerations." *ADE Bulletin* 91 (Winter 1988): 52–55. Print.

Graham, Marilyn Long. Rev. *The Magic Shell*, by Nicholasa Mohr. *School Library Journal* 41.10 (October 1995): 138. Print.

Greengrass, Linda. Rev. *All for the Better: A Story of El Barrio*, by Nicholasa Mohr. *School Library Journal* 39.5 (May 1993): 118. Print.

Haviland, Virginia. Rev. *Felita*, by Nicholasa Mohr. *The Horn Book Magazine* 56.1 (Feb. 1980): 56. Print.

Heins, Paul. Rev. *El Bronx Remembered*, by Nicholasa Mohr. *The Horn Book Magazine* 52.1 (Feb. 1976). Print.

Janeczko, Paul. Nicholasa Mohr. *From Writers to Students: The Pleasures and Pains of Writing*. Ed. M. Jerry Weiss. Delaware: International Reading Association, 1979. Print.

Kevane, Bridget A. and Juanita Heredia, eds. "Pa'lante: An Interview with Nicholasa Mohr." *Latina Self-Portraits: Interviews with Contemporary Women Writers*. Albuquerque: New Mexico UP, 2000: 83–96. Print.

Koss, Jaon D. Rev. *The Puerto Rican Woman*, ed. Edna Acosta-Belén. *The Journal of Psychoanalytic Anthropology* 7.3 (Summer 1984): 320–22. Print.

Lauter, Paul ed. "Interview with Nicholasa Mohr." *Heath Anthology of American Literature, 5th Edition*. Vol E. Boston: Houghton Mifflin, 2005. Print.

M.M.B. Rev. *Nilda*, by Nicholasa Mohr. *The Horn Book Magazine* (April 1974): 153. Print.

Maldonado, Lionel A. Rev. *The Hispanic Experience in the United States: Contemporary Issues and Perspectives*, by Edna Acosta-Belén and Barbara R. Sjostrom. *Contemporary Sociology: An International Journal of Reviews* 18.6 (Nov. 1989): 877. Print.

McCracken, Ellen. "Latina Narrative and the Politics of Signification: Articulation, Antagonism, and Populist Rupture." *Critica: A Journal of Critical Essays* 2.2 (1990): 202–07. Print.

McCullers, Carson. *Illumination and Night Glare: The Unfinished Autobiography of Carson McCullers*. Ed. Carlos L. Dews. Madison: Wisconsin UP, 1994. Print.

——. *The Ballad of the Sad Café. Ballad of the Sad Cafe and Other Stories.* New York: Bantam, 1991: 3–74.

McHargue, Georgess. Rev. *In Nueva York*, by Nicholasa Mohr. *New York Times Book Review*, 22 May 1977. Print.

Miller, John C. "Nicholasa Mohr: Neorican Writing in Progress." *Revista/Review Interamericana* 9.4 (1979–80): 543–49. Print.

——. "The Emigrant and New York City: A Consideration of Four Puerto Rican Writers." *MELUS*, 5.3 (Fall 1978): 82–99. Print.

——. "The Concept of Puerto Rico as Paradise Island in the Works of Two Puerto Rican Authors on the Mainland: Nicholasa Mohr and Edward Rivera." *Torre de Papel* 3.2 (1993): 57–64. Print.

Mohr, Nicholasa. "A Special Gift." *Kikiriki: Stories and Poem in English and Spanish for Children.* Ed. Sylvia Cavazos Pena. Houston: Revista Chicano-Riqueña/Arte Público Press, 1981. 91–100. Print.

——. *All For the Better: A Story of El Barrio.* Ed. Alex Haley. Austin: Raintree Steck Vaughn Publishers, 1993. Print.

——. An Awakening ... Summer 1956. *Woman of Her Word: Hispanic Women Write.* Evangelina Vigil. ed. Houston: Arte Público Press, 1983. Print.

——. "An Open Letter of Friendship and Welcome for Antonio Martorell." *The Americas Review* 22. 1–2 (Spring–Summer 1994): 179–82. Print.

——. *El Bronx Remembered.* New York: Harper, 1975. Print.

——. *Felita.* New York: Dial, 1979. Print.

——. *In Nueva York.* New York: Dial, 1977. Print.

——. "Puerto Rican Writers in the United States, Puerto Rican Writers in Puerto Rico: A Separation Beyond Language." *Americas Review* 15.2 (1987): 91. Print.

——. *Rituals of Survival: A Woman's Portfolio.* Houston: Arte Público Press, 1984. Print.

Nilsen, Alleen Pace. "Books for Young Adults: Keeping Score on Some Recent Winners." *The English Journal* 67.2 (1978): 98–100. Print.

——. Rev. *In Nueva York*, by Nicholasa Mohr. *Contemporary Literary Criticism* 12. 447. Print.

Ocasio, Rafael. "An Interview with Judith Ortiz Cofer." *The Americas Review* 22. 3–4 (Fall–Winter 1994): 84–90. Print.

Olmos, Margarite Fernandez. "Growing Up puertorriqueña: The Feminist *Bildungsroman* and the Novels of Nicholasa Mohr and Magali García Ramis." *Centro: Bulletin of Centro de Estudios Puertorriqueños* 2.7 (1989): 56–73. Print.

Ortiz, Miguel A. "The Politics of Poverty in Young Adult Literature." *The Lion and the Unicorn* 2.2 (Fall 1978): 6–15. Print.

——. Rev. Nilda, by Nicholasa Mohr. *Contemporary Literary Criticism* 12. 448. Print.

Pena, Sylvia Cavazos., ed. *Kikiriki: Stories and Poem in English and Spanish for Children*. Houston: Revista Chicano-Riqueña/Arte Público Press, 1981. Print.

Pérez-Firmat, Gustavo. *Literature and Liminality*, Durham: Duke UP, 1986. Print.

Redburn, Maria. Rev. *The Song of El Coquí and Other Tales of Puerto Rico*, by Nicholasa Mohr and Antonio Martorell. *School Library Journal* 41.8 (August 1995): 137. Print.

——.Rev. *El Bronx Remembered*, by Nicholasa Mohr. *Guidelines for the Future— Human and Anti-Human—Values in Children's Books: A Content Rating Instrument for Educators and Concerned Parents*. CIBC Racism and Sexism Resource Center for Educators, 1976. 251–52. Print.

——.Rev. *Felita*, by Nicholasa Mohr. *Kirkus Reviews* 48.3 (Feb. 1980): 127. Print.

——.Rev. *Going Home*, by Nicholasa Mohr. *Publishers Weekly* 230.4 (July 1986): 190. Print.

——.Rev. *In Nueva York*, by Nicholasa Mohr. *Kirkus Reviews* 45.7 (April 1977): 360. Print.

Rochman, Hazel. Rev. *The Song of El Coquí and Other Tales of Puerto Rico*, by Nicholasa Mohr and Antonio Martorell. *Booklist* 91. 19&20 (June 1995): 1779, Print.

——. Rev. *The Magic Shell*, by Nicholasa Mohr. *Booklist* 91.22 (August 1995): 1947. Print.

Sachs, Marilyn. Rev. *Nilda*, by Nicholasa Mohr. *New York Times Book Review* 7 Nov. 1973: 27–28. Print.

——. Rev. *El Bronx Remembered*, by Nicholasa Mohr. *New York Times Book Review* 16 Nov. 1975: 30. Print.

Shepard, Ray Anthony. Rev. *Nilda*, by Nicholasa Mohr. *Contemporary Literary Criticism* 12. 446. Print.

Slade, Tomelene. "Growing Up Hispanic: Heroines for the 90's." *School Library Journal* 38.12, 1992: 35. Print.

Spivak, Gayatri Chakravorty. *The Postcolonial Critic: Interviews, Strategies, Dialogue*. London and New York: Routledge, 1990. Print.

Sutherland, Zena. Rev. *Going Home*, By Nicholasa Mohr. *Bulletin of the Center for Children's Books* 30.11 (July–August 1977): 178. Print.

——. Rev. *Going Home*, by Nicholasa Mohr. *Bulletin for the Center for Children's Books* 34.9 (May 1986): 175.

Williams, Denise M. Rev. *Going Home*, by Nicholasa Mohr. *Booklist* 82.21 (July 1986): 1615. Print

——. Rev. *Felita*, by Nicholasa Mohr. *Booklist* 76.7 (Dec. 1979): 559.

Zarnowski, Myra. "An Interview with Author Nicholasa Mohr." *The Reading Teacher: A Journal of the International Reading Association* 45.2 (October 1991): 100–06. Print.

Jester's Mercurial Nature and the Hermeneutics of Time in McCullers' *Clock Without Hands*

Craig Slaven

Carson McCullers' final novel, *Clock Without Hands*, belongs to a sort of deuterocanon. As one early reviewer astutely put it, McCullers "has had to write with the albatross of reputation hung around her neck and the thumping signboard of 'genius' staring her in the teeth" (Martin 3). The general verdict, at the time of its release in 1961, was that *Clock Without Hands*, while good, did not measure up to McCullers' more prodigious masterpieces. The novel, many agreed, failed to find structural cohesion. By abruptly shifting focus from one narrative thread to the next, the novel neither integrates the discrete plotlines nor satisfactorily develops them in their own right, suggested Irving Howe, who described the text as "an unadorned and scrappy scenario for a not-yet-written novel" (5).

Fourteen years later, Charlene Clark suggested that the earlier failure to appreciate the novel's literary achievement denoted a misperception of McCullers' political agenda, so that readers "dismissed it as a quasi-propaganda piece for civil rights." On the contrary, she wrote, "[t]he novel in the final analysis has to do with … the individual's attempt at self-discovery through knowledge of the past both public and private" (16). This observation, while valid, too readily depoliticizes and decontextualizes the process of negotiating identity through "public and private"

C. Slaven (✉)
University of Kentucky, Lexington, KY, USA

© The Author(s) 2016   251
A. Graham-Bertolini, C. Kayser (eds.), *Carson McCullers in the Twenty-First Century*, DOI 10.1007/978-3-319-40292-5_15

pasts, which is necessarily contingent on the political climate and cultural contexts informing the text.[1]

Rather than offer an apologia for the novel's perceived aesthetic short-comings, I suggest that the text situates the familiar story of self-discovery in relation to national narratives of cultural production in the 1950s and that the incompleteness observed by reviewers reflects a heightened sense of discord between personal, regional, and national narratives of self-hood. Using McCullers' established literary accomplishments as a rubric for reading *Clock Without Hands* obscures the contextual significance of the interim between her 1940 debut and her 1961 coda.[2] That interval carries autobiographical significance—as it is connected to the deaths of McCullers' husband and mother, as well as her own declining health—but it also encompasses global, national, and regional paradigm shifts, both ominous and hopeful. This was a period of reductive national narratives that pitted democratic heroism against communist villainy, but it was also a time when such metanarratives, such *H*istory, proved inadequate for containing the excess *h*istories of disenfranchised groups.

The Supreme Court's deliberation over desegregation looms large in the background of the novel. Set between the summers of 1953 and 1954, the citizens of Milan, Georgia, anxiously contemplate the imminence of integration, and the tension finally breaks, near the conclusion, when the radio announces the Court's ruling. Thus, the story of a seemingly insular town is caught up in the national drama of civil rights, just as the nation was engrossed in the global drama of the cold war. As Mary Dudziak argues, Jim Crow hindered the American-led effort to contain the communist threat globally. How could a nation that tolerated legal segregation at home be entrusted to spread the gospel of democracy abroad? The nation's initial response was to veil the problem through containment narratives that "presente[d] American history as a story of redemption," of a "gradual and progressive social change which was described as the fulfillment of democracy" (49). Despite these optimistic accounts, the reactionary backlash against civil reform made it increasingly difficult to avoid confronting racial oppression. The cold war, therefore, "was simultaneously an agent of repression and an agent of change" (250); it created a need to conceal racial oppression that tarnished the nation's exceptional image, and when those efforts failed, it ensured that global victory would depend on the success of the civil rights movement. An unfortunate consequence of this entanglement, however, was that when the cold war ended, the interest in domestic reform also receded (Dudziak 251).

While McCullers could not have predicted this outcome, she could certainly look back at the Reconstruction period in the South and draw parallels with the "new reconstruction" (Dudziak 53) that cast premature pronouncements of democratic triumph in a skeptical light. In the novel, Judge Clane, an eighty-five-year-old former congressman, dreams of running for office again, and even more unrealistically, plans to convince Congress to remonetize Confederate currency, of which he has plenty in his attic. This implausible obsession figures the Judge as temporally irrelevant, out of step with the progressive nation; however, the novel also problematizes the assurance of inevitable progress. As Margaret McDowell writes, "The clock that monitors social progress is almost always without hands." Thus, "McCullers, with modulated irony, implies that this day was not the turning point the Judge understood it to be. The foolish Judge, who thinks the clock of the South is tolling midnight, was wrong, but the people who thought the clock marked a new dawn because of this (the Court's) decision were just as wrong" (102). The "new dawn" narrative was necessary for the restoration of American innocence; however, triumphalism potentially hindered a more vigilant effort to reform the justice system and enforce progressive legislation. The novel, rather than dismissing the Judge's outlandish Lost Cause ideology, warns against narratives of unstoppable progress by interrogating the intricate relationship between time and the narrative structures we rely on to imbue time with meaning.

McCullers draws troubling parallels between the Judge's Lost Cause rhetoric and that of American exceptionalism. On the surface, the two seem to be opposing paradigms, the former signifying a futile search for meaning and tradition in a never-realized Southern victory and the latter naively defining itself in terms of yet-to-be-realized democratic aspirations. Further consideration, however, reveals an unlikely marriage between national and regional expressions of innocence. In *Civil Rights in the White Imagination*, Jonathan W. Gray discusses this surprising correlation: "although the South lost the conflict on the battlefield," he writes, "it won political and rhetorical control over the war's ultimate meaning after Reconstruction by encouraging a deliberate forgetting of the actual causes of the war" (4). Rather than deal with the persistence of racial oppression, it was more convenient for white Americans, Southerners and Northerners alike, to believe that "the nation went to war over a disagreement that centered on differing interpretations of the proper role of government" (5). During the civil rights movement, moreover, a similar convergence occurred when some Southern authors who publically supported the goals of the civil rights movement simultaneously "permitted the successful recuperation of the premise of white American innocence at precisely the moment when a reinvigorated emancipationist narrative—the civil rights narrative—challenged the basis of that innocence" (6). This analogy between the Lost Cause cooptation of Reconstruction and American Exceptionalism's cooptation of civil rights reform, both antithetical affirmations of innocence in the face of exposed national and regional transgressions, resonates throughout *Clock Without Hands*. In this light, the untenable scheme to redeem Confederate currency appears as a more viable threat, reminiscent of the so-called Southern Redeemers' religiously-intonated campaign to end sanctions imposed by Reconstruction.[3]

In *Clock Without Hands*, McCullers exposes the cultural processes by which such narratives are reproduced and propagated. To accomplish this point, McCullers employs the Judge's grandson, Jester, who appears as a welcome counterpoint to his grandfather's white supremacy. As I will demonstrate, however, Jester unwittingly reaffirms white innocence throughout the novel. Jester, as revealer and concealer of meaning, becomes a true trickster figure, both questioning and reconstituting the prevailing order. As Vicki K. Janik writes, the figure of the jester "uses language to alter perception, and he seems both involved in and alienated from the prevailing social structure, participating but always commenting and evaluating" (20). Jester clearly fits the bill of one whose partial detachment from the prevailing order grants him a unique exegetical perspective: an aspiring pilot, he hovers over the fictional community and examines it from a readerly distance; the narrator describes him as an outsider—"Some people were content to live their mortal lives and die and be buried in Milan. Jester Clane was not one of those" (101); and at the novel's climax, when white citizens gather to plot an act of racial terrorism, Jester, like the reader, eavesdrops from the shadows, not participating in but privy to the conspiracy (221).

While the trickster's peripheral vantage allows him to examine what other characters cannot, he frequently reaffirms the very order he disrupts. In his chapter on the archetypical trickster Hermes, William D. Doty notes, "Typically the trickster helps humans by stipulating social boundaries, even if he does so by metonymically transgressing them" (Hynes and Doty 55).[4] Similarly, Jester's subversive transgressions, including homosexual fantasies and his defense of integration, consistently precipitate the reaffirmation of his innocence, implicitly confirming the categorization of such thoughts and actions as transgressive. Through Jester, *Clock Without*

Hands deconstructs and reconstructs the cultural narratives of innocence that tempered, rather than addressed, civil unrest in postwar America.

Jester resembles many of the adolescent characters central to the bildungsroman narratives of McCullers' earlier works. He is socially clumsy and insecure. His sense of self—his convictions, aspirations, desires—are ambiguous and unformed, always in process. But Jester's inner conflicts, more than those of his antecedents, allegorize the historical moment in which his story takes place, when the South, like Jester, was in an adolescent stage of change and confusion. In this turbulent setting, Jester's protean nature proves to be an exegetical asset: as a character in the process of becoming, he models for the reader the way in which private narratives of self-determination always relate to prevailing cultural narratives.

Like the mythological trickster Hermes, or Mercury, whom Frank Kermode identifies as the patron god of the hermeneutical arts,[5] Jester's ambiguities give him the ability to cross boundaries that inhibit characters who are confined to their culturally prescribed roles. According to William Hynes, these figures engage in a sort of "metaplay" that "ruptures the shared consciousness, the societal ethos, and consensual validation—in short, the very order of order itself" (215). Often depicted as naïve and overly sensitive, however, Jester's deviant nature stems precisely from his undeveloped sense of selfhood. An unwitting jester, he lacks the cunningness of the conventional trickster, but he nevertheless defies and transgresses the discursive boundaries that govern others, likening him to the subtype Janik identifies as the "innocent or holy fool" (3).

The novel, however, opens and closes not with Jester, but with J. T. Malone, a middle-aged druggist who in the opening pages learns he is dying of leukemia. Given a one-year prognosis, Malone must come to grips with his mortality and try to find some meaning to his mundane existence. Terrified by "what would happen in those months ... that glared upon his numbered days," he "was a man watching a clock without hands," the omniscient narrator reports (25). Significantly, Jester enters the text when he interrupts an ongoing conversation between Malone and the Judge. From his first appearance, Jester's hermeneutical function of disrupting narratives emerges, and the conversation that he stumbles into is just as significant. Devastated by his prognosis, Malone seeks consolation from his cherished friend, the out-of-time caricature of the Southern gentry who constantly bemoans the Old South, espouses white supremacist beliefs, and blames his troubles on the meddlesome federal government. The Judge is also in poor health, having suffered a stroke ten years prior, but he is a consummate denialist, skeptical of doctors, and he comforts Malone by telling him that the prognosis is probably wrong. The Judge, the arbiter of Southern heritage who wishes he had written *Gone With the Wind* and given it a happier ending, dismisses Malone's existential concerns and resituates him, momentarily, in the sentimental fiction of Southern romance.

When Malone tells the Judge about his blood disease, the Judge responds, "A *blood* disease! Why, that's ridiculous—you have some of the best blood in this state." The Judge's comment briefly suspends Malone's trepidation, so that he "felt a little chill of pleasure and pride that passed almost immediately" (15). When Malone again stresses the diagnosis, the Judge tells the story of how he outlived his own "alarmist" and "fallible" doctor, and he prescribes the pharmacist an alternative regiment of "fried calf liver and beef liver smothered in onion sauce," "sunlight," and alcohol (16). The conversation then shifts to a "blue-eyed Nigra," who had startled the already-unnerved Malone in the alley recently. "I never saw such strange eyes," he tells the Judge, who identifies the stranger as Sherman Pew, a "woods colts ... something wrong between the sheets. He was left a foundling at the Holy Ascension Church" (20–21). The sign of miscegenation clearly unsettles the Judge as it does Malone, but the Judge uses pastoral idioms of Southern innocence to repress rather than confront the precarious foundations of (white) Southern tradition. Malone's prognosis brings all of these latent fears to the surface, which jeopardizes the Southern romance that the Judge, as authority and author, compulsively reconstructs. As the narrator reports, "Malone felt that the Judge had left some tale untold but far be it from him to pry into the manifold affairs of so great a man" (21). The need to uphold the stature of this patriarch overrides an interrogation of the unstable foundation of his greatness.

It is in the middle of this dialogue, in which Southern romance provides a temporary diversion from Malone's, and the South's, imperiled existence, that Jester enters the text. "Jester—speaking of the devil" (21), exclaims the Judge, as if discursively summoning absence into presence. Jester's announced devilment signifies his function as a mischievous figure. Indeed, Jester literally descends into the text like the winged Hermes, having just arrived from the airport: "I soloed, Grandfather," he announces. The Judge explains to Malone that "a few months ago this little rapscallion just announced to me that he was taking flying lessons ... But with not so much as by-my-leave" (22). The exchange is an affectionate one, but Jester's learning to fly without his grandfather's leave—like a baby bird leaving the nest—establishes Jester's internal drive to distinguish himself from the man who raised him, to shape an independent identity.

That Jester's shapelessness relates to questions of interpretation becomes evident in his first full exchange with the Judge. Jester questions his grandfather's white supremacy: "I can't see why colored people and white people shouldn't mix as citizens," he says. The Judge, unable to accept his beloved grandson's "act of incipient lunacy," tells Jester he is "too young to have learned the pattern of thought. You are just deviling your grandfather with foolish words" (29). Jester's assertion is thus rendered permissible and nonthreatening. The Judge is always ready to pardon his grandson, who remains innocent in his youthful folly to the same extent that such folly is impermissible for black adolescents, who are always already guilty and menacing. "How would you like to see a hulking Nigra boy sharing a desk with a delicate little white girl?" he asks. After Jester's open defiance, the conversation shifts to a seemingly less touchy subject, a pastoral painting of a "Nigra shack" and a peach orchard painted by Jester's aunt. Jester asks, "Do you see there between the shack and the trees a pink mule?" and the Judge adamantly responds, "Why naturally not" (30). Like the childhood activity of discerning shapes in amorphous clouds, Jester makes out a mule, and this racially charged image[6] returns the conversation to the topic that the Judge was so relieved to have left behind. "All my life I had seen the picture like Aunt Sara had intended it," Jester says, "And now this summer I can't see what I'm supposed to see in it" (30). Jester, true to his role as embedded exegete, explains that his altered perception of the painting is a "symbol of this summertime": "I used to have ideas exactly like everybody else. And now I have my own ideas," he clarifies (31), announcing an emerging identity in contradistinction to that of his grandfather.

As confident as Jester appears in his proclamation, Jester immediately reveals how uncertain he really is in the words he uses: "'A symbol,' Jester said. He repeated the word because it was the first time he had spoken it in conversation, although it was one of his favorite words in school compositions" (31). Jester is in the process of acquiring a more mature vocabulary; his speech, like his identity, is malleable and unformed. Thus, Jester is liberated from his grandfather's rigidity not by conscience or mere contentiousness but, surprisingly, by a poor proficiency in the language of the narrative at hand. Not having mastered the patterns of thought—the paradigms—he has not been fully indoctrinated by his grandfather's ideology. Jester's linguistic fluidity often surfaces in his malapropisms—when, for instance, he tells his grandfather, "I had to tell you, otherwise you would have taken it for granite I was like I used to be." Jester, in fact, should neither be taken for granted nor for granite, because his character lacks assurance of a permanent form. When Sherman calls Jester "fatuous," Jester replies, "I'm not a bit fat." "I didn't say fat," Sherman says; "I said fatuous. Since you have such a putrid and limited vocabulary, that means fool ... fool ... fool" (84). Jester's foolishness, again, relates to verbal inaptitude.

The Judge regards deviations from the rigid patterns of thought as devilment, but Jester's devilment falls within a permitted form of defiance, a privilege of his presumed innocence. Jester's seemingly firm position on race, in fact, becomes an expression of his innocence. His developmental experimentation with "different feelings, different thoughts" are, the Judges says, "only natural" (30). This sanctioned deviance results from his privileged subject position in the community. Jester soon falls in love with Sherman, whom the Judge hires as a personal servant and amanuensis, but Jester's innocent transgressions contrast to Sherman's impermissible insubordination to the Judge, his moving into a white neighborhood, and indeed his very existence as the product of interracial desire. Whereas the novel codifies Jester's rabblerousing as an adolescent inclination to test boundaries as he transitions into adulthood, Sherman faces dire consequences when he tests the racial boundaries of his community.

Other parallels between Jester and Sherman accentuate Jester's permissible aberrances. The Judge reveals very little to his grandson about Jester's deceased father, Johnny Clane. This profound mystery generates for Jester a drive to discover himself by uncovering his hidden past. Like Jester, Sherman is an orphan, and he, too, tries to establish an identity through speculations about his unknown parentage. Both characters eventually discover the truth about their intertwined pasts. Jester's father, a lawyer, commits suicide after unsuccessfully defending Sherman's black father for the self-defensive slaying of his white lover's abusive husband. Johnny falls in love with the widow, but after she gives birth to a boy she curses Johnny, with her dying breath, "for being a fumbling lawyer" (200). While Jester learns these secrets directly from the Judge, Sherman accidentally uncovers his origins when the Judge sends him to the courthouse on an unrelated errand: "I want to read my clippings from the newspapers. Little as you know, I am great man," the Judge tells Sherman. Having the keys to the courthouse gives Sherman a sense of importance and a form of public access heretofore forbidden. Ignoring the Judge's instructions not to "monkey around" with other documents, Sherman stumbles across the court proceedings of another man named Sherman (211). On this errand to retrieve clippings that publically praise the Judge as "*a glory to this fair state and to the South*" (212), Sherman discovers the truth of his own past from his father's criminal record. For Sherman, the public recognition of his private self cannot occur without self-incrimination, and he is deemed valuable to the Judge (and the public) only as long as he acknowledges the Judge's public accolades. Sherman can never fully belong to this "fair" (read, white) state, yet he is expected to recite the precise public narratives that exclude him, a task that Sherman "was too broken not to obey" (212).

While these revelations instill in Jester a newfound desire to become a lawyer like his father, they infuriate Sherman, who had up to then loathed his own white blood, thought to have come from his imagined black mother's white rapist. The shocking revelation provokes Sherman to rent a house in a white neighborhood, a final protest that seals his fate. Unlike Jester's hermeneutical flexibility, Sherman's interpretive role is confined to that of amanuensis: he can inscribe that which is dictated to him by a white judge, and he can read about his past in long-filed criminal proceedings. His eventual refusal to write the Judge's letters and his ultimate transgression of dictated racial boundaries ensure his tragic death just as the same revelation about the murder trial puts Jester on a sure path to self-discovery. Jester thus fulfills the court jester's paradoxical function of transgressing and gesticulating boundaries, breaking ranks with the Judge's racism but fluidly evading the penalties that Sherman, in his stead, must suffer.

Jester's affinity for flight further reinforces his mercurial qualities.[7] Jester is an aspiring pilot and so obsessed is he with this pastime that he tells Sherman, "flying's fun and I look on it as a kind of moral obligation that everyone ought to learn to fly" (75). Sherman refuses to be impressed, in part because of his fear of heights but also because he could never afford, and would not likely be permitted to take, private flying lessons like Jester: he "was sick about talking about something he couldn't do" (76). If Jester's power of flight signifies the text's self-referential reflections on cultural interpretation, then the text seems to deny Sherman access to this means of self-understanding. In another of Jester's malapropistic insights, he tells Sherman, "this summer I'm taking flying lessons. But that's just an advocation" (75). The conflation of avocation and advocacy reconfigures Jester's foray into the racial taboos that his grandfather deplores as a low-stakes social experiment or hobby. After all, Jester's moral pursuit of flying is an expression of his "summer vacation freedom." On the same day that Sherman begins his summer *vo*cation as the Judge's amanuensis, Jester goes leisurely to the airfield to pursue his moral *a*(*d*)*vocation*: "Jester did not race but took his mortal time, for after all it was summer vacation and he was not going to any fire" (98).

Jester's obsession with flying also troubles Malone. Malone spies Jester waiting for the bus to the airport: "Happy, confident, free, he lifted his arms and flapped them for a moment." Seeing this odd "gesture" (an apt homophone for "Jester") through the window, Malone "wondered if, after all, the boy was dotty" (98). After his flight, Jester returns to the drugstore and orders a coke from Malone, and while he waits, he gets on a nearby scale. "Those scales don't work," Malone tells him, and Jester awkwardly replies, "Excuse me." The broken scales reflect the sensation of weightlessness he still feels from his flight. But Malone responds as he had before: "wasn't it a dotty thing to say, apologizing because the pharmacy scales didn't work" (101). Malone sees the "prancing" teenager as queer in every sense, but the association of his eccentricity with his power of flight reveals that Malone is unsettled by the fact that Jester is not quite grounded in the social categories that make other residents of Milan legible. Further, Jester's gravity-defying nature and lack of a properly grave demeanor come across as eccentric to the dying druggist who himself longs to be grounded in the world of the living. In addition, the fact that Jester apologizes for the broken scales seems dotty to Malone because Jester is a privileged white boy apologizing for the figurative broken scales of justice. To acknowledge fault belies Malone's and the Judge's romanticized ideal of Southern innocence; however, that threat to innocence is also contained by the image of the broken scales, because Jester's levity tips the scales, presumably in his own favor.

The name "Jester" does not immediately describe the adolescent who desperately wants to be taken seriously and is frustrated when others infantilize him. For instance, Jester is in love with Sherman, who ridicules the overly sensitive boy's gestures of affection. Sherman calls him "[i]nnocent, dopey, the very living image of a baby's behind." To the last charge, Jester protests, "I'm not innocent" (139). Far from a crafty and purposeful jester, Jester becomes an ironic trickster: the more he demands to be taken seriously, the more of a jester he becomes. After Sherman emasculates him, Jester, fearing further belittlement, hides in his pocket a jar of caviar he had bought as a gift for Sherman. As a result, "he had to sit gingerly in a sideways position" (139). The very action taken to preserve a manly image intended to impress Sherman forces him back into an unmanly posture, and the result is ostensibly humorous. But Jester's perpetually reinscribed innocence is no laughing matter. On the contrary, it shows how interpretive acts conceal as much as they reveal. Jester's defiance of social boundaries may seem consonant with civil rights activism; however, Jester has a tendency to reinforce the very order he appears to break, which I have suggested is the jester figure's ancillary function. By consistently reaffirming Jester's innocence, the novel reimposes order on whatever havoc he wreaks. By alternately transgressing and reinscribing boundaries between adolescence and manhood, innocence and culpability, Jester negotiates the production, disruption, and reproduction of romanticized narratives of American and Southern innocence.

The most compelling example of this pattern of undercutting and reconstituting innocence is Jester's inadvertent role in the death of another young black teenager called Grown Boy. Grown Boy often accompanies Wagon, a crippled black man who begs for money downtown. Frustrated that Wagon refuses to share his fried chicken, Grown Boy snatches the coins from Wagon's cup and runs. Witnessing this, Jester impulsively pursues the culprit, but when nearby mill workers spy "a white-coated white man running after a nigger," they automatically follow suit. By the time Jester grabs Grown Boy and tries to fetch the stolen money, "more than half a dozen people had joined in the fray, although none of them knew what it was about" (103). An intervening cop strikes Grown Boy on the head with his club, killing him instantly. Jester's inadvertent role in the racially charged narrative of an officially coated white man chasing an implicitly guilty black fugitive (a less redemptive form of flight) causes other whites to follow suit. They each play a role in the prescriptive racial drama with little sense of volition. When the cop takes Jester's statement, Jester says, "It was all my fault. If I hadn't been chasing him and those people piling in on top of us ... and why did you hit him so hard?" The cop responds, "When you are breaking up a crowd with a billy stick you don't know how hard you are hitting. I don't like violence any more than you do. Maybe I shouldn't even have joined the force" (104).[8] Both Jester and the cop express a sense of guilt, but they also evoke the strange sensation of having involuntarily participated in a narrative they neither condone nor comprehend. Despite the fact that Jester is often construed as innocent and inexperienced, it is a "white-coated white *man*" that the crowd sees chasing Grown Boy. Jester dons the "unaccustomed coat" earlier to appear manlier. On his way to the bus stop, a well-known banker tips his hat to Jester, "very likely because of the coat," he imagines (99–100). Jester's guise grants him a sense of authority that, on the one hand, causes important people to recognize him; on the other hand, it legitimizes the black fugitive narrative that facilitates Grown Boy's death.

But the narrator contains the disruptive revelation of fault within a larger narrative of redemption:

> The next few moments would be forever branded in his brain ... Later Jester knew he was responsible for the murder and the knowledge of that fact brought further responsibility. Those were the moments when impulse and innocence were tarnished, the moments which end the end, and which, months later, were to save him from another murder—in truth, to save his very soul. (101–2)

Guilt, in this way, reinscribes innocence: the remembrance of his role in the death of a black man prevents his subsequent murder of a white man, Sammy Lank, whose spared life redeems Jester's tarnished soul. As Clifton Snider observes, "Grown Boy is a flat character, symbolic of the random brutality of the South ... and a catalyst to Jester Clane's growth" (42). While Grown Boy has reached his severely limited potential for mental and spiritual growth, his death facilitates Jester's growth, which, tautologically, leads to Jester's exoneration from complicity in the very death that allows him to grow. If the Judge's scheme to redeem Confederate currency seems far-fetched, more insidious perhaps is the redemptive invocation of white innocence in Jester's heroic act of mercy that ironically represses the ongoing civil crisis revealed by Grown Boy's death. Sherman also spares another's life when he replaces the Judge's insulin shots with water for three days but cannot follow through with the murder (215), but this is not represented as an act of mercy and does not anticipate Sherman's redemption in the same way that Jester's last-minute decision not to kill Sammy saves Jester's soul.

Sammy, the recipient of Jester's soul-saving gesture of compassion, appears late in the novel. When news gets back to the Judge that his former servant has moved into a white neighborhood, the Judge convenes a secret meeting at Malone's drugstore, and the gathered men plot to bomb Sherman's house. With the Judge presiding "as the *chief* citizen of this town" (218, emphasis added), this secret lynch meeting parodically inverts Chief Justice Warren's and the Supreme Court's concurrent deliberations over *Brown v. Board*. When Malone, afraid of damning his soul, dissents, Sammy Lank, the poor and uneducated man from the same white slums where Sherman has moved, volunteers. Meanwhile, Jester, from the shadows, overhears and goes to warm Sherman, who refuses to leave and dies at the hands of Sammy. Determined to avenge his friend's death, Jester, carrying the pistol that his father had used to kill himself, offers to take Sammy up in his airplane. During the flight, Sammy, terrified of heights like Sherman, nervously tells Jester about his triplets and how he and his wife had read about quintuplets in Canada: "rich, famous, mother and daddy rich and famous too ... We almost hit the jackpot," he continues; "and every time we did it we thought that we were making quints. But we only had triplets and twins and little ole singles" (232). Sammy is driven by the same desire for social recognition as his victim. In his house hangs the framed article from the *Milan Courier* about his triplets, his greatest achievement prior to killing Sherman. "The grotesque pity of the story made Jester laugh that laughter of despair," the narrator reports; "And at once having laughed and despaired and pitied, he knew he could not use the pistol" (233). With this redemptive act, Jester's "odyssey of passion, friendship, love, and revenge was now finished," and he lets Sammy believe "he is such a well-known man now that even Jester Clane had taken him up on an airplane ride" (234).

Sammy's misreading of Jester's intentions demonstrates how Jester's return to innocence also redeems the pawn of racial terrorism. As Cicely Palser Havely observes, "Thus ironically a small choice against violence comes to be seen as a gesture approving it. The progress of justice is almost invisibly slow" (170). What slows such progress, however, are the cultural narratives that set the tempo, and tacit resignation to this gradualism lay at the heart of a Southern white liberalism that emerged in the 1950s. As Richard H. King writes, "The tendency in political and social analysis of that period was to theologize political and social concerns" (283), leading, in the case of Robert Penn Warren, for instance, to a "tendency to abstract his works from historical reality" (284) by replacing concrete attention to social reform with a kind of "moral therapeutics" (285) that emphasizes spiritual redemption of the individual over the political condemnation of the region or nation at large. While my analysis of the reproduction of narratives of innocence in *Clock Without Hands* potentially places McCullers in Warren's company, Jester's *unwitting* capitulation to reclaimed innocence seems to belie a more witting, and therefore more critical, awareness on her part of such liberalism's untimely focus on white redemption.

On the heels of Jester's last flight, the radio announces the Supreme Court's *Brown v. Board* ruling, and the outraged Judge assures his dying friend, "There are ways we can get around it ... Writing it in laws is one thing but enforcing it is another" (239). The Judge goes to the radio station to address the Court's decision in what he believes will be a "historic speech" (239). He gets so worked up, however, that he cannot put his anger into words: "The ideas were so chaotic, so inconceivable, he could not formulate his protests ... Words—vile words, cuss words unsuitable for radio— raged in his mind" (240). Flustered, the Judge can only think of Lincoln's Gettysburg address, which he knew by heart from law school (240). On the surface, the irony of the Judge's self-defeating speech humorously appears to dismiss the Judge's archaic ideology. As Havely explains, "Even a dyed-in-the-wool reactionary like the Judge must now march to ... Lincoln's tune, the last thing in the world he wants" (170). But this interpretation only delineates *part* of the "modulated irony" of the scene, to repeat McDowell's phrase. That the Judge's intended vitriol is "unsuitable for radio" suggests that the public broadcast must project a censored, sanitized image of innocence, and this is in keeping with other public records of the Judge's greatness—like the *Milan Courier's* description of the Judge as "*A fixed star in the galaxy of Southern statesmanship. A man of vision, duty and honor*" (212). Indeed, he is a "fixed" star in the sense that his image, paradoxically, is secure and stable precisely because it is fixed or corrected to suit the ever-changing and unstable political climate. The public record's assertion that he is a "man of vision" contrasts with his failing eyesight, just as his recitation of Lincoln's address contrasts with his white supremacy.[9] In both cases, the public image retains a form of innocence that conceals a darker side. Thus, while the Judge's words contradict his political agenda, they symbolically ratify his belief that he is "as innocent as newborn babe," as he says regarding his role, as presiding Judge, in the death of Sherman's father (198).[10]

Clock Without Hands, more than an ad absurdum critique of the Judge's political backwardness, reveals how dominant cultural narratives construe public consensus in a way that preserves images of exceptionalism. The dominant narrative, rather than ruining the Judge's reputation, preserves it by resituating him in the historical order of American innocence. To be certain, this is not the Southern restoration he envisioned, but neither is the South's reintegration into the narrative of American innocence at cross purposes with the Judge's vision that Southern white resistance to change will endure beyond the formal end of Jim Crow. In some ways, it ensures it, pre-memorializing an ongoing political struggle as an already-won victory.

NOTES

1. For Alan Nadel, "[p]ersonal narration is required for any form of historical narrative and also, necessarily, disrupts it. While the more pervasive, cultural narratives are echoed and reiterated ... with a contagion that resembles viral epidemics, personal narration oscillates, situationally, between identification with and alienation from a historical order." Thus, "the American cold war is a particularly useful example of the power of large cultural narratives to unify, codify, and contain—perhaps *intimidate* is the best word—the personal narratives of its population" (3–4).

2. Cicely Palser Havely similarly observes that, while McCullers' earlier works excel in their "subtle delineations of eccentric inner landscapes," this novel goes "beyond her earlier achievement by relating four such inner landscapes to each other and to the complex social and political situation which involves them all. The unwilling desegregation of the South is not mere 'context.' It impinges directly and violently on her characters' lives even though the particular events they are involved in have little historical consequence. The novel achieves a rare and impressive balance between the demands of private feelings and the claims and pressures of the public world" (169).

3. Daniel W. Stowell explains that, with slavery abolished and the South's greatest sin "removed," white Southerners more readily asserted the South's spiritual superiority to the "atheistic North," whose political control and occupation of the South they egregiously equated to slavery (140).

4. Chris Jenks likewise writes, "To transgress is to go beyond the bounds or limits set by a commandment or law or convention, it is to violate or infringe. But to transgress is also more than this, it is to announce and even laudate the commandment, the law or the convention. Transgression is a deeply reflexive act of denial and affirmation" (2).

5. Kermode writes, "Hermes is cunning, and occasionally violent; a trickster, a robber. So it is not surprising that he is also the patron of interpreters. Sometimes they proclaim an evident sense, like a herald, but they also use cunning, and may claim the right to be violent, and glory in it. The rules of their art, and its philosophy, are called 'hermeneutics'" (1).

6. As the hybrid offspring of a female horse and male donkey, the mule—etymologically related to "mulatto"—is a common image for racial mixing and racist attitudes toward interracial sex. The Judge recognizes this connotation when he tells Jester, "... this talk about mixed races and pink mules is certainly—abnormal" (31).

7. Easily the most bewinged Roman god, with his winged helmet, staff, and shoes, Mercury flies between divine and human realms, another indication of his role as mediator.

8. "Joined the force," in this context, has the double meaning of joining the police force and unthinkingly going along with the mob's momentum and policing the boundaries of dominant narratives.

9. The evocation of Lincoln in the Judge's intended rebuttal of federal intervention is scarcely a novel trope. The conflation of cavalier and Yankee was central to Southern redemption, and Henry Grady and other promoters of the "New South" memorialized Lincoln as the ideal combination of Northern and Southern virtues: Lincoln, Grady announced, "was the sum of Puritan and Cavalier, for in his ardent nature were fused the virtues of both, and in the depths of his great soul *the faults of both were lost*" (28, emphasis added). This composite cultural hero *conceals* "the faults" of the nation and the South.

10. In another act of public sanitization, the Judge, as "not only the leading citizen in Milan but the most responsible one," bans "the *Kinsey Report* from the public library" so that "innocent eyes are not offended" (94). The Judge had read the obscene book himself, hidden "behind the covers of *The Decline and Fall of the Roman Empire*" (92).

WORKS CITED

Dudziak, Mary L. *Cold War Civil Rights: Race and the Image of American Democracy.* Princeton, NJ: Princeton UP, 2000. Print.

Clark, Charlene. "Selfhood and the Southern Past: A Reading of Carson. McCullers' *Clock Without Hands.*" *Southern Literary Messenger.* 1.2 (1975): 16–23. Print.

González, Constante Groba. "Ivan Ilych in the Jim Crow South: Carson McCullers and Leo Tolstoy." *Literature and Belief.* 24.1 (2004): 118–133. Print.

Grady, Henry. *The New South and Other Addresses.* New York: Haskell House, 1969. Print.

Gray, Jonathan W. *Civil Rights in the White Literary Imagination: Innocence by Association.* Jackson: UP of Mississippi, 2013. Print.

Havely, Cicely P. A Materialist Reading of *Clock Without Hands. Critical Essays on Carson McCullers.* Ed. Melvin Friedman and Beverly Lyon Clark. New York: G.K. Hall, 1996. 166–71. Print.

Howe, Irving. "In the Shadow of Death." Rev. of *Clock Without Hands* by Carson McCullers. *New York Times Book Review.* 17 Sept. 1961: 5. Print.

Hynes, William J., and William G. Doty. *Mythical Trickster Figures: Contours, Contexts, and Criticisms.* Tuscaloosa: U of Alabama Press, 1993. Print.

Janik, Vicki K. *Fools and Jesters in Literature, Art, and History: A Bio-Bibliographical. Sourcebook.* Westport, CT: Greenwood Press, 1998. Print.

Jenks, Chris. *Transgression: Critical Concepts in Sociology.* New York: Routledge, 2006. Print.

Kermode, Frank. *The Genesis of Secrecy: On the Interpretation of Narrative.* Cambridge, MA: Harvard UP, 1979. Print.

King, Richard H. *A Southern Renaissance: The Cultural Awakening of the American South, 1930–1955.* New York: Oxford UP, 1980. Print.

Martin, Jean. "Ways of Telling It." Rev. of *Clock Without Hands* by Carson McCullers. *Nation.* 18 Nov. 1961: 3. Print.

McCullers, Carson. *Clock without Hands.* Boston: Houghton Mifflin, 1998. Print.

McDowell, Margaret B. *Carson McCullers.* Boston: Twayne Publishers, 1980. Print.

Nadel, Alan. *Containment Culture: American Narrative, Postmodernism, and the Atomic Age.* New Americanists. Durham, NC: Duke UP, 1995. Print.

Stowell, David W. "Why 'Redemption'? Religion and the End of Reconstruction, 1869–1877." *Vale of Tears: New Essays on Religion and Reconstruction.* Eds. Blum, Edward J. and W. Scott Poole. Macon, GA: Mercer UP, 2005. 133–46. Print.

Snider, Clifton. "On Death and Dying: Carson McCullers' *Clock Without Hands.*" *Markham Review* 11 (1982): 43–47. Print.

NOTES ON CONTRIBUTORS

Lin Bin holds a PhD from Peking University and specializes in women's literature. She is a professor of English at Xiamen University, P.R. China, who has been researching and writing about Carson McCullers for more than ten years. Bin is the author of *Spiritual Isolation and Textual Analysis: A Post-feminist Study of Gothic Elements in Carson McCullers's Fiction of the 1940s* (Tianjin People's Press, 2006) and has published several McCullers papers. She is currently writing a monograph about McCullers' works to be published by Peking University Press. She is the leader of two major McCullers research projects in China: "Studies of Carson McCullers' Fiction," Ministry of Education Project of Humanities and Social Sciences; and "A Study of McCullers and Southern Writing of Modernity in the US," National Social Science Fund Project of China. In 2013, she worked with the Beatrice Bain Research Group on "Carson McCullers: Gender and Southern Modernity" at the University of California, Berkeley.

Carlos Dews was the founding director of the Carson McCullers Center for Writers and Musicians and the founding president of the Carson McCullers Society. He edited *Carson McCullers: Complete Novels* for the Library of America and his edition of Carson McCullers' unfinished autobiography, *Illumination and Night Glare*, was published by the University of Wisconsin Press. He is chair of the Department of English Language and Literature at John Cabot University in Rome, Italy.

© The Author(s) 2016
A. Graham-Bertolini, C. Kayser (eds.), *Carson McCullers in the Twenty-First Century*, DOI 10.1007/978-3-319-40292-5

Temple Gowan is an M.A. candidate, Department of English, University of Mississippi. Her primary interest as a scholar is how we can improve our ethical relations with both other species and our own by taking the presence of animals in literature seriously. Her master's thesis focuses on the intersections of gender, race, and sexuality with posthumanism in novels by 20th century American authors Carson McCullers, Charles Johnson, and Ruth Ozeki.

Alison Graham-Bertolini is an assistant professor of English and Women's Studies at North Dakota State University. She researches and writes about contemporary American literature, especially literature written by women. Her first monograph, *Vigilante Women in Contemporary American Fiction* (Palgrave Macmillan, 2011), is about female protagonists who take extra-legal action in response to violence that women experience on a daily basis: domestic violence, restrictive laws, and lack of political recourse. Graham-Bertolini has published in the *Eudora Welty Review*, *The Southern Quarterly*, and in a variety of collections. She serves currently as the vice president of the Carson McCullers Society.

renée c. hoogland is a professor of English at Wayne State University in Detroit, where she teaches contemporary literature and culture, critical theory, visual culture, and queer theory. Hoogland is the editor of *Criticism: A Quarterly for Literature and the Arts*. Her third book, *A Violent Embrace: Art and Aesthetics after Representation*, was published by the University Press of New England in January 2014.

Casey Kayser is a clinical assistant professor of English at the University of Arkansas, where she teaches courses in literature and medical humanities. Her research specialties include narrative medicine; modern and contemporary American literature and drama; southern literature, drama, and culture; folklore; and gender studies. Her work has been published in *Midwestern Folklore*, and she has essays forthcoming in *Mississippi Quarterly* and *Pedagogy*. She is working on a book focusing on gender, race, and regional identity in the work of southern women playwrights. She currently serves as the President of the Carson McCullers Society.

Kiyoko Magome has been teaching at the University of Tsukuba in Japan since 2007. Her publications include *The Influence of Music on American Literature Since 1890: A History of Aesthetic Counterpoint* (Edwin Mellen, 2008) and "Edward Said's Counterpoint" (*Paradoxical*

Citizenship: Edward Said (Lexington Books, 2006). Supported by the Japanese Society for the Promotion of Science (Grants-in-Aid for Scientific Research, 2008–2018), Magome has been researching modernist musico-literary quartets and has published Japanese translations of contemporary American novels, such as Claire Vaye Watkins's *Battleborn* (Iwanami Shoten, 2015).

Melanie Masterton Sherazi is a University of California President's Postdoctoral Fellow in English at UCLA, specializing in twentieth-century modern and contemporary American literature. She is currently working on a study of African American expatriate culture in postwar Rome, with an archival emphasis on the papers of the late author William Demby. She is also developing a project that explores the ethics and aesthetics of posthumously published mid-century literature by such authors as Carson McCullers and Ralph Ellison. Her writing on Faulkner has been published in *Mississippi Quarterly*, and an article on Ralph Ellison is forthcoming in *MELUS*.

Miho Matsui is a senior assistant professor of English at Sapporo City University, Japan. Her doctoral dissertation at Hokkaido University (2014) was "Passing into the Darkness: Sexuality, Race, and Integration of the Segregated in the Works of the Southern Renaissance." She has published several essays on southern writers including Frances Newman, Julia Peterkin, William Faulkner, and Carson McCullers in Japanese literary journals. At the Carson McCullers Interdisciplinary Conference in 2011, she presented "Exploring Southern Queerness: Desire and Identity in *Reflections in a Golden Eye*," which was published as an essay titled "Reflections in a Filipino's Eye: Southern Masculinity and Colonial Subject" in *ANQ: A Quarterly Journal of Short Articles, Notes and Reviews* in 2013.

Kristen Proehl is an assistant professor of English at SUNY-Brockport, where she teaches courses in children's and young adult literature. She has recently published articles on Louisa May Alcott's work in two different essay collections: *Romantic Education in Nineteenth-Century American Literature* (Routledge, 2014) and *Sentimentalism in Nineteenth-Century America* (Fairleigh Dickinson UP, 2013). She is currently revising her book manuscript, *Battling Girlhood: Sympathy, Social Justice and the Tomboy Figure in American Literature*.

Barbara Roche Rico is a professor of English at Loyola Marymount University, where she has taught since 1989. She holds a doctorate from Yale University. Her research interests include comparative studies of Renaissance authors and, more recently, work on Nicholasa Mohr, Judith Ortíz Cofer, Esmeralda Santiago, and other writers of the Puerto Rican Diaspora. The textbook she co-edited with Sandra Mano of UCLA, *American Mosaic: Multicultural Readings in Context*, is in its third edition. She has presented her work at conferences in the United States (including Puerto Rico) and in Mexico. Her other publications include essays in *Frontiers: A Journal of Women's Studies* (reprinted in Latino/a Writing [Routledge]) and *Short Fiction in Theory and Practice*. Transatlantic exchange is a focus of her research and teaching, which have been supported by internal and external grants. She has recently completed a term as a member of the National Networking Board of the Lilly Foundation.

Stephanie Rountree is a PhD candidate in American literature and Provost's Dissertation Fellow at Georgia State University. Her scholarship has appeared or is forthcoming in *Ethos*, *Mississippi Quarterly*, *south*, and *Word and Text*. She serves as co-editor of *Small-Screen Souths: Interrogating the Televisual Archive* (LSU Press, forthcoming Fall 2017). In 2014, she co-founded the Emerging Scholars Organization, an affiliate of the Society for the Study of Southern Literature, and served as its inaugural President (2014–16). Her dissertation, entitled "American Corpus: The Subversion of National Biopower in Post-Emancipation Literature," investigates public policies that relegate citizens' bodies as mechanisms of U.S. (neo)liberalism in literature and history, 1865–2011.

Craig Slaven teaches English at Auburn University. He earned his PhD from the University of Kentucky, where he taught classes on southern literature, African-American literature, and the Bible as literature. His dissertation examines the proliferation of cultural narratives of redemption, from Reconstruction through the twentieth century, that helped rebrand the South as the "Bible Belt" in the popular imaginary. In 2014, he was a participant at Dartmouth's Futures of American Studies Institute and one of three presenters at the St. George Tucker Society's Cleanth Brooks Forum. He currently serves as the Secretary of the Carson McCullers Society.

Carmen Trammell Skaggs, Associate Dean for Academic Support in the College of Humanities and Social Sciences at Kennesaw State University in Kennesaw, Georgia, is the author of *Overtones of Opera in American Literature from Whitman to Wharton* (LSU Press, 2010). Dr. Skaggs's interest in Carson McCullers developed while she lived in Columbus, Georgia—McCullers' birthplace—while previously serving on the faculty at Columbus State University. Her work on McCullers also appeared in *ANQ: A Quarterly Journal of Short Articles, Notes, and Reviews.*

Jan Whitt is a professor of literature and media at the University of Colorado at Boulder and the recipient of the 2013 Edward R. Murrow Teaching Award and the 2014 Boulder Faculty Assembly "Excellence in Research and Creative Work" awards. She has published numerous journal articles on American literature, media studies, popular culture, and women's issues. Her books include *Allegory and the Modern Southern Novel, Burning Crosses and Activist Journalism: Hazel Brannon Smith and the Mississippi Civil Rights Movement, Dangerous Dreams: Essays on American Film and Television, Rain on a Strange Roof: A Southern Literary Memoir, Reflections in a Critical Eye: Essays on Carson McCullers, Settling the Borderland: Other Voices in Literary Journalism,* and *Women in American Journalism: A New History. The Redemption of Narrative: Terry Tempest Williams and Her Vision of the West* (Mercer University Press) is in press. A book about Truman Capote's *In Cold Blood* (Rowman & Littlefield) is in progress and is part of the "Contemporary American Literature" series.

INDEX

© The Author(s) 2016
A. Graham-Bertolini, C. Kayser (eds.), *Carson McCullers in the
Twenty-First Century*, DOI 10.1007/978-3-319-40292-5

CPSIA information can be obtained
at www.ICGtesting.com
Printed in the USA
LVOW04*1600021117

554681LV00012BA/92/P

9 783319 402918